The League of Orbis Novus

The League of Orbis Novus

A novel by

C.C. Prestel

ISBN-13: 978-1-7336663-3-6 (paperback)
ISBN-13: 978-1-7336663-2-9 (eBook)

Cover design by Bookcoversart.com.

This book is dedicated to my mother, who always encouraged me to write. I wish that she could read it.

Contents

Prologue

Jack sat in a patch of dirt with his legs crossed in front of him and replayed the past hour in his head. A part of him wondered if it was simply a bad dream. If that was true, then he had the misfortune of waking up to find himself in the middle of another. He looked over his shoulder toward the old brick building behind him. It was real, and there was still a faint florescent light originating from the corridor leading from the glass front door. There was no sign there of the man he left behind just a few minutes earlier.

A crescent moon was veiled by a thin blanket of clouds. Its feeble rays combined with the light from the corridor to marginally illuminate the surroundings. They revealed that he and the building sat in a clearing encircled by complete darkness. Maybe it was a forest that surrounded him—the sound of distant animal noises suggested that the area was home to several species. Or perhaps he was in a desert that hosted its own nocturnal creatures. The December breeze was cool but not cold, and provided no meaningful clues of his location. Other than the far northern and southern latitudes, he could rule out nothing.

He desperately wanted to evacuate the area, yet there was nowhere to go, at least not until daylight. It wasn't as if he feared imminent danger. In fact, he felt quite assured that the parties responsible for his whereabouts lay lifeless inside the building. What he desired to flee were the memories of the torment and anguish he had endured there over the past two weeks, which culminated in the surreal, ghastly events of the past hour.

Although the stranger he left inside was still very much alive, he posed no immediate threat. Adimu had called the man by his name in those final moments, yet Jack was too terrified to process the information at the time. Now in the calm of the aftermath, he could not recall it. He also couldn't fathom why the man was there at all, and he certainly didn't want to contemplate the burdensome quandary which the stranger now faced. Jack assumed that the man was left with only one option, and he didn't wish to be around to witness it.

And so he turned his head away from the building and attempted to focus on something else. It wasn't as if he could block the past two weeks completely from his mind, so he reached a compromise with himself and pondered the improbable circumstances that led him to the patch of dirt on which he sat.

What makes Jack's story so compelling is the sheer unlikeliness of his participation in it. Almost any of us could have found ourselves in his predicament if happenstance had dealt the cards of randomness differently. There was nothing extraordinary in his personal background that set him upon his fateful journey. Nobody would have mistaken him for an adrenaline junkie and he certainly wasn't the kind of person who would actively seek out adventure or peril. He was sharply averse to any drama that wasn't occurring on a stage or screen.

One might point to his heightened curiosity toward an ambiguous internet proclamation that was largely ignored by the rest of the world. Yet most of us have stumbled onto arcane fascinations—especially since the rise of the internet—and delved into researching them with an inexplicable fervor. In our own cases, these efforts amounted to little more than passing fancies for our brief attention spans. Jack was possibly a little overly zealous in his initial pursuit of the mystery. Nevertheless, the circumstances by which he was pulled into a tangled web of secrecy, riddles, and genocide were undoubtedly beyond his control—and probably his imagination.

At the time that Jack sat alone in the darkness, there were few people on the planet who were unaware of the impact that the League of Orbis Novus had on the world. Most knew the story as it was fed to them by bureaucrats, politicians, and so-called experts via the endless stream of television programs and news articles that saturated the airwaves and the cyber world. From there, facts and figures were sometimes churned, reshaped, and stretched into rumors and speculation, then recirculated into the news cycle. Millions of people felt the impact directly. If a person did not have a friend or family member affected, then he surely knew someone who did.

In spite of the devastation they had unleashed upon the world, nobody at that time knew much about the organization itself. Its members would be identified, one-by-one, and in due time. Strangely, their methods and motivations would both unite and divide, bestowing upon the world a dichotomy of the ends versus the means that likely predates civilization. The enigmatic organization's legacy would endure in a paradoxical cloud of heartless villainy and transcendent wisdom for centuries to come.

The stories of undisputed heroes across the globe would soon come to light as well. Their ranks would number in the hundreds and include brilliant scientists, quick-thinking medical professionals, and shrewd law-enforcement officers. The lives they saved could be counted in millions. Yet even among this group of leaders were those who understood the league's rationales, and secretly admired their courage, even if they condemned their methods.

It is neither my intent nor my wish to expound upon or deliberate the moral questions surrounding the league's actions. Furthermore, I have no desire to recount the stories of the world-renown heroes and notorious villains referenced above, about whom you can learn anything you desire on sites such as Wikipedia. My purpose for this narrative is to shed light upon a small cast of unheralded yet critical players in the saga of the League of Orbis Novus. These people have been omitted from the historical record for various reasons, which will become apparent in this story. Jack Kurry is one of them.

Nobody remembers the day that the message first appeared on an obscure, fleeting website, though few would escape the far-reaching tentacles of its authors:

> *"All hope abandon ye who fail to heed this warning."*

\- The League of Orbis Novus

1

"I'm such a stereotype that it isn't even funny," Jack Kurry said to an old friend one evening a few weeks after his twenty-eighth birthday. The occasion was his ten-year high school reunion just outside of Dayton, Ohio. His classmates were delighted to see that Jack had retained the self-deprecating style of humor with which he once entertained students and teachers alike. In this particular conversation, he was responding to the question that is ubiquitous at these gatherings: "What have you been up to since high school?" Those who recalled his affinity for the drama club and ardent participation in the school's theatrical productions asked the more pointed question: "Are you still acting?" They knew he had not made it big and were curious to learn if he was still chasing the dream.

Jack had recently concluded that he was at a crossroads in his life. He had some regrets about the path he had chosen and had no qualms about sharing them with his peers. The remark he made to his friend was in reference to his pursuit of an elusive acting career that began after graduating from college.

"I spent three years waiting tables in New York," he said with a sigh, "followed by two more in Los Angeles, during which I wasted a lot of time at auditions and a lot of money on acting classes."

His tragic flaw with respect to his career choice was one that plagued most of the aspirants in his position: he wasn't handsome enough to play the hero, not quirky enough in appearance to be a character actor, not obese enough to play the jolly fat guy, and not ethnic enough to fill certain stereotypical roles. He often noted that he was not talented enough to overcome any of those barriers. He was simply a face in the crowd. Obtaining work as an extra was never a problem.

Nor was he destined to be a leading man off the stage, which suited him just fine. As is true with many actors, he shied away from attention outside the theater with the same earnestness with which he craved the spotlight within it. He was bestowed with a set of genetic attributes that rendered him difficult to distinguish from the "everyman." This might have suited him well for acting in commercials, but that notion did not appeal to him. He stood a hair under six-feet tall, weighed about a hundred and seventy-five pounds, and wore one of those faces that evoked within complete strangers a feeling that they knew him from somewhere.

"It's funny," he mused with his former classmate. "Those who wasted years trying to make it wish they hadn't, while those who didn't go for it wish they had."

"But a lot of people are successful," suggested the classmate.

"I wouldn't say *a lot*," replied Jack, then added with a grin, "Maybe zero point zero, zero, zero, zero one percent, but I'm way too jealous of those lucky bastards to talk about them."

An attractive young woman approached with two bottles of beer and handed one to Jack.

"Thanks," said Jack, then he turned to the classmate. "This is my girlfriend, Jeanine. Jeanine, as you can see by his nametag, this is Jeff."

"He makes you fetch his drinks?" asked Jeff playfully.

"Only here," joked Jeanine. "It's his reunion and I don't know anybody, so I offered. It's *much* different back home."

Home was Las Vegas. "Homes" would be more accurate, for the couple resided in separate apartments, having only met a few months earlier. Their fortuitous meeting occurred a few days after Jack relocated to the city. He had arrived in Las Vegas as the result of a slight detour from the aforementioned crossroads. In order to explain how he arrived there, this story requires a detour of its own.

Jonathan Wesley Kurry was born in the middle-class community of Kettering, just south of Dayton. He came to be known as Jack for the same inexplicable reason that anybody calls someone named John, Jack. His father, Donald, was a mechanical engineer by trade, though he made his living as a converted software engineer. He was an employee of Lockheed Martin (or some pre-acquisition variant thereof) for his entire career. Don was a product of neighboring Indiana but remained in the Dayton area after graduating from the city's eponymous university. He met a captivating young woman from Cincinnati named Diane two years later and married her within a year. As Don liked to put it, this was before she came to her senses. She was also a graduate of Dayton University, though the two Flyers had not known each other while attending college. Diane stayed at home with the children until Jack reached his freshman year in high school, at which time she gained employment as a civilian finance specialist at nearby Wright-Patterson Airforce Base. Jack's older sister Mindy, born two and a-half years before her brother, rounded out the nuclear family.

Perhaps a harbinger of his nondescript early adulthood, Jack's childhood was pleasantly uneventful. He is described by former schoolmates and neighbors as having been an amiable kid with lots of friends, though he failed to maintain any of his Ohio connections outside of his family upon his subsequent move to New York. He was an active and average participant in intramural sports throughout his childhood. Far less than a passion, sports were just a way for him to hang out with his buddies. He discovered what he once characterized as his "true calling" upon arriving at Kettering High School at the age of fourteen, where he joined the drama club at the behest of his friend Billy.

"I just wanted to meet girls," said Billy years later, "and I figured that would be a good place to start. I dragged Jack along with me—he really wasn't interested at first."

The two boys soon fell in love—independently—Jack with acting and Billy with a girl named Deanna who broke his heart "several times over" before they graduated.

Jack was a decent student, though his mother had to crack the figurative homework whip from time to time to keep him focused. His parents enjoyed watching their son perform in various high school productions, ranging from a spirited *Twelve Angry Men* to an abridged version of *Les Misérables*, in which Jack displayed a remarkable ability to carry a tune as the steadfast Javert. His vocal talents were a delightful surprise to his parents, who had never heard him sing a note. They were far less pleasantly surprised when Jack informed them that he was planning to forgo college in order to pursue acting professionally.

It was the evening of his seventeenth birthday when he broke the news to them. Like any good actor, he had prepared a carefully-written speech. He had also (correctly) anticipated their reticent reaction and was armed with a list of successful actors hailing from Dayton. This included the brothers Lowe—Chad and Rob—and Jonathan Winters. Jack didn't know much about the latter persona, but he hoped the name might appeal to his parents' generation. Don and Diane recognized their son's diligence. They listened cordially and quietly until he was finished with his spiel before denouncing it. Had they more time to prepare, they might have utilized the tried-and-true good-cop/bad-cop approach. Instead, they instinctively fell back on the less effective bad-cop/bad-cop strategy.

The negotiations droned on for weeks before the parties reached a compromise. The covenant tilted slightly toward his parents' position: Jack would attend college and pursue a minor degree in theater arts. He was to select a major that would provide a suitable fallback option if the acting career failed to pan out. By the time of his high school graduation, Jack had decided that the fallback major would be journalism. Privately, his parents were skeptical about the choice. They questioned the future of journalism in light of the recent meteoric rise of the internet and social media. Still, they were happy with the compromise and didn't want to press their luck. What they failed to recognize at the time was how much journalism would evolve and explode on the engine of the world wide web, albeit at the cost of diluted integrity.

Jack gained admission to the Scripps School of Journalism at Ohio University in Athens and departed for the campus in the fall after his high school graduation. His parents made the two-hour drive with him, helped him move into the dorm, and reminded him that his major was journalism—not acting—before heading home. Jack devoted just enough time to his core curriculum to maintain a B average. He spent nearly all of his free time engrossed in theater-related courses, productions, and parties. The close-knit society of theater students (majors, minors, and grad students) became his de facto co-ed fraternity and accounted for most of his social life in college.

By the start of his junior year he was winning significant roles in university productions and nearby community theater shows. He received accolades for most of his performances and was considered an above-average actor by his teachers and peers.

"Being a big fish in a very small pond isn't bad," he remarked to a fellow student after starring in a production of *Cat on a Hot Tin Roof.* "For now, at least."

Jack flipped burgers at a local fast-food restaurant back in Dayton during the summer following his freshmen year, then spent the subsequent three summers delivering pizza and performing on stages in Columbus. He obliged his parents' entreaties by accepting an unpaid internship with a small newspaper during his final year of college. At his graduation ceremony, he admitted to his parents that he liked journalism, but that it simply wasn't his passion. He was headed for New York and stardom, and nothing could change his mind. Once again, his parents made the trip with him, helped him move into a small Brooklyn flat that he shared with three other aspiring actors, and reminded him that he had a fallback plan before heading home.

At the ten-year high school reunion, Jack recounted his years in New York to a classmate who had inquired about life in the Big Apple. Jeanine listened intently as well. She had yet to hear most of these stories.

"You could say that I honed my acting skills, but it was mostly in classes—and at my own expense," he told them. "What I really excelled at was waiting tables. I started out at a breakfast diner and worked my way up to a four-star restaurant. The money was pretty good."

"You can make a lot of money as a waiter in Manhattan," said the classmate, who had visited there once. Jack found it amusing how so many people who had been to New York once or twice seemed to know so much about it. He kept his observation to himself.

"Maybe so, but that wasn't in my plans," he responded to the classmate.

Passing three years of his life in Brooklyn without landing a role that was even remotely considered to be off–off Broadway was also not in Jack's plans. He decided that his talents might be better suited for the screen—big or small. He packed up his meager belongings and drove to

Los Angeles in a rented minivan. His parents flew out to meet him there and helped him move into a small apartment in Burbank. In an anticipatory maneuver, he gave a proclamation to his parents before they left for the airport.

"I'm giving this thing two years—tops. If it doesn't work out, I'll give it up," he declared. His father nodded and wished his son the best of luck.

"There's a lot of good jobs back home," said Don. Unbeknownst to his father, Ohio was no longer home for Jack and never would be again.

In reality, Jack's parents were not overly concerned about their son's prospects. It wasn't as if they believed he would find success in the movies—it was because he had saved a considerable amount of money in New York and was in pretty good shape financially. His New York theater connections had yet to lead to acting work in LA, yet they had landed him a lucrative job at a swank eatery in Fairfax. He would not be going hungry. In fact, he had put on a few pounds since graduating college and resolved to get back into shape. The icing on the cake of his new California lifestyle was that his sister Mindy lived down the I-5 in nearby San Diego. She had married a captain in the Marine Corps a few years earlier and the couple had decided to remain in that area following the completion of his service.

Jack had not dated much in New York—just a few on-stage romances that carried over off-stage for a month or so after the run. His first significant relationship since college commenced only a few weeks after arriving in Burbank, when he crossed paths with a young television production assistant at a local gym. This launched a string of brief romances that spanned between three and six months each. Like many millennials, he was torn between his professional aspirations and the instinctive call of the wild.

Marriage and children were not on the table. He supposed they might happen someday, far down the line and well after he was established. Yet it was difficult to resist the urge to be with a woman—and not just physically. Jack enjoyed the companionship and social avenues that a relationship brought—until he didn't. Perhaps committing to a woman, and thus a family, meant giving up the dream of stardom. At the end of each cycle he would resolve to remain single, though the firmness of his intent always waned after a few weeks, when the grass on the other side suddenly seemed a little greener, and he forgot how much he enjoyed his independence.

The untimely death of his mother came traumatically—and swiftly, from Jack's perspective. His parents had suppressed the news of her tumor from him and his sister until it had become unmanageable. Why parents choose to withhold such paramount information from their adult children is moot; whether it is an act of compassion or self-indulgence is not a matter for this narrative. Although Jack was informed of his mother's illness only a few weeks before she died, he managed to spend more than two weeks with her in Dayton, including a week at her bedside before she was rendered semi-catatonic with morphine and other sympathetic pain killers. She died a merciful death shortly thereafter.

He remained with his father in Dayton for a few weeks following his mother's passing. An incidental upside of not finding work as an actor is the luxury of having ample free time. Don eventually convinced his son that he was fine and urged Jack to resume his own life in Burbank. Jack complied, though the two grew closer in the wake of Diane's death and spoke on the phone two or three times per week in the years that followed.

The two years in California passed quickly. Jack found himself three months into his latest dalliance and looking for a way to bow out of it gracefully, as if that was ever possible. He was sitting in the trusted old recliner he had purchased from a used furniture store in Dayton years ago, when a calendar reminder popped up on his smartphone.

"Did you make it?" read the message.

He knew what it meant, and he knew that the answer was 'no.' It was the reminder he had created exactly two years prior, for the purpose of reflecting on his progress toward his goal. His attempt at a professional acting career had not been a complete failure. He had appeared in small roles—often non-speaking—in various television shows, and he had performed professionally in local dinner theaters. He could have probably eked out a living, perhaps if he supplemented it with restaurant work, but that wasn't going to be enough. That wasn't the goal.

Jack had seen this day coming for quite some time and had already begun preparations for a life change. He wasn't sure where he would find work, yet he knew that it would not be in Los Angeles. As if the exorbitant taxes and cost of living were not enough of a deterrent, he couldn't bear to live so close to the dream that he abandoned. He surmised that watching others chase the elusive pot of gold might be too tempting. Nearly every one of his Los Angeles friends was in the business, or aspiring to be. He needed a fresh break from them, as well as his current girlfriend, to whom he soon broke the news that he would be returning to Ohio—alone. She took it well. *Perhaps a little too well*, thought Jack. He wondered if he might have soon found himself on her own chopping block.

He still didn't have many possessions to his name, though he had accumulated more odds and ends than a rented minivan could hold. So, he sold his little car and rented a truck. The first stop was for a brief respite in Las Vegas. A friend, Mike, had invited Jack to stay with him for a few days. Mike was originally from Texas, by way of Los Angeles, where he had abandoned his own dreams of stardom a year earlier. Following three months of specialized training, Mike had become a professional poker dealer in one of the mega-resorts in the city. He resided in an apartment complex west of town that, by some odd chance, was teeming with beautiful women. Most of them seemed to reside directly on the patio surrounding the pool, though they were never seen in the pool itself.

The serendipity of his decision to stop in Vegas was not lost on Jack, and the brief respite expanded into an extended vacation. He began to gush about how much he loved the city to his friend.

"Why don't you just live here?" asked Mike one day as they sat by the pool sipping margaritas. "We have newspapers here too, you know." Jack didn't have to be told twice. Las Vegas would become his new home and the site of his new career, though he feared that it might be difficult to find a job in his fallback field.

Fortunately, they had restaurants in Las Vegas too, and plenty of them. The city had finally emerged from the disastrous consequences of the Great Recession and tourism was picking up. The tourists had never really stopped coming, but they were spending money once again. Now having to compete with casinos across the country, Las Vegas had slowly transformed itself into a "destination," where gambling accounted for less than half of the tourism revenue. Restaurants and shows had once been afterthoughts—mere perks thrown in to sweeten the pot for gamblers. Now they were high-end and high-cost attractions. Every resort boasted at least one signature restaurant with the name of a famous chef tied to it. ('Famous' to foodies and fans of reality cooking shows, at least.)

A few days later, Mike set up Jack with an interview at one such restaurant located within the casino resort where he worked. With his credentials, Jack had no trouble landing a job at the upscale steakhouse. Thus, the holdover plan in support of the fallback plan was in place. He would work as a waiter in Vegas until he could find a position in the field of journalism. Mike also welcomed Jack as a roommate until he could find his own place.

2

Jeanine was nothing like the women who seemed to reside on the patio surrounding the pool. She lived in the same complex and could measure up against any of those ladies, yet she had little time for lounging around. She had recently met Jack Kurry at the small fitness center adjacent to the pool where the two hit it off. Jeanine possessed an independent streak of her own and was in no hurry to settle down. The long-term prospects for their relationship were bolstered by the fact that they didn't see each other more than once or twice per week. Jeanine was finishing up law school at UNLV and working as an intern for a bustling downtown firm. They mostly met up in the fitness center, where she could usually be found when not in school or at the office. She only managed to get away to Ohio for Jack's reunion weekend because the recent semester had ended.

Like nearly half of the city's residents, Jeanine was not born there. A few years younger than her suitor, she was one of the transplants in the growth wave that followed the Great Recession. Her intent was to remain in Las Vegas for law school then head back to her home town of Tucson, where she would seek employment with the district attorney's office. She and Jack never discussed long-term plans nor the commitments such plans might precipitate, though friends described their budding romance as close and exclusive.

To his surprise, Jack found a journalism job before he found an apartment, and just one day after he purchased a used Honda Civic from Mike's brother. He had not even begun to look for his own place, having grown fond of his proximity to Jeanine and his friendship with Mike. He was a bit disappointed that he had found employment in the fallback career so quickly. Not only would Mike expect him to find his own apartment, he would also be forced to take a pay cut. He decided to stay on at the steakhouse and work two nights a week. The hours were brutal but the tips were too lucrative to relinquish.

Grant Lewis was Jack's editor and hiring manager at the *Las Vegas Chronicle*. Throughout the initial interview, Grant described the small newspaper in various ways, including "upstart," "alternative," and "targeting a younger crowd." Jack would come to recognize those descriptions as euphemisms meaning "not the top-selling publication," which was the popular *Las Vegas Review-Journal*. None of that mattered to Jack. It wasn't as if he held any leverage over the *Chronicle*, as it was the only publication to offer him a position. The job title "cub reporter" was long since passé. In Jack's case, it had been replaced with the very blunt "entry-level journalist."

Grant's enthusiasm about the *Chronicle* was genuine and it bubbled over during both of his interviews with Jack. Even if Jack had other options, Grant's passion and optimism surrounding the small publication's future would have likely won him over. The editor was well into his forties and displayed the physical signs of wear and tear one might expect from a newspaper person who had spent two decades chasing leads and sweating deadlines for large city papers. Any dedicated reporter knows that sensible meals usually yield to carbs and coffee in order to get a story done on time. Grant was no exception. At least he had quit smoking a few years earlier, once his kids had grown old enough to chastise him for it.

He was particularly excited about the online potential for "the Chronic," as it was known within the office walls. The paper had been around for fifty years, yet it was a little behind the curve with respect to the internet. Grant had been hired to refocus the aging dinosaur on a more youthful readership, which meant creating content for shorter attention spans and smaller displays, as on smartphones and tablets. He was intrigued by Jack's life experiences in New York and Los Angeles. They outweighed his concern that Jack's journalism degree was more than five years old and mostly untapped.

"Why are you here?" asked Grant when Jack showed up for his first day of work. The new reporter was taken aback, having been under the impression that this particular ground had been covered during the interview process.

"And don't give me any bullshit about wanting to make a difference," added Grant before his protégé had a chance to respond.

"I'm here because I need a job, and apparently, I suck at acting," replied Jack.

"Ha!" howled Grant with cavernous smile. "That's what I wanted to hear—complete honesty. I'll make a reporter out of you yet, Kurry."

The newest member of the *Chronicle* team settled into his job over the next few weeks. He was initially tasked to "watch and learn" over the shoulders of Grant and the seasoned staff reporters. Following the brief bootcamp, Grant dispatched him to cover various human-interest events around the greater Las Vegas metropolis, about which he wrote articles for the online edition of the paper. Around this time, he secured a one-bedroom flat in the same complex as Mike and Jeanine. His relationship with the latter continued smoothly in a once-a-week groove, neither thriving nor waning. His friendship with the former was bolstered by a newfound interest in poker.

Mike taught his friend the ins and outs of Texas Hold'em, providing a unique perspective from a professional poker dealer. Jack embraced his new hobby and soon became a regular player at Mike's casino, participating in the entry-level, no-limit cash games. He quickly rose through the ranks of the above-average players. He won slightly more than he lost, though his losses and winnings never amounted to more than a few hundred dollars per session. Jack found that he enjoyed the social interactions with tourists and locals alike, and made several casual friendships over the ensuing months.

After he had been living in Sin City for a month or so, he received an unexpected call from his father—unexpected in that he had just spoken with him a few days earlier. The call brought sad news of another death in the family. The newly deceased was a great uncle, a man whom Jack had only met a few times. The elderly miser and life-long bachelor had reached the age of ninety-two and had accumulated a small fortune along the way. Don informed his son that he was to be the recipient of a sizeable portion of the inheritance—in the neighborhood of twenty-thousand dollars. Jack suppressed his excitement in consideration of his father's endearment to his uncle. Don couldn't see how much Jack's eyes lit up upon hearing the news.

"If you ask me," started Don, which was his way of saying that whatever followed should be carefully adhered to, "you should invest the money and save it for a rainy day—maybe a down payment on a house or something." The entry fee for the upcoming World Series of Poker tournament flashed through Jack's mind, but he quickly discarded the notion in light of his father's advice. The check arrived a month later, after which Jack treated Jeanine to a five-star meal at the Cosmopolitan Hotel and invested the remainder of his inheritance in a conservative mutual fund. The World Series of Poker would have to wait another year or two.

On the following Monday morning, Jack found an email from his boss in his inbox.

"Have you seen this?" read the first line of the message. He clicked on the link Grant had included with the text. His browser popped up and displayed a popular social media site, where someone had posted an implausible story about elderly men and women being snatched from assisted-living facilities and held for ransom. Those for whom no ransom was received were allegedly sold off to scientists in South America where they were subjected to torturous experimentation. The story was allegedly relayed to the author by someone who knew the family of one of the victims.

Jack recalled receiving a junk email message with a nearly identical story a few days earlier. Its author warned its readers that the epidemic was rapidly spreading and told them to be ever-vigilant of their elderly loved ones. The admonition was supposedly confirmed by the Indiana state police, where the first instance of the horrific crime had allegedly occurred. The author's friend of a friend had been forced to pay a hefty ransom for his misfortune.

"Come talk to me about this," wrote Grant at the bottom of the email message. Jack rose from his chair and walked into his boss' office.

"Ah, you read it?" asked Grant.

"It's a hoax," said Jack.

"Of course, but it's a very popular hoax. A whole lot of people are obviously buying into it."

"How do people fall for this stuff?"

"That's what I want you to find out. It's your next assignment."

"You want me to write about this internet rumor?"

"Not just this one. Find out what keeps these things alive—how they propagate so widely and rapidly. And speaking of rapidly, you've got a week to write it."

It was just another fluff piece, yet something about it excited the neophyte reporter. He surmised that it would require research, and perhaps interviews with experts. He returned to his cubicle and dove in.

3

At first, the sound of knuckles rapping on the door was a figment of Sydney Carter's dream. The aggravating noise slowly roused him into the conscious world, where he was welcomed with a wicked headache and various other symptoms of a hangover, feelings not unfamiliar to him.

"Doctor Carter," said the Spanish-accented voice from the other side of the door, "are you ready to go?" He continued to knock as he spoke.

Sydney glanced at his wristwatch, which he had failed to remove the night before. It displayed the time as 8:15. He remembered having told his guide, Manuel, that he wanted to leave the hotel by 7:30 a.m.

"Hold on a sec," grumbled Sydney. He lifted his aching body and sat on the edge of the bed with his head buried in his hands. The toothy smile of the cartoon burro on the empty bottle of tequila stared back at him from the floor. He spied the remote control next to the bottle and switched off the muted television. "Give me fifteen minutes. I'll meet you downstairs," he shouted to Manuel.

Sydney had only himself to blame for his nausea. There had been no welcome dinner, drinks at the bar, nor wild party in his room the night before. Manuel had picked him up unceremoniously at the airport and dropped him off at the Radisson Hotel in Guatemala City after confirming their plans for the following day. Sydney had purchased the bottle at the hotel gift shop before retiring to his room and ordering a hamburger to be delivered. He could not remember anything past ten o'clock.

He managed to brush his teeth and take a quick shower. Next, he picked up a can of shaving cream, stared at his reflection, then replaced it onto the counter. Shaving could wait until tomorrow. He put on a neatly-pressed pair of khaki pants and a light blue button-down shirt. The necktie remained in his luggage. After taking a quick inventory of the contents of his leather case, he carried it downstairs and found Manuel seated in a comfortable lobby chair. Sydney couldn't resist flopping down in the chair next to him.

Manuel stood up. "We have to go, Doctor Carter. We have a long trip ahead of us, and we are already late."

"Just give me a minute."

Manuel sized up Sydney, who was presently slumped in the chair with his arms dangling over the sides. He was concerned that his client might fall asleep there, and wondered if his eyes were already closed beneath the dark sunglasses. Manuel observed that his client looked older than a man in his mid-thirties, which is what he had been told to look for at the airport. His client appeared to have lived a rough life—especially considering that he supposedly worked as a research scientist and had a doctorate degree, no less. Portions of his physique still resembled the athlete he once was, though most of it was covered with a layer of flab. His dark-brown hair was prematurely gray near the temples.

"How far?" asked Sydney, without moving anything other than his lips.

"About a hundred and fifty kilometers, sir."

That didn't sound too far to Sydney. "Alright then, let's go—and please don't call me 'sir'."

The drive took more than six grueling, hungover hours. The roads grew more rustic and bumpier with each mile they advanced into the northern region of the country. Sydney admonished his guide, albeit mildly, for the underwhelming air conditioning system in the car. He might have been more appreciative had he known that the vehicle would provide his last smidgen of air conditioning before returning to Guatemala City.

"I am sorry, Doctor Carter," said Manuel. I have not had a chance to repair it."

"It's Sidney."

"I am sorry, Doctor Sydney."

They eventually came to a group of mobile trailers about twenty miles from the highland city of Coban late in the hot, humid afternoon. The camp had been established a few weeks earlier by the Guatemalan Ministry of Public Health to house a team of scientists and medical officials. They were responding to a recent outbreak of an unidentified illness in a nearby village. All of the team members were from Guatemala, though a few scientists from the World Health Organization (WHO) had visited earlier, during the first days of the outbreak. They had subsequently concluded that the illness did not pose a threat to the greater world and departed. The remaining members hurried out to meet Sydney, brimming with enthusiastic smiles and waves.

"Welcome, Doctor Carter," greeted a thirtyish Guatemalan man as they shook hands. His English was impeccable. "I am Doctor Rudy Jimenez. I don't know if you remember me. I interned with you at the CDC while I was a graduate student at Duke. I assisted you with the preparation of a lecture. The topic was 'Lipid Rafts and HIV Pathogenesis'."

Sydney couldn't remember the lecture, let alone meeting Dr. Jimenez. He shook his hand and pretended that he did. Following the introductions, the doctors moved into the largest trailer and brought Sydney up to speed on the outbreak. From what Sydney could tell, not much had changed since the briefing he received before leaving Atlanta, though it was difficult to hear amid the noisy fans.

"Would you prefer that we turn those off?" asked Jimenez.

"God, no," replied Sydney. His shirt was already soaked through.

The news was mostly positive. No new cases of the mysterious illness had appeared in more than a week, and the nearby village of Tanchi remained under quarantine. There were six fatalities since the illness first appeared last month. Two other villagers had presented with the flu-like symptoms and had since recovered. The disappointing news was that the team of scientists had been unable to identify the pathogen. This was the primary reason for Sydney's trip. He was an expert in pathogenesis and was currently working in the burgeoning field of viromics, a study of the viral genome. The Centers for Disease Control had offered his services and the Guatemalan government eagerly accepted.

"You are from the CDC?" asked a woman in broken English after Jimenez concluded the introductory briefing.

"I work for Emerson–Lee University in Atlanta," replied Sydney. "We have a contract with the CDC." The woman returned a confused expression, to which Jimenez responded with an explanation in Spanish.

"Ah, yes" said the woman with a smile.

"How soon can I take a look at the samples?" asked Sydney.

The entire group relocated to a smaller and even hotter trailer next door. For two hours, the Guatemalan doctors huddled behind Sydney as he examined numerous samples of lung tissue, blood, and stool using various microscopes. Other than jotting down notes and muttering a few words here and there, he mostly withheld his findings until the process was completed.

"Can we go back to the other trailer?" he asked.

The larger trailer felt like a desert oasis compared to the mobile lab they had just vacated. As his eager audience settled in for the report, he couldn't help but wonder why they had not simply mailed the samples to his comfortable lab in Atlanta. He already knew the answer: the CDC wanted him to examine the bodies as well, and they also wanted to show their support to the Guatemalans in the form of boots on the ground. As an expert in the field of viral pathogenesis, Sydney's boots were the logical choice.

"Unfortunately, I can't tell you exactly what it is," started Sydney. The enthusiastic expressions among the audience languished in response. "But I can tell you what it *isn't*, and that's very important too." He looked for a positive reaction. There wasn't one. "It isn't bacterial, which you already knew. As for the virus, I know you've been expecting to find H3N2 or some variant of it," he continued. "And I can see why you might have thought that, but I'm pretty sure it isn't there."

He proceeded to expound on his findings for an hour before moderating a discussion among the scientists. Sydney's professional opinion was that the virus was a newly-evolved strain that could not survive outside of a host long enough to thrive. The villagers who contracted it must have been in very close contact with each other, or with the original source of the pathogen. The latter could have been something they ate, such as undercooked chicken.

"In all likelihood, it's already extinct," proclaimed Sydney. "Another dead-end branch on the tree of viral evolution." Nevertheless, he requested samples to take back to Atlanta for further testing. It was important to identify and catalog all known viruses, though he fully-intended to hand the task off to an underling upon his return home.

The workday concluded with a dialogue concerning the quarantine and other steps to be taken. As they adjourned, Sydney saw that his colleagues were visibly disappointed that the expert from the CDC had not furnished the answers they desired. He pulled Dr. Jimenez aside.

"I'm sorry that I couldn't provide more answers, Rudy. I'd like to talk to some of the villagers when I examine the bodies."

"You were very helpful, Doctor Carter. I'm so glad that you came here. In fact, when the CDC offered to send someone, I requested you specifically. We already suspected that the virus had gone extinct, and now you have confirmed it."

"I wouldn't say that I *confirmed* it," said Sydney. "Honestly, Rudy, I need to take a closer look. We need to investigate beyond the lungs. Something tells me that you've got a blood-borne virus here."

"Then it is definitely viral?" noted Jimenez.

"Probably… yeah, definitely. Just keep your eyes peeled, my friend. This one didn't have the stones to survive, but the next one might. That's all I'm saying."

"Stones?"

Sydney patted the young doctor on the back. "Gonads… it lacked the physical composition to survive." He noticed that his hangover had finally been displaced by hunger. "What's for dinner?"

"We'll have dinner in my trailer," replied Jimenez. "There's a cot set up for you in there as well."

"Thanks."

"Oh—and I've got some local beer for you to sample."

"Excellent. You read my mind."

That night, the two scientists shared a twelve-pack over dinner and the ensuing discussion about viral pathogenesis. Rudy accounted for two of the bottles, while Sydney downed the other ten. He dozed off sometime after eleven o'clock and woke once again to the sound of Manuel rapping on the door. The inside of the trailer was brightly lit by the morning sun, and Rudy was already up and gone.

Though he was tired and physically drained, Sydney felt a little better than he had twenty-four hours earlier. "Come in, Manuel."

"Are you planning to stay here today, Doctor Sydney?"

"We're going to visit the village today. Where is everybody?"

"They have already left. Doctor Jimenez is in the laboratory."

Sydney found Rudy alone in the small, muggy trailer. The Guatemalan doctor confirmed that the team had departed for the village an hour earlier. He told Sydney that they didn't want to wake him.

"They should have," said Sydney. "But that's okay—we can catch up to them."

"You do not look well, Doctor Carter. There is no reason for you to stay here. We'll ship the samples to your office."

"What about the bodies?" asked Sydney.

"There's really nothing for you to see. We'll send you the tissue samples."

The advice sounded good to Sydney. He never wanted to leave Atlanta in the first place. He turned to Manuel, who was standing just outside the door.

"Can I book a flight out for tonight?"

Rudy answered the question. "There's a flight to Los Angeles in the morning. I take it often."

"Alright. Then let's get back to the hotel."

Sydney collected his notes, thanked Rudy for his hospitality, and climbed into the stuffy car. Manuel appeared distracted.

Sydney prompted him politely. "I'm all set."

"Sorry," said Manuel. He started the car but left it in park. Then he looked at Sydney inquisitively. "Where did you and Doctor Jimenez go last night?"

"What do you mean? We didn't go anywhere."

"You were not with him?"

"What are you talking about?"

"I could not sleep last night," continued Manuel, "I came outside my trailer around midnight for some fresh air and saw Doctor Jimenez walking with someone up that path." He pointed to a dirt path leading up from the camp. "I thought it was you."

"Well, it *wasn't* me. Which way is the village?"

"That way," replied Manuel, pointing in the direction opposite from the path.

"I don't know. Maybe Rudy couldn't sleep either."

"Of course. I am only asking because I am responsible for your safety. There are dangerous animals in the jungle up there." Manuel put his car into gear and headed toward the main road. He soon noticed that his client was in slightly better spirits than he had been on the drive up.

"Are you happy to be going home, Doctor Sydney?"

"Sure." Sydney rested his head against the passenger window and closed his eyes. Manuel assumed that his client had fallen asleep. After several minutes, Sydney broke the silence, though his head remained against the window and his eyes remained shut.

"Are you married, Manuel?"

"Yes."

"Are you happy?"

"Yes, Doctor Sydney. We are very happy."

"My wife asked me to move out."

"I'm sorry to hear that, Doctor Sydney."

4

There was no shortage of websites dedicated to debunking internet hoaxes, though they were not nearly as plentiful as the hoaxes themselves. Jack Kurry discovered that the deluge of fabricated stories and ominous warnings was greater than he had imagined.

He parsed through hundreds of them. There was the ubiquitous Nigerian prince who always managed to find himself in a bind that could yield great dividends to the random Samaritan willing to lend a helping hand. There were the savage gang members who drove around in cars at night with their headlights turned off, then brutally murdered anyone who tried to alert them by flashing their headlights. There were numerous tales targeted toward the elderly, with the most recent being the one that Grant had forwarded. There was an entire subset of hoaxes that centered on the perils of babysitting.

Jack found one website, called Hoax Hunters, to be particularly informative and insightful. It categorized each hoax in several different ways so that users could search for groups that shared similar attributes, such as those involving a phony police car. It also rated each hoax on a scale of one to ten, where a one represented a story that was proven to be false, and a ten meant that the story was likely to be true. Most of them scored at or near a one. The Hoax Hunters provided a narrative for each hoax that speculated on its origins. Jack learned that many had evolved from previous incarnations, and some derived from actual crimes dating back to the 1950s and earlier.

After two solid days of researching the breadth and depth of internet scams and fairytales, Jack decided to start writing the article, though not before checking out one or two more examples. He had nearly reached the point of obsession—not that he believed any of the scams. He found the sheer gullibility displayed by many of his fellow internet users to be astonishing. One alleged hoax caught his attention. It was a relatively new entry on the site, and the Hoax Hunters had little information to convey about it.

There was something peculiar about this particular item. There was no story—it was merely a statement. Like the others, it presented a warning, yet not one borne from a narrative about some poor, unsuspecting soul upon whom a menacing tragedy befell. It was simply a warning, albeit an ambiguous one. According to the Hoax Hunters, the statement could be traced back to a few temporary internet sites that existed just long enough to be indexed by the mammoth search engines, such as Google, before they disappeared without a trace. The message was subsequently proliferated via email forwarding, though not as widely as most hoaxes.

As shown on the Hoax Hunters site, the statement read as follows:

June 1

> *"There is nothing more difficult to take in hand, more perilous to conduct, or more uncertain in its success, than to take the lead in the introduction of a new order of things."*

On December 1st, six months from today, opioids will no longer render their desired effect. The time has come to rid the planet of this toxic pestilence.

This is your first warning. Subsequent messages will follow. All hope abandon ye who fail to heed this warning.

- The League of Orbis Novus

A quick search revealed that only two mainstream media sites made so much as a passing reference to the warning, and dismissed it as another spurious prank at the hands of a bored teenager. Why wouldn't they? The internet was saturated with outlandish proclamations, manifestos, and predictions. That this one would be rebuffed or simply fall through the cracks was nothing unusual.

Jack could find no reference to a person or organization called Orbis Novus beyond the message itself. It didn't take a Latin scholar to recognize that the name translated to something akin to "new world." This coincided with the reference to a new order contained in the quote from Machiavelli at the beginning of the message. The final line appeared to be a modified portion of a line from Dante's *Inferno*, referring to the gates of Hell: "Abandon all hope ye who enter here," though this might have been a coincidence.

He bookmarked the Hoax Hunters page describing the Orbis Novus message and put it out of his mind for the moment. The clock was ticking toward the article's deadline and he needed to obtain some insight and quotes from experts. The Hoax Hunters home page indicated that the site managers were located in San Diego. He found Grant in his office and requested permission for a fact-finding road trip to visit the Hoax Hunters. Grant questioned why an interview couldn't be conducted over the phone, to which Jack replied that he would stay at his sister's house.

"A good reporter always questions his sources in person, right?" Jack asked rhetorically.

"Alright," said the frugal editor, "but no per diem—just mileage on this one."

"Deal."

Jack invited Jeanine to accompany him on the two-day jaunt to Southern California, but she couldn't pull herself away from the internship or her summer course in advertising law which had commenced the previous week. Jack was disappointed, though not surprised. He tossed a backpack into the backseat of his Civic and headed south on the I-15 under the hot desert sun. He hoped that San Diego would provide a welcome respite from the scorching Las Vegas summer heat, to which he had not yet become accustomed.

His sister and her husband, Ron, greeted Jack at the front door of their small home in the community of Torrey Highlands, about twenty miles north of downtown. The air wasn't quite as cool as Jack had anticipated, as the town lay inland from the coast. Still, anything was better than Vegas in July, he thought. Torrey Highlands split the difference between La Jolla to the south, where Mindy worked as an academic advisor for UC–San Diego, and the Northrop Grumman offices a few miles north, where Ron was employed as a program manager. Jack was well acquainted with their charming little home, though this was his first visit since moving out of the state. He tossed his backpack onto the guestroom bed before the trio left for dinner at a nearby pizza parlor.

In between slices, Jack brought his sister and brother-in-law up to speed on the reason for his visit. Ron took an immediate fancy to the topic and asked if he could tag along for the interview, which was scheduled for the following evening. The retired Marine captain and tank commander glowed with the excitement of a child on Christmas morning when Jack okayed the request. It was no wonder that Mindy referred to her husband as her big teddy bear.

"It probably isn't very professional to have you along," said Jack, "but it's just a human-interest story. I don't think my boss would mind."

"Especially if he doesn't know," added Ron.

Toward the end of dinner, Mindy changed the subject to a secret that appeared ready to burst out of her gut if she didn't reveal it soon. She had been waiting for the right moment, then realized that she couldn't quite define what the right moment would look like. Now was as good a time as any.

"We have some news of our own," she announced. Before Jack could ask what it was, she blurted, "Ron and I are going to adopt a child from Guatemala."

Jack expressed his congratulations and Mindy proceeded to fill him in on the details: why they chose Guatemala's adoption program, the schedule for identifying and taking custody of a child, and so forth. Jack knew through his father that his sister had been trying to conceive a child for several years. He did not pry into their reason for adopting, though he surmised that the couple had probably received confirmation of an infertility issue with one of them. None of that mattered, and he was excited about the prospect of having a little niece or nephew. The adoption conversation dominated the remainder of the evening.

The next morning, Mindy dropped Jack off near the beach at La Jolla on her way to work, where he passed the day exploring the area. He confirmed the interview with the Hoax Hunters while sitting on a bench and watching a pair of friendly seals rollick in the surf. He called the website manager with whom he had spoken two days earlier, a man named Chuck. Chuck's enthusiasm was so pronounced—even through the phone—that Jack wondered if the man had ever been interviewed about anything. Not only would Chuck be there, his Hoax Hunter partner, Craig, was going to attend as well. The plan was to meet at their favorite watering hole after they left work. Jack caught a rideshare back to his sister's house and waited for Ron to return home.

Chuck and Craig had met several years earlier while working as system administrators for a large corporation in San Diego and became fast friends. They discovered that they shared interests in role-playing games, beer, and just about anything to do with network administration. The latter eventually led to the creation of the Hoax Hunters website. The impetus for the hobby was the technical challenge of creating and maintaining a website on their own server. The concept of documenting hoaxes and scams was initially just a means to an end—practically chosen at random—though they quickly developed a passion for the subject.

"We're not ashamed to admit that we're a couple of geeks," Chuck announced following the initial greetings with Ron and Jack. The four men sat a table near the back of the restaurant/bar at which Chuck and Craig were members of the establishment's beer of the month club. Jack noted to himself that the two men could have passed for brothers, if only because they wore similar scruffy beards and nearly identical eyeglasses. They might have looked completely dissimilar without the facial hair and spectacles. Modest guts bulged from their t-shirts, divulging their love for ales and lagers. They were otherwise slender and somehow managed to look both fat and skinny at the same time.

The contrast of their appearances with Jack's brother-in-law was stark, if not comical. Ron was five years retired from the Marine Corps but still looked the part. He kept his hair in a tight crewcut and across his broad shoulders he wore a form-fitting, short-sleeved t-shirt—with an emphasis on short. His exposed arms revealed a large navy blue Marine Corps tattoo. Yet the former tank commander, who served two tours overseas, sat wide-eyed on the edge of his seat, completely enthralled with what the two engineers had to say. He asked as many questions as Jack did at the interview, during which Chuck and Craig fervently professed everything they knew about internet hoaxes, often talking over each other in the process.

"The internet allows them to spread more quickly, but urban legends have been around since the dawn of civilization," noted Craig.

"It's just modern folklore," added Chuck.

The men proceeded to elaborate on the history of these myths. Prior to online social media, they spread via traditional media sources, such as newspapers. Some passed on through the years relatively unchanged, while others evolved to adapt to modern society. Surprisingly, many are rooted in a grain of truth.

"You know the one about the guy who woke up in a bathtub with a kidney missing after a night of partying with strangers, right?" asked Chuck.

"Yeah!" said Ron excitedly. "They drugged him and stole his kidney to sell on the black market."

"Correct," continued Chuck. "We know it's complete bullshit, but did you know there was an illegal kidney harvesting case in Turkey back in the eighties? It wasn't exactly the same, because the victims agreed to sell their kidneys—they just got ripped off. But you can see how the urban legend might have spawned from a real incident. The facts get further blown out of proportion with each successive iteration of the story."

Jack asked how it was possible for these myths and hoaxes to spread so widely even if most people know that they were fake.

"Most people *don't* know that they're fake," replied Craig, "or at least they're unsure. Even if they suspect—deep down—that it's probably not true, they figure they should warn their friends and family anyway."

"Kind of a 'better safe than sorry' thing, huh?" asked Ron.

"Yeah. That's how these things spread—just like any other rumor. It's not because of sinister intentions—except for the outright scams."

The men discussed the differences between the internet scams and urban legends. The scams mostly preyed upon the naïve, whereas the urban legends appealed to the vivid imaginations in everyone.

"How often have you said to yourself, *it could happen*, even if a big part of you knows that it didn't?" suggested Chuck.

The four men became so engaged in the conversation that the

meeting morphed into a full-blown dinner, including dessert and several microbrews recommended by the bearded connoisseurs. They delved into the backstories of several popular urban myths, including Walt Disney's cryogenically frozen head, the babysitter who receives a phone call from a killer who is inside the house, and the photo of the guy posing on the observation deck of the World Trade Center, where the first jet about to strike the tower is seen in the background.

"You can see why that one would be so widely circulated," Craig said about the 9/11 photo. "Who wouldn't want to share it with his friends in the wake of such a world-changing event?"

They talked about the histories and evolutions of hoaxes, how most are variants of earlier incarnations. The victim might change from a brother to a sister, or the physical location of the event might change, while the gist of the legend remains the same. That is, the moral of the story is constant, and often involves the unfortunate consequences of trying to do the right thing or behaving immorally—helping a stranger on the side of the road, babysitting, visiting a prostitute, and so on.

"They all have one thing in common," proclaimed Craig as the evening was wrapping up. "They are held to be true accounts by the storyteller."

"It's the old 'friend of a friend' gimmick," added Chuck superfluously, so that he might have the last word on the subject.

In the parking lot, just after the parting handshakes were completed, Jack remembered that he had wanted to ask about the curious warning message he had come across on the Hoax Hunters site. The guys could not recall precisely the item to which he was referring, so Jack accessed it on his smartphone and showed it to them as they stood under a street lamp.

"Oh, that one," remarked Craig. "I found that one a few weeks ago and posted it on the site."

Chuck had not yet seen it. He quickly read the warning message and Craig's brief description that accompanied it. "That's altogether a completely different beast," he said. "We call those 'spurious random threats'."

"Spurious random threats?" repeated Ron.

"Yeah. The web is full of them—random warnings and threats geared to the ills of society. This guy obviously has a grudge against opioids."

"The League of Orbis Novus is just one random guy?" asked Jack.

"Probably," said Chuck. "It looks better if it has a fancy, mysterious name attached to it, but it's probably some dude sitting at his computer in his tighty whities."

"Maybe he lost someone to an overdose or something," chimed in Craig, "and now he wants the world to stop using opioids."

"It reads as if they plan to do something about four-and-a-half months from now," said Jack.

"Yeah, and the Mayan calendar said that the world would end in 2012," remarked Craig. "I wish I had a dollar for every one of these warnings."

"But you have it rated as a two, instead of a one. Does that mean that it might be legitimate?" asked Jack.

"Nah. It just means that we can't prove it to be false. We'll have to wait until December 1st before we lower it to a one," replied Craig.

"It *is* kind of unusual in that it doesn't have a predecessor," remarked Chuck. "It's what we call an orphan. I can't see where this particular message evolved from an earlier hoax—not one that I can recall."

"Would you classify this as a classic doomsday hoax?" Craig asked his partner.

"Maybe, but the guy didn't provide any details of the consequences. He didn't mention anything about a doomsday."

"That's because he doesn't *have* any consequences," Craig noted smugly.

The deliberation over the Orbis Novus message petered off a few moments later and the men parted ways. The dismissive attitude displayed by Chuck and Craig wasn't enough to put it completely out of Jack's mind. Something about the ominous warning was glued to the forefront of his imagination and would remain lodged there for some time to come.

Back at his sister's house, the prevailing subject of conversation was once again the upcoming adoption, which the couple hoped would be transacted within a couple of months. They had recently made a trip to Guatemala for the purpose of meeting with adoption officials. Now they were awaiting the selection of a child. Jack reaffirmed his happiness for them, pledged to help in any way he could, then went up to bed.

He arrived back in Las Vegas in time to meet Jeanine for a quick lunch at a local taco joint near her downtown office. His head was still swimming with the nuts and bolts of urban legends and internet hoaxes. The meeting with the Hoax Hunters had stoked a flame of fascination within him—nearly to the level of his brother-in-law's excitement. Jeanine did not seem inclined to share in his zeal.

"It's just a bunch of nonsense that can be easily proven false, right?" suggested the aspiring attorney.

"That's the whole point. If that's true, then how come they don't go away?"

"Because people are generally idiots."

"It's not that simple. The guys told me that it has a lot to do with our vivid imaginations making us believe that the stories might be true. They're a product of our evolution."

"How's that?" asked Jeanine. A conversation about anthropology was a bit more appealing to her than silly urban legends.

"Think about it. Let's say that a prehistoric man hears a rustling noise in the tall grass. Nine times out of ten it's just the wind, but that one other time it's a sabretooth tiger. The prehistoric man with the vivid imagination will assume it's the tiger every time and run away. The man without the imagination will assume it's the wind. He'll eventually be killed when that one-in-ten chance occurs."

"So, you're saying that our imagination is an evolutionary advantage?"

"It once was. Now it provides us with good artists, musicians, writers, actors, and liars."

"And gullible idiots who like to spread internet myths?"

"Yeah."

Jeanine was intrigued by the notion, yet not so much entertained by it, so she changed the subject to their plans for the weekend. Specifically, the one night of the weekend that they would spend together.

"I've got to get this story done before Monday," said Jack. "I think I'll need to cancel for the weekend."

Jeanine politely displayed an expression of disappointment, though inside she wasn't really *that* disappointed. She had a lot of studying to do on the ins and outs of advertising law.

On Monday, Grant Lewis made a handful of minor edits to the fluff piece and affixed a headline to it that read "America's Obsessions with

Internet Hoaxes and Myths," before approving it for publication in the online version of the *Chronicle*. Jack was a little disappointed with his boss' appraisal of the article as being "adequate," until the other junior reporter on the staff, who was six months his senior, assured him that a rating of adequate from Grant was very respectable.

"He might tell you that your article was good if you won a Pulitzer," said Jimmy, "with an emphasis on *might*." Everyone at the *Chronicle* knew the slight, freckled-face young man as Jimmy, an homage to his uncanny resemblance to Jimmy Olsen, the cub reporter at the *Daily Planet* in the Superman comics. Some of the office staff didn't even know that his real name was Richard. He was much younger than Jack, having accepted his position at the *Chronicle* upon graduation from journalism school a year earlier. Despite having a few months more experience in the field, Jimmy looked up to Jack as the older brother he never had.

Jack didn't have long to dwell on any hidden meanings within Grant's middling assessment of his work. He was next assigned to research a myriad of affairs related to the start of the upcoming school year in Clark County. These included a new elementary school opening in Henderson, the teachers' union's dissatisfaction with the county, the county's dissatisfaction with the teachers' union, and the best places to find deals on school supplies. He kept tabs on his internet article and saw that it had spawned several reader comments over the first few days following publication. Grant also took notice of the numerous online responses—an indication of interest in the article—and provided his protégé with a figurative pat on the back in the form of an email telling him to "keep it up."

Covering the commencement of the school year wasn't up to the challenge of distracting Jack from his burgeoning obsession with internet hoaxes—and one hoax in particular. Or more accurately, Orbis Novus was becoming too large a distraction from his assigned task of documenting the new school year. It didn't help that Chuck and Craig had begun sending him twice- or thrice-daily email updates concerning the latest developments in the world of internet myths. None of their messages included anything about the haunting Orbis Novus declaration, yet it remained cemented in Jack's mind—a small voice that called out to him during brief lapses of concentration.

He continued to investigate the source of the message on his own time as well as a fair portion of his work time. This included a conversation with the administrator in charge of the *Chronicle*'s IT network and equipment. The young woman struck Jack as being very knowledgeable in the ways of the internet—both above board and below. Sensing Jack's technical ignorance, and delighted to have the audience of someone who wasn't there to complain about the performance of his PC, she spoke in the somewhat condescending tone for which IT administrators are infamous.

Jack provided her with one of the website addresses that the League of Orbis Novus used to broadcast its warning message. Despite having boastfully hinted at having some experience in the shadier side of network manipulation, i.e., hacking, she admitted that tracking down the location of the site would likely prove futile.

"If they know what they're doing," said the administrator, "then it will be impossible to trace them."

She tried to explain the challenge to Jack in what she described as layman's terms, though she came across as someone addressing a kindergarten class. The gist of the lecture was that criminals use proxy servers and other means to disguise their site locations and provide anonymity. Their server might appear to be located in Cairo, but actually be located in Sydney, with a chain of five other proxy servers in between. She pointed out that in this particular case, the website and its host server disappeared within twenty-four hours, rendering it nearly impossible to forensically investigate.

"*You're* not gonna find them," proclaimed the administrator. She purposely phrased it in such a way so as not to admit that *she* wouldn't be able to find them, though Jack accurately concluded as much.

"These guys don't want to be found," she told him.

5

The next few weeks passed in a slow simmer for Jack. Seemingly unrelated matters in his life slowly ascended into new levels of significance and connectivity, and could only be recognized as such in hindsight. An ambiguous feeling pervaded his psyche at that time, one which he ascribed to being in a personal rut. He couldn't pinpoint the precise cause or causes. The symptoms were similarly vague—favorite take-out meals seemed less tasty, popular sitcoms seemed less funny, Mike's sarcastic sense of humor seemed less witty, and Jeanine's pragmatic disposition seemed less appealing, if not a little caustic.

Playing poker at Mike's casino had become Jack's go-to distraction, yet even it had proven to be less effective in recent days. Called the Monaco Palace, the sizeable resort hotel and casino occupied a sixty-acre lot in the heart of the coveted Summerlin neighborhood to the west of downtown. It catered to locals and vacationers who preferred the relative serenity of the off-Strip properties. It was a short ten-minute drive from the apartment complex in which Mike and Jack resided.

Jack was engaged in a low-stakes cash game on a particular Thursday night when a strange feeling of self-realization came over him. The poker-playing stereotypes whom he normally found mildly amusing were suddenly crawling under his skin. There was the grumpy older man who seemed angry at the cards dealt to him—not only by the dealer, but by the world as well. He distributed his displeasure equally among his fellow players, the dealers, and the cocktail waitresses in the form of an unintelligible grumble. Next to him sat the self-appointed expert who felt compelled to explain his strategy following each hand as if providing a tutorial for the rest of the group. In reality, he was simply trying to convince his fellow players that he was better than the dwindling stack of chips in front of him suggested.

In the seat to Jack's right was the verbose windbag who consistently proclaimed that he knew what his opponent's cards were after the fact (and after they were revealed), despite having raised the pot and lost the hand. On Jack's left sat the antithesis of the windbag: the young wannabe professional, wearing the shadow of a beard, and decked out in dark sunglasses and hip-hop earphones. A sweatshirt hoodie had originally covered his head, but he had been forced to remove it in accordance with house rules. Everything about him reflected the stylish pros he had watched on television, except for his skills. Rounding out the stereotypes was the senior citizen who couldn't manage to stay awake long enough to fold his cards, which he almost always did after being prodded by the dealer.

Jack's realization was that these players should not have bothered him to such an extent as they were that night. Furthermore, he attributed his unusually sizable losses on the evening to a lack of focus and concentration. Rather than study the habits and tells of his competitors, Jack browsed the internet between hands using his smartphone. A timely email message from Craig the Hoax Hunter spurred an idea. The content had nothing to do with the League of Orbis Novus, yet it was enough to trigger a notion.

He deduced that his preoccupation with Orbis Novus was beckoning him to write a follow-up article—one that would focus on this specific example of an internet hoax. He would delve into the history of opioids and the recent explosion of their abuse. He could research the intentions of the mysterious organization. Was their warning merely an admonishment or were they planning a tangible response to the epidemic? Jack thought it was a great idea for his first in-depth article and it would serve as a bridge into serious journalism. It would also require a green light from Grant.

"Big blind, sir," repeated the dealer, while tapping her hand on the table in front of Jack and bringing him back into the reality of the present. It was Jack's turn to post the blind bet.

"Sorry," replied Jack. "I'm cashing out." He picked up his short stack of chips and left the table.

Jack arrived at the offices of the *Chronicle* earlier than usual the next morning and found his boss dispensing a cup of coffee from the single pod machine in the kitchen. His excitement prevented him from waiting any longer, so he pitched his idea to Grant under the guise of waiting to make some coffee for himself—a beverage for which he cared little. He was forced to sip the bitter concoction while listening to Grant's response.

"I like your initiative," started Grant. He ran his fingers through his hair while searching for his next words. "But I just don't see how this one obscure warning warrants its own story."

Jack emphasized, again, that the story would also cover the opioid epidemic in great detail.

"That's been done," replied Grant. "I hate to sound callous, but that's yesterday's news. Just look into our own archives. We've published several articles already. Until something changes, there isn't much to tell that hasn't been told."

Jack shifted gears and pushed the angle of tracking down the League of Orbis Novus and digging into who they were and what motivated them to create the warning. Grant's armor started to crack, ever so slightly. He was reluctant to dampen the spirits of his junior reporter.

"First you'd have to find them, and I suspect that would be next to impossible," he told his protégé. "*If* you were able to, *and* their backstory was compelling enough… Well, then I might—*might*—let this move forward."

"So, I can research them?"

"Hold on there, scout. You can use the paper's resources—on your own time. If you come up with anything, let me know."

It wasn't exactly the endorsement for which Jack had hoped, yet it also wasn't the outright rejection he had feared. He decided not to press his luck and agreed to the terms. He waited for Grant to leave the kitchen, then dumped his coffee into the sink and headed for his cubicle.

In light of the extra workload he had created for himself, it was not the best time for his sister and her husband to visit. There wasn't much he could do about it and they were not exactly visiting *him* so much as they were visiting Las Vegas. As Mindy had worded it in her text message, she and Ron wanted one last shindig before they connected with their new daughter in Guatemala. Although Jack had graciously offered the use of his apartment for their stay, they had decided to stay at a resort on the Strip, "in the heart of the action," as Mindy put it.

Jack was relieved to be off the hook with respect to hosting Mindy and Ron, but his sister made it explicitly clear that his presence was required for dinner on at least two of the three evenings they were in town, to include bringing his latest girlfriend (whose name had escaped her) to one or both of the dinners. Furthermore, his and the girlfriend's presence, though optional, were desired at the Cirque du Soleil show on the second night of their stay. Jack had always found it difficult to defy his older sibling. When they were kids, it carried the consequence of a strong punch in the arm. At this stage in their lives, he missed spending time with her and didn't want to forfeit the opportunity. The death of their mother had brought them closer as adult siblings. Thus, he agreed to her terms and put aside his extracurricular research for the weekend.

He would have to take a night off from his moonlighting job at the steakhouse as well. Following a few days of internal deliberation, he decided that it was the right time to permanently relinquish the table-waiting business. The tips were great and the extra money came in handy, but he had been wrestling with the notion of focusing on the career for several months, and Orbis Novus was the perfect catalyst.

Jack felt a little touched emotionally when he informed the restaurant manager of his resignation. It signified the end of an era—a kind of transition to adulthood that was long past due. Waiting tables was the relic of the acting dream that had already perished, and Jack relived it for one final moment there in the manager's office. For his part, the manager didn't appear to be all that shaken-up about losing Jack. He even agreed to extend the employee discount to him for one last dinner.

Jeanine freed her schedule to attend the meal at the steakhouse and the acrobatic show that followed. Once again, the upcoming adoption fueled the dinner conversation. Mindy and Ron were scheduled to fly into Guatemala City one week later, where they would sign the final paperwork and permanently unite with their fifteen-month-old daughter, Bella.

"Are you worried about traveling there, given what's happened recently?" asked Jeanine.

"Nah," replied Ron. "That was in a village a hundred miles to the north. We won't be anywhere near there."

Jack had no idea of the incident to which they referred. He was embarrassed for being the only journalist at the table and the only one of the four who had not heard about the situation in Guatemala. He was about to reveal his ignorance then decided to ride it out. He acknowledged the discussion points in the form of a few corroborating nods and said nothing.

"We also looked at the State Department's travel advisory," said Mindy. "It basically said that there was no threat to travelers with respect to the mysterious deaths, but they recommended staying away from that particular village."

"The level of crime there still sucks, though," added Ron. "We won't be leaving the hotel much."

Jack saw an opportunity to jump in.

"How many people died in all?" he asked in a tone that suggested he had once known the number but had subsequently forgotten.

"Six," said Ron. "There haven't been any new cases in more than a month."

"Did they figure out what caused it?" asked Jeanine.

"Nope," continued Ron. "At first they thought it might be the Bird Flu or something called the Mayberry Virus—"

"*Marburg*, honey," said Mindy, while placing her hand on Ron's in a motherly fashion.

"Right, Marburg. I guess the symptoms were similar but the tests were negative."

"What's the Marburg Virus?" Jeanine asked.

"Something you don't want to get," Ron said smugly. He didn't know any more than that.

"Anyway," concluded Mindy, "The whole thing seems to be over, and it isn't an issue for us." She had already convinced herself of this and didn't want to hear anything that might change her mind. They were going to get their daughter and nothing would stand in their way. "So, tell us about your job, Jeanine," she said, successfully diverting the dialogue.

Following the show and a friendly disagreement over the origins of Cirque du Soleil's unique performers, the two couples parted ways.

(Ron had read an internet post claiming that many of the performers were purchased from Russian labor camps in Siberia.) It was after midnight by the time Jack pulled into the apartment complex. He invited Jeanine up to his place, but she politely declined, citing an upcoming early-morning study session. He escorted her over to her own building and returned home, where he promptly logged into his laptop. He wanted to bone up on the inexplicable Guatemalan deaths—not because of a thriving interest in the incident so much as wanting to be prepared in case the subject arose at the office. Grant often preached that a good reporter was always on top of the headlines, and Jack felt that he had so far dodged a bullet on this one.

His mail icon indicated the arrival of a new message, and he pulled up the mailbox to see that it was from Craig. The subject line read, "Thought you'd be interested in this." Jack found it amusing that the professional debunker would use a subject line that was so common among the junk email messages that propagated internet hoaxes. He was a little surprised that Craig's message had not gone directly to his spam folder.

The body of the message consisted entirely of an html link—more evidence of an internet chain message or phishing scam. Jack doublechecked that the email had indeed come from Craig before clicking on the link. Upon doing so, a very spartan webpage popped up in his browser. It read as follows:

September 1

> *"If you want a picture of the future, imagine a boot stamping on a human face, forever. The moral to be drawn from this dangerous nightmare situation is a simple one: don't let it happen. It depends on you."*

On December 1st, three short months from today, opioids will no longer render their desired effect. The time has come to rid the planet of this toxic pestilence.

This is your second warning. One final warning

```
will follow. This could be heaven or this
could be hell. You decide.

- The League of Orbis Novus
```

The leading quote rang a bell with Jack, yet he couldn't place it. A quick web search revealed that it came from the George Orwell novel, *1984*. Jack immediately recognized the sentence near the bottom as an excerpt from the Eagles song "Hotel California." The combination of the two quotes struck him as an odd pairing. Most of the remaining text was nearly identical to the previous message, updated to reflect that it was the second of three warnings. He downloaded a copy of the webpage to his desktop and went to bed. The first thing he did upon waking in the morning was to try the link again. He received the universal "404 Not Found" message. The webpage was gone, as he suspected it would be.

Prior to the arrival of the second warning, Jack's research efforts had faltered. To say that they had stalled or hit a wall would imply that they had once yielded fruit, which they had not. A few days earlier, he had picked the brain of a seasoned investigative reporter at the *Chronicle*. The reporter listened patiently to Jack's verbal inventory of the facts before telling him that he simply had too many dead ends and nothing left to pursue. Jack had come to the brink of giving up the chase and admitting to Grant that the exercise was a complete failure. The appearance of a second message now rekindled the withering flame. He sauntered into the office armed with fresh ammunition, unaware that the puzzle of Orbis Novus would soon grow even more intriguing.

Grant studied a printout of the warning message that Jack laid upon his desk. He leaned back in his chair and clasped his hands on top of his head.

"This is interesting, Jack, but it isn't much different than the first message."

"I know, but it demonstrates that this wasn't a one-time hoax," suggested the protégé.

"Right. It's a two-time hoax. What's the difference?"

"The guys from the Hoax Hunters site said that—"

He was suddenly interrupted by a knock on the doorframe. Jimmy, the other cub reporter on the *Chronicle*, poked his head inside the door to Grant's office.

"Jack—you're the Orbis Novus guy, right?" he asked.

"Yeah, why?"

"You didn't see the billboards?" Jack and Grant exchanged curious glances.

"No… what billboards?" asked Jack. Jimmy entered the office and stood over Grant's shoulder.

"Check the wire," he said.

Grant launched his interface to the Associated Press content services and typed in a search for Orbis Novus. There was a blurb about a series of puzzling billboard notices that had appeared in several major cities on the previous day. The wire noted that billboards were seen in New York, Los Angeles, London, Paris, Berlin, Prague, Mexico City, Buenos Aires, Beijing, Bangkok, Tokyo, and Sydney. Each contained the identical message written in the country's native language. The wire article included the English version of the billboard message.

"It's identical to this one," said Jack, pointing to his printout from the website, "except that the Orwell quote is missing."

"There's no room for the quote on a billboard," said Grant. "They wanted to keep the message simple."

The brief article concluded with a sentence stating that the funding sources for the billboards had not been identified and that there was no official record of the League of Orbis Novus.

"Who's talking about this?" asked Grant. He was referring to the major news outlets.

"Just a few mentions online. Nobody's taking it very seriously," replied Jimmy.

"I wouldn't expect them to," Grant speculated. "But you boys have piqued my interest. Let's see if you two can put together an in-depth piece on this Orbis Novus thing. Who knows? Maybe we'll get a scoop."

Grant did not truly believe that there was anything behind the warnings. Nonetheless, the incorporation of international billboards indicated that Orbis Novus was more than just a high school kid operating out of his bedroom. The two young men looked at their editor with wide-eyed expressions that conveyed both excitement and indecision. Grant recognized the look and knew that the junior reporters didn't know where to begin.

"Jack, you'll be the lead on this," he instructed. "Find an expert—a scientist of some kind—who can expound on what this group might have in mind with respect to opioids." He pivoted slightly and pointed his index finger at Jimmy. "See if you can find out who paid for the billboards. Start with the one in L.A."

They had just stepped into the hallway when Grant called out to them.

"And one more thing," he said loudly. "Find out what the FBI has to say about this."

Jack hustled back to his cubicle, plopped down in his chair, then stared blankly at his computer monitor for several minutes. Grant's instructions seemed pretty straightforward, yet he found himself struggling to figure out how to begin researching the scientific angle of the story. He decided to tackle the FBI first. He looked up the number for the main office in Los Angeles and called it from his desk phone.

He identified himself as a member of the press to the FBI operator and was subsequently forwarded to the local communications director, a man named Carl Dignasiak. Dignasiak's phone went straight to voicemail, where Jack left him a message detailing the purpose of his call. He was a little surprised when Dignasiak called him back an hour later, having presumed that he would need to leave a few more messages before receiving a response.

Dignasiak sounded familiar with the billboard. Jack wondered if this was merely the result of having dug into it upon receiving his voicemail message. Nonetheless, the FBI agent was very cordial and appreciative of Jack's inquiry. On the record, he told Jack that the FBI takes the threats very seriously and is investigating the possible sources of the billboard warning and their potential ties to known terrorist organizations. Off the record, he called Jack's attention to several other "quirky" advertisements in Los Angeles that admonished its citizens or prophesized of impending doom.

"There's currently a sign above an abandoned gas station off of Melrose that's been forecasting the end of the world for two years now," he said.

"Do you know who paid for it?" asked Jack. He read from a short list of questions he had jotted down before calling.

"In that particular case, we do. It's a Pentecostal church in the neighborhood."

"So, that's a different situation."

"Maybe," said Dignasiak.

"Is there anything about the Orbis Novus warning that strikes you as being different in some way?"

"Different… in what way?" replied Dignasiak. His patience with the reporter was beginning to wear thin, yet he maintained his politeness, as any professionally-trained communications director would.

"I was referring to the subject—opioids."

"I guess it's the first time we've seen a group of wackos targeting the opioid crisis, but that's a relatively new issue." He took a deep breath then continued. "Honestly, those billboards are expensive. I doubt that it will still be there in a week, but if it is, we'll figure out who's behind it."

Jack thanked him for his time, to which the agent responded that he could reach out to him any time.

At the end of the long day, Jack synced up with Jimmy. His partner had made little progress in tracking down the funding source of the billboard in Los Angeles. As they suspected, the bill was paid in cash. The advertising agency would not comment further on the customer nor the duration of the ad. The woman at the agency had hinted that the buyer was probably anonymous, though she would not confirm that on the record. Jimmy had spent most of the afternoon tracking down the agency that managed the advertising space for the New York billboard. When he finally reached them, they had nothing of value to say. The reporters were stumped and looked at each other with the same blank stares they had cast to Grant earlier that morning.

"I really want to write this story, man," said Jack. "We've gotta come up with something."

"How about the scientific angle?" asked Jimmy. "Why don't you reach out to someone at UNLV?"

"Yeah. I've been thinking about that. I've got a better idea."

6

On that same day, Gina Alvarez opened the massive spreadsheet on her desktop display and marveled at the number of entries contained within. There were 37,393 in total, representing a five-year period. Each row contained the attributes, or metadata, of a specific phone call, and each needed to be analyzed for the case. The thirty-year-old FBI special agent then directed her attention to her email inbox, in the hopes of finding a quasi-legitimate excuse to delay the tedious task that would surely occupy her time for weeks to come. Her rationale for procrastination was soon provided by an unlikely source—the same person who assigned the job to her.

Daryll Jameson was the special agent in charge of the Las Vegas FBI field office. Although he was well into the second half of his storied career, he still cast an imposing figure, despite his reputation for equanimity. He lost his temper about as often as he smiled, which was almost never. He cared about the careers and well-being of the junior agents in his command—they just didn't know it. Nevertheless, they respected their sturdy, six-foot three-inch boss and were grateful to be working under him.

Daryll walked into the small office that Gina shared with another agent. "Are those the Poison Ivy phone records?" he asked, referring to the name of the case to which Gina was assigned. It was one of the largest cases the FBI was working at the time, and most of the agents in the Las Vegas office were involved. Vegas was one of several offices investigating the case nationwide.

"Yes, I was just about to dive in," replied Gina, somewhat truthfully.

"That might have to wait."

Daryll ate, drank, and slept the Poison Ivy case. Whatever it was that was taking her away from the phone records must also be related to the case, Gina deduced. She was right.

"Metro found the body of one of our CIs," continued Daryll. He was referring to the Las Vegas Metropolitan Police and a confidential informant for the Poison Ivy case. "Jacobs is already there, and I'm about to head over. Do you want to come with me?"

Daryll had a way of disguising his orders in the form of questions. Gina had no choice, but she was happy to go along. She had not been out of the office for a case in weeks and could barely contain her enthusiasm. Without a word, she quickly locked her computer and followed Daryll into the hallway before he might change his mind. Her officemate, Shawn, gave her a thumbs-up as she left the room. He was happy for her and a little envious.

The short car ride over to the Church-Noblitt neighborhood east of downtown was a quiet one. Gina couldn't figure out why her boss wanted her along since she was one of the lowest-ranking agents from Las Vegas assigned to the case. She presumed that it was simply for her own experience and she wasn't about to question his decision.

Daryll pulled into the parking lot of a low-rent apartment complex where they saw Agent Jacobs speaking with a uniformed Metro sergeant. The building resembled an old motel more than apartments. The two-story, U-shaped structure surrounded a concrete courtyard containing two crooked palm trees. In the middle of the courtyard sat a cracked, dried-out pool that a couple of teenagers were using as a skateboard park. Nearby, orderlies from the coroner's office were carefully loading a body bag into a van as a few residents looked on.

The sergeant waved to Daryll as they approached. Daryll seemed to know every law enforcement worker in Las Vegas—or at least, they knew him. Having only been assigned to Las Vegas for a year, Gina knew very few people beyond her limited professional circle. She assumed that her job was to listen and learn, and she remained quiet following a brief introduction to the Metro officer.

"Was it a homicide, Paul?" asked Daryll.

The sergeant seemed a little surprised by the question. "She OD'd," he said, then showed the others a small paper strip. "See this pink line?

There was fentanyl in the heroin. It only takes a little bit."

"Is it possible that someone could have targeted her—maybe spiked her heroin with the fentanyl?" pressed Daryll.

"I guess it's *possible*, Daryll," replied the sergeant. "But I wouldn't rule out the more likely scenario. This is the fifth overdose in this neighborhood in three days. They probably all stem from the same batch of fentanyl-laced heroin."

"She was working for us on a trafficking case," said Daryll.

"Heroin?"

"Human. She danced at the Kitten Klub. Did any of the other overdose victims dance there?"

"I really don't know, Daryll. You have to understand that this is pretty common around here. I mean, we see this all the time. She fell into the trap and she died. It's pretty straightforward. Sad, but straightforward."

"Why cut heroin with fentanyl?" asked Jacobs.

"Who knows? It makes the product stronger… It's cheap… I guess it boosts their profits."

"And kills their customers," added Daryll.

"Tell me about it," said the sergeant. "My district had more than 1500 ODs last year alone. A lot of them died."

Daryll looked over toward a young woman speaking with a Metro officer. "Is that the roommate?"

"Yeah," said the sergeant. "She told us that they bought from their usual guy. We know who he is. We'll talk to him."

"I'd like to be there when you do."

"Sure, Daryll."

Daryll then turned to Gina. "Agent Alvarez, why don't you talk to the young lady and see what you can find out?"

Gina now understood why she was there. Daryll hoped that the roommate might open up to the young female agent about the circumstances surrounding the CI's death. Gina greeted the roommate and brought her over to a tattered wooden bench where they sat down, away from the others.

The woman, whose name was Sarah, was scared and still in a state of shock—not just from the loss of her friend, but because she had come within seconds of her own death. If the victim hadn't exhibited the signs of an overdose so quickly, Sarah would have soon taken a hit from the same batch and met with the same fate. Gina also perceived that Sarah was experiencing symptoms of withdrawal, and took note of the woman's frail, underweight physique. Nevertheless, she had a job to do and she questioned Sarah about the victim's employment at the Kitten Klub.

"She never talked much about it," said Sarah. "She kept telling me how she was gonna save money and go home to Provo."

"Did she mention anything about being threatened?"

Sarah began to shiver, though it was very warm outside. She clutched her body and rocked back and forth. "I told you. I don't know anything about that."

"Did she start hanging around with anybody new recently?"

Sarah ignored the question. "She went to college, you know. That's where she started."

"Started what?"

"Using. She told me that she broke her leg riding a bike. The doctor gave her oxy."

"How did she end up here?"

Sarah looked at Gina as if she must have recently arrived from another planet. "How does anybody end up here?"

Gina nodded sheepishly. They spoke for a few minutes longer, during which Gina deduced that Sarah knew nothing about the CI's involvement with the case. She felt compelled to help the young addict.

"Is there someplace you can go?" she asked.

"Yeah, back inside my apartment," answered Sarah nastily. "Can I go now?"

"Of course, and thank you."

Gina returned to Daryll and Jacobs and briefed them on her conversation, concluding with, "I don't think she knows anything."

The drive back to the office was as awkwardly quiet as the ride over. Daryll was preoccupied with his paramount case and seemed unconvinced that the CI's death was accidental. Gina silently disagreed, though she had nothing to offer in support of her opinion. Throughout the day, she couldn't stop thinking about Sarah. She wondered how long it would be before the frail woman became another overdose victim. She told her officemate about the experience.

"It's strange," said Gina. "That woman is only a few blocks away from here, but she's living in a completely different world from us. Her whole life revolves around getting a fix, just so she can feel normal. It isn't even about getting high."

"I know," said Shawn. "Metro has their hands full." The highly-trained law enforcement officer tended to look at things from a criminal angle.

"She went to the University of Utah," noted Gina.

"Who?"

"The CI. She dropped out and came here."

"Then she never should have left."

Gina was curious about Shawn's apathy, yet decided not to push the dialogue further. There was work to be done, and the Poison Ivy phone records were hanging over her head like a dreaded college term paper.

7

Jack Kurry placed a call to his sister before he left the office late that evening. As soon as she answered, he launched into a breathless monologue about the emergence of the second warning. Mindy halted him in mid-sentence, implored him to slow down, and informed him that she didn't have the slightest idea what he was talking about.

"Ron didn't tell you about Orbis Novus?" asked Jack.

"No. What's an orbit's novice?"

Jack reminded himself that the world was paying little attention to the league's dubious warnings. He went backward a few steps and briefed his sister on his assignment to write about the mysterious internet messages and billboards.

"They put up billboards?" asked Mindy in disbelief.

"Yeah, all over the world."

"What do they plan to do on December 1st?"

"That's what I'm calling you about. Do you think you could put me in touch with someone at UCSD who might be able to help?"

"I guess so. What kind of help are we talking about?" Mindy was eager to assist her kid brother but she was still a little confused with respect to what he needed. He didn't exactly know either. His boss wanted the opinion of a scientist, and his sister worked with a lot of scientists. That was the extent of the logic behind the call to her.

"Well, let's see..." Mindy thought aloud. "Opioids come from opium poppies... poppies are plants... drugs are chemicals. I'm thinking you'll want to talk to a biochemistry professor."

"I assume you have plenty of those at UCSD, right?"

"Uh, yeah," she replied sarcastically. "You could say that."

Mindy proceeded to roll through a mental list of the professors she thought might be of help, partially aloud and partially to herself. When she didn't feel satisfied with any of the options she had conjured, she pulled up a faculty list on her smartphone.

"Ah! Here we go. Muriel Smithson. I don't know why I didn't think of her in the first place. You'll like her." She assured Jack that she would reach out to Dr. Smithson first thing in the morning and try to set up a meeting for the same day. She then brought her brother up to speed on her and Ron's upcoming trip to Guatemala before saying goodnight.

"Good luck with the Orbis… what is it again?"

"Novus. It's Latin for new world."

"Whatever."

Jack received the go-ahead from his sister at 9 a.m. the next morning, telling him that Dr. Smithson would be happy to meet with him in her office at two o'clock that afternoon. There was no need to stay in San Diego overnight. He could leave directly for UCSD from the *Chronicle* office and make it back home well before midnight. So, he jumped into his Civic and hit the road without thinking to stop by Grant's office first. He phoned his boss from his car about an hour later and explained why he was calling from Interstate 15. Grant verbally approved the mileage reimbursement then coached his cub on the dos and don'ts of interviewing scientists. Jack did his best to make mental notes, though only about half of it sunk in.

He eventually arrived at an open door and found Muriel Smithson sitting in a tiny square office, behind a tiny desk hidden under layers of notebooks and loose paper. She was an older woman, though her face appeared younger than the advanced age suggested by her silver hair. It had been that color since her late thirties. At the moment, her long, straight hair was pulled back into a tight ponytail—more for utility than style. She appeared to be lost in concentration, though Jack could not determine which of the scattered papers in front of her was garnering her attention.

"Hello," he said softly, as if politely rousing her from a deep sleep. She raised her head and surveyed Jack with inquisitive eyes.

"Yes?" she replied, while trying to remember which of her classes the young man standing before her was taking.

"I'm Jack Kurry… from the *Las Vegas Chronicle*," he said, making it sound a little bit like a question. Her expression immediately changed from mild annoyance to delight.

"Oh, right! Come in. Please, sit down." She stood and quickly cleared a small stack of books from the chair in front of her desk. The jeans and button-down shirt she wore seemed well-suited for her slender frame, and Jack wondered why he had imagined her wearing a white lab coat.

"Your sister told me a little bit about your story," she continued. "Something about opioids?"

Jack was encouraged by the professor's zeal. She was amicable by nature and genuinely eager to help. She was also grateful for anything that diverted her from grading papers. Jack presumed that she had no knowledge of Orbis Novus. Upon her validation of his assumption, he proceeded to show her copies of the internet warnings and spent a few minutes briefing her on their history.

"This part here, Dr, Smithson, also appeared—"

"Muriel," she interjected.

"Muriel," continued Jack while pointing to a segment of the message. "This part also appeared on several billboards around the world this week. That's when my paper decided to write a story about it."

"This isn't exactly my area of expertise, but let's see what we have here," she said while trying not to sound too discouraging. She re-read the message to herself while silently moving her lips.

"Hmm. It's interesting that they say 'opioids' instead of 'opiates'," she noted.

"Why is that?"

"It might just be a semantic oversight, but I would think that their target is opiates."

"What's the difference?" asked Jack. Muriel paused for a moment to formulate a response in layman's terms.

"Opiates are naturally derived from opium poppies—like morphine and heroin. Opioids include all of the opiates plus the synthetic compounds that can act upon the same receptors in the body. That includes Vicodin and Oxycodone—you probably know it as OxyContin."

She continued to speak on a tangent explaining the chemical and biological constructs of opioid receptors. With each passing minute, her layman terminology gradually yielded to nomenclature more suited for graduate students. Jack listened politely until she took a deep breath.

"So, why would they only want to target the natural opioids?" he asked.

"Well, think about," she replied, reverting back to a level of detail better suited to her novice audience, while retaining the tone of a teacher educating a student. "They could achieve a wider impact by going after the source instead of the finished product."

"The source?"

"The opium poppy fields. If these threats are genuine, they'd probably try to poison, destroy, or otherwise tamper with poppy fields," said the teacher.

"That sounds like a pretty tall order," observed the reporter-turned-student.

"Not as difficult as attacking the finished product."

"Heroin? Yeah, it's distributed all over the world."

"And in the hands of some very dangerous people—mostly the cartels, I would think," added the teacher.

"I imagine that the poppy fields are pretty well-guarded too," noted the student.

"Exactly. That's why the whole notion of a group like Orbis Novus is… well, outlandish. Even if they managed to disrupt a few poppy fields here and there, the effect would have short reach and be short-lived. Governments attempt that approach all the time."

"With little success," added the student.

"True. I don't think that isolated incidents of toxic heroin would make the kind of difference they're suggesting in their warnings."

"So, why do you think somebody would post warnings like these if they aren't for real?" asked Jack.

"Now you're *definitely* beyond my area of expertise," replied Muriel with a smile. "We have a psych department two buildings over."

The professor next steered the conversation back into her own neighborhood, and explained the biochemistry behind drug addiction. Jack took copious notes but soon found himself swimming in the details. His page was filled with terminology that would require extensive follow-up research if he was going to cover this angle of the story. His takeaway from this portion of the meeting was that scientists were constantly making new discoveries that caused them to rethink the complex inner-workings of the brain. This was especially true with respect to the neurotransmitter called dopamine. Dopamine seemed to play a crucial role in reward-related learning, which was at the heart of addiction. He circled the word on his notes.

Jack graciously thanked Muriel for her time then walked out of the building feeling a little dejected. His article was not intended to be about the science of drug addiction. There were thousands of those already in circulation and he lacked the qualifications to write one anyway. Muriel's professional opinion on the Orbis Novus warnings was a resounding rejection of their authenticity. There was little that anyone could do to stem the supply of illegal opiates. The bloated and corrupt governments of the world had already proved that.

He tried to recapture some of his momentum on the long drive home. *Maybe Jimmy has dug up something about the billboards?* A quick phone call to his partner revealed otherwise. The news was disappointing though not surprising. There was no point in stewing over it any more that night, so he turned on his satellite radio and searched for a good diversion. He flopped onto his bed soon after arriving home and managed to fall asleep about two hours later.

It was early when he pulled into the *Chronicle* parking lot the next morning—so early that he beat Grant there, and Grant was usually in by 7 a.m. The door to his boss' office was open, so he plopped down behind the desk and waited. Grant was more surprised to find Jack at such an early hour than he was to find him sitting in his desk chair.

"Judging by the look on your face, I'd say things didn't go so well yesterday," suggested the senior editor as he placed a brown lunch bag into a compact refrigerator behind his desk. Jack relinquished the chair to his boss, then filled him in on his progress—or lack thereof.

Grant leaned back and smiled. "Why are you moping about this? So, the FBI isn't really concerned and the professor thinks its hogwash. Those aren't exactly surprises."

"I just thought I'd find more to write about," said Jack.

"That's it, then? You're finished?" asked Grant. He leaned forward and put his elbows on his desk, as he always did before launching into a teaching moment. "Jack, there's still a newsworthy story here, just maybe not one for the front page. Did you think this was going to be your own personal Watergate? Those are pretty rare. You can have a long rewarding career as a reporter and never stumble onto anything close to that."

"I didn't think that," replied Jack defensively. "I guess I'm a little stuck, that's all."

"That's fine. That's why I'm here. Now, show me what you've got."

Jack went over his notes from the meeting with Muriel Smithson and his call with the FBI communications director in Los Angeles. Grant reclined once again and rested his hands on his protuberant stomach.

"Okay—here's what you do. Delve into a history of previous vigilante attempts to thwart the drug trade. The DEA can probably help with that and I know a guy there you can call. Find out what Interpol thinks about it too. This is an international story now."

"Sounds good," said Jack. He wasn't just telling his boss what he wanted to hear. He truly felt better about the story again.

"And don't worry too much about the science. This isn't a story about drug addiction. It's about the frustration people have with the failure of their elected officials to do anything about it. Orbis Novus might be a hoax, but there's a deep-seeded motivation behind it. They bought friggin' billboards, for chrissakes. What would provoke someone to do that? Your job is to get the readers talking about it."

"Can I quote you on all that?" quipped Jack.

The day flew by. Jimmy pitched in by helping to research vigilante efforts. Much of what he found was centered upon local citizens standing up to the cartels, such as the Avocado Army in the small Mexican town of Tancítaro. Southeast Asia was riddled with examples. Villagers in Myanmar had taken up arms against opium traders, and vigilante movements in the Philippines had been making headlines for years. A group of fed-up Russian citizens had taken matters into their own hands as well.

There was a lot of useful supporting data and Jack wrote extensively about it. Yet when he took a break and reviewed what he had written about the vigilantes, something was missing. The examples didn't seem to connect to the Orbis Novus warnings. The vigilante efforts were localized militia responses to violence and thuggery in their own neighborhoods. Humans had been doing that since the dawn of civilization. Orbis Novus was global, and their declarations mentioned nothing about cartels and violence.

Jack wondered if this difference was perhaps the angle for which he had been searching. The point of his article would be that Orbis Novus was unique. Was this the beginning of a new trend? What might they have in store for the world?

The call with a German Interpol liaison was helpful. The man was aware of the billboard in Berlin and seemed genuinely concerned. He said that his organization was enabling the exchange of information between local authorities in the various cities where the billboards appeared. That was essentially the mission of Interpol.

"It isn't like the movies," he said with a slight accent. "We are not an international police force. Our job is to facilitate cooperation among police services around the world." He offered to provide Jack with the phone number of his contact within the Berlin police department. "You should speak with him. They took down the billboard there," he added.

Jack spoke with the police contact in Berlin who confirmed that the billboard had been deemed "menacing," which provided the city government with the authority to take it down. After several calls to London and Paris, Jack learned that officials in those cities had taken similar courses of action. The proactive responses in the European metropolises spawned another angle to the story. What rights do citizens have when issuing public warnings like the Orbis Novus messages? Is it free speech? He posed the question to Tom Hardesty, the *Chronicle*'s lead attorney and legal consultant.

"It's not like yelling 'fire' in a public theater," said Hardesty. "In my opinion, their message is too vague to be considered a genuine threat to society or even a public nuisance—at least, here in the U.S. The European governments probably have more leeway in these matters. My guess is that the billboards in L.A. and New York will disappear on their own."

He was right. Exactly a week after they appeared, the billboard messages in the two American cities were replaced with conventional ads. Jimmy confirmed that they had only been funded for a week. This was on the very same day that the *Chronicle* ran Jack's story in the Special Features section of the paper's print edition. A link to the online version was featured on the site's home page. Grant composed the title: "The League of Orbis Novus: Hoax or Heroes?" Jack received the byline and Jimmy was noted as a contributor at the end of the article.

"This is a decent article—very adequate," Grant told his two junior reporters as he perused it in between bites of his Chick-fil-A sandwich—a leftover from the previous night's dinner. "It's okay not to have all the answers. Sometimes an article needs to raise questions."

The number of internet comments received over the next few days indicated a below-average readership of the story. Jack wasn't dissuaded by the underwhelming response. Grant was pleased with his effort, and the experience gained in researching and writing the article was invaluable to someone who had only just dipped his feet into journalism. Jack was starting to enjoy his fallback career, and the League of Orbis Novus warnings were no longer haunting him. He looked forward to his next assignment.

8

Sydney Carter pulled into the driveway of the small suburban home in the Sandy Springs neighborhood of Atlanta, near the famous Perimeter Center north of the city. He stepped out of his ten-year-old Ford Explorer and stood for a moment, surveying the front of the house and the tall trees that surrounded it. The leaves were just starting to display shades of burnt-orange and red. It would not be long before they would blanket the lawn and fill the gutters. He noted a small tear in the screen door and that the lawn needed cutting too—perhaps the final mowing of the year.

As he approached the front door, it flung open and two little girls burst out, donned in matching t-shirts of Arch Black and Bulldog Red. The University of Georgia alumnus responsible for the girls' attire stood just inside the door and watched with a reserved expression. She was a short, shapely woman in her early thirties with long dark hair that was presently resting on her shoulders. Her own bright-red Bulldog sweatshirt reflected the sun through the screen door.

"Hi Daddy!" shouted the older girl as she hugged Sydney's waist. The younger sibling embraced one of his legs and mimicked her older sister. "Hi Daddy!"

Sydney stooped down and pulled them into his chest. "Hi Lexi, hi Amanda. It's so good to see you."

"Girls, wait for your father inside," said the woman as she came outside onto the sidewalk. The girls ran inside in the usual order, with the younger copying every move of her older sister.

"How are you?" asked Sydney. He administered a half-hug which was neither reciprocated nor acknowledged.

"I'll be watching the game at Ellie's," said the woman. "I'll be home before eight. Thanks for watching them."

"Jesus, Pam. They're my kids too. You don't have to thank me. I'm not a babysitter."

She continued as if he hadn't spoken a word. "There's plenty of food in the fridge—and no Play-Doh this time. I don't want to come home to a huge mess."

Sydney called out to his wife as she continued toward her car. "I'll see if I can fix that screen while I'm here, and I can come by tomorrow to cut the grass."

His words froze Pam in her tracks. She paused for a moment then returned to Sydney. "I can handle it."

"It's no problem, I'll just stop by—"

"Syd—no." She released a heavy sigh. She had hoped to avoid a conversation with her estranged husband. "Are you still sleeping on Bill's couch?"

"Yeah, he's been pretty good about it. We ride to work together sometimes. He said I could stay until… well, you know—until we figure this out."

"There's nothing that *we* need to figure out, Syd. *You* need to figure it out." She walked a few steps past him, then reluctantly turned around again. "Are you sober?"

"God, Pam. Of course, I'm sober. I wouldn't come here if I wasn't."

"You know what I mean. Are you *sober*?" She already knew the answer. She didn't need to see his disheveled appearance or the bags under his eyes. She just knew. They had been through this too many times over too many years.

Sydney considered his words for a moment before responding. He couldn't tell her what she wanted to hear, but he could spin it in his favor, as he was prone to do. "It's under control. Ask Bill. I'm getting to work on time and just having a few drinks at happy hour and stuff like that."

"You should find your own place, Syd."

"Come on. You don't mean that. If you saw how I—"

"We're not having this conversation again." She spoke without looking back as she continued to her car.

Things did not go any better for Syd when his wife returned a few hours later. His attempts to incite a dialogue ignited another squabble instead. Teeming with disenchantment and frustration, he pulled into the parking lot of a popular sports bar to unwind for a short while before returning to his friend's condominium. A burger and a beer led to a shot of Jack Daniels with the guy seated next to him, who was still celebrating the earlier victory of his beloved Georgia Bulldogs. Sydney had earned his own undergraduate degree from their rival Georgia Tech, but that did little to dampen the festivities. He didn't follow college football very closely anyway. He stayed and watched another game with his latest friend-in-passing. Neither man cared much for who won, though the game grew more and more interesting to them with each drink. Just before midnight, Sydney decided to call it a night. In his deluded mind, he had tempered his imbibing and even felt proud of his newfound self-control. He paid his check, patted his new buddy on the back, and exited to the parking lot.

The officer sat in his patrol car a block down from the bar, as he often did on fall evenings after a full-slate of college football games. He had a good view of the foot traffic coming in and out of the sports pub, and a particular gentleman piqued his policing intuition. There was something about the way the man carried himself. When the driver of the Ford Explorer failed to signal coming out of the parking lot, the officer pulled him over.

This was Sydney's second DUI in five years. He spent the night in a cell at the Dunwoody Police Station, which he shared with two other drunken drivers. His cellmates mostly slept and didn't notice the tears that Sydney strained to hold back throughout the night. His roommate Bill picked him up the next day and drove him over to the impound lot. Nothing was said for several minutes until Bill could no longer hide his concern.

"Syd, I work with a lot of smart people, and you might be the smartest."

Sydney waited for his friend to continue, yet Bill couldn't find the words.

On his lunch break two days later, Syd met with a lawyer named Thad Morton, whom he had located on the internet. Morton specialized in DUI offenses and painted a bleak picture of the consequences to his potential client. Syd's first offense had occurred less than five years earlier, which implied stiffer penalties for the second. The attorney rattled off a litany of punishments, including jail time, a suspended license, community service, an ignition interlock device for his car, and a hefty fine. Syd was more interested in discussing whether the officer had pulled him over unlawfully. He wanted to enter a not-guilty plea and have the case dropped.

"I've been doing this for more than twenty years," said Morton, "and it's my professional opinion that you have a zero percent chance of making that happen. You need to negotiate a plea option."

Sydney reckoned that the lawyer was merely using scare tactics to secure his business as a client. In Sydney's mind *he* was the victim, and it was the overreaching, corrupt government that needed to be held accountable. He thanked Morton for his time and stood up to leave. The seasoned attorney had seen this level of stubbornness and blind arrogance countless times before. He recognized it as a symptom of the disease.

"Mr. Carter, I don't care if you hire me or not," he told Sydney as he scribbled notes on a piece of paper. "But you need help, and I don't just mean legal help. Find an attorney as soon as possible, and call this man when you're ready to deal with your problem." He handed him the paper, which Sydney shoved into his pocket without reading.

Two days and two attorney meetings later, Sydney finally conceded to requesting a plea deal, though he still felt that he had been wronged. Nevertheless, he considered Morton to be the most qualified to assist him and returned to his office for the purpose of rehiring him. Morton didn't appear surprised to see him and treated him graciously.

"Have you had a chance to call that number I gave you?" he asked at the end of their session.

"No. Let's deal with the real problem here, Thad: keeping me out of jail."

When the case was settled two weeks later, Morton kept his client out of jail. Nevertheless, the conviction agreement carried many of the other penalties about which Morton had forewarned his client. Sydney surrendered his driver's license for twelve months, paid the maximum fine of $1000, and agreed to attend the state's DUI Risk Reduction program.

Sydney had not told his wife or anyone at Emerson–Lee University other than Bill about his DUI predicament. It was his intent for nobody else to ever know about it, and now the loss of his driver's license rendered that goal practically impossible. Bill offered to drive his friend to work when their schedules aligned, but there were periods when they worked at different facilities and on different schedules. Bill was employed as a lab technician supporting multiple CDC contracts and was often called to facilities beyond the campus.

The solution came in the form of a used bicycle that Sydney could ride to the Dunwoody MARTA station—one of the northern stops on the Red Line of the Atlanta mass transit system. From there he could ride the train downtown and catch a bus to the campus. He lied to his coworkers, telling them that he was trying to get into better shape while simultaneously saving gas money. Most of them inferred the true reason for his revised commuting habits and kept their opinions to themselves.

Sydney knew that he was rapidly wearing out his welcome with Bill. The living arrangement was supposed to be temporary and the incommodious occupation of his friend's living room was driving an awkward wedge between them. His solution was to come clean to Pam in the hopes that his contrition might prompt her to take him back in the house.

His wife agreed to meet him for lunch at a restaurant near their home where she found his spiel underwhelming. Having failed to convince her, he resorted to pleading, followed by chastising her for not giving him a chance to prove that his drinking was "under control." He was oblivious to how far apart they actually were in the negotiations. He thought that ordering iced tea at lunch showed great promise and commitment; she would settle for nothing less than complete abstinence, and was already near the point of no return. Neither party conveyed their position clearly, for honest communication had never been a pillar of their relationship. Pam did make one thing clear before leaving the restaurant prematurely: she had hired an attorney to pursue a formal separation.

Sydney remained in the booth for another hour, searching on his smartphone for apartments near the Dunwoody Station. He was unfamiliar with the rental market in the pleasant suburb and found the prices to be astounding. After a few days of looking, he signed a lease for the basement apartment of an older home closer to the city and within walking distance of a train station. The cheaper flat was small, dark, musty, and several miles away from his daughters. He would have to ride the train north to see them. He convinced himself that the situation was temporary, now that his drinking was under control. He stocked the small refrigerator with beer, having resolved to stay off hard liquor.

During the turbulent period following the DUI, his professional life suffered from a lack of focus and ambition. He was able to skate by on his remarkable intellect, and his job was not in jeopardy. Still, lesser items fell through the cracks. One of them involved the blood and tissue samples from the Guatemalan outbreak. The world had already forgotten about the incident, in light of such an insignificant number of deaths and the complete disappearance of the pathogen. That it happened in a third-world country probably rendered the story even less newsworthy.

Sydney's trip to the outbreak site was not within the scope of his contract. His services were a gesture of goodwill from the University toward the CDC, with whom they held many government contracts. As such, nobody at Emerson–Lee followed up with him after reading his brief trip report, save for a passing question one day from a coworker a few weeks after he returned.

"What did you find in those blood samples from Guatemala?" she asked.

Sydney had not thought about the samples since submitting his report to the CDC and they had not sent any follow-up questions. He realized then that the samples had never arrived. He subsequently left a voicemail message with his contact at the CDC. Nobody from the CDC responded to his message and he soon forgot about the matter once again.

Two weeks after his plea deal, Sydney attended the first session of the DUI Risk Reduction program, colloquially known as DUI School. The first component of the program was an individual assessment—a questionnaire designed to evaluate his alcohol use. As is typical with many people suffering his affliction, he approached the evaluation with a contemptuous attitude and answered the questions disingenuously. He was convinced that the program was ill-suited for him, having been wrongfully convicted of the crime.

The seasoned professionals administering the evaluation saw through his veneer and required Sydney to attend a 20-hour course designed to educate offenders about drug and alcohol abuse. Even such a modest time commitment slighted Sydney, who felt that a suspended license and fine were more than enough retribution.

"I have a doctorate in molecular pathogenesis," he told Thad Morton over the phone. "I think I understand something as basic as the effects of prolonged alcohol usage on the human body."

"Take the class, keep your mouth shut, and be thankful that you're not in jail," instructed his attorney. Sydney reluctantly adhered to Morton's advice and sat through the course, albeit in silent protest.

He soon found that public transportation afforded him an opportunity to practice his beer-only approach to regulating alcohol intake without the threat of legal ramifications. Nor was he fettered by the active governance of his wife or the passive oversight of Bill, both of whom he felt underestimated his willpower and physical constitution. Over the coming weeks he would see each of them less and less, reaching the point where he barely spoke to Bill and saw his wife only during supervised visits with his daughters.

He began to surround himself with new friends—people who sympathized with him and validated his new approach to drinking. One of his new compadres was a man whom he met in DUI School, and he passed most evenings swapping philosophies with him and others in neighborhood bars. In Sydney's eyes, his career was progressing just fine and he had settled into a new groove. Those in his former circles might have defined the groove as more of a downward spiral searching for a rock-bottom.

9

Jack Kurry returned to writing articles about festivals, celebrations, and major conventions in Las Vegas, of which there were many. The only immediate reward for his efforts covering Orbis Novus was a promise from Grant to gradually transition him over to the *Chronicle*'s crime beat. Grant did not specifically define what he meant by 'gradually.'

Jack planned a trip to meet his new niece such that it coincided with his father's visit for the same purpose. He even timed it so that he could pick up his father at the San Diego airport. The two men arrived at the home of Mindy, Ron, and little Bella on a cool afternoon in early October. Bella had already made herself quite at home under the vigilant eyes of her proud and doting parents. The family room was so littered with toys that Jack found it difficult to recall how it had looked pre-Bella. The couch in the family room also served as his guest bed, given that the number of vacant bedrooms in the house had been cut in half, and his father outranked him for the sole remaining one. Jack reckoned that it was probably a good thing that Jeanine had been unable to attend. They would have probably had to stay in a nearby hotel if she had accompanied him.

The Orbis Novus story could not have been much further from Jack's mind when Ron asked him about it as they sipped beers on the backyard deck.

"What's going on with those opioid guys?" he asked. Before Jack could answer, Ron turned to his father-in-law. "Did you read the article,

Don?"

"Of course. I thought it was very interesting," replied Don. Jack couldn't determine if his father genuinely felt that way or if he was merely being polite.

"I guess we'll find out what they have in mind," said Ron. "When is it supposed to happen, Jack?"

"December 1st. They said that there would be one more warning."

"Will you be covering that for the paper?" asked his father.

"Nah. Honestly, I doubt we'll ever hear from those guys again."

Ron had suddenly grown weary of the topic and pivoted to another without the slightest segue. That was typical of his conversation style and the others just rolled with it.

"Where's Jeanine, Jack? How come we never see her?"

"I barely see her myself."

"Is that a good thing or a bad thing?" asked Don wryly. This was a subject that Jack had no desire to discuss with his father and his nosey brother-in-law. Fortunately, Bella came outside in Mindy's arms and stole the attention of her father and grandfather. Neither topic came up again before Jack headed back to Las Vegas two days later.

Having quit his moonlighting job at the steakhouse and with Jeanine bogged down between school and the law firm, Jack found himself spending more and more time at the poker table. He had played for about three hours each on five consecutive nights since returning from San Diego. He met up with Jeanine for dinner on the following night, then returned to the poker room the next day, which was a Sunday.

He preferred playing on the weekends because it brought a mix of tourists and casual players. It was nice to see new faces at the table, especially if they belonged to mediocre poker players. He was still at the table and up about a hundred dollars around four in the afternoon when a new player took the open seat on the dealer's right. Jack was sitting in the sixth position of the ten-person table, which placed him directly across from the newcomer.

Jack instinctively sized-up the new player to see if he fit any of the poker stereotypes, and to determine if he was intoxicated. The middle-aged man was lean and muscular. He was not overly large in stature, yet he had a somewhat intimidating demeanor, even if it was unintentional. He wore the shadow of a beard below a stylish, layered haircut. Jack noted to himself that the guy resembled a high-roller blackjack gambler more than a low-stakes poker player. The newcomer brought a mixed drink to the table with him but did not appear to be under the influence of anything. He wore fancy jeans and an untucked, long-sleeved button-down shirt. The sleeves were loosely rolled up to his forearms, revealing several tattoos.

The man greeted the table as he sat down. "What's up, fellas?" One or two players mumbled a half-hearted response or nodded. The others ignored him, which is typical at Texas Hold'em tables.

The game continued uneventfully. After several hands, Jack had sized up the new guy as being an average player and a little loose, meaning that he tended to take risks that outweighed the potential rewards. He appeared to be someone who simply wanted to enjoy a few hours—win or lose. Jack loved playing against that type of player and waited for an opportunity to take down a pot at the expense of his new opponent. It happened about thirty minutes later when Jack's set of queens outranked the man's pair of tens. Jack thought it was a little strange that the man had played the hand so poorly, when it should have been obvious that he had the better cards. Nevertheless, he was glad to take the man's money.

"Nice hand," said the man as he patted the table in front of him—a sign of respect.

"Thanks," replied Jack.

"Do you live in Vegas?" asked the stranger. It was not unusual for players to strike up conversations in between hands or after they had folded the current hand. Jack replied in the affirmative, to which the man responded that he was from Cleveland, and was currently in Las Vegas for business.

"Really? I'm originally from Dayton," said Jack with raised eyebrows. He didn't meet people from his home state very often.

The banter continued off and on for the next hour. The man, who had since introduced himself as Frank, seemed fairly amicable in contrast to the tough, though polished, exterior he displayed. The two players swapped stories about growing up in Ohio. Frank knew a lot about the Dayton area as well as his hometown of Cleveland. He was a fan of the Browns football team while Jack followed the rival Bengals. They discussed the current point spread for the upcoming game between the two teams. It was nothing more than an every-day poker table conversation. Jack remained until half past six then decided to call it a day.

"Take it easy, buddy. It was nice meeting you," said Frank as Jack stacked his chips into a clear plastic rack.

"Yeah, you too. Good luck," replied Jack. He took his chips over to the cashier, exchanged them for bills, then headed home to his apartment. On the way, he touched base with Jeanine. The two decided to get together for dinner and a movie on the following evening.

The date didn't exactly go as planned. After the fact, neither Jack nor Jeanine could put a finger on the impetus for the serious conversation on Jack's couch that followed the movie. Perhaps it was the impractical Hollywood ending in the romantic comedy juxtaposed with their own colorless relationship, or maybe it surfaced on its own accord, buoyed by the allure of greener grass. For both of them, the greener grass was the nostalgia of independence, absent of the loneliness that often accompanies it. Neither party had intended to have such a weighty discussion on that particular night, yet neither was particularly regretful that it had transpired.

It began as an innocuous discussion about their plans for the upcoming week, then slowly escalated into a full dissolution of the relationship. They fed off of each other. Perhaps each sensed where the conversation was headed and hoped to preempt the other in order to save a little embarrassment or to claim the title of "initiator." There were no hard feelings on display. The two parties agreed to the terms in a very business-like manner. One might have thought it truly was a meeting between business partners, if not for the brief hug Jeanine gave Jack before leaving his apartment.

Jack sat alone in silence on his couch after she left. He was not a hundred percent certain that they had just broken up. (The confirmation would not occur until a few days passed with zero communication between them.) After mulling the development for a few minutes, he reached for the remote control. There was no sense in dwelling on the decision, nor did he feel compelled to do so. He slept well that night, as did his former girlfriend.

Over the next month, the greener grass of independence would slowly morph into the greener grass of finding the elusive perfect woman. For the time being, Jack adjusted his routine to include spending more time with his friend Mike and more time at the poker table. He briefly contemplated returning to the steakhouse for a night or two per week, then quickly extinguished the notion. Those days were long behind him and he enjoyed his leisure time.

Three Saturdays later, Jeanine was a distant memory and Jack found himself at the Monaco Palace early in the afternoon. The poker room was filled with casual players—mostly college football fans who were monitoring their wagers on the television screens that plastered the room like wallpaper. Occasional shouts of joy or dismay rang out across the poker tables, coinciding with a touchdown, turnover, or other significant play in a marquee game. An hour or so into his session, a familiar face sat down next to him.

"Hey, it's Jack, right?" asked the man. "I'm Frank." He wore a nondescript dress shirt and khaki pants that blended him in with the crowd.

"Sure, I remember. Still in town, huh?"

"I just got back. I had to return for a follow-up meeting."

"Good luck."

"I'll need it, playing against you," said Frank. Jack thought the comment was a bit patronizing. It was not unusual for players to butter-up their opponents like that.

"Yeah, right," he replied with a smirk.

The game did not go very well for either player. After two hours, Jack was down about a hundred and fifty dollars. Frank had lost twice that amount, yet seemed as amiable as the moment he had first sat down to the table.

"That's it for me," Frank abruptly announced after folding his cards a few hands later. "Take it easy." He left the table and disappeared into the crowded casino before Jack had a chance to respond. Jack figured that the guy must have been more frustrated with his losses than he had let on. He played a few more losing hands until his own frustration convinced him to call it quits as well.

The last rays of sunshine were fading as the sun dropped below the Spring Mountains when Jack emerged from the air-conditioned Monaco Palace and entered the warm, stuffy parking garage. A familiar voice called out to him.

"Hey, Jack."

He turned to see Frank quickly approaching. Frank smiled and waved as if he was both surprised and delighted by the serendipitous encounter. Jack thought nothing of the chance meeting at first, then wondered why someone from out of town would be in the parking garage. Maybe he had a rental car?

"Do you have a minute?" asked Frank.

Ugh, thought Jack. *This guy is gonna try to sell me something, or maybe he wants a ride.* He stopped and waited for Frank to approach. The notion that Frank might attempt to rob him flashed through his mind. After all, they were standing in a casino parking garage. But there were plenty of people coming and going, and Jack had very little cash left in his wallet.

"What's up?" asked Jack.

"I read your article," said Frank. He was no longer smiling.

Jack was thrown off kilter and paused in bewilderment before responding. "What article? How do you even know who I am?"

"Are you Jack Kurry?"

Jack looked around the garage. Suddenly there weren't so many people coming and going. "Yeah. Can we go back inside?"

"Okay," said Frank. "Let's get some coffee."

They stopped at a small coffee shop just inside the hotel from the parking garage. Frank purchased two cups of black coffee for them. Jack was too preoccupied with the mysterious aura that now surrounded Frank to tell him that he didn't like coffee. He followed Frank to a small round table where they sat down.

"What's this about?" asked Jack. "Are you referring to the Orbis Novus article?" Frank studied the reporter for a moment before responding with a question of his own.

"Let me ask you something, Jack. Do you think it's just a hoax?"

"I don't know if it's a hoax, per se, but I have a hard time believing that they could make any difference," answered Jack.

Frank shook his head slightly. His response appeared to be something in between disagreement and disapproval. "What if I told you it was legit?"

Jack rumpled his eyebrows in a show of curiosity and disbelief.

Frank surveyed his immediate surroundings then leaned in. "It's true, Jack," he said in a solemn tone. "The League of Orbis Novus is a real thing."

"How do you know?" asked the reporter. Frank responded by widening his eyes and casting a knowing glare. Jack smirked in disbelief and said, "Oh—you're a part of it?"

"Maybe."

"Look, if this is some kind of joke…"

"It's no joke, Jack."

"Are you really from Cleveland?"

"That's not important, but I am here on business. You're my business."

Now Jack felt compelled to survey the surrounding area. Frank's sobering demeanor was making him restless.

"Are you a member of the league?" asked Jack.

"No more questions. That's not why I'm here." Frank took a sip of his coffee and studied Jack for a moment before continuing. "We need you to get the word out. Your paper was the only one that published anything more than a dismissive reference to our warnings."

"You said 'our' warnings. You're one of them."

"Let's just say that I'm associated with them," said Frank. "We need you to write another story."

"That isn't my decision. You'll have to speak with my editor." Jack reached for his phone. "I can call him right now."

Frank put his hand on top of Jack's, preventing him from using his phone. "That's not how this is gonna work. What if I was to take you there?"

"Take me where?"

"Let's call it the Orbis Novus facility."

"It's near here?" asked Jack in disbelief.

Frank ignored his question. "We leave right now."

Jack felt a surge of adrenaline course through his excited veins. This could be a huge story—even if Orbis Novus still turned out to be a hoax. "Okay. I'll follow you there in my car."

Frank smiled in a smirky sort of way. "It doesn't work that way, Jack. We'll take you there."

"Who's 'we'?"

"It starts by you handing me your phone right now."

"What if I say 'no'?" asked Jack, though he had little intention of saying no.

"Then I walk away, and you learn nothing. You'll never see me again."

Like a poker player, Jack leaned back and feigned mulling over the decision he had already made before pushing his phone toward Frank.

"Let's go," said the junior reporter. The pot odds were greater than the risk. He was all in.

Frank powered off Jack's smartphone and slipped it into his own jacket pocket. "You do everything I tell you, or the deal's off," he instructed.

"What exactly *is* the deal?"

"We'll give you something to write about," replied Frank as he stood up. "Walk with me to the garage and don't say a word." He took a step closer to Jack and added quietly, "Now listen. This is gonna take a while. You have to trust me. You're in no danger as long as you do everything I tell you."

A second rush of adrenaline poured through Jack. This one was borne of fear. Frank was an intimidating character, and the word "danger" coming from his lips felt particularly threatening. Nevertheless, he couldn't turn back. There was too much to be gained. He nodded silently to Frank and the two men began walking.

They rode the elevator to the sixth level of the parking garage. Jack had never been on that level before, as there was always ample parking lower down. Frank led him to a large black SUV that was parked in a dark, secluded spot in a far corner of the near-empty lot. Jack made a mental note of the make and model—a Lincoln Navigator. Frank opened the passenger door on the driver's side and extended his arm, beckoning Jack to get in first. Jack climbed nervously into the dark interior and slid into the middle of the bench seat. Frank followed him. Before Jack's eyes could adjust, a black hood was thrown over his head. He reacted instinctively and tried to pull it off. A pair of strong hands held it in place.

"Easy now, Jack," said Frank. His voice seemed to be coming from the opposite direction of the strong hands. Jack sensed that there was another man on his right.

"This wasn't part of the deal," exclaimed Jack.

"The deal is you trust me and you'll be safe," said Frank. "We can't let you see where we're going. Just relax. We'll have you back here before lunch time tomorrow."

"What? Tomorrow? I—"

"Just relax," repeated Frank, slowly and sternly. "No more questions."

The SUV drove smoothly and quietly for several minutes. Jack tried futilely to mentally track their route for a few miles before giving up.

"How long are we going to be driving?" he finally asked.

"Jack…" replied Frank in the same calm, yet threatening tone that a father might use with his child. The sounds of the city soon gave way to the sounds of the suburbs, which eventually faded as well. An hour or so later, the truck pulled onto what felt and sounded like a dirt road, as the tires flung pebbles into the wheel wells. It continued slowly for a few minutes before coming to a halt, though the engine remained running.

"This is our first stop," announced Frank. "It's a short one." Jack reached for the hood covering his head. A large hand met his and held it firmly at bay. "Not yet," said Frank.

He helped Jack out of the SUV and guided him for about fifty paces before they stopped. "We're getting on a plane now," he said. "You'll walk up five steps then duck your head." This development had not crossed Jack's mind as he sat in the SUV pondering the possible destinations for the clandestine excursion. Now the comment about having him back before lunch time tomorrow made more sense. Oddly, the notion of flying in an airplane with Frank and his cohorts did not make Jack more apprehensive. It somehow legitimized the endeavor.

Jack didn't need his sight to know that it was a small aircraft, yet it was not until the engines powered up that he realized it was a jet. Frank sat him down in a cushy leather seat—much larger and more comfortable than those on a commercial airliner. He heard some murmuring between Frank and another man but couldn't make out what they were saying until Frank said, "I'll check."

"Do you need to take a leak, Jack?"

Not only did Jack need to relieve himself, he also saw an opportunity to have the hood removed, if only for a minute or two. "Yes," he responded.

Frank took him by the arm and led him to the rear of the small cabin. He pivoted him a quarter-turn and removed the hood, before quickly nudging him into a small lavatory.

Jack was able to catch a quick peripheral glimpse of the cabin before the door shut behind him. The seats and walls appeared creamy white in color, with a faux wood veneer. The interior of the lavatory had a similar motif. Jack had never been inside a private airplane, but this one matched his preconceived image of a fancy business jet. He carefully surveyed the inside of the bathroom one more time before leaving. He wanted to soak in every detail for the article he was destined to write. He opened the door to find Frank waiting for him, ready to place the black hood over his head.

Jack found it difficult to track the passage of time during the flight. His best guess was that it lasted for something between two and three hours. The plane taxied for a few minutes upon landing, after which the engines droned to a halt. Jack expected to hear the typical sounds of an airport tarmac—the engines of other jets, vehicles, passengers—yet there was nothing but an eerie silence. Frank helped him to put on a jacket before exiting the plane.

"It's cold out there, huh?" asked Jack. He didn't expect an answer and didn't receive one.

Even through the hood, he could tell that it was dark outside. His foot stepped off the stairs onto a firm, gravelly surface, similar to the one which he had left a few hours earlier. The air felt cooler, though the jacket rendered it difficult to determine how much. They walked for about ten minutes, alternating between grass and gravel. During the walk he could hear two sets of footsteps in addition to his own. One belonged to Frank, who held a firm grasp of his arm. The other presumably belonged to the man who had sat next to him in the SUV.

They eventually stepped onto smooth pavement and came to a halt soon thereafter. Frank held Jack in place with a hand on his shoulder. It sounded as if the other man was opening a door. They entered an airconditioned building and proceeded into another room. Through his hood, Jack saw the light disappear when the door shut behind them.

"Sit here," said Frank. He helped Jack into a seat that felt similar to his desk chair at the *Chronicle*. The hood was suddenly yanked from his head.

There was just enough light for Jack to see that he was seated at a large conference table. Several shadowy figures joined him around the oval table, though the chairs on either side of him were vacant. Someone stood behind him and slightly to the left—he assumed it was Frank. The faint lighting in the room was provided via a single window on the wall opposite from him. Rays of moonlight shone through the spaces between the horizontal blinds and rendered the other occupants as silhouettes. He wondered why they had not simply left the hood over his head. Perhaps they wanted him to catch a mere glimpse of the people involved.

"Welcome, Mr. Kurry," said the voice of an older woman from the far end of the table. He reckoned her accent to be German or Eastern European. "I trust your journey was not too uncomfortable?"

Jack hesitated before replying. "It was fine," he said tensely.

"Excellent," said the woman. "Frank has told you why you are here?"

"Not exactly," replied Jack. He was beginning to acclimate himself to the gravity of his situation.

Frank's voice came from behind. "I told him that he needs to write another story."

"And I told Frank that it's not my decision," said Jack with a hint of nervous anger.

"Do you know how many people perished from opioid overdoses last year?" asked the woman.

"No."

"More than 200,000 worldwide. Do you think that is a problem?"

"Of course."

"Then we will give you what you need to write a story," continued the woman. "Your newspaper will publish it."

"Who are you people?"

"Hold it, Jack," said Frank, while placing his hand on the reporter's shoulder.

"It is alright," said the woman. "We are a group of concerned citizens who have come to together to rid the world of a plague."

"But *who* are you?" pressed Jack.

"We come from all over the world," said a voice belonging to a Latino man. "We cannot provide you with our identities, but I assure you that we are experts in our fields."

"We know what we're doing," added a gruff American man, "and the world needs to take notice."

"What are your fields of expertise?" asked Jack. He was starting to feel a little emboldened. The people at the table seemed to need him—they *wanted* him there. A short silence ensued, followed by some whispering.

"That would be too much to reveal at this time," said the German-sounding woman. It was obvious that she was in charge of the meeting. "Rest assured that we are in full control of our actions, and we are very serious."

"Can you tell me why?"

"*Why?* Have you been living under a rock?" asked the American.

"The most expensive housing in the world is found in emergency rooms and prisons," said a female voice that sounded African or Caribbean to Jack. She spoke in a compassionate tone. "They are not the answer. There is also the cost of treating babies born with addiction, and the spread of HIV and hepatitis. We have to stop it at the source."

"You're vigilantes, then?" asked Jack. "You're going after the cartels?"

The American man let out a disdainful laugh. "We're scientists, man. We—"

"He means to say that our solution is a scientific one, not militaristic," interrupted the German woman. Jack sensed that the league might not have been in complete agreement about how much they were willing to divulge.

A new voice chimed in. She sounded younger and had a slight Asian accent—probably Chinese, Jack thought. "Our intentions are noble, Mr. Kurry. We want to save as many lives as possible."

"From addiction to opiates?" asked Jack. The question spurred another round of unintelligible whispers. Jack wondered if the muffled discussion centered on his use of the term "opiates" instead of "opioids."

"Yes," replied the German woman. "We will cure the world of its addiction to these deadly chemicals."

"I'll need to know how you're planning to accomplish it—for my story."

"We can't provide you with details at this time," said the Latino voice. "If we reveal too much, we risk being thwarted by the authorities."

"Ignorant morons," added the gruff American.

"People who mean well but do not see the big picture," said the Asian woman, attempting to soften her cohort's comment. "They continue to address the symptoms. We will eliminate the cause."

"Like I said," continued the American. "Idiots who coddle the addicts—"

"Enough," said the German woman. "Mr. Kurry, we understand your desire to know more about our operation. Perhaps we can meet again soon. But for tonight, would it be helpful to show you portions of our facility?"

"Sure."

Without another word, Frank placed the hood over Jack's head and a heavy hand upon his shoulder. The room filled with the sounds of people pushing back their chairs and standing up. Nobody spoke.

"Wait," implored Jack in a raised voice. The room quieted abruptly. "Are you still on schedule? Will something happen on December 1st?"

After a pause, a new voice answered. She sounded Russian. "We are. It has taken much longer than we had hoped, but we are confident that our solution is ready. That is why we need more traction with our warnings. We will not delay any longer."

"They've had enough warnings," came a whisper that Jack was not supposed to hear.

"That's it for questions," said Frank, as the others left the room. The two men waited for another minute or so before he led Jack down a corridor and into another room. Jack saw the fluorescent lights come on from underneath the hood, then was temporarily blinded when Frank removed it. When his eyes adjusted, he found himself alone with Frank in some kind of laboratory.

"What is this?" asked Jack.

"Exactly what it looks like," said Frank.

"What am I supposed to learn from seeing this?"

"That this isn't some kind of joke—or hoax, as you called it."

The room was loaded with scientific equipment: beakers, microscopes, tubes, burners, and lots of fancy equipment that Jack could not identify. It was clear that the area had been highly sanitized too. The whiteboards on the walls were blank and there were no papers lying around. Nothing containing writing of any sort was visible. Jack scoured the room from top to bottom in search of clues that might reveal their location, or anything else about the League of Orbis Novus.

"You won't find anything," said Frank, recognizing his captive's intent.

"Who paid for all this?"

"Money? That's no issue at all. You'd be amazed at the number of wealthy people willing to fund such a worthy endeavor."

"Like who?"

"Ha. That's not for me to say."

With the black hood back in place, the men returned to the waiting jet. Jack managed to doze off on the flight back to Las Vegas. He felt a little safer now that he was heading home, and the long, exhausting day had caught up to him in the comfort of his leather seat.

"Let's go," said Frank with a nudge after they landed. The SUV was waiting for them as if it had never left. At least, it seemed to be the same SUV. It retraced the route back to the casino, though it stopped short of the parking garage. Instead, Frank exited the truck and opened the door on a deserted side street nearby. After Jack followed him out, Frank closed the door and removed the hood.

"See? You've still got time for a late breakfast."

"How do I get in touch with you?" asked Jack.

"You don't."

"Of course," said Jack sarcastically.

"And you don't talk to anybody else about this either," added Frank.

"Like who?"

"You know who."

"What happens when they come to me?" asked Jack. He knew that Frank was referring to the police. "They'll want to talk to me after the story comes out."

"Everything you know will already be in your article. You've got nothing else to tell them."

Jack nodded reluctantly to Frank's bewildering answer. He knew that he would not be able to dismiss the authorities so easily. He also knew that Frank wouldn't provide any useful advice, so he started to walk away.

"Hey Jack."

"Yeah?"

"You'll probably want this." Frank tossed Jack's cellphone to him, opened the door, and climbed back into the SUV. As the vehicle sped off, Jack craned to get a glimpse of the license tag. There wasn't one. While walking to the parking garage, he powered up his phone and informed Grant of his excursion.

"How soon can you get here?" asked his boss.

Jack stopped at his apartment for a quick shower before heading to the office. He stood under the hot streaming water and marveled at how surreal the past twenty-four hours now seemed. Although his junket felt like a dream, the League of Orbis Novus was now very real.

It occurred to him that he should contact the police, in spite of Frank's warning. But then he thought, *What crime has been committed?* He concluded that the best course of action was to get to the office asap. *Grant will surely know what to do next.*

Within an hour, Jack had briefed Grant on the recent developments regarding Orbis Novus. Also present were the *Chronicle*'s managing editor and his coworker, Jimmy. Dialed in for the conference was Tom Hardesty, the legal consultant who also happened to be the newspaper's lead counsel.

"Should I start writing the article?" asked Jack.

"Whoa. Hold on a minute," said Grant.

"What do you think, Tom?" asked Janet Holmes, the managing editor.

"Well, I think that Jack and I need to pay a visit to the FBI," replied the voice on the speakerphone. "Today."

Jack cringed in anguish. "The guy—Frank—warned me not to do that."

"Did he threaten you?" asked Tom.

"Not exactly. He just told me not to talk to anyone. It definitely *felt* like a threat."

"Jack, I understand you concern," continued the attorney, "and the *Chronicle* will do everything in its power to protect you. But we have a responsibility to inform the authorities. It's not for us to decide how serious this matter might or might not be."

"After you meet with them, we can talk about publishing another piece," added Janet, as she patted her cub reporter on the back.

"And let's keep this entire episode to ourselves for the time being," instructed Tom.

10

On the morning of October 27th, Gina Alvarez awoke to the sound of her cellphone blasting a fifteen-second audio loop of "All that She Wants" by Ace of Base. Just like the previous twenty or so workday mornings, the FBI special agent cursed the song and vowed to load a new one into her alarm clock app, then subsequently forgot to do so once she was out of bed and on with her day. She shuffled half-asleep into the kitchen of her small home in the Las Vegas community of Southern Highlands and turned on the coffee machine. The next stage of her routine required her to lumber back upstairs and take a shower.

The aforementioned routine had been in place for nearly three years at this juncture, following the separation and consequent divorce from her ex-husband. The marriage had lasted for six years. In retrospect, this was three years longer than Gina would have preferred, and two more than her ex-husband would have preferred, meaning that the final two years had been particularly grating on their nerves. Their relationship since the divorce had been very much improved, owing *partially* to the fact that they had produced no offspring, and *mostly* to the fact that they had practically lost touch with each other.

At the urging of her girlfriends, and having quite recently celebrated her thirty-first birthday, Gina was just beginning to explore the wonders of online dating, albeit with little success. She sometimes wondered if her girlfriends, both married, enjoyed the pastime of perusing online profiles more than she did. She had been flooded with requests from potential suitors since joining the dating site. This was undoubtedly an indication of her physical beauty, as represented by the photos posted by her girlfriends, as well as her background and personality, as described in the profile narrative written by her girlfriends. The data that her girlfriends had posted was perhaps excessive yet not deceitful (unlike so many online dating profiles). She was indeed remarkably attractive and well educated. She was also shy, and often did not see herself in the same light that others did.

The product of Cuban-born grandparents on her paternal side, and a mix of Mexican, Italian, and Irish blood on her maternal side, Gina was a true representation of America's twenty-first century melting pot. As a result of her dark hair, brown eyes, and light-brown complexion, recent immigrants sometimes addressed her in Spanish. She usually responded with a brief "no hablo espanol." If she was feeling particularly feisty, she might reply in French, in which she was nearly fluent.

Her profile on the dating site highlighted that she enjoyed traveling and playing sports such as soccer and volleyball. The photos selected by her girlfriends supported these claims by depicting a well-dressed Gina at various cruise-ship destinations, and an athletically-built Gina in action on the intramural soccer field. As such, most of the men that had reached out to her via the site were, in her own words, "muscle-bound pretty-boys," and not at all what she was hoping for, though her girlfriends enjoyed reviewing their photos.

And so, on this late October morning, she cruised to work in her white Toyota Rav4, very much appreciative of the light traffic. She was used to much worse, having grown up in San Mateo, part of the highly-condensed network of cities that blanketed California's Bay Area. She had spent her undergraduate years at UCLA, sharing the roads with eighteen million fellow Los Angeleans, then endured five years navigating the circular parking lot known as the Washington Beltway. The latter sacrifice was made in service to her fellow citizens, first as an analyst, and more recently as a special agent, both for the FBI.

Following a posting in Houston, and the aforementioned dissolution of her marriage that occurred therein, she applied for an opening in the Las Vegas field office. Upon receiving the job, she packed up her Rav4—a gift to herself in celebration of her divorce—and moved to Sin City. She had no real affinity for the desert or the flashy oasis that it boasted, other than its proximity to her friends and family in California.

Yet over the past year, the heterogenous mix of people, predictable weather, abundance of entertainment, and relatively light traffic had grown on her.

The Las Vegas field office was not as large as one might have guessed, given the nature of the city's primary industry. In terms of FBI-related crime, Clark County, Nevada was one of the smaller markets when compared to other major cities. As such, Gina found herself in a position that was slightly more junior than she would have preferred, and with limited opportunity for advancement. She knew that she would need to relocate again within a few years—preferably to San Francisco next time. But for the time being, she felt reasonably content with her situation.

Gina was especially content to be sitting in her office late that morning, snacking on a granola bar while sifting through thousands of online phone records in support of the intricate case referred to as Poison Ivy, which had the entire office on its toes. Her officemate, Shawn, was busily engaged in a Poison Ivy task of his own and much less talkative than usual. Gina was grateful for this anomaly, though she dared not tell him so and risk ending the silence. Shawn was the only special agent in the Vegas field office over whom Gina could claim seniority. In contrast, Shawn viewed his officemate as something of a peer, and often bent her ear for extended periods of time, recounting the ebbs and flows of his personal life. Gina had learned that the best response was to semi-ignore him and allow him to peter out on his own.

The quietude that morning was ultimately interrupted, albeit not by Shawn. Daryll Jameson, the senior agent in charge of the office, poked his head into the open doorway.

"Hey guys. I need one of you to sit in on a meeting with me," he told them. "It's with a reporter from the *Chronicle*. He claims to know something about an anti-drug vigilante group."

Gina and Shawn exchanged apathetic glances then turned back toward Daryll. There was something about meeting with a newspaper reporter that dampened their enthusiasm.

"Don't everybody jump at once," said the senior agent.

"He wants to interview us about it?" asked Shawn.

"No. He wants to provide us with information about an organization called…" He looked down at the paper in his hands. "Orbis Novus—

wait—The League of Orbis Novus. He thinks they're cooking up something in response to the opiate trade."

"Sounds interesting," said Gina facetiously. "You should go, Shawn."

"Oh, no," replied Shawn. "I wouldn't want to deprive you of such an exciting opportunity."

Daryll was not amused by their interchange. "Look, I don't care which one of you comes with me. Do you want me to choose?"

Gina sighed and stood up. "I'll do it. But you owe me, Shawn."

They had a half-hour before the meeting with the reporter was scheduled to begin. Daryll used the time to brief Gina on the research he had done that morning. To her surprise, Gina found the case more alluring than she had presupposed. She sat at a small round table in Daryll's office and reviewed copies of the Orbis Novus warnings, the *Chronicle*'s article about internet hoaxes, and the memo that the paper's lead counsel had submitted in advance of the meeting.

"I don't understand this part," she said to Daryll. "Did they kidnap this guy Kurry?"

"No, he went along willingly. I'm told that the *Chronicle* is planning to write a story about his experience."

The receptionist called Daryll's office a few minutes later to inform him that his visitors had arrived and were waiting for him in Conference Room B. Gina followed her boss into the meeting room where she found two gentlemen rising from the table to greet them. She knew instantly which one was the reporter and which one was the attorney. Although they were both dressed in business suits, she could easily discern which of them donned one on a regular basis. It was not as if the younger man appeared the slightest bit disheveled or unkempt, it was just that his clothes looked a little more off-the-rack. She also thought he was much cuter than his counterpart.

Gina's countenance revealed no inkling of these impressions as she shook hands with the men. When the obligatory pleasantries had finished, the four participants sat down at the large conference table to discuss the matter at hand. The reporter, who had been introduced to her as Jack Kurry, provided a lengthy synopsis of what had transpired thus far. The attorney, a man by the name of Tom Hardesty, chimed in redundantly from time to time, with the sole purpose, Gina surmised, of justifying his presence at the meeting.

Daryll was masterful at guiding the next phase of the conference. He expressed his sincere gratitude to Jack for having the courage to speak with them. He assured the young man that he was not presently in any danger, then added that the government would afford him any security if, in the remote chance, it might become necessary. Next, Daryll noted that the FBI received hundreds of tips each year regarding threats from fringe organizations, then conceded that this case was somewhat unique in light of Jack's recent airplane ride.

"We take this very seriously," said Daryll. Gina noticed a slight reaction in Jack's eyes and wondered if he really believed Daryll. "We'll delve into this from all directions," continued Daryll. "My hunch is that we'll be able to connect Orbis Novus with an established anarchist movement."

"They didn't seem like anarchists," said Jack. "They said they were scientists, and they spoke like scientists too."

"Okay, okay—that's good," said Daryll, trying to sound supportive. Gina was getting the impression that her boss was not buying into the notion that scientists were behind the scheme.

"Now tell us more about your visit to the facility," instructed Daryll. He glanced at Gina, and then her notepad, which was his way of telling her to take copious notes. Jack recounted everything he could about his visit to the alleged Orbis Novus facility.

"You said the flight lasted two to three hours?" asked Gina, while reviewing her notes.

"Yes."

"That gives us a radius for their location," she continued. "It's probably west of the Mississippi."

"But that's still a huge area," added Daryll, for the purpose of level-setting expectations. "Finding them would be nearly impossible, and maybe not the wisest use of our resources at this point." Gina could see that Daryll's use of the hypothetical "would" versus the definite "will" was not lost on Jack.

"And you met this guy Frank at the Monaco Palace," said Gina, "which is really kind of strange."

"Why is that?" asked Jack.

"Because they'll have lots of video footage of him. He had to have known that."

Daryll proceeded to outline the steps that the Bureau would take in order to determine if there was a legitimate threat. He advised Jack to keep them apprised of any developments. "Ms. Alvarez will give you her contact information. She'll be our lead person on the investigation."

Her boss had not yet informed Gina that she would be handling the case, though she was not surprised to hear it now. She also knew that "lead person on the investigation" really meant that she would be the *only* person working the case, and that she would be doing it without relinquishing her other responsibilities.

Following the meeting with the two gentlemen from the *Chronicle*, Gina followed Daryll into his office for a post-meeting conference.

"I know you're busy, Gina," said Daryll before Gina had a chance to speak. "But can you take this on? It shouldn't demand a lot of your time. We're up to our ears in Poison Ivy."

"No pun intended?" asked Gina.

Daryll understood the joke but did not crack a smile. "Nope."

She knew that Daryll's request was an order in disguise. "Where should I start?"

"See what you can dig up on Orbis Novus, but I doubt you'll find anything. And you can run down the guy from the casino—uh, Frank. Maybe you'll get lucky. Our only hope is to find someone we can question."

"What if we can't?" asked Gina.

"Then we hand it off to DHS."

"And *they'll* forget about it before we do," she added with a sneer. Daryll nodded in affirmation and returned to his computer monitor. Gina recognized her cue to leave, though something else had occurred to her.

"What about Kurry?" she asked.

"What about him?"

"Do you think he's in any danger?"

"No, I don't. These guys just want the *Chronicle* to run another story about them. They'll be finished with him after that." Daryll sensed that Gina wasn't satisfied with his response. "Alright, check in with him on a regular basis. See if he's noticed anything suspicious."

As she was walking out of the office, Daryll gave her one final instruction.

"Agent Alvarez, Poison Ivy is still your top priority—understood?"

"Got it."

Gina returned to her desk and sat down. Her hand reached for the desktop mouse, then she leaned back and crossed her arms. She didn't feel much like pouring through Poison Ivy phone records at the moment.

"How did it go?" asked Shawn.

"I don't know. It was kind of weird."

"How so?"

"Well, I need to get the surveillance video of some guy at the Monaco Palace."

"What's the charge?"

"That's the problem," said Gina. "There is no charge. I want to question him about these vague threats." She handed some printouts to Shawn.

"They won't let you see the video without a warrant," noted Shawn as he took the papers. "It sucks nowadays. A few years ago, we could have waltzed right in there and looked at any footage we wanted. Now they have to cover their own asses. No warrant, no dice." He looked the papers over for a few seconds then added, "Who exactly are these guys threatening?"

"I don't know—the opium growers maybe? The cartels?"

"Ha. Just tell the guys at the Monaco Palace that you're trying to protect some drug lords," quipped Shawn.

"Yeah," snickered Gina. "I'd better go warn the growers. Do you wanna come with me to Afghanistan? We can stop in Thailand too."

"There *are* opium growers in the U.S.," Shawn noted with a hint of sincerity.

"What am I supposed to do? Track them down and warn them about some ambiguous threats from the lunatic fringe?"

"Yes, then arrest them for growing illegal opium," added Shawn. "Tell them it's for their own safety."

The lighthearted banter continued for a few more minutes until Gina had enough, upon which she initiated her semi-ignoring mode and turned to face her desk monitor. To her disappointment, the phone records had not magically disappeared from the spreadsheet.

After a tedious hour spent combing through the insufferable haystack of records and finding no sign of the needle she sought, Gina decided to turn her attention to her new case. It was as good an excuse as any to take a break from the monotony of Poison Ivy. Maybe she could find something about the mysterious organization that had taken Jack on the bizarre field trip, though she harbored no serious aspirations of locating their so-called secret lab. And if she somehow found it, what then? Perhaps the source of the billboard funding was a better route to pursue. Jack had provided details about his conversation with Interpol. *Interpol?* she thought. The idea of a worldwide conspiracy seemed like a stretch to her. The most logical step, and also the easiest, would be to visit the Monaco Palace. But Shawn was right—the casinos were unlikely to cooperate without a warrant.

She leaned back and folded her arms. The phone records were summoning her once again.

11

Jack and Jimmy sat in the two chairs facing Grant's cluttered desk and watched their editor as he stared at the wall behind them in deep thought. Jack's eyes appeared significantly redder and puffier than Jimmy's. The former had been struggling to sleep since returning from his clandestine visit to the Orbis Novus facility; the latter was secretly relieved not to have had his name on the byline of the previous article. Jack's friend Mike had offered him the use of his guestroom—Jack's former bedroom—and the protection of his "Smith & Wesson security system." Jack declined, citing that the feds had assured him that he was in no danger. He was not completely sold on their position, but he was too embarrassed to admit to his friend that he was afraid.

"I think I've got it," said Grant, still staring at the wall. "We'll call it 'My Visit with the League of Orbis Novus.' It'll be a straight narrative. Write it exactly the way you experienced it."

"What's our position with respect to their warnings?" asked Jack. "Do we lend them any credence?"

"This isn't an editorial," replied the seasoned editor. "Just write about what happened to you—step by step. The readers can draw their own conclusions."

"Do you need me?" asked Jimmy.

"Not on this one."

"Sounds good," replied Jimmy, trying to disguise his relief. When he was already halfway out the door, he added, "Let me know if you if you need any help, Jack." Jack thanked him, though Jimmy was already too far down the hallway to hear him.

Jack returned to his cubicle and started typing. The article was easy to write in terms of the research, or lack thereof, it required. Yet he struggled to find the right words to convey his experience. He couldn't help but wonder how Frank would want the story to read. More precisely, he worried about what Frank might do if the league didn't like the story. Within an hour, he found himself back in Grant's office.

"You're overthinking this," said the editor. "A good journalist isn't compromised by his fears."

"Right, and I'm not a good journalist yet. You've implied as much in the past."

"Come on, Jack. Just write what happened. You're not saying that the warnings are real, but you're also not saying they're a hoax."

"I guess so," said the protégé. He didn't seem convinced.

"Look—I shouldn't be saying this, because it shouldn't matter, but the Orbis Novus guys will be okay with the story. They put you on a jet, for chrissakes! If that doesn't show how real they are, or how real they *think* they are, then I don't know what does."

Jack did not feel completely relieved by Grant's pep talk. He also knew that he couldn't keep whining to his boss—having done so twice already was pushing it. He returned to his desk and labored through the story until he reached the point where he met with the FBI. He opened up a desk drawer and retrieved the business card that the female agent had given to him. For some reason, he was hesitant to call her, though he certainly had a legitimate reason to do so. *Why are you so nervous?* he asked himself. He decided to call her desk phone instead of her cellphone, and leave a voicemail message. To his dismay, she picked up the call.

"Oh... hi. This is Jack Kurry... from the *Chronicle*?" He didn't expect to have a live conversation with her, and he had not rehearsed an opening line. It showed.

"Yes, hello," she responded.

"I'm sorry to bother you, but—"

"It's okay," she interrupted. She sounded a little nervous as well.

He proceeded to tell her that he was writing an article about his recent visit to the Orbis Novus facility and he needed to know what he was allowed write in reference to his meeting with her and the other agent. (The name of the other agent escaped him at the moment.)

Gina thought about it for a moment then gave her directive. "You can say that you met with us and we're investigating the incident."

"Okay, thanks. I'll—"

She interrupted again. "But Jack, maybe you shouldn't mention the meeting with us at all."

"No?"

"Well, I'm not saying that you have anything to worry about… But you don't want to piss these guys off either."

"Okay…" Then an idea occurred to him. "You know, it might be easier if you insisted, officially, that I not mention our meeting."

Gina laughed. "I don't think your editors are going to care about that. I can't give you a gag order."

Jack tried to play it off as if he were joking. "Yeah, I know."

"How are you doing?" asked Gina. She realized that the question sounded a little personal and quickly added, "Have you seen anything suspicious?"

"Nah," replied Jack. He tried to make it sound as if it wouldn't have been a big deal if he had.

"Good. Let me know if you do."

"I will. Have you found anything?"

Gina was hoping that he wouldn't ask. She had not spent as much time on the case as she could have. "No, not yet. I'm afraid that we don't have much to go on. Plus, no crime has been committed, remember?" She replayed her response in her head and it sounded like a cop-out.

"Sure. Okay then, well… thanks for your time."

"You're welcome. Thanks for your… time."

After hanging up, they each felt as if they could have performed better on the phone, then wondered why they even cared. After all, it was a professional conversation.

Later in the afternoon, Jack emailed his article to Grant, then followed up with him fifteen minutes later.

"It ends where they drop you off at the Monaco Palace," noted Grant. Jack sensed there was a question hidden in his statement.

"Yes, I thought it would be interesting to end it right where it began."

Grant's dubious expression indicated that he was not fooled. Jack waited for him to ask about the FBI, yet his boss simply nodded and said nothing. Instead of letting it go, Jack allowed his paranoia to get the better of him. Maybe Grant was testing him.

"I *could* mention the meeting with the FBI, if you think it would add something to the story," he suggested. He tried to make it sound as if it was merely an oversight. Grant studied his computer monitor for a moment.

"Did they say anything worth printing?" he asked without diverting his eyes from the screen.

"Just that they're investigating it."

"I don't see what it adds to the story," said Grant, while appearing to read something on his monitor. Jack now knew with certainty that his boss was letting him off the hook. He changed the subject.

"I was thinking I might take a few days off to go home and visit my father. I haven't seen him for a while."

Grant turned and faced him again. "What are your assignments for the rest of this week and next?"

"You haven't given me anything yet."

"Then I guess it's an opportune time to take a vacation."

The article appeared in the Special Features section of the *Chronicle*'s print edition on the following day. Jack picked up a copy after going through security at Las Vegas' McCarran Airport. Grant had made a few minor edits, but it otherwise appeared precisely how he had written it. Having been distanced from it for several hours, the article now came across to him as a sort of mystery novel. Frank's interpretation of it crossed his mind once again. *He shouldn't have a problem with this*, Jack thought.

Given the last-minute notice of his son's visit, Don Kurry was unable to take off work on the day he arrived. Although he typically enjoyed a high degree of flexibility with his job, on that day there happened to be a critical design review scheduled for the project he managed. Nevertheless, he would take off the following day, which was a Friday, and spend a long weekend with his son. They made no specific plans, which meant that they would likely end up in front of the television watching football, and that was agreeable to both. Don had sensed a little apprehension in his son's voice during their brief phone conversation and decided that a few days of mindless relaxation was the correct prescription.

Jack landed at Dayton International Airport just after noon and headed to the rideshare pickup zone. The airport brought back memories of his mother. The fact that the so-called international airport had no non-stop international flights seemed to irritate her, and she made it a point to mention the absurdity whenever she was there. The rest of the family would tease her about her frivolous obsession and she would always end up laughing at herself.

Although his father was still at work, Jack's childhood home was not empty when he arrived there. Flyer, the spunky little Pomeranian-Yorkie-Pug mutt, was waiting eagerly inside the front door. Jack didn't consider himself a dog person, yet Flyer held a special place in his heart. His mother had rescued the dog from a shelter shortly after she was diagnosed with breast cancer. Flyer had provided some much-needed comfort and diversion to his mother, and now he kept his father company. Don claimed to despise having to take care of the dog, while incessantly doting on the little guy.

Jack was the last of the home's three occupants to wake up on the following morning. He came downstairs to find the other two hanging out in the kitchen. His father was reading a newspaper while his little canine companion studied his master's every move.

"That's the *Chronicle*, right?" asked Jack. It was their running joke.

"No, but I did read your article online," replied Don. The thought had not even occurred to Jack. The trip to Dayton had already placed the subject of Orbis Novus onto a backburner within his mind. Although he had previously told his father all about his visit to the secret facility, the article provided a more detailed account of the adventure.

"It reads like a spy novel," noted Don.

"Yeah, that's the way my editor wanted me to write it," replied Jack. "It wasn't as scary as it sounds." Actually, it had been *very* scary to Jack, but he didn't want to alarm his father. Don was a big fan of the crime scene investigation programs that saturated the airwaves at the time. As such, he asked Jack a lot of questions about the SUV and the airplane, as if conducting his own investigation. Jack appreciated his father's interest in the story, even though the whole point of his visit to Dayton was to forget about it for a while.

"The FBI says that they probably won't be able to find them," he said, hoping that his father would take the hint. *If they can't find them, you won't be able to either.*

Don seemed surprised. "Really? I would think that they could figure it out."

"The truth is, dad, they aren't even looking for them. There really isn't anything they can do. I mean, it was a good story—there just isn't much for the feds to do about it."

"Maybe in December, huh?"

"Yeah, we'll see."

Don suddenly remembered that he had picked up a box of his son's favorite cereal. His father looked so proud to have remembered, that Jack didn't have the heart to tell him that he no longer ate cereal and that the particular brand he purchased had not been his favorite since the seventh grade. He soon discovered that it still tasted pretty good after all these years. When he was well into his third bowl, his phone chimed with the receipt of a new text message. He lifted it off the table and saw that the message came from an unknown phone number. He unlocked his phone and displayed the message. It contained a photo, followed by a brief message that read, "Cute dog."

Jack studied the photo then glanced over at his father, who had moved into the adjacent family room to continue reading his newspaper. He was wearing the same clothes that were shown in the photo of him. The dog referenced in the message was Flyer.

"Did you walk Flyer this morning, dad?"

"Yes, why?"

"No reason… I just thought I'd take him out," lied Jack. The photo of his father and Flyer had obviously been taken earlier that morning and from just across the street.

"By all means. He'd love to go out again."

Jack tried to hide the jitters he felt in light of receiving the cryptic message. "Sure, um, maybe later." Then he decided that it really would be a good idea to take Flyer out for a walk. Perhaps he could figure out what was happening without alarming his father.

Jack stood on the front porch and surveyed the neighborhood while Flyer waited patiently on his leash. He wondered if somebody was watching him at that very moment, and thought it best that he not appear too suspicious. "Let's go, boy." They proceeded down the front steps. As soon as Jack's foot touched the sidewalk, his phone chimed again.

"Cute girl," read the message. It also came from an unknown phone number. The photo showed an attractive young woman getting into a car in a parking lot. The woman was Jeanine, and the building in the background was her apartment building in Las Vegas. Jack looked around again, as if the sender might be standing nearby to observe firsthand his reaction upon receiving the latest message. The suburban street was empty. Flyer's limited patience had waned and he began to tug on his leash. Jack remained fixated on his phone as he commenced walking in the direction Flyer pulled him. He knew that the messages were no joke, yet he struggled to make any sense of them beyond the obvious supposition.

Flyer guided Jack to his favorite destination—the neighborhood playground three blocks away. The small park was mostly deserted, as it was a school day in Montgomery County, Ohio. One young mother pushed her toddler on a small swing. Another figure sat on a bench at the far end of the playground. As they approached, Jack's phone chimed for a third time.

"Cute family."

Although unexpected, the third photo lacked the shock value of the first two. It stood to reason that the perpetrator of this warning would include a photo of his sister and her new daughter. The image portrayed Mindy holding little Bella inside a grocery store. Ron could be seen in the background, pushing a shopping cart. The lack of astonishment upon receiving the third message did not diminish the gravity of what it implied.

Jack looked up from his phone and scrutinized the male figure on the park bench. He did not appear to be associated with the woman and child over at the swing set. The revelation that a fourth message might be delivered in person shot a chill down his spine. He considered turning back before concluding that it was better to face the danger rather than bring it back to his father's doorstep. When he came to within a few feet of the bench he halted and fixed his gaze on the playground, as if waiting for his dog to do its business. Peripherally, he studied the man seated on the bench. His first thought was of a longshoreman. The bearded man wore a navy-blue peacoat and black knitted cap. Jack had half-expected to find Frank on the bench. This behemoth of a man clearly was not Frank.

The imposing stranger must have caught Jack studying him, and for a moment they locked eyes. The former nodded to the latter then turned his eyes downward toward his knees. Having decided that the man had nothing to do with his current plight, Jack turned back toward the direction whence he had come and pulled Flyer behind him. After two steps, a voice with a Middle Eastern accent broke the silence.

"Jack, leave the dog."

Jack looked behind him to see the man on the bench extending his hand toward him. The stranger spoke calmly—almost politely, while his visage conveyed a very serious and menacing demeanor. As Jack stood motionless and stared at the stranger, an SUV turned onto the street from the opposite corner of the park. It was similar to the one that had picked him up at the casino except that it was white. He knew instantly that it was coming for him.

The man on the bench beckoned with his fingers. "The leash."

Jack knew that there was no point in scooping up Flyer and taking off. He needed to address the issue and hopefully resolve it forthwith. He slowly walked over to the stranger and handed him the leash. The SUV stopped near the bench and the rear passenger door cracked open. Nothing was said as Jack climbed into the truck, where Frank was waiting for him. Frank's well-dressed appearance contrasted with that of his longshoreman associate. Whether intended or not, it suggested a good-cop, bad-cop scenario. The only other person in the vehicle was the driver. The young man's eyes remained glued on the street in front of him during the conversation that ensued, as if oblivious to anything behind him.

"You broke our deal," said Frank. His tone matched that of his associate on the park bench.

Jack was unnerved and also confused. "Deal? What was our deal?"

"We show you our facility and you write another story about us."

"I did write a story. And I never agreed to any—"

"You went to the FBI," interrupted Frank. "I specifically told you not to."

"That was our lawyer's idea. I had no choice."

"You always have a choice, Jack, and some are much easier than others."

Jack had no response to Frank's ambiguous declaration. He waited for Frank to continue.

"What did you tell them?" asked Frank.

"Nothing much," replied Jack. He saw an opportunity to placate his captors. "There wasn't much I *could* tell them."

"Are they looking for us?"

"Honestly, I don't think they're doing much of anything about it. They don't seem too interested in you." Jack was not exaggerating and his sincerity carried over in his words. Oddly, he and Frank shared a similar frustration with the lack of attention paid to the League of Orbis Novus.

"For your sake, I hope they aren't," said Frank.

Jack's worry was slowly becoming augmented by a growing irritation. *Why am I in the middle of this?* he thought. He worded his response a little differently. "Why are you threatening me and my family now? What's done is done."

"Stay away from the authorities," warned Frank. "And don't tell anyone about this meeting or the photos we sent you."

"Trust me, I want nothing to do with any of this anymore," claimed Jack. "Just leave my family and friends alone. They're not involved. And that woman—she's not even my girlfriend anymore."

"Sometimes a few of the guiltless need to be sacrificed for the greater good of the human race," said Frank. "We'll take no joy in it, but we won't hesitate to do what needs to be done."

Jack's budding journalism instincts were beginning to overtake his fear. "What's so bad about telling the FBI?" he asked. "What better way to get your message out to the public than having the FBI recognize you as a genuine threat?"

"It's too early for that. We can't allow them to get in our way."

"But they could help prevent people from taking opiates."

"This conversation is over, Jack. Get out."

"Do you want me to write another article?"

"Get out."

As Jack exited the vehicle, Frank added a final warning. "If you see me again, it won't end well for you."

The longshoreman handed the leash to Jack before joining Frank in the SUV. As the truck pulled away, Jack noticed that like its predecessor, the vehicle displayed no license plate. He instinctively looked around the park to see if the woman and child had witnessed the incident. They were gone. It was not as if they could have offered any future assistance with respect to jurisprudence. There was nothing to witness. Gina's words rang in his head. "No crime has been committed."

Jack and Flyer slowly made their way back to the house. Jack recognized that Frank's admonition was no idle threat. The hesitance in each physical step he took reflected his internal strife in contemplating the figurative steps he should take next. He started to call Grant then returned the phone to his pocket. He knew that his father would provide sound advice, but he was warned not to tell anyone. How would they know? By the time he reached the front door he had changed his mind several times.

His father greeted him in the entrance hall. "How was the walk?"

Jack was still clouded with indecision. The best course of action was to do nothing. "Okay."

"What's the plan for today?" asked Don. "Do you still want to go to Churchill Downs?"

"Sure."

Don had taken his children to see the thoroughbreds race down in Louisville once before, when Jack was ten. The purpose of that trip was simply a family outing to see the beautiful animals up close. The father and son had often talked about returning for some good old-fashioned handicapping and wagering since Jack had become old enough to place a bet. Although they had never followed through, the idea had never quite fizzled out over the years. Don had suggested the day-trip on the previous evening as a great way to spend a Friday away from work.

The racetrack was a short two-and-a-half-hour drive away. In the car, Jack did his best to disguise his angst and participate in the conversation as if the lives of his family had not just been threatened by an international gang of terrorists, or at least, some nutjobs from the lunatic-fringe. Don sensed that something was bothering his son and he figured that Jack would tell him about it if, and when, he wanted to.

This dynamic persisted for the remainder of the ride south, throughout all ten horse races, and during the walk back to the car. Jack had enjoyed a few moments of excited distraction interspersed among long periods of consternation. His mood seemed to parallel the races—two minutes of excitement with approximately thirty minutes in between. It was not until they crossed the Ohio border that the guilt reached its breaking point within Jack. He had no choice but to tell his father that his life had been threatened.

Although he was now firmly resolved to disclose the incident to his father, Jack opted to downplay certain elements of the story. He emphasized the fact that the threat was only implied, and he did not mention the photos that were texted to him. Don kept his gaze fixed on the road ahead, as if he wasn't surprised to hear the news. In truth, he was, but thirty-plus years as a parent had trained him not to alarm his children.

"What exactly did the guy say?" he asked.

"He told me not speak with the authorities and not to tell anyone about my meeting with him this morning."

"So, this conversation we're having right now never happened?"

"Yeah, I guess so."

"And you haven't told anyone else?"

"No, definitely not. I wasn't even gonna tell you."

A small part of Don wished that he hadn't. Blissful ignorance certainly would have made his life a lot easier. Nevertheless, he was glad that Jack had confided in him and he was more than willing to shoulder some of the tension that was burdening his son.

"Let's not tell anyone else," he instructed, "until we figure this out."

"Definitely," affirmed Jack.

They stopped and dined at a popular gourmet burger joint on the outskirts of Dayton and mulled over their plight in between bites. Although Jack was not fond of eating red meat, this occasion warranted comfort food, which also came in the form of a giant vanilla malt.

"First of all," started Don, having had a couple of hours to digest the news, "you did nothing to cause this. This isn't your fault." He took a sip of his diet soda. "Secondly, you shouldn't tell your boss. He might insist on printing a follow-up article, which isn't a good idea. I don't give a damn about your journalistic obligations or anything like that."

Jack trusted Grant to do the right thing. Nevertheless, he agreed that the safest course of action would be to tell his editor nothing—for now.

"What about Mindy?" asked Jack. "She and Ron should know about this."

Don concurred and suggested that he be the one to tell them. When he called his daughter later that evening, he downplayed the threat, which had already been downplayed to him. The effect of this dilution, similar to copying a copy, was that Mindy and Ron felt only a little apprehension. Don assured them that Jack would comply with the wishes of Orbis Novus, and there was nothing to be concerned about. Back at the restaurant, this left the question of Jeanine.

"I don't know," said Jack. "She might go straight to the police. I probably would if some ex-girlfriend came to me with a crazy story like this."

"That would put all of us in danger. The question," pondered Don, "is whether she has a right to know."

"She does, right? I mean, somebody threatened her. On the other hand, what can she do about it?"

"Short of leaving the country," added Don.

"Which isn't likely," continued Jack. "And this whole threat will be over in a month—assuming these guys actually do something."

The dilemma concerning Jeanine would not be resolved at the burger joint, nor anywhere else over that weekend. The father and son were torn between what seemed to be the appropriate thing to do and what felt like the safest course of action to protect the most people.

Whether by coincidence or the direct result of Frank's threat, the two men spent most of the weekend inside the house watching football. That Saturday evening was Halloween and the old neighborhood was overrun with the latest generation of trick-or-treaters. Each time the doorbell rang, a small chill rushed through Jack. He knew that it was merely another batch of children, though a small part of him half-expected Frank to show up to ensure that he was keeping his mouth shut. Jack had no doubt that he was being watched, and could not help but canvass the neighborhood each time he opened the door to hand out candy.

On the following evening, Don dropped his son off at the airport.

"Don't forget—call me if anything happens or if you just feel like something isn't right. Don't talk to anybody else about this," he advised.

"Okay, thanks dad."

"Remember, it's only for a month."

12

A week after returning from Dayton, Jack sat at his desk and replayed the message on his cellphone for a third time. The voice said that she was following up to the message she had left two days earlier, then repeated what she had conveyed in the original one: that she wanted to check-in and see if everything was okay. He had not replied to Agent Alvarez's first message, and he had no intention of responding to this one, in spite of the shame he felt for such rude behavior. The notion that the alluring agent might think he was ignoring her simply because he had no interest in speaking with her troubled him more than it should have. Nevertheless, he could not take the risk of calling her—or even texting. He deleted the voicemail message and set his phone aside.

If not for Gina's messages, Jack might have been able to distract himself from Frank's threats more capably. There was plenty on his plate at the *Chronicle*, as Grant had assigned him to cover a genuine news story. The Culinary Workers Union was engaged in heated contract negotiations with one of the smaller casino resorts in Las Vegas. More than 1500 guest room attendants, bartenders, food servers, porters, bellmen, cooks, and kitchen workers were on the verge of striking. Jack knew that if the stalemate had involved one of the colossal, multi-property conglomerates such as MGM, then he would not be covering the negotiations. Yet even this lesser story was a significant step forward in his career and he was very grateful to his boss for the opportunity. He was equally appreciative of the much-needed preoccupation.

He arrived at his apartment complex that evening and pulled into a vacant parking space that was a little closer to Jeanine's building than his own. He remained in his car for several minutes and gazed, just as he had done every night that week. Perhaps he was subconsciously protecting her out of guilt, scouring the area for operatives lurking in the shadows. He saw none.

Consciously, he spent the minutes pondering the pros and cons associated with disclosing the threats made against her. As usual, there were no new arguments discovered that evening, for or against telling her. A subsequent phone conversation with his father also yielded nothing. He sensed that his father was leaning against informing Jeanine—or was that just a wishful perception, given that he dreaded having the conversation with his ex-girlfriend? In the end, as is the case with so many of life's quandaries, the inactiveness of his indecision became his decision. Taking no action was by default, an action, and with each passing day it took deeper root. By the end of the following week he was parking in front of his own building again, having convinced himself that it was too risky to speak with Jeanine.

Poker was another quasi-effective distraction, albeit a much costlier one than working on the union negotiation article for the *Chronicle*. Jack found his concentration constantly diverted by a need to survey his surroundings in search of Frank or any other suspicious characters. On several occasions, dealers had to prompt him for action, causing him to act hastily, and before formulating a proper strategy. In short, he was hemorrhaging money. Worse still, he had become "that guy"—the person who slowed the game down for everyone else. Whether the muffled grunts and groans of his fellow players were real or imagined was moot; they affected his game nonetheless.

He tried other casinos, even the busiest poker rooms on the Strip. Playing with an entire table full of unfamiliar faces only amplified his paranoia. The league was surely watching him, he reasoned, and anyone of the strangers at the table could be an agent of Orbis Novus. He finally concluded that poker would need to be postponed until after the first of December, and he regretted not having made that decision several hundred dollars earlier.

Gina's third voicemail message, received three days after its predecessor, was just enough to nudge Jack over the threshold. It occurred to him that his silence might prompt her to contact him in person, which could be disastrous. In light of this epiphany, Jack decided to send her a brief text message.

"Can't talk. Too busy. Everything's fine," he wrote. It took him only a few seconds to compose the message. After another ten minutes spent deciding whether or not to include a smiley-face emoticon, he sent the message—without one. He didn't want to come across as seeming too chummy, though once again, he didn't know why it mattered so much to him. She responded with a text several minutes later. "OK." She opted to include the smiley face, which evoked a similar reaction on Jack's actual face.

The following day was a Saturday, and Jack spent most of the afternoon at the nearby apartment belonging to his friend, Mike. The two men had met up with a few of Mike's coworkers from the Monaco Palace in the morning for some vigorous hiking over in the Valley of Fire State Park. Mike had recently dedicated himself to losing a few pounds, though any calories burned that morning were likely offset by the impromptu pizza and beer party that followed at his apartment. Jack knew most of Mike's friends and welcomed the respite from the seemingly omnipresent restlessness in his life. Unfortunately, it was waiting for him when he returned to his own quiet apartment just before sunset. An hour later, the chime of his cellphone roused him from a pizza-induced nap on the couch.

"Can u come over for a minute? Need help with something," read Mike's text message.

Jack wondered what his friend could possibly need help with. There were still a few of Mike's buddies there when he left a little while ago. "Help with what?" replied Jack.

"Need to move some furniture," read Mike's next message.

Jack could only think of two large pieces of furniture in Mike's apartment and could not imagine how they might be rearranged in the tiny space. "Move furniture??????" he wrote back.

Mike's response arrived almost immediately. "Dude, just come over—pls!"

Now fully-awake and with a piqued interest in his friend's peculiar request, Jack walked over to Mike's building and pushed the doorbell next to his front door. He heard the chain lock unfastening before the door opened, which compounded his curiosity. Mike opened the door to reveal a silent, seemingly uninhabited room behind him—completely opposite of the festive scene which Jack had left earlier. Mike beckoned Jack to enter with a sideways nod.

"You need me to help you move—" Jack started to ask before noticing Gina seated on the couch. Mike quickly closed the door behind him. "What are *you* doing here?"

"Sorry to be so cloak-and-dagger," said Gina. "I didn't mean to alarm you. I was a little concerned about you."

"But why are you here at Mike's?"

"I sensed that you were avoiding me and I wanted to make sure you were okay. I didn't want to show up at your place."

"Why not?" asked Jack. The agent seemed to be confirming his worst fears.

Gina looked at Mike, who was earnestly soaking up the conversation as if he was watching a crime drama on television. "Would you mind giving us a minute?" she asked.

"Sure, I'll just be in here," replied Mike as he headed into his bedroom and closed the door. He was a little disappointed at the dismissal, though confident that his friend would fill him in later.

"What's going on?" Jack asked anxiously. "Is somebody watching me?"

"Other than me—probably not," Gina replied calmly.

"You've been watching me?"

"I was today. I saw you come over here, so I waited until everybody else had left before asking your friend to bring you back over."

"Why didn't you come to my place?"

"You tell me. I was just being overly cautious. Are you in some kind of trouble?"

Jack stood quietly and carefully contemplated his words. He was hesitant to say anything at all.

"Sit down, Jack," said Gina after waiting a moment. "Tell me what happened."

Jack plopped down into the recliner next to the couch. "They told me not to talk to you." He proceeded to disclose everything that had happened on his trip to Dayton, and showed her the photographs in his cellphone. Gina listened intently with a concerned, yet confident expression. Jack released a heavy sigh and leaned back in the easy chair when he had finished unloading his burden.

"First of all," started Gina, "they don't know that we're talking to each other right now. You don't have to worry about that. Secondly, I don't think that you're being followed and I seriously doubt that they've tapped into your phone. But just to be safe, don't use your home wi-fi network to call or text."

"How did they know that I talked to the FBI before?"

"They might have just been guessing or maybe they followed you for a few days after your visit with them. That was weeks ago. I've been with you all day—including at Valley of Fire—and I didn't see anybody watching you."

Jack was visibly impressed and a little more relaxed. "You drove all the way to Valley of Fire?"

"Like I said, I was a little concerned—and it's my job. This is my case."

"How's the case going?" asked Jack.

Gina detected a hint of friendly sarcasm in Jack's voice and cracked a wry smile. "I'll be honest with you. We don't have much to go on. You know that."

"Yeah."

Gina leaned forward. "But this is a serious development Jack. You've been threatened."

"So, what now?"

"Well, I need to talk with my superiors. For now, just keep doing what you've been doing—nothing. You'll be alright." She leaned back again. "These guys don't want anything to do with you. They just want you stay out of their way."

"That's a plan I can live with." Jack was beginning to feel a burgeoning sense of relief in having confided to the FBI, when the other matter, the greatest contributor to his recent apprehension, abruptly interrupted his relief. "What about Jeanine—my ex-girlfriend?"

"Have you spoken with her about it?"

"I haven't talked to her since we broke up," said Jack. "It's been more than a month." He didn't know why he felt compelled to add the second part.

"She deserves to know," said Gina, causing Jack's heart to sink with dread. "But I'll take care of it," she added. He felt a mix of guilt and reprieve in having Gina handle his dirty work. She could see his anguish and tried to mollify it by telling him that it was better for the authorities to deal with it. Although it was the absolute truth and the proper way to handle the situation, she also felt a slight comfort in knowing that Jack would not be seeing his ex-girlfriend again.

Jack accessed Jeanine's contact information on his cellphone and wrote it on a piece of paper. After handing it over to Gina, the two sat quietly for a moment. Professionally, she was glad that he had the information on hand. Personally, she wondered why he still had it in his phone.

"I guess that's it then?" asked Jack. He called Mike back into the room, where the awkward silence continued. Gina finally perceived the misunderstanding.

"You need to leave first, Jack," she said. "If somebody *is* watching you—and I don't think anybody is—then *you* need to return to your apartment first, so there won't be any eyes on this place when *I* leave."

The logic made sense to Jack, though it also made him a little uncomfortable. What would she and Mike talk about while waiting for enough time to lapse? He couldn't help but feel a little envious of his handsome (and single) buddy.

"Okay," he replied.

"Is somebody gonna fill me in?" asked Mike as Jack approached the door.

"He can talk to you later," said Gina.

As he walked back to his building, Jack attempted to reconnoiter the area inconspicuously. The resulting display could hardly have appeared less conspicuous, though he did not notice anything out of the ordinary. Upon returning to his apartment he sat on the couch and continued to cogitate a mixture of relief and guilt, now with a tinge of jealousy. The guilt eventually morphed into dread, in the form of anticipating an angry phone call from Jeanine. It never came.

Two hours later, Mike showed up to discuss the events of the day. Jack attempted to casually inquire about what had happened after he left the apartment. "Just out of curiosity," he said.

"We mostly sat there and said nothing," answered Mike. "I asked her some questions but she kept deferring me to you. Then she left, so here I am."

Jack was happy to hear that there was no spark between his friend and the agent, though he wasn't sure why it mattered. The reason he saw no harm in telling his buddy about the latest developments surrounding what he now referred to as the "Orbis Novus case," is unclear. Perhaps he felt that he owed him as much, in exchange for the surreptitious use of his apartment. Or maybe it was simply the temptation of sharing such a fantastic experience with a friend. Nevertheless, he swore Mike to secrecy.

"Of course, man," said his friend. "I won't say a word. And you can use my apartment any time."

That night, Jack experienced his first fully-satisfying sleep since returning from Dayton. He reached his desk at the *Chronicle* earlier than usual the next morning feeling refreshed. He desperately wanted to call Gina and find out how the conversation with Jeanine went, but felt that he should wait until at least nine o'clock, so as not to appear too anxious. At three minutes past, he picked up the desk phone, only to replace it in its holder. Three minutes past might seem too obvious. He placed the call exactly four minutes later.

"I'm calling from the office phone," he told her, as if she didn't know.

"Good."

Gina described her meeting with Jeanine as having gone "pretty well." She told Jack that she had made Jeanine aware of the threat without having to go into great detail. She also assured Jack that Jeanine harbored no ill-will toward her ex-boyfriend.

"She even joked about taking a two-week vacation to the Bahamas," added Gina.

Next, Jack inquired about Gina's aforementioned discussion with her superiors.

"I've only had a brief meeting with my boss so far this morning," she said. "He has some ideas… but Jack, the less you know, the better. You're not talking to us, remember?"

"Right."

After hanging up, Jack shifted his mental gears back to the Culinary Workers Union and rolled up his sleeves.

13

"Sydney!" said the loud voice. This was the first time he heard his name and the third time that the coworker had spoken it. He lifted his head from his folded arms that lay on the desk.

"Oh, sorry," Sydney Carter said to the young graduate student who stood in the doorway to his small office. "I must have fallen asleep. I've been up late all week working." The student smiled and nodded. She had her doubts about Sydney's explanation, having been working late herself and seeing no sign of him in the building past 5 p.m. It was not her place to say anything.

"I just emailed the influenza results to you," she said before walking away.

It was the peak of flu season, and Emerson–Lee held a seemingly perennial contract with the CDC to compare strains of the virus with previous years. Sydney had been assigned to the effort a few weeks earlier. It was not the cutting-edge research to which he had become accustomed over the years and which had won him community-wide respect. He viewed the task as little more than babysitting grad students. Nevertheless, he had not protested when his manager informed him of the transfer. In fact, he welcomed a break from the constant travel, lectures, and pressure associated with identifying new and deadly pathogens, which he reckoned to be a contributing factor to his recent lethargy and dreariness. He had recently griped to his new bar mates about being in a funk.

He certainly had reasons to feel sorry for himself. The upcoming

Thanksgiving was the first he would spend without family. His estranged wife was planning to take his daughters to her parents' house in Savannah for the holiday, which he viewed as a spiteful maneuver to avoid an awkward dinner with him. He had considered visiting his own parents in Florida, yet opted instead to attend the "Thanksgiving Football & Fowl Extravaganza" at Harold's Pub, a favorite haunt of his within biking distance of his flat.

He passed most of the four-day weekend in and out of Harold's and other establishments. He adhered to his beer-only policy for the first half of the weekend, then decided that holidays represented a legitimate exception, and bought a round of Wild Turkey bourbon shots for his companions. By Sunday afternoon, he was languishing alone in his apartment, trying to sober up for the upcoming work week. On Monday morning he realized that he needed a few more hours to nurse a surprisingly persistent hangover, and he finally made into the lab around noon.

He arrived there on Tuesday only about an hour earlier than he had on Monday. Happy hour at Harold's the evening before had morphed into dinner, which was followed by Monday Night Football. There were no particular reasons to account for his arriving late to the lab on Wednesday and Thursday, and it was not unusual for him to do so. In recent weeks he had grown accustomed to a later schedule, deciding that it better suited his lifestyle and career. As he explained it to his coworkers, his mind was much more vibrant and prolific in the afternoon. He typically remained in the office until 6 p.m. or until the last of his peers departed for the day—whichever occurred first. He was irritated when overzealous grad students worked late, forcing him to remain, lest it appear that he wasn't working a full day.

Sydney's latest self-professed groove proved to be short-lived. His manager and a representative from human resources came into his office shortly after lunch on November 28th and closed the door behind them.

The manager kicked-off the awkward conversation. "We're very concerned about you, Syd." He then handed the reins over to the HR representative, a young man whom Sydney had never met. He appeared to be fresh out of college.

"The University has determined that you present a risk to its ability to perform its contractual obligations," stated the HR rep, as if reciting from a legal document. He was, in fact, partially quoting from one of the University's written policies. Sydney soon deduced that his employer was more concerned with its own liabilities than his personal well-being. He was not sure if it was because of this, or in spite of this, that they were not firing him. Instead, they were forcing him to use his sick leave, followed by an unpaid leave of absence. He was strongly urged to spend this time in an alcohol rehabilitation program that would be covered by his medical insurance.

Sydney pushed back. "I know how it looks," he reasoned. "The truth is, I haven't been feeling very well recently. I'll take a few days off, see a doctor, and come back rejuvenated."

The HR rep politely intimated that there was no room for negotiation. He made it clear that Sydney faced two options: rehab or termination.

Sydney reacted angrily and directed his animosity toward his manager, whom he felt had betrayed him. He folded his arms in a defensive posture. "I can't believe you're doing this, Phil. Emerson–Lee can't afford to lose me—not with my reputation."

His manager, Phil Rogers, did not take the attack personally and was genuinely sympathetic. He recognized that his employee was in a state of denial and knew that sugarcoating the situation would prove counterproductive. "Frankly Syd, your reputation isn't what it once was. Don't get me wrong, I know you can get it back—with the proper help."

"Spare me the intervention," said Sydney, before telling the men where they could shove it.

In the end, Phil's persistence, patience, and empathy won the day. Seeing no other viable option, Sydney reluctantly agreed to the leave of absence and rehab. The HR rep remained with him for a while to go over the details, before Phil escorted him downstairs and into the courtyard.

"I'll need your office key, badge, and building pass," said Phil as cordially as he could muster. "I'll hold them for you until you get back."

Sydney reluctantly handed the items over, then added a final, albeit weak, protest. "I'm telling you that I don't have a problem, Phil."

"Then rehab will be a piece of cake," replied his manager. "Do yourself a favor, Syd. Embrace the process."

Sydney considered continuing the dialogue with a snide remark before walking away in disgust. The notion of thanking his manager and long-time coworker did not cross his mind, though perhaps it should have. It was Phil who had convinced the university administrators to give Sydney one last chance.

Per the agreement, Sydney was to enter the rehab facility on the following morning. That evening, he packed a suitcase and polished off the beer in his refrigerator, justifying the binge by convincing himself that the apartment needed to be devoid of alcohol upon his return. Concerned that he might oversleep his alarm, he stayed up all night before catching a MARTA train to the East Point Station in Southern Atlanta the next morning. After walking several blocks, he checked himself into the Breland Recovery Center. They were expecting him.

During the intake and evaluation processing, the Breland staff confirmed that Sydney should be enrolled in an inpatient program, and determined that a medically-supervised detoxification was in order. He had no choice but to accept the diagnosis or reject the treatment outright, which would likely result in his termination from Emerson–Lee.

Sydney began to experience the first symptoms of withdrawal about twelve hours into his detox, including sweating and insomnia. These served to fuel his most prominent symptom, which was irritability. The doctors provided medications to ease his suffering, and one nurse was particularly impressed when her patient requested them by their chemical name.

"Got any benzodiazepines?" grumbled Sydney.

The nurse administered Ativan, and a lengthy conversation between them ensued. At first it was more of a lecture, in which the scientist described the biochemical reactions that were causing his withdrawal symptoms, right down to the cellular level. Next, he detailed the molecular process in which the Ativan counteracted the symptoms. The nurse glanced at the clipboard near his bed and mentally noted her patient's occupation and highest level of education. She knew that the disease affected all walks of people, regardless of intellectual achievement, and this person appeared to be one of the smartest she had ever met. Although most of his terminology went over her head, she was happy to help with the diversion from his suffering by nodding and smiling at appropriate intervals.

The nurse was eventually able to work a few questions into the conversation. "I see that you haven't listed any friends or family for visitation," she said. "I can add someone for you."

"Nah, there's isn't anybody," replied her cranky patient.

She was not surprised by his response. It was common for detox patients to avoid friends and family during the process which many found embarrassing. What she didn't know was that Sydney had no true friends left, and that he had barely spoken with his parents in recent years.

"No problem," she said. "We can always add someone later."

Sydney responded well to the detoxification procedure. At thirty-five, the former high school lacrosse player's body retained just enough of its youthful strength and vitality to carry him through the process faster than the average patient. After three days, the Breland staff began speaking to him about the next steps in his treatment process. In fact, the individual therapy sessions had commenced when he entered the facility. The casual conversations with staff members were by design, and they had already begun to devise a framework to address Sydney's social situation and underlying psychological issues.

Sydney was not oblivious to the center's stealthy tactics. He was aware of the process and knew that he faced a few weeks of therapy as an inpatient. Yet he was amazed at how well he felt after four days of detox. He downplayed the effects of the medications and attributed his physical restoration to his own will and determination.

He participated in his first group therapy session on the following morning, where he remained mostly silent. By the middle of his second session on the next day, he had already diagnosed the underlying issues of his group mates and concluded that he was nothing like them. They had *real* problems, whereas he drank merely to take the edge off of a stressful day. Having identified his own trigger for drinking, he felt that he was perfectly capable of suppressing it.

This is precisely how he described his situation to the therapist in a private session later in the afternoon. In summary, he informed the therapist that there was no plausible reason for him to continue as an inpatient. He was willing to attend outpatient sessions, but he would no longer be sleeping at the center, beginning with that night.

The therapist was all too familiar with this reaction—that of a patient unable to recognize himself in the mirror of his fellow addicts. He strongly advised Sydney to reconsider his decision. As Sydney packed his things, staff member after staff member implored him to stay. Sydney thanked them for their concern and assured them that he had it all under control. He implied that the Breland staff had never dealt with a patient of his intellectual fortitude and self-awareness. They had, of course, and advised him that intellect, willpower, and addiction were very different animals, not to be confused with each other.

In the end, they reluctantly agreed to accept Sydney as an outpatient, given the alternative of never seeing him again. His therapist warned him that Breland would be forced to notify his insurance company of the change, and they would surely notify his employer. Sydney dismissed the threat, telling him he would be back at work before it became an issue. The affable nurse he met on his first day escorted him into the parking lot.

"Is there anything I can say to make you stay?" she asked.

"Don't worry," replied Sydney. "I'll see you tomorrow. I promise."

Sydney kept his promise. He attended his therapy session on the next day, December 5th. After that, she never saw him again.

14

On a November evening, a few weeks before Sydney's leave of absence commenced, Don Kurry pressed the 'end' button on the kitchen phone and placed it into its base. The news of Jack speaking with the FBI in Mike's apartment was distressing, though he understood that it was beyond his son's control. Adding to his discomfort was the notion of the FBI briefing Jack's ex-girlfriend on the situation. He understood the necessity of this development as well. There just seemed to be a little too much communication in defiance of the secretive group's warnings, and he was concerned that it might put his family in harm's way. After all, the organization had demonstrated that it had the wherewithal and the resolve to make their intentions known to Jack. They were certainly not a hoax.

As the evening wore on, Don began to wonder if he wasn't over-worrying a little. He had spent his entire career supporting the Department of Defense, which had instilled in him a confidence in his government's ability to deal with threats to national security—*and this Orbis Novus situation is hardly that*, he thought. Although he had never worked with the Justice Department directly, his trust in the DoD encompassed the FBI, an organization with an unimpeachable reputation. He assumed that they were doing everything they could to protect his family.

What Jack said at the end of their phone conversation provided more solace: "The agent told me that Orbis Novus wants nothing to do with me. They just want me out of the way."

Don wondered why it had not occurred to him earlier. *Maybe we should all get out of the way for a while.* December, and the supposed cessation of the threat, were only a few weeks away. He concluded that it was high-time for a family vacation—the first since the death of his wife, and long overdue.

He devised a plan to spend two weeks visiting various beaches and theme parks in Florida, culminating in a Thanksgiving feast at a restaurant in Miami Beach. The destination was far away from the reaches of Orbis Novus and also a sentimental choice, for he and his wife had honeymooned in Magic City more than thirty years earlier.

The plan was riddled with alterations from the very start. Mindy and Ron were excited and onboard, but they could not commit to abandoning their careers for such a long period. Thus, the two weeks were reduced to nine days, and the Disney portion of the vacation was eliminated. (Mindy noted that Bella would not be old enough to remember it anyway.) Jack signed on as well, though only for the extended weekend that included Thanksgiving. He cited too many deadlines with the *Chronicle* as the impediment to a longer vacation.

After coordinating the schedules of his children, Don set forth to make reservations and discovered that he was very late in the game, given the time of year. It seemed that a lot of northern families had embraced the tradition of visiting their snowbird relatives in the warmer climate for Thanksgiving. After several phone calls and internet searches, he secured lodging in a few mediocre hotels, including a property on the western shore of Biscayne Bay, which an online review noted as being "decent but in dire need of an update into the twenty-first century."

The bayfront hotel is where Jack intended to catch up with his family on the eve of Thanksgiving. As he stood nearly shoulder-to-shoulder in the crowded terminal at McCarran Airport, a text from Gina caught him off-guard. Nearly three uneventful weeks had passed since their meeting in Mike's apartment, and although she was hardly the furthest thing from his mind, he had not expected to hear from her. Upon seeing that she was the sender of the message, he wondered if she was perhaps wishing him a happy Thanksgiving. The warm feelings this notion evoked were washed away when he read the text.

"Look at this," it read.

He selected the html link that followed her words. The final warning from the League of Orbis Novus was more concise than its predecessors:

```
November 23

  "Thunder may sound a warning, but it's too
  late for the lightning."

The abuse of opioids has befouled the human
race. Our solution will free the world from
its pernicious clutches. The level of
sacrifice required for our success is up to
you.

This is your final warning. Ignore it at your
own risk. The lightning will strike one week
from today.

- The League of Orbis Novus
```

He was reluctant to call Gina from his cellphone, yet felt that the circumstances outweighed his fear of reprisal. The first thing he asked her was if the FBI could trace the message's origins.

"The guys in cyber forensics are looking into it," she said, "but they told me ahead of time that it would be difficult to track down."

"What about your boss?" asked Jack.

"I'm going to meet with him in a few minutes." After a brief pause, she continued. "Jack, there isn't much to go on here. I just wanted to make sure that you had seen the message."

"So, we just wait to see what happens next week?"

"*You* wait, and do nothing, remember? We'll do what we can on our end."

They both knew that there was little the Bureau could do and the conversation ended quickly. Gina's tone was polite yet unusually terse. Jack sensed that she was swamped and he wanted to make another call before he boarded his flight. He wished her a happy Thanksgiving then texted the link to Grant before calling him. He found it difficult to hear his editor's voice amid the increasing cacophony of terminal noises, as his fellow passengers gathered to board the flight.

"Say that again," he asked, after covering his open ear with his hand.

"I said that there isn't anything to print. Let's see what happens next week," repeated Grant in a raised voice.

"Then I should go?"

"Yes, go. Have fun in Miami."

"What?"

"Go!"

The family gathered in the Miami hotel room shared by Don and Jack following an early Thanksgiving dinner at a Brazilian steakhouse near the beach. Only little Bella seemed interested in the football game that was playing out silently on the television. The adults were busy deliberating the intimations and undertones of the latest Orbis Novus publication. The discussion had commenced the night before when Jack showed his father the message at the Miami airport and it carried through the next day. When there was finally nothing left on which to speculate, and the tryptophan, wine, and carbohydrates had begun to weigh in, the conversation yielded to naps, football, and a walk on the beach.

Gina spent the holiday in San Mateo after driving late into the night in order to dodge the tidal wave of traffic that preceded her into California. Unlike the Kurrys, there would be no mention of Orbis Novus during her brief visit with her parents and siblings. The unseasonably warm weather lured the horde of nieces and nephews into their grandparents' spacious backyard for most of the day. The adults took advantage of the unexpected tranquility indoors to interrogate Gina about her life in Sin City. As the only single child among her parents' four offspring, and the only one residing outside of the Bay Area, she had anticipated the questions and was fully-prepared with canned answers. There was no boyfriend. The job was fine. The weather was perfect this time of year, and so on.

Later in the evening, after the horde had departed and the dishes were cleaned, she reclined on the living room couch and unlocked her smartphone. Something drew her attention back to the text messages she had exchanged with Jack on the previous day. She pulled up the webpage containing the latest Orbis Novus warning, which she had saved before the link disappeared.

"Too late for the lightning," she read to herself. The quote seemed exceptionally ominous. She recalled the reaction of her senior agent, Daryll, when she showed him the message the previous day.

"It's rather tumultuous for an organization aiming to rid the world of a so-called pestilence," were his exact words, coated in sarcasm. His only direction was for her to follow-up with Interpol and see if any other law enforcement agencies had learned anything new. Interpol had nothing of value.

"They're operating within your country," the Interpol agent had told her, in reference to Jack's hooded field trip. "Everybody wants to know what the FBI is doing."

"Unfortunately, not much," was her response.

On Friday, while most of Miami's citizens were battling crowds in department stores or scouring the internet for irresistible bargains, the vacationing Kurry family was enjoying an afternoon at the surprisingly uncrowded Jungle Island eco-park. Don readily volunteered to watch Bella while his adult children and son-in-law partook in a ziplining adventure. Jack did not want to risk dropping his cellphone while zipping over the lush, fabricated jungle, so he left it with his father for safekeeping.

"Your phone's been ringing off the hook," Don said to Jack when they returned from the ziplines. Jack took the phone and found a secluded spot in the shade where he could read its display. He had received three calls in the space of thirty minutes. They were from a private number, and the caller left no voicemail messages. He felt a tingling in his spine. *Could it be Frank? He has no reason to call me.* He hoped that it was some kind of robocall solicitation. If it was something important, the person would surely call back.

It was later that night when the private number summoned him again. Jack was relaxing in his hotel room and on the verge of turning in for the night. His father had already dozed off in the adjacent bed. Jack muted the television and answered the phone. A brief pause followed his greeting of "hello."

"Is this Jack?" asked a woman's voice. It sounded vaguely familiar.

"Yes. Who is this?"

"I am…" her hesitation conveyed that she had not thought it through. "You don't know me. I'm from Orbis Novus." Her voice was hushed, as if there might be others close by whom she did not want listening in.

Jack's initial reaction was one of journalistic skepticism. He quickly rattled off a mental list of those familiar with his connection to the league. Mindy? Jeanine? Mike? Gina? No, it couldn't possibly be a prank. If it was, the prankster was pulling off an Oscar-worthy performance.

"Why are you calling me?"

Following another pause, the voice replied softly, "I need your help."

Jack detected an Asian accent—perhaps Mandarin. It called to mind the voice behind one of the shadowy figures seated at the conference table that day at the Orbis Novus facility.

"My help? How?"

Jack caught sight of his father, who was awake and mouthing the words, "Who is it?" He shook his head and shushed is father silently, while trying not to spook the caller.

"You need to tell them… it is going to be bad—very bad," warned the voice.

"Tell who?"

"Everybody."

Having dismissed the notion that somebody was putting him on, his thoughts then turned to Frank's threats. "Is this some kind of test? I didn't go to the FBI." Technically, that was a true statement. The FBI, i.e. Gina, had approached him.

"No, no—forget about that," said the woman. Her voice, though still muted, was growing frustrated. "It changed. A lot of people are going to be hurt. You have to stop this."

The questions rolled off of Jack's tongue as they streamed through his mind. "What changed? How can I stop it? Why don't *you* stop it?

Call the police," he said. He was wary of cooperating and imagined Frank standing next to the caller with a sinister grin on his face.

"I cannot," replied the woman.

Jack decided that he was entitled to some answers before collaborating with the phantom caller. "Were you there that day?" Silence. "What exactly is going to happen?" Silence. "Where are you now?" Silence. "Look, you have to give me something."

The voice lowered to a barely-audible level. "Tell them… Tell them not to look at the plants. Look at the people."

Jack scribbled the riddle down on a pad of paper lying on the nightstand. "What does that mean?" Instead of a response he heard a shuffling noise in the background of the call.

"I have to go," said the voice.

"Can you call me back?"

Several seconds of silence ensued. "Tomorrow. Three o'clock. Your time."

"My time—" started Jack, but the call had ended. He wondered what she thought his time zone was—did she presume he was in Las Vegas?

He sat the phone down and turned to his father with the intent of filling him in. The expression on his father's face intimated that he already had the gist of the conversation.

"That was someone from the group?" asked Don.

"Yeah. She was there the day I visited. I recognized her voice."

"What now?"

"I gotta get home. She's gonna call back tomorrow, and I want Gina—the FBI agent—to be there."

While Don watched his son diligently manipulate his smartphone in an effort to reschedule his flight, he pondered the effect of the secretive phone call on him and his family. He understood Jack's obligation to work with the authorities. The rest of his family needed to stay clear of Orbis Novus. In the morning he would implore Mindy and Ron to extend their stay in Florida for another week.

Jack phoned Gina before he departed for the airport the next morning. He needed to speak with her in private, and not in the presence of a nosey Uber driver. It was not until after the phone started ringing that he remembered the three-hour time difference. It was 5 a.m. in California when a groggy voice answered the call.

"Jack?"

"Sorry. I'm in Miami."

After taking a moment to gather her wits, she said through a yawn, "I'm in San Mateo. What's up?"

After listening to Jack's depiction of his conversation with the mysterious caller, Gina provided him with some instructions then set upon revising her own schedule and putting it in motion. The foremost item on the agenda was to apprise Daryll Jameson of the situation. For the first time since the initial meeting with Jack and the *Chronicle*'s lead counsel, her boss seemed genuinely engrossed in the matter. Although there was still little evidence upon which to act, the verbal threat of multitudes being injured warranted immediate attention from the government.

At two o'clock that afternoon, nearly two hours hour after touching down in Las Vegas, Jack rapped on the door to Mike's apartment. His friend greeted him with a sober expression and a single nod, as if admitting him to the meeting of a secret society. Jack was surprised to find two strangers sitting with Gina at Mike's kitchen table. Gina was speaking to a middle-aged woman while a younger man fiddled with a laptop and some electronic equipment that sprawled across the table. Both women wore smart business outfits that seemed better suited for a board meeting. The man was clad in a button-down shirt with an open collar. A tweed sport coat was draped over his seatback. All three rose to meet Jack.

Gina introduced her colleagues as agents Milford and Wickham. The former proceeded to describe herself as a behavioral analyst and said that her primary role was to create a psychological profile of the caller. Her confident demeanor and graying hair suggested decades of experience.

The younger Wickham identified himself as a surveillance specialist, adding, "I'm the geek." He was preparing his equipment to record the conversation and track its origin— "if possible." All three agents were tasked with finding actionable intelligence.

Jack was impressed with the show of force. He was also disappointed that his preconceived image of Gina and him sitting alone in a dimly-lit room would not become a reality. Still, a romantic notion of the two of them against the world had alighted somewhere in his subconscious and would remain aflame there. He felt a morsel of consolation when Mike was banished to his bedroom just before three o'clock.

Jack's cellphone rang promptly on the hour. Despite having been connected to a recording device, the conversation played through the speakerphone, as normal.

"This is Jack."

"It's me," said the muted voice. Jack pictured the woman hiding in a dark closet. Gina signaled to him with a nod.

"I have people here with me," said Jack. "They want to hear what you have to say. Is that okay?"

Following a long silence, the woman asked, "Police?"

"The FBI," replied Jack. "This is what you wanted, right?"

Another quiet interlude transpired. Jack feared that she might have disconnected the call. "Yes," came the meek reply.

"My name is Nancy," said Agent Milford. Her voice sounded like something one would expect to hear from a grandmother depicted in a Norman Rockwell painting. "I'm here with a woman named Gina. What should we call you?"

"Nothing."

Jack cringed upon hearing the curt reply. Milford gently placed her hand on his, accompanied with a reassuring glance. "That's fine," she said into the phone. "What is it that you would like to tell us?"

Jack noticed that Wickham was busily scribbling notes on a pad of paper. He tried to read Wickham's words upside-down from across the table. One of them read "cell phone." Wickham then shifted into a higher gear, alternating between jotting down notes and hurriedly tapping on his keyboard. All of this was done without making a sound, and he seemed oblivious to anyone else in the room.

"It is wrong," said the Asian woman hesitantly. "This is not what was supposed to happen."

"You need to be more specific," pressed Milford. "Who is in danger?"

"Everybody."

Milford heaved a quiet sigh before adopting a new approach. "Yesterday, you told Jack to look at the people, and not the plants. Can you tell us what that means?"

"His article—"

The conversation was suddenly interrupted by muffling sounds, as if the receiver was being buried under something. Jack, Gina, and Milford exchanged curious glances. Even Wickham looked up for a moment.

"Are we still connected?" Milford asked quietly. Wickham nodded in affirmation.

After nearly a minute of silence, the voice returned. "His article was incorrect. It is not the drug trade… that is not the target."

The muffling sounds returned. "I have to go," said the woman in a frantic whisper.

"Am I being followed?" interjected Jack.

"I don't know." A familiar clicking sound indicated that the line was now dead. Wickham relaxed his fingers and clasped them over his head as he leaned backward.

"Any luck?" asked Gina.

"No," replied the specialist. "I could have used a few more minutes."

"She sounded genuine," said Milford. "She really believes that a catastrophe is imminent."

"What now?" asked Jack.

"She'll call you again," replied Milford confidently. "I sensed a lot of remorse. She feels compelled to right a wrong."

"So, we just sit here and wait?"

"For a while," added Gina. "Let's see what happens."

Over the next three hours, Jack divided his time between watching television in Mike's bedroom and chatting with the agents. His phone rang once during the span, at which time he sprang into the kitchen, only to see his father's name on the display. He assured his father that everything was fine during a very brief interchange. Not long after sunset, Mike ordered out for pizza, which the agents graciously covered at the taxpayers' expense. An hour later, when Wickham nodded off on the couch, Gina decided to call it a night.

"If she calls, try to arrange a time for her to call you back when we can all be present," instructed Milford.

Per the safety protocol, Jack left the apartment first. The agents waited thirty minutes before following. The women helped Mike tidy up the clutter while Wickham scarfed down the last slice of cold pizza and resumed his nap on the couch.

Jack received no more phone calls that night.

15

Jack had been to Grant's home in Henderson, Nevada, once before. The purpose of that previous visit, a barbecue, starkly contrasted with his reason for driving there on the chilly Sunday morning of November 27th. The suburban home blended in seamlessly with the other houses in the neighborhood, each varying only in the shade of beige that covered the exterior stucco. As with most neighborhoods in Clark County, the homes were crammed together on small lots demarcated by high block walls. The footprint of the Lewis home nearly enveloped the entire lot upon which it sat, save for tiny yards in the front and back, and slivers of land on the sides. They had somehow managed to shoehorn a pool and patio into the backyard.

The interior was beautifully appointed, courtesy of Mrs. Lewis. The Victorian-esque furniture was a more recent touch, added after the youngest of their two daughters departed for college. As a full-time bank branch manager, Mrs. Lewis ran a tight ship both there and within her spotless home. Even the little Yorkie knew better than to leave any clutter lying around. Upon entering, Jack removed his shoes without being prompted. Mrs. Lewis was visibly impressed with the young man's gesture, not realizing that it was the result of her unintended maternal intimidation.

"Grant is in the den, Jack. Go on in."

Their meeting was a follow-up to a phone conversation from the previous night when Jack brought his editor up to speed on the latest developments. Grant felt that an in-person strategy session was imperative. Jack pulled up a chair in front of Grant's home desk, which was even more cluttered than his office desk. Just as it had done to Gina's boss, news of the mysterious phone calls piqued Grant's interest in Orbis Novus.

"Any more phone calls?" he asked.

Jack placed his cellphone on the desk. "Not yet."

"Alright then. Let's outline a follow-up piece."

Jack felt compelled to remind his editor of the directive that Gina imparted the night before. "We can't print anything. They don't want to compromise the informant."

"Yes, we can't print anything *now*," clarified Grant. "We need to be prepared for when we can."

Throughout the ensuing strategy session, the young reporter couldn't help but notice his editor's preoccupation with the cellphone he had placed on the desk. It was as if Grant was willing the woman to call back. Jack wondered if that was perhaps an ulterior motive for why he had been summoned to the house—so that Grant might be present when the next call came through.

If that was the case, then Grant didn't get his wish. Whereas the meeting did not conjure a phone call, it did yield some good ideas for an article. The men decided that Jack should reconvene with Muriel Smithson, the UCSD professor with whom he had met a couple months earlier. They agreed that she might shed some light on the caller's riddle about focusing on people versus plants.

Grant missed the much-anticipated call by a matter of minutes. Jack's phone lit up shortly after leaving the neighborhood.

The words "private call," appeared on the Honda's dashboard display and a dull ring tone displaced the music that was playing through the car's audio speakers. Jack was prepared for this moment. He immediately pulled over to the side of the road and switched off the car's Bluetooth connection before picking up the phone and answering.

"This is Jack."

"I do not have a lot of time," said the soft, familiar voice.

"Okay, but let me conference in Agent Alvarez. This won't take long."

Anybody who has ever tried to conference-in a third party on a cellphone knows that it can be a tricky endeavor, often resulting in the loss of one or both of the connections. Fortunately, Jack had practiced the maneuver with his father and sister before retiring to bed the night before.

Gina answered her phone after one ring. She had anticipated a call from Jack, but had not expected to be conferenced in with the informant.

"Gina, this is Jack. I have… um, the person from Orbis Novus on the line."

Gina took a moment to collect herself. "Okay, is the event still scheduled for December 1st?"

"Yes."

"Then you have to tell us everything you can," Gina implored. "We don't have much time."

"London," said the voice. She sounded more resolute and prepared this time.

"Is that where you are?"

"No. That's where the… event will be—one of the places."

"It's going to happen in multiple locations?" asked Gina.

"Yes, as far as I know."

"Where else?"

"I cannot say… exactly. I only know about London for sure. They don't tell me everything."

"Where are you?"

"Close. Maybe closer than you think."

"Are you with the others?" There was no response to this question. "I don't understand why you're being so covert," pressed Gina. "What's so secretive about curing the opioid epidemic?"

"Cure?" The voice became louder and more animated. "No, there is no cure. You don't understand."

"Okay then. What don't I understand?" asked Gina calmly. "Tell me."

The woman sounded on the verge of tears. "We could not make it work. It's different now. It's…"

"It's what? You have to tell me."

"It's about killing."

"Killing who?" asked Gina, without skipping a beat. The steady hum of background noise suddenly disappeared. Jack looked at his phone and confirmed that the line had dropped.

"She's gone."

Gina and Jack waited for a minute or so then hung up and re-established a connection between the two of them.

"You could have given me a heads-up that you were going to conference me in," admonished Gina.

"Sorry. The idea occurred to me late last night."

"It's alright. I'm glad you did this."

They discussed the newly-acquired intelligence for a few minutes before Gina begged off, citing the need to inform her boss of the developments. Jack felt obliged to disclose his plans regarding the professor at UCSD. He prefaced his admission by reiterating that there would be no article published until later.

"I'm going to follow-up with the scientist who contributed to my original article on Orbis Novus—hopefully tomorrow. We think she might be able to help decipher the 'people instead of plants' message."

"You mean *killing* people instead of *killing* plants," said Gina, calling attention to the tip from their most recent conversation with the informant.

"I guess so."

"Are you meeting her in person?"

"That's my plan."

"I should go with you. Let me check with Agent Jameson and get back to you."

Jack arrived at the *Chronicle* earlier than usual the next morning. The office looked deserted at that hour, as many of his coworkers were still recuperating from the long Thanksgiving weekend. To the few people who were there, Jack appeared purposefully engaged with his computer. In reality, he was far too restless to accomplish any meaningful work. At five minutes before 8 a.m., he rose from his desk and walked over to Grant's office. After exchanging a few words with his editor, he proceeded to the rear of the building and waited beside a window near a seldom-used backdoor.

A white Toyota Rav4 soon pulled into the alleyway and stopped near the door. He exited the building and opened the front passenger door.

"You should probably get in the back," said Gina. Without saying a word, Jack climbed into the rear seat. "I'm sure this is overkill," she continued, "but slouch down—just in case." Before pulling away, she picked up a small walkie-talkie, and spoke into the receiver. "We're ready here. How does it look?"

"All clear," replied a staticky voice.

Gina noticed Jack's reaction to the radio chatter and answered his question before he had a chance to ask it. "We've got someone watching the front of the building," she told him. "Just in case."

The Rav4 traversed a few city blocks then pulled into an underground garage.

Gina looked at Jack in the rearview mirror and smiled. "Thanks to you, I get to park in the special parking space. You can sit up now."

After taking an elevator to the third floor, she led Jack into the same conference room in which his initial meeting with the FBI had been conducted, and left him alone there. Notepads and bottles of water were laid out for the meeting's participants, though none of them were yet present. A few minutes later, a wave of agents barged into the room. Jack inferred that they had been meeting amongst themselves before joining him. There were six in all, including Gina. He recognized agents Jameson, Milford, and Wickham. The other two were clean-cut, middle-aged gentleman sporting nearly identical blue suits and red ties.

Gina had provided a high-level verbal agenda to Jack during the ride over. Her presence at the meeting, seated by his side, made him feel more comfortable amid the no-nonsense dispositions of her colleagues. He had to remind himself that he was not in any trouble with the feds.

Daryll Jameson noticed Jack's apprehension and attempted to put the young reporter at ease. "Jack, we're really glad that you can help us today. Thanks for coming."

On cue, the other agents nodded and smiled. Following brief introductions, Daryll launched into the first item of business. Jack felt as if he was coming into the middle of an ongoing meeting. Nobody summarized the situation for him or revealed the Bureau's strategy for dealing with Orbis Novus. He was clearly there to provide them with information, and it was a one-way street.

The first line of questioning was centered upon the identity of Frank. After answering several questions about Frank's appearance and demeanor, one of the blue-suited agents presented a collection of headshot photos for Jack to review. None of them bore any resemblance to Frank.

"What about the casino videos?" asked Jack.

"Good news and bad news," said the other blue suit. "The Monaco Palace switched to digital storage six years ago. They retain the surveillance videos of their gaming tables indefinitely. The bad news is that the poker room footage is only retained for fourteen days."

"As well as the video from the non-casino areas and the parking garage," added Daryll. "I'm guessing that your friend Frank knew that."

The session continued for another solid hour, during which the agents questioned Jack about every detail surrounding his jet-plane ride and the Orbis Novus lab facility. Jack was tempted to point out that his memory of the events was much clearer a month ago, then thought better of pissing off the FBI. *At least something is happening now*, he thought.

Following the meeting, he was left alone in the conference room once again. Gina returned fifteen minutes later.

"Are you ready to go?" she asked. It was already ten o'clock—only seven hours before their scheduled meeting with Muriel Smithson at UCSD. As it was, they had left little margin for traffic delays. The slightest issue on the I-15 could thwart their plans, and it was the Monday after Thanksgiving, to boot. Fortunately, the California freeway gods were merciful that day. The trip took longer than usual, though only by an extra hour.

The duo passed the first hour of the drive discussing the case. Now seated comfortably in the front passenger seat, Jack peppered Gina with questions about the Bureau's tactics—specifically in regard to Orbis Novus. She answered his questions, though he sensed that she was somewhat reticent, which he attributed to his need-to-know, or lack thereof.

"I'm just glad that the FBI is finally taking action," he told her. "That looked like a pretty good team in there."

Gina cringed inside and attempted to mask her qualms beneath a phony smile. She was finding it increasingly difficult to toe the company line. She initially opted to say nothing in response, but was soon overcome by an inexplicable desire to be honest with Jack.

"I think you're looking at the entire team going forward," she confessed. "Those other agents are back to working on other cases."

"What about everything we talked about in the meeting?"

"That was the culmination of their efforts over the past twenty-four hours. We didn't come up with enough to keep them on the investigation."

"Oh."

"If it makes you feel any better, I'm assigned to this full-time now," said Gina.

"What—you weren't before?" asked Jack with a chuckle.

"Actually, it's pretty cool. I was up to my ears in grunt work for a major case, and now I'll be heading to London."

"Really?"

"Yeah. You heard the informant—London is ground zero."

"I don't remember her using the term 'ground zero'."

"No, but it's the only location we have to go on," replied Gina.

"Why are *you* going there?" asked Jack. "I didn't think FBI agents ever left the country."

"Sure, we do. I mean, not *me* so much—until now. We have an attaché office over there in the embassy and Daryll wants me to be his eyes and ears there in case things heat up here in Nevada. He cleared it with some bureaucrat in Washington, and that guy talked to someone at the British National Crime Agency, and yada, yada, yada, I'll be packing my bags. Everyone's involved now."

"So, they are concerned after all."

"Don't confuse *involved* with *concerned*," said Gina. "This is just protocol. If Daryll was seriously concerned, then he'd be going over there instead of me."

"What did the Brits say?"

"I think we piqued their interest a little, but what can they do? We'll see what happens on Thursday."

The conversation gradually drifted into more casual topics. Two near-strangers can learn an awful lot about each other when confined in an automobile for six hours—especially when both participants, a reporter and an FBI agent, are trained in the art of interrogation. What began as awkward small talk to pass the time morphed into a heartfelt dialogue. They each fostered a genuine interest in the other's personal affairs, though each tried unsuccessfully to conceal it.

Jack found himself disclosing deep-seated feelings about his mother's death. Gina reciprocated with a visceral account of her divorce. This was the first time that either had opened up to anyone about these pivotal, life-changing events. They lowered their guards in the way that one might open up to a therapist, or perhaps two young adults on a first date that was exceeding expectations. Alone in his bed later that night, Jack would replay the conversation in his head. His candid revelations would surprise him, yet he would feel no regret. Gina would experience a similar self-assessment.

They arrived at Muriel Smithson's office just before sunset. The professor greeted them cordially then introduced the man who stood beside her. His name was Ted Frankovic. He was a professor of botany, specializing in plant biochemistry. He appeared younger than Muriel, though still old enough to be Jack's father.

"I hope you don't mind," she said. "I think Ted could answer some of your questions better than I would."

"Of course, thank you." replied Gina.

Jack couldn't help but wonder how a botanist would help them to focus on people rather than plants, per the informant's advice. His concern was soon validated. Ted fervently addressed their questions and was able to convey his thoughts in a way that was easily understood by the two lay persons in the room. Yet he seemed unwilling, or perhaps unable, to venture beyond his area of expertise. Ted was convinced that the League of Orbis Novus was intent on spiking the London supply of heroin, or a portion thereof, with a toxic additive, and Muriel concurred. He had evidence to solidify his opinion, having once worked as a consultant for the DEA. In short, he had seen it all before.

Jack attempted to steer the discussion down alternative avenues. He made an indirect reference to the informant, which earned him a stern glare from Gina.

"We were told to look at the people, and not the plants," said Jack.

In spite of this, Ted pulled him back into the realm of plant biochemistry, as a teacher might guide a student toward the correct solution. Ted seemed so earnest and intent on helping, that Jack eventually abandoned the notion of discussing other scenarios. He sat quietly until the meeting was over. Worse still, Gina seemed eager to buy everything that Ted was selling. Maybe it was the criminal aspect of Ted's theory that appealed to the FBI agent.

Jack left UCSD feeling unfulfilled—not unlike he felt following his first visit with Muriel. He and Gina had a long drive back to Las Vegas ahead of them. He would have offered her a guest bed at his sister's house, but Mindy and Ron were still in Florida, riding out the potential storm with his father. They decided to stop for a quick Tex-Mex dinner before hitting the freeway, and swapped mental notes about the meeting in between bites of their tacos.

"I don't know," said Jack. "It feels like we're still going down the wrong path."

"How do you mean?"

"We're still focusing on plants, not people."

"Poisonous heroin could hurt a lot of people," posited Gina.

"Yeah, but it doesn't mesh with their rhetoric. Spiking heroin would be a very localized and temporary effect. How would that rid the world of a pestilence?"

"I see what you mean. Even if they targeted heroin supplies all over the world, it would still be a temporary solution. They couldn't sustain the attack."

"And why is everyone so fixated on heroin?" asked Jack. "Opioids are much broader than that. Most of them are taken legally and with good intentions."

"Okay then, let's break it down," suggested Gina. "Who takes opioids, other than addicts?"

"People recovering from surgery—like Percocet and Morphine."

"People with chronic pain, maybe?"

"People in hospices, too," added Jack, recalling his mother's final days.

"So," pondered Gina. "What do these people have in common?"

"I don't know. Nothing? Everything?"

Gina dropped Jack off in the alley behind the *Chronicle* building just before 1 a.m. They agreed to touch base later in the day, though not before Gina warned Jack against getting his hopes up. She reminded him that the FBI would likely take no action beyond dispatching her to London, and that her trip would probably amount to little more than a boondoggle. Jack's hopes *were* on the rise, but they had little to do with the League of Orbis Novus.

As the Rav4 pulled away, he discovered that the backdoor was locked for the night. He walked around to the front of the building and approached his car, which sat alone under a bright streetlamp in the parking lot. It was not until he was half-way home that he recognized the risk he had just taken, and was surprised at his calmness.

December is just three days away, he said to himself. *I'm no threat to them anymore.*

Gina checked in with Jack on Tuesday afternoon before her flight departed for London. The brief conversation amounted to little more than her reporting that there was nothing to report. He wished her a safe trip then resumed his previous task, which amounted to little more than staring at his computer screen. He scoured the internet for anything related to the ominous warnings and discovered nothing new. Here it was two days before December 1st, and Orbis Novus had become Orbis Nothing in the eyes of the world once again.

After a long, unproductive day at work during which minutes seemed like hours, he headed straight for the Monaco Palace and secured a seat at a no-limit poker table. He had convinced himself that it would be a good way to blow off steam, yet somewhere deep down he was hoping that Frank would make an appearance. He departed for home four hours later without a sighting, and not before losing roughly a hundred dollars per hour.

He lay in bed at midnight, exhausted but unable to sleep. He decided to check in with his father in Florida—it would be three hours earlier there. He learned that the family had decided to trek up to Orlando over the weekend and was enjoying a few fun-filled, albeit crowded, days in the Magic Kingdom. Even his father seemed to have lost sight of the reason he was in Florida.

"Just keep your nose down," said Don in response to his son's apprehensive remarks concerning their safety. "In two days, the threat will be over—if there ever was one."

Jack knew that his father was referring to the personal threat against his family. Nevertheless, he couldn't help but feel that the world was turning a blind eye toward a looming danger.

"You think this whole thing is a hoax?" he asked.

"I don't know," replied Don. "Maybe it isn't a hoax, but London is far away from us." Jack could have reminded his father that London was only one of multiple possible locations for the alleged event. He decided not to worry his family about something they could do nothing about.

For Jack, the last day of November started out like its predecessor. He sat at his desk, ostensibly working on a style piece for the weekend edition of the *Chronicle*. The subject was the recent and sizeable population growth in the city. Las Vegas was booming again and the *Chronicle* was pondering whether it might be too much, too soon in the wake of the Great Recession. Jack's was one of three articles covering various angles of the story. It was a substantial and alluring assignment, yet Jack had written all of one paragraph. His eyes re-read it over and over while his mind was thousands of miles away, across the Atlantic. Jimmy stood behind him for nearly a minute before he realized that he was not alone in his cubicle.

"Writer's block?" asked Jimmy.

His voice startled Jack back into reality. "Huh? Oh, yeah—I guess so."

"Do you want some help? I've got some ideas."

"I'll tell you what," said Jack as he abruptly stood up. "You write it."

He found Grant in the breakroom, watching the final drops of his coffee slowly trickle from the dispenser into his mug.

"It's true, what they say," said Grant upon seeing Jack. "A watched coffee machine never finishes."

"Do you have a minute?"

Grant wiped the smile from his face. He could see the conviction in Jack's expression. "Sure."

Jack launched into his objective as soon as they were seated in Grant's office. "I want to cover the Orbis Novus event. I want to write another article."

"You will," replied Grant. "If there is an event. Let's see what happens."

"I want be in London when it happens."

"We don't even know what 'it' is. It could be nothing."

"Either way, I think there's a story," pitched the young reporter. "Either I cover a major crime or I write a human-interest story about the whole experience, dating back to September."

Grant released a deep breath through his mouth and buried his face in his hands, in order to buy a few seconds of introspection. The last thing he wanted to do was squash the enthusiasm of his junior reporter.

Jack interpreted it as a sign of frustration. "You think it's a bad idea?"

"No," replied the editor, "but I can't afford to send you to London—not for this."

"I thought about that," said Jack. "What if I pay my own expenses?"

Grant leaned back in his chair and placed his hands on top of his head. It was a familiar pose to Jack and it signified that his boss was at least considering his idea.

"I don't know how that could work," said Grant. "What about your obligations here?"

"Okay then. I'll quit." The words just came out, unfiltered and without contemplation. "One way or another, I'm going to London."

Grant quickly leaned forward and smiled. "Whoa, whoa. Just hold on there, buddy."

A few minutes later, Janet Holmes, the *Chronicle*'s managing editor, was in Grant's office and already knee-deep into the affair.

"We can't pay you to be over there," she said. "But I'm not going to let you quit either. There *is* a way we can do this."

"How's that?" asked Grant.

She directed her comments toward Grant, as if Jack wasn't even in the room. It reminded Jack of the discussions he had with his parents years ago about being a professional actor. Just like mom and dad, his professional parents were also eager to find a suitable compromise.

"Jack takes a temporary, unpaid leave of absence," suggested Janet. "We hold his position for him—for a while. We can pick up stories from the wire to cover his workload."

"What about the story?" asked Grant.

"He writes it freelance. It'll be a good learning experience for him—one that we can't afford to pay for."

"And you'll buy my story?" asked Jack.

"Maybe," replied Janet. "But Jack, we'll give you two weeks, tops, then we need you back here in Vegas."

"I don't want to be nosey," said Grant, "but can you afford this?"

"My late, great uncle took care of that," replied Jack with a grin. Janet's arrangement sounded like a good deal to him.

As he left Grant's office, Janet shrugged. "I hope that kid knows what he's doing."

Jack stopped at Jimmy's desk on the way back to his own.

"Be careful what you wish for, my friend. The article is all yours."

"How come?" asked Jimmy.

"I'm going to London. Freelance." He didn't stick around to see watch friend's baffled reaction. There were too many arrangements to be made.

First and foremost was the question of informing his father. He quickly dismissed the notion in favor of preserving his father's nerves. Secondly was Gina. It made sense to stay in the same hotel, though he worried about sending the wrong message. (Or was it perhaps the right message, but the wrong time?) He decided on waiting to inform her until he was en route. He would book a hotel near the American embassy, assuming that she would be staying nearby. Google Maps identified the Plaza on the River as a reasonable hotel choice, just down from the embassy on the bank of the river Thames.

The flight was nearly as easy to arrange. He had not realized how popular Las Vegas was as a destination for British tourists. There were several options for that day, though they were all red-eyes departing late in the afternoon. He ultimately booked a flight that would land him in London's Gatwick Airport at ten o'clock on the following morning. There was just enough time to head home, shower, pack, and dig up his passport. His passport had been used only once, for an excursion to Oktoberfest in Munich nine years earlier, and it was only a year away from expiring. He said a quick goodbye to Jimmy and Grant on his way out of the office. A woman from human resources caught up with him near the front door. She needed him to sign some papers regarding the leave of absence.

"Can we do this over email?" asked the anxious young reporter.

"Sure," replied the woman. She had years of experience dealing with reporters on the move. "Just sign this one here, and I'll send you the rest."

"Thanks."

"But don't forget to send them back," she yelled as he bounded out the door, "or I'll have to come looking for you."

He waved his hand in acknowledgement but didn't look back. London awaited.

16

Gina awoke to the pattering of a cold London rain on the penultimate day of November. She had only just arrived a few hours earlier, and the strains of jetlag were beginning to take hold. Although her eyes had been closed for most of the long plane ride, she had enjoyed no deep sleep. Her attempt to catch up amid the city sounds of a London weekday, amplified by the wet air, was doomed to failure. Thus, she diverted to the time-honored strategy, as old as jet travel itself, to soldier through the entire day without sleep in the hopes of adapting to the local schedule.

The FBI's legal attaché office, better known as Legat London, consisted of a few offices and a small bullpen area on the third floor of the U.S. embassy. Gina arrived there shortly after lunch and introduced herself to the Bureau's legal attaché in London, a woman named Courtney Roberts. Roberts had been informed that an agent from Las Vegas would be spending some time in her office, but that was about the extent of it. She requested a quick summary from Gina, then interrupted her fifteen seconds into the briefing.

"Oh, you're here about the heroin threat," said Roberts. "And why does Las Vegas need somebody here for that?"

"Opioid threat, yes," replied Gina politely. "We think it's more than just heroin. The group responsible is thought to be located somewhere in the western U.S. and my office has the lead."

Roberts was unaware of that factoid and subsequently requested a more comprehensive briefing from Gina on the spot. After three interruptions courtesy of two phone calls and a report in need of a signature, Roberts punted the briefing and deferred the young agent to one of the five assistant "legats" stationed in the office. She called out to the man in the bullpen area just outside her office.

Gina recognized the agent from a firearms course they jointly attended seven years earlier at the training academy in Quantico, Virginia. He recognized her as well, and noted to himself that she had not lost the physical allure that had garnered the secret admiration from many of the men in the class. Neither agent could recall the other's name.

"I know we took the close-range course together," said Gina, "but I don't remember your name. I'm Gina Alvarez."

"Alvarez, right," replied the agent. "I'm Nate Simmons." He led her to a vacant desk near his own. "This is for visitors. Sorry that it isn't much."

"It'll do," said Gina. The workspace appeared to be the result of an oversight or afterthought. It consisted of the detached, smaller section of an L-shaped desk normally found within a cubicle, with a tiny pedestal of drawers wedged underneath. Simmons pulled up a chair and listened to Gina's summary of the Orbis Novus threat. He suggested a meeting with his contact at the British National Crime Agency then moved on to small talk.

"Have you ever used your firearm outside of training?" he asked.

"Nah, just at the range."

"Me too. We can't even carry them here," continued Simmons. "My Glock is back home in Louisiana."

Gina began to recall more about the legat's background. "You played football there, right?"

"Yeah. Cornerback at Louisiana–Lafayette."

Had she been better acquainted with the handsome agent, Gina might have remarked that he looked as if he could still suit up. Her consummate professionalism disallowed any flirtation, along with the wedding band on his left ring finger.

Simmons' next remark confirmed that there would be no budding attraction between them. "Do you have plans for dinner? You should join me and my family."

"Should you check with your wife first?"

"Nah, we already have plans to go out. She'd love for you to join us—my daughter too. They don't get to see many people from the States. In fact, we'll show you the English version of American cuisine. You'll get a kick out of it."

"Sure, thanks," said Gina. As Simmons walked away, the business at hand re-captured her attention. "Hey, you're going to set up that meeting for tomorrow, right?"

"Roger that."

Following a pleasant evening with the Simmons family at a restaurant called The Damn Yankee, Gina returned to her room at the DoubleTree Hotel on the opposite side of the Thames. The pint of stout and pseudo-American cheeseburger weighed heavily in her stomach. There would be no trouble falling asleep this evening.

She woke in a jet-lagged haze eight hours later. The meeting with the Brits was to commence in less than two hours, and she had to meet Simmons at the embassy first. After an abbreviated shower and a short ride in a London cab, she found him waiting at his desk.

"You look like you just flew in from Vegas," he joked. "The time difference is a real bitch."

"Which way to the coffee?" she asked.

The National Crime Agency (NCA) was only a few miles away from the embassy and they passed Gina's hotel along the route. She realized that she could have simply met Simmons there and enjoyed a proper shower. *Next time*, she thought.

Two men from the NCA attended the meeting: a representative from the Specialist Capabilities Command and a liaison to Interpol. The former was only vaguely familiar with the Orbis Novus warnings and seemed intent on passing the buck over to the Metropolitan Police Service—the London police. The gentleman was polite with his deflection, stating that his organization typically handled major, far-reaching crimes such as human trafficking and organized crime.

"If this turns into something like that," he told the FBI agents, "we'll be there."

The NCA's Interpol liaison, a man named Nigel Peters, was more engaging and was clearly up-to-speed on the international threats made by the fringe group. Nevertheless, he agreed with his coworker that the MPS was the appropriate organization to deal with a drug-related issue in the city.

"You should check in with them," advised Nigel. "I'll take you over there. They won't be too interested in sharing information with a couple of feds from across the pond, but I've got some friends there."

Nigel was right on all counts and had, in fact, downplayed his connections within the force. He took them to the desk of a Special Inspector by the name of George Hendricks. Along the way, the trio passed through several doors where they were required to identify themselves and state the purpose of their visit. It was obvious to Gina that the journey would have been frustrating and arduous without Nigel there to grease the skids. She found out later that the graying, fifty-something liaison was a retired member of the force. He and Hendricks appeared particularly chummy, as indicated by the ribbing they heartily dispensed upon each other. It also helped that Inspector Hendricks was a big fan and frequent visitor of Sin City.

Gina politely entertained several of his gambling anecdotes before delving into the reason for her visit. She asked if the police had taken any precautions for the following day, December 1st.

"We've asked our men and women in uniform to put the word out," said the inspector. "They're warning people in the high drug-use areas about possible supplies of tainted heroin."

"That's good," replied Gina diplomatically. "But there might be more to it than that."

"More to it?" asked the gruff inspector. His thick eyebrows and bushy mustache rose in unison.

"It might involve more than just heroin," chimed in Simmons, anxious to assist his comrade. "The organization's threats made reference to all opioids."

"That could mean the legal forms as well," added Nigel. "In hospitals and the like."

"Well, I suppose we could talk to the hospitals too," said Inspector Hendricks. "What should they be looking for?"

"We're not exactly sure," replied Gina. "That's the problem."

"Perhaps an odd reaction to opioids," suggested Nigel. "They'd know how to recognize tainted drugs better than we would."

"We'll do what we can, Nigel. It's all a bit vague, though, isn't it?"

"I'm afraid it is, George. Hopefully it's just a false alarm—much ado about nothing."

The trio left the busy inspector to his tasks and ventured to a nearby eatery for lunch. The discussion oscillated between the threat of Orbis

Novus and the two men's recommendations for tourist attractions that Gina should take in while in the city.

"How long are you going to be in London?" asked Nigel.

"That depends on what happens tomorrow—if anything," replied Gina. She was about to expound on her travel plans when her phone buzzed with an incoming call. It was Jack. She assumed that he was merely looking for an update and sent the call to voicemail, not wishing to be rude to her lunch companions.

"What does Interpol think is going to happen?" she asked.

"I'm afraid the rest of the world isn't too concerned," replied Nigel. "They've got real problems staring them in the face—tangible problems that they can define. They'll wait and see if anything happens here. London is the target, correct? That information came from your office, did it not?"

"Yes. I spoke to the informant myself," said Gina, "but she hinted that other cities will be affected as well."

"Have you heard from her lately?" asked Simmons.

"Not since last Sunday."

"Any idea of her identity?" inquired Nigel.

"Only that she claims to be a member of the organization. Maybe a scientist of some kind."

"And you said that she was close to you—in Vegas?" asked Simmons.

"More or less," continued Gina. "Their facility is within a two- to three-hour flight from Vegas. Not much else to work with."

Nigel parted ways with the FBI agents on the sidewalk in front of the pub, but not before insisting that they stay in touch on the morrow. They thanked him for his generous help and returned to the embassy.

Gina was sitting at the tiny desk in the legat office when Jack's second call came in, and she realized that she had forgotten to listen to the voicemail he had left a few hours earlier. The choice between answering this one or continuing with the tedious internet research into London's opium trade was easy.

"Jack?"

"Hi. Did you get my message?"

"No, sorry—I haven't had a chance to listen to it yet."

"You must be really busy."

Gina did not want to maintain a façade with Jack, and she assumed that he would figure it out eventually. After all, he was a trained reporter. "Honestly, I was having lunch when you called then I just forgot about your message," she confessed.

"So, you're not too busy then?" he asked.

"Not really."

"Then why don't you meet me for dinner and get me up to speed?"

Gina pulled her cellphone away from her ear and glared at it with a scrunched face, as if the phone itself was the source of confusion. She took no issue whatsoever with his dinner invitation; it was the logistical challenge of it that baffled her. She returned the phone to her ear. "How are we supposed to do that if I'm in London?"

"So am I."

"What?"

"I'll explain when I see you."

In lieu of searching for a decent restaurant on the internet, or taking a minute to ask Simmons for a recommendation, Gina asked Jack to meet her at the Damn Yankee at six o'clock.

"I was really hoping for some authentic English food," teased Jack when Gina found him waiting in the restaurant lobby. He was grasping for some humor to counterbalance the awkward handshake between them.

"I thought you might miss American food by now," retorted Gina.

The hostess showed them to a booth in the style of an American diner, complete with cushy, bright-red upholstery.

"Ah, you were right," Jack said with friendly sarcasm as he glanced at the menu. "I can get a tasty grilled chicken sandwich—and a milkshake, too."

Gina noticed the dark circles under her dinner companion's tired eyes and worried that her own face looked as haggard. "What are you doing in London, Jack?"

"Writing a story."

"On Orbis Novus? You told me that your editor didn't think there was a story."

"I'm not here for the *Chronicle*. I'm freelancing."

Gina looked at him inquisitively before responding. "You paid your own way?"

Jack explained the situation, though he omitted the part about wanting to investigate the threats alongside Gina. He had not yet consciously admitted it to himself. Gina couldn't help but feel partially responsible for Jack's trip to England. The part about his inheritance made her feel less culpable, and it certainly didn't bother her that he was sitting in the booth with her at that moment. Despite the budding ulterior attractions, the dinner conversation remained on point. Gina apprised him of her meetings with the NCA and Metropolitan Police Service.

"So, what now?" asked Jack.

"I sit tight tomorrow and see what happens. What about you?"

"I don't know. I guess I'll take in some of the sights and check in with you throughout the day," said Jack. "Is that alright?"

"Sure. I'll pick up if I can. Hopefully there won't be anything to report."

Jack played his gag about craving American food to the hilt and downed a large vanilla milkshake with his chicken and bacon sandwich. He could barely keep his eyes open following the sizeable meal.

Gina did not take it personally and was ready for bed as well. "Go get some sleep, Jack."

"Sorry. I've been up for more than thirty hours."

"I know the feeling."

The Damn Yankee was not far from the DoubleTree, so Jack escorted Gina back to her hotel then caught a cab to take him across the Thames. It turned out that Gina wasn't staying as close to the embassy as he had guessed. He glanced at his watch as the cabbie drove across the Vauxhall Bridge. In just a few hours it would be December 1st in London.

17

The misty rain and below-average temperatures could not dampen the spirits of the diners and dancers in Soho on that Thursday evening. The narrow streets were full of tourists and residents alike. Some were wrapping up an afternoon of early Christmas shopping while others were coming to London's West End for a nice dinner or to experience the scene in one of the many clubs.

Mixed in with the crowd traversing Carnaby Street was a large man dressed in neat black jeans and a tight leather jacket. His attire prompted some of his fellow pedestrians to guess that he hailed from Russia or Eastern Europe. His shaved head and rugged demeanor likely contributed to the stereotype. Nobody asked him where he came from, nor did he speak with anyone as he walked along the popular thoroughfare of boutique shops, restaurants, and pubs.

Contradicting his hard-boiled appearance was his use of a vape pen versus traditional cigarettes. He sucked on the device incessantly, as if this was his final waltz with tobacco before finally quitting for good. The man stopped at various intervals, joining small crowds flocked around street musicians, or blending in with clumps of window shoppers. He eventually entered a crammed pub on a busy corner and took a seat at the bar in a patio area where smoking was permitted. He occasionally sipped his vodka on the rocks, though most of his attention seemed fixated on exhausting the vape pen. When the cartridge ran out, he reached into his jacket pocket and replaced it with a fresh one.

After an hour or so on the brisk patio, he exited the pub and worked his way back up Carnaby Street and entered a busy Thai restaurant. Once inside, he requested a seat at the crowded bar, where the bartender asked him to stop vaping—politely at first, then more curtly for the third time, despite being intimidated by the man's menacing appearance. The stranger finally adhered to the demand, paid his bill, and left the establishment.

His final stop for the evening was a popular dance club, as indicated by the line of partiers waiting outside. The man took his place in line, though he looked more like one of the bouncers than a clubber. After spending about thirty minutes waiting in the queue, he entered the building and maneuvered his way across the crowded dance floor and outside into a walled-in veranda. He remained in the smoker's area and wielded his vape pen for an hour or so, switching cartridges once more and nursing a bottle of lager. At one point, a young woman approached him and asked for a light. He dismissed her by raising his vape pen and telling her that he didn't use a lighter. When she remained and engaged him in further conversation, he pretended to receive a phone call and politely excused himself to a quieter corner of the veranda.

Upon returning to the inside of the club, he once again weaved shoulder-to-shoulder through the jammed dance floor on his way toward the front door. In the cramped confusion, a young man bumped into the foreigner incidentally, causing the young man to spill his cup onto his own shirt. The bald man immediately apologized, though the contact clearly was not his fault. Perhaps the young club goer misconstrued the incident, or was merely looking for an excuse for a confrontation. Regardless of which, and emboldened by alcohol and whatever stimulant he might have ingested, the slighter man immediately confronted the larger stranger by getting into his face. His girlfriend, a petite woman of Indian descent, gasped in fear. She recognized, as did the other bystanders, that the bald man could probably make short work of her boyfriend.

The hot-blooded boyfriend apparently compensated for his slight build with bodily décor. His arms were fully-sleeved in tattoos that snaked up to his shoulders and completely encircled his neck. His face was tattoo-free, though several piercings adorned his ears and nose. He wore his hair in a faux-hawk that looked as if he had shaved it himself. His sadistic appearance might have intimidated many others in the club, yet the bald man seemed unphased. Nevertheless, the larger man begged for pardon once again.

"I want no trouble with you, my friend," he said in a French accent, as he reached into his pocket and retrieved his wallet. He held out a ten-pound note and continued, "Please, let me pay you for your drink."

The offended man seemed uncertain of how to respond to the affable gesture, but his girlfriend was not. She immediately stepped between the men, accepted the money, and thanked the Frenchman. Then she pulled her boyfriend away as the foreigner turned and continued toward the exit.

The Soho streets were mostly deserted at 1 a.m. on the frigid morning of December 1st. The man zipped his jacket up to his throat and walked southward for several blocks until he came to St. James's Park. He took a seat on a bench facing the small lake of the same name. After staring into the water for a few moments, he threw his vape pen into it. Then he reached into his pocket and pulled out a pack of cigarettes and a lighter. He lit a cigarette, took a long drag and blew a large cloud of smoke into the air above him.

18

The day which Jack Kurry had anticipated for months came and went without the slightest inkling of any transgressions at the hands of an organization calling itself the League of Orbis Novus. He spent his time wandering about the city and checking in with Gina at regular intervals. He was at one endpoint of a telephone relay that extended from Gina to Nigel Peters of the NCA and ultimately to Inspector Hendricks of the London Police.

Late in the afternoon, Hendricks informed his old friend that the number of overdoses in the city was more than usual but "certainly not *unusual*." Nigel had nothing extraordinary to report from the Interpol channels that reached into the far corners of the Earth.

Gina passed the day at the tiny workstation in the legat office. She even reverted to supporting the Poison Ivy case for most of the afternoon, at the suggestion of Daryll, who had strongly hinted that the case's phone records were easily accessible over the secure FBI network. She eventually grew tired of the monotony and blew off the busywork to meet Jack at the Tower Bridge. On her way out, she informed Nate Simmons of her plan to see the famous icon before sunset.

"Um, yeah," Simmons called behind her. "You might be a little disappointed."

She came outside and discovered what he meant—the sun had already set. It was barely four o'clock in the afternoon. *Oh well, I'm sure it looks pretty nice at night*, she thought.

The nighttime view of the bridge and its surroundings did not disappoint. She found Jack waiting for her at their appointed meeting place—the fountain near the St. Katherine Pier.

"Can we eat at an *English* restaurant tonight?" he asked when she was still several yards away.

"Yes."

"Good, because I've already made us a reservation."

"I hope it isn't too fancy. I'm not really dressed for that."

"You look great, and who cares? We're tourists tonight."

They had no difficulty adhering to the tourist vein for most of the evening. There was little business to discuss, and both were finally feeling rested enough to enjoy the evening. A part of Jack was disappointed that nothing attributable to Orbis Novus had transpired, though he wasn't willing to admit it out loud. They had an hour to kill before the reservation, so the pair strolled along the north bank of the Thames, heading west past the Tower of London and other lighted attractions. At one point, Jack realized that they were walking in the opposite direction of the restaurant. They turned around and hustled back, making it early enough to grab a drink at the bar before being seated.

Following a more traditional English meal consisting of roasted pollack, stuffed tomatoes, and walnut cake, they departed for a leisurely walk to the DoubleTree, which was about a mile-and-a-half away. A chill came over Jack as they approached the doorman. He had not thought this moment through. He didn't want to appear presumptuous, nor did he want to squander an opportunity. He wondered if they were on an actual date.

To his great relief, Gina must have read his mind. "Are we on a date?" she asked.

"It definitely *could* be," replied Jack, while carefully reading Gina's non-verbal response.

"Why don't you two head over to the lobby bar and figure it out?" suggested the doorman, who had been patiently holding the door open for them. They took his advice and went inside.

It was at the bar where the discussion briefly returned to Orbis Novus, though neither participant had really intended it to. Perhaps one of them had brought it up in order to fill an awkward gap in the conversation.

"Yes," Gina replied in response to a query from Jack, "nothing unusual—no significant increase in overdoses."

"But we didn't really expect to see overdoses, did we?" suggested Jack.

"No, I guess not. What did you think would happen?"

"I'm not sure. Something big."

"We'll see what happens tomorrow."

That was the extent of the shop-talk for the evening. They soon found themselves exchanging histories, fears, and goals. Each was wallowing in that sweet spot of alcohol consumption, where inhibitions are lowered, but regrettable decisions are still avoided. Neither regretted having spent the night together in Gina's hotel room when they awoke early the next morning. Jack lay in bed as Gina prepared to shower.

"How long are you staying in London?" he asked.

"If nothing happens today, then Daryll will probably want me back in the office on Monday. I'll leave tomorrow."

When she emerged from the bathroom several minutes later, Jack was fully dressed and ready to leave. "No chance of you taking the day off, huh?" he asked.

"I'd like to, but I can't. I'm here on business."

"I suppose I am too."

After a quick but heartfelt embrace, Jack headed for the door.

"I'm glad you're here," said Gina.

He turned around and smiled. "In London?"

"In my hotel room, you moron." She paused for a moment. "The thing is, I'd really like to see where this goes, but until this case is over…"

"Yeah, I get it. Me too." He renewed his grin and added facetiously, "Hey, we'll always have London, right?"

"You're such a goofball. I'll talk to you later."

Gina spent the first half of the second day in December in the same manner that she had spent the second half of the first—studying phone records in support of the interminable Poison Ivy case. Just after 2 p.m., Nate Simmons called over to her from his desk nearby.

"Gina, Nigel Peters wants us to meet him in Haringey."

"What's going on?"

"He wasn't specific. He's at a hospital up there."

In the taxi, Simmons explained that Haringey was a borough in

North London, and that it was an area known for significant drug activity. They pulled up to the Accident and Emergency entrance of Newham General Hospital and spoke to a woman at the reception desk. Upon mentioning Nigel's name, she directed them to a small room down an adjacent corridor. As soon as they entered the room, Nigel raised his open hand toward them, as a means of tempering their expectations.

"I don't know if this is anything yet," he proclaimed.

Gina was surprised to see that the man from the NCA Specialist Capabilities Command was also present, as he had shown little interest during their meeting a few days earlier. *It must be something if he bothered to show up*, she thought. A female uniformed police officer was also with them.

Nigel dispensed with some hasty introductions. "You remember David Hughes from NCA, and this is Constable Morgan of the MPS." He turned to the constable and continued, "These are agents Simmons and Alvarez of the FBI."

"What's the situation?" asked Simmons.

"A DOA arrived late this morning," said Nigel. "He died in the ambulance on the ride over. A twenty-two-year-old male."

"Overdose?"

"Unlikely. The cause of death is still being determined. He had been complaining of severe flu-like symptoms."

"So why are we here?"

"The paramedics found heroin all over his flat, and his blood tested positive for it," explained Nigel. "The MPS has the hospitals on alert to call them with any drug-related suspicious illnesses or deaths. Word reached Inspector Hendricks and he called me."

"What do you think?" asked Gina.

"We don't think anything yet," said Hughes. He seemed intent on downplaying the potential ramifications of the young man's death.

Another constable ducked his head into the doorway and interrupted the conversation. "She's here."

"Bring her in here," responded Nigel, then he turned back to the FBI agents. "Your timing is good. We're going to speak with the man's girlfriend."

The male constable returned shortly with a young woman who appeared to be just shy of her twenties. She was frightened and trembling. Her red, puffy eyes were running short of tears. The female constable sprang into action. Rising to meet the girl, she placed her arm around her shoulders and led her to a nearby chair. Gina surmised that the officer's role was to calm the girl and gain her confidence.

"We're so sorry for your loss," said the constable as she handed the girl a tissue. "You aren't in any trouble. We just want to find out what happened to Michael, okay?"

The girl nodded as she wiped her eyes and sniffled.

Nigel leaned over and placed his elbows on the table in a friendly posture. "Lucie, my name is Nigel, and I'm going to ask you a few questions. Remember that we're not here to accuse you in any way. We just need your help." The girl nodded again.

Nigel continued in a tone that reminded Gina of the way her grandfather used to speak to her. "Now, when did Michael use the heroin? Was it this morning?"

"Last night."

"Okay, approximately what time?"

"Maybe around eleven," answered the girl in between sniffles.

"Did he shoot it with a needle?"

"He snorted it."

"Did you take any?"

The girl hesitated. Constable Morgan placed her hand on the girl's back and said, "It's alright, Lucie. You're not in any trouble."

"A little bit."

"And you don't feel sick at all?" asked Nigel.

"No."

Nigel proceeded to question the girl about her boyfriend's illness. She told them that he was fine when they went to bed around midnight, but that he woke her early in the morning complaining of a severe headache. He soon started vomiting repeatedly and mentioned aching all over his body. He collapsed in the bathroom shortly thereafter, and she called for an ambulance. After twenty minutes of questioning, Constable Morgan escorted the distressed girl out of the room.

"We've sent the heroin that we found in the flat to the lab for testing," said Nigel.

"She used the heroin too, and she's fine," noted Simmons.

"Yeah, maybe the poor lad just caught some kind of flu," suggested Hughes.

"But to go to bed with no symptoms, then die from it just a few hours later? That doesn't sound like the flu to me," said Gina.

"It's certainly an unusual case," said Nigel. "Let's see what the medical examiner and the lab have to say. No sense hanging around here. We'll keep you posted."

Back at the legat office, Gina found it difficult to concentrate on the tiresome phone records. She was happy to see an incoming call from Jack, then hesitated to answer it. What could she tell him about an ongoing investigation? Knowing that she couldn't avoid him all day, she decided to answer.

"Hi."

"Hey," said Jack. Following a brief interchange of pleasantries with no mention of their sleepover, Jack asked if there was anything happening with Orbis Novus.

"Possibly," said Gina reluctantly. "That's all I can tell you."

"What happened?" pressed Jack.

Gina looked around to see if Simmons or anyone else might be within earshot, then lowered her voice. "Come on, Jack. You know I can't disclose the details of a case. It's probably nothing anyway."

"I thought I was *part* of the case," said Jack. "Can you tell me anything off the record for my story?"

"Let's just see if anything comes of this, then I'll ask Daryll about it." She turned to find Simmons standing in front of her.

"Got another one," he told her.

"Jack, I've got to go. I'll call you later."

Their destination this time was the North Middlesex Hospital, only a few miles away from Newham General. Nigel met them outside. He was alone this time.

"He's still alive. Same symptoms as the other man."

Inside the waiting area, Nigel explained the situation further. The patient was known to local police officers as a drug addict who had been living on the streets for months. He had walked into an urgent care facility in Finchley complaining of flu-like symptoms, mainly in his respiratory system. He also had a very high fever. The staff there quickly recognized the severity of his situation and transferred him to the Middlesex Accident & Emergency Center.

"The bobbies tracked down a few of his friends," Nigel told them. "There's no question that he used heroin in the past twenty-four hours."

Not long after they arrived, a doctor approached and informed them that he was unable to save the patient. Nigel asked the physician if he knew the cause of death.

"Not precisely," replied the doctor. "The man was violently ill and dehydrated. If he had come to us a few days earlier, we probably could have treated him."

"According to what my officers tell me, the lad wasn't sick until today," said Nigel.

"I find that difficult to believe," said the doctor. "His body was ravaged."

Nigel made a phone call and arranged for the corpse to be examined by the same coroner who was handling the earlier case.

"Since you're here," he said to the agents, "come with me to the lab."

Nigel drove them over to one of the MPS toxicology labs, where Inspector Hendricks was waiting for them, along with a uniformed sergeant. Hendricks introduced the sergeant to Gina and Simmons.

"I appreciate, the rush job on this, George," said Nigel.

The five law enforcement officers entered the lab and debriefed the technician who had analyzed the heroin found in the first victim's apartment. They learned that there was nothing unusual about the sample.

"Typical street grade," the technician told them. "No toxins detected. No fentanyl."

Nigel turned to the sergeant. "Do you think you can find a sample from the lot used by the Finchley victim?"

"Unlikely, sir," replied the sergeant. "Gettin' those drifters to talk is hard enough. Askin' 'em to hand over their drugs? Unlikely. 'What drugs?' That's what they'll say. 'What drugs? I 'ave no doubt.'"

"You'll give it a go, though, won't you?" asked Nigel.

"Of course, sir."

The group reconvened in the hallway outside the lab.

"How soon until the medical examiner's reports?" asked Nigel.

"It'll take a couple of days, even if I put some pressure on them," replied Inspector Hendricks. "Do you think they're connected? Some kind of flu epidemic?"

"Unknown," said Nigel.

"All the same, you should give the PHE a heads-up," advised the inspector. "You don't want to be stuck holding the bag if this turns into something."

"Right, will do. Thanks, George."

Nigel offered to drop Gina and Simmons off at the embassy.

"What's the PHE?" asked Gina as they sat in the heavy London traffic.

"Public Health England," answered Nigel. "They'll want to know if we've got a new strain of the flu going around—especially one this deadly."

"It doesn't seem to have anything to do with the heroin," suggested Simmons.

"No, but it's good that we're getting a hold on it early. The PHE will track it if they think it's a problem."

Nigel dropped Gina and Simmons off outside of the embassy gate, where they vowed to keep in touch with him. The agents stopped by the office of Courtney Roberts, the Bureau's legal attaché, before returning to their desks. She listened to a summary of the day's events while displaying little reaction.

"Sounds like a problem for public health," she said. "Keep me posted."

Daryll Jameson responded similarly to Gina when she called him, though he agreed that she should extend her trip by at least another day. Then he asked her if she had made any progress with the Poison Ivy phone records.

She was slightly peeved but tried to remain calm. "I've been in hospitals all day."

"I understand," replied Daryll. "Whatever you can get done would be appreciated."

It was very late in the day when the conversation with Daryll ended. Gina yawned, then leaned back and folded her arms across her chest. Any trace of motivation for reviewing phone records had long since dissipated. She dialed Jack's number.

"Before you say anything, I can't tell you what's going on," she declared.

"Alright," said Jack, "how about I tell *you* something?"

"What?"

"Actually, it'll be easier if I just show you. Can we meet at your hotel?"

Over the phone, Gina could not discern if he had something serious to share with her or if he was merely flirting. Either way was fine, though her preference was for the latter.

She was in her hotel room an hour later when Jack knocked on the door. She checked herself in the mirror before answering. Her hair was still a little wet from the long, steamy shower, but it would have to do. They greeted each other with a hug that was nearly as awkward as the handshake from their first encounter in London. As with most new relationships, they would take a step backward for every two steps forward, though each was secretly longing for a giant leap ahead.

"I want to show you something," said Jack as he walked over to a small table near the window. He pointed to Gina's personal laptop, which was recharging on the table. "May I?"

"Sure." She opened the laptop and unlocked it.

Jack sat down, opened a web browser, and typed in a few words of search criteria. "Here it is."

Gina pulled a chair up next to him and looked at the screen. The browser displayed a story from the online version of a Dallas newspaper. The headline read, "Death of Prominent Research Scientist is Probable Suicide."

"I just stumbled onto this today," said Jack. "Read the first paragraph."

The article was an updated version of a prior story reporting the death of the scientist three days earlier. She had been discovered by her landlord at the behest of a concerned coworker. An empty bottle of wine and an empty container of Vicodin were found on the bed near her body. The name of the thirty-six-year-old woman was Natalie Wu Lan. She was a member of the research faculty at the North Texas Medical Center.

"Now look at this," Jack instructed, as he scrolled down the article to the end. "She specialized in molecular biology."

"Okay, I see where you're going, but what makes you think she had anything to do with Orbis Novus?"

"Because it gets more interesting. Check this out." Jack pulled out his smartphone and started playing a video he had cued up. "I googled her. She gave a TED talk three years ago." The video showed an Asian woman addressing a large audience at one of the organization's popular information-sharing conferences. "Just listen."

Gina leaned her ear toward the phone and listened keenly for a few seconds. "Wait—you think…?"

"I know it's her. I won't forget that voice for a long time."

"I can compare it to the recording we made of her second phone call tomorrow at the embassy.

"Go ahead, but I already know it's the same voice."

"What else do you know about her?"

"She emigrated from China when she was eighteen. She seems to be very well known and she's published lots of material. I haven't had a chance to look at any of it yet."

"I can look into this tomorrow," said Gina. "If she's connected—and that's a big 'if'—then this could be significant."

"The question is why she would kill herself," posited Jack.

"She sounded remorseful, remember? Maybe the gravity of it was too much for her to handle."

"Or maybe it wasn't suicide."

"Maybe not."

"I did good, didn't I?" asked Jack in a more playful tone. "Does this mean that you'll tell me what happened in London today?"

"It does not."

They spent another thirty minutes or so researching Wu Lan before their appetites for dinner and other proclivities took control of their frontal lobes. They ordered room service and stayed in for the entire night.

19

On the morning of December 3rd, most of the planet's inhabitants were still oblivious to the cataclysm that stood at its doorstep. Authorities in scattered locations throughout the world were just beginning to connect the dots that formed the web of Orbis Novus.

The ringtone of her cellphone roused Gina from a deep sleep at 6 a.m.

"A lot has happened overnight," said Nigel Peters. "Where are you now?"

"In my hotel room," she replied sheepishly. Although it was such an early hour of the morning, Nigel's tone somehow made her feel guilty for not being at the embassy.

"I'll pick you up out front in forty minutes," said Nigel. He ended the call before she could confirm, let alone ask for more details.

"What's going on?" asked Jack in a groggy morning voice.

Gina was already in the bathroom. "I've gotta go. You can stay here as long as you like."

"That's okay. I've got a lot to do as well," said Jack, now fully-awake and out of bed. They parted ways with a brief, less awkward hug in the lobby thirty minutes later.

"Let's keep in touch throughout the day," suggested Jack. "I'll tell you what I find out, and you tell me whatever you can."

A few minutes after Jack's cab disappeared down Pepys Street, Nigel's car pulled into the hotel's narrow pickup zone.

"Where are we headed?" asked Gina as she climbed in.

"Back to Newham. Two patients died there overnight. Same symptoms."

She called Nate Simmons while Nigel weaved in and out of traffic. Simmons informed her that he was booked in unrelated meetings for the morning and that he would touch base with her later in the day.

They were a little ahead of the peak rush hour volume, but the twenty-mile trip to the hospital still took more than an hour. Nigel revealed other noteworthy developments during the drive. He had posted an advisory on the Interpol network before leaving his office on the previous evening. Reports of similar, inexplicable flu-like deaths in Hong Kong and Rio de Janeiro had since come into Interpol in response. China was concerned about another SARS outbreak.

"They're probably unrelated," tempered Nigel. "Hundreds of people die of the flu every day. We'll just keep it in our back pocket for now."

Gina wondered how much sleep her older colleague had managed to obtain over the previous night. It could not have exceeded more than a few hours, yet Nigel appeared spirited and resilient as he piloted his car like a seasoned London cabbie. Conversely, she was physically dragging and yearned for a cup of coffee. She had stayed up a little too late relishing in the excitement of a new relationship, and her lingering jetlag was now mixed in with a smattering of Jack-lag.

They found David Hughes of the NCA inside the main entrance of Newham General where he was speaking with a woman. Her confident demeanor was bolstered by her smart business suit, and she introduced herself as Betty Wilshire from Public Health as they walked briskly to a conference room down the corridor. Waiting for them inside were several administrators from the hospital, including its chief operating officer and medical director. Brief introductions were made, during which the hospital staff politely compelled Gina to explain why an agent of the American FBI was in attendance.

"We're investigating the possible connection of these deaths to a radical element based somewhere in the United States," she told them.

"You think this is some sort of bioterrorism?" asked the COO with raised eyebrows.

"We don't know," replied Gina. "We have to consider all of the possibilities." Nigel then came to her aid and briefed the attendees on the League of Orbis Novus and their internet warnings.

"What we have is a severe outbreak of the flu," claimed the hospital's medical director.

"Two deaths of this nature in one hospital over such a short time span is quite unusual," said Betty Wilshire. "Have you identified the specific influenza virus?"

The medical director briefly glanced at the COO before answering. "*Three* deaths now, and no, we haven't. Isn't that your job?" He sounded a little on edge.

"Sorry," said Betty. "I was merely wondering if you recognized the symptoms."

The hospital staff revealed that all three victims were inpatients and housed in the same ward. A decision to quarantine the ward had been made just prior to the meeting. The victims had only begun to display symptoms a few hours before dying. None had been hospitalized for life-threatening conditions, and none were known to be drug addicts.

"Were any of the patients administered opioids in the hours preceding their deaths?" asked Nigel. The medical director was unable to answer the question and appeared puzzled about why it was asked. "It's imperative that we find out as soon as possible," added Nigel. In response, the COO immediately dispatched one of the staff members to find out.

Following the meeting, Betty Wilshire from Public Health reconvened with Gina and the two NCA officers in the main lobby. Her first order of business caught Gina by surprise and spurred a rush of fear throughout her body.

"I suggest we continue this discussion outside," advised Betty. "They have already implemented their quarantine protocol for one ward. They might lockdown the entire facility soon, and we wouldn't want to be stuck inside."

Gina had been so focused on finding an opioid connection to the deaths that she had not considered the probability that this was a flu outbreak—possibly of epidemic proportions. Perhaps hanging around at ground zero was not the wisest choice, she thought.

"Are we in any danger here?" she asked.

"I don't know what we're dealing with," replied the slender, middle-aged woman with the hint of smile. "But I'd rather be locked out then locked in." Without further deliberation, the group hurried out to the parking lot while trying not to display any outward alarm to the visitors, patients, and staff they passed along the way.

After a brief discussion outdoors, they reconvened at the headquarters of Public Health England on Waterloo Road, where a large meeting room was designated as the focal point for the budding health crisis. Before long, the room was buzzing with PHE epidemiologists, managers, and other staff. Gina was amazed at the fluidity in which they interacted with each other, as if they were used to dealing with similar situations on a daily basis. She even wondered if they were not prone to overreacting, though she recognized that as a positive attribute for a public health ministry.

She approached Betty. "Is it okay if I stay here? I'd like to remain in the loop."

"Of course," replied Betty. "We'll set you up with a desk outside."

A young IT administrator showed Gina to an empty cubicle near the situation room. He seemed enthralled with the task of assisting a real-life FBI agent. When he asked to see her firearm, she told him that she didn't bring one and suggested that he might have watched a little too much American television. He lingered near the cubicle long after she was set up and online, before yielding to her not-so-subtle hints for privacy.

It was too early to call Daryll Jameson in Las Vegas, but she was able to reach Courtney Roberts at the legat office in the embassy. Roberts seemed more concerned about Gina's health—and her own—than any possible connection between the deaths and FBI interests.

"Stay away from the hospitals," she said. "We don't want you getting sick."

As the day wore on, concern within the PHE slowly morphed into crisis. News of events poured in from various sources. One of them was Jack. He texted an html link to Gina then immediately followed up with a call.

"Did you see the link I sent you?"

"Hold on a sec." She retyped the link into her desktop browser. It led her to a story from the Kansas City Star with a headline reading, "Four Bodies Found in Ingleside House." She started to read the article before Jack saved her the effort by providing an abridged version.

"Last night, they discovered four bodies in a boarded-up house known for drug activity," he said. "At first they assumed the deaths were overdoses. Now they've ruled it out and suspect tainted heroin."

"It doesn't look like there were any witnesses around," said Gina as she scanned the article. "No surprise, but it would be nice to know what their symptoms were."

"Do you have anything for me?" asked Jack.

Gina carefully considered how to frame her words before responding. "Keep looking for stories about similar deaths. Search here *and* world-wide." Upon ending the call, she discovered Nigel Peters in a nearby cubicle. He wanted to stay near the action at PHE as well.

In response to her report of the deaths in Kansas City, he said, "That sounds a lot like the two bodies they just found here in Camden."

"Heroin?" asked Gina.

"It's not just that. I heard back from Newham General. All three victims had been given Percocet or Oxycontin in the hours preceding their deaths. They just had a fourth patient die and the facility is now on a complete lockdown." Gina asked about any news from Interpol.

"Thanks for reminding me," he answered. "It's been a couple of hours since I checked in." Gina listened to Nigel's side of a phone conversation with one of his colleagues back at the National Crime Agency. The colleague appeared to be doing most of the talking, with occasional interruptions from Nigel, such as "I see," "when?," "how many?," and "what else did he say?" It was obvious to Gina that the situation was escalating worldwide.

"There are more cases in Hong Kong and Brazil," he told her. "Paris now, as well."

Inside the PHE situation room, Betty Wilshire was alarmed by the news of the additional deaths yet unwilling to seriously consider a correlation to opioids. As she put it to Nigel and Gina, they were receiving far more dots than connections. The most obvious explanation was a flu epidemic, and until it could be ruled out, it would remain the working theory.

"Is it normal for a new strain of the flu to appear simultaneously in distant parts of the world?" asked Nigel.

"No, it isn't," responded Betty. "We've ruled out a bacterial infection, and our rapid diagnostics tests for influenza have come up with nothing."

"You haven't found the flu virus?"

"Generally speaking, with these tests it helps to know what kind of virus you're looking for," explained Betty. "We've looked for specific antigens that the body produces to fight influenza, and they are not present."

"But you still think it's a virus?" asked Gina.

"I do. There are more intensive tests we can run. Everything we're seeing in the lungs and respiratory tracts of the victims points to an influenza virus, but it simply isn't there. For all we know, the cases in other parts of the world are unrelated. The Chinese believe that they have a resurgence of SARS."

When Gina finally reached her boss in Las Vegas, he reminded her that it was a public health issue with no confirmed criminal linkage. There was no new message from Orbis Novus or any other organization claiming credit for the mysterious outbreaks. He assured her that the Centers for Disease Control and World Health Organization were monitoring the situation.

"What do you want me to do?" she asked.

"Stay with the Brits and call me again in two hours."

"Oh, I almost forgot," added Gina. She was about to mention Jack's name, then caught herself. "A scientist in Dallas was found dead of an apparent suicide. I found a video of her on YouTube, and she sounds like the voice on the recording we made of the informant."

Daryll sounded dubious. "That seems like a stretch. What made you connect her to Orbis Novus?"

"Just doing my job, boss. She was a Chinese-American research scientist—world renown for biochemistry."

"Alright. Email me everything you have on her."

By mid-afternoon, news of a newly-branded "superbug" had proliferated throughout the English news media outlets. From the window of the hotel restaurant, Jack noticed a few pedestrians wearing the odd combination of a business suit and surgical mask. For the first time in two days, he thought of his family. He reached his father at his office in Dayton.

"Have you seen the news?"

"What news?" replied Don.

"About the flu outbreak."

"Oh. That's mostly in London, right?"

Jack decided to not disclose his present location. "Yes, but I think it might be connected."

"Connected to…?"

"Orbis Novus."

"Really?" said Don.

Jack understood his father's incredulous tone. It was December 3rd and he could see how the Orbis Novus warnings might appear to have been frivolous. "Just do me a favor and don't take any prescription opioids, okay?"

"I wasn't planning to."

"Seriously, Dad. Promise me."

"Alright."

Jack couldn't trust his father to warn his sister, so he took it upon himself. Mindy was much more aware of the so-called superbug, yet she had also forgotten about Orbis Novus. Jack convinced her not take any chances.

"What if I break my leg?" she asked, half-jokingly.

"Just don't be a klutz," advised her brother. "But if you do, then you'll have to tough it out with ibuprofen."

"Ugh. Okay, I've gotta get back to work."

It was not as if Jack was convinced that Orbis Novus was behind the outbreak. He worried about catching the flu and decided to spend the rest of the day secluded in his hotel room, but not before purchasing the last bottle of hand sanitizer from a nearby drugstore. He remained in his room, alternating his attention between his laptop browser and the television news. Even after filtering out the hype that was common among the twenty-four-hour cable news networks, he could see that the superbug was quickly becoming a serious worldwide problem.

The London news outlets reported twelve more suspicious deaths between noon and 5 o'clock. All but two occurred in city hospitals. Citizens were being advised to remain at home until the source of the illness could be confirmed. The death tolls in China, Brazil, and France rose as well. Medical experts were not conceding that the deaths were related, but everybody else seemed to be. At six o'clock, the Kansas City Police Department released a statement concerning the deaths of three more drug users. The victims had complained of flu-like symptoms before dying.

Jack noted that there were no reports of anyone surviving the illness. So far, the death rate was one hundred percent. He phoned Gina.

"Are you still at the health ministry?"

"Yes. Where are you?"

"My hotel. It's crazy out there. More than fifteen people have died in London."

"It's worse than you think." She hesitated before continuing.

"Just tell me," said Jack. "It's not like I'm gonna write a story and quote you. At this point, it's just me you're talking to."

"It's a lot higher than fifteen."

"What are they doing about it?"

"They're trying to identify and isolate the flu virus but they haven't been able to do it."

"What does the FBI want you to do?"

"They want me to wait here. They're more concerned about me getting sick than anything else."

"It's funny," said Jack. "I'm not as worried about catching it as I probably should be. I can't help but think that this whole thing is related to Orbis Novus."

"I know the feeling," said Gina. "There's a connection to opioids. It's obvious to me because I came here with that mindset. Nobody else sees it—except for maybe Nigel."

"Who's Nigel?"

"Nigel Peters. He works for the British NCA as a liaison to Interpol. He's here too."

Something on Jack's laptop prompted a change in subject. "I'm looking at Google Maps. You're only about a mile away from my hotel. You can walk here."

"I need to stay here tonight," said Gina.

"You have to sleep sometime. It's room 513."

"If I get too tired, I might come over."

At 2 a.m. that night, Jack awoke to the sound of someone knocking softly on his door. Within minutes, the attractive and exhausted FBI agent was asleep by his side.

20

Jack awoke at 5 a.m. on December 4th and immediately switched on the television in his hotel room. Stories of rising death tolls in cities spanning the globe plastered the early morning news. Not surprisingly, panic levels were rising in equal proportions. He reached for his phone and noticed that he had received a text overnight from his acquaintance, Craig the Hoax Hunter.

The text consisted of an html link, preceded with a line reading, "Maybe they're for real?"

He nudged Gina awake. "Look at this."

She took his phone and scanned the web page he had pulled up using Craig's web link.

December 3

> *"If your right eye makes you stumble, tear it out and throw it from you; for it is better for you to lose one of the parts of your body, than for your whole body to be thrown into hell."*

What are you waiting for? Stop using opioids.

You were warned. How many more have to die before you wake up?

- The League of Orbis Novus

"I don't have to look that quote up," she said. "It's from the Sermon on the Mount."

Jack leaned in and briefly examined the words. "That's what he told me."

"Who?"

"Frank, when he visited me in Dayton. He said that sometimes a few of the guiltless need to be sacrificed for the greater good."

"So did Natalie Wu Lan, the informant," said Gina. "Remember? She said, 'It's about killing'."

Jack stood up and walked to the window. He pulled the curtain open and turned back toward Gina. "That's why they're not telling us how they're doing it," he told her. "They want people to die first."

"How many?" Gina asked rhetorically. "I need to get over to the PHE."

"You're gonna wear the same clothes?"

"Why not? I'm sure I won't be the only one."

"You can borrow my toothbrush."

Gina cringed a little. "Thanks, but I'll use my finger."

As she prepped in the bathroom, Jack flipped through the cable news channels. He came across a panel of talking heads discussing the theory of poisoned opium. The conventional wisdom among many of the so-called experts had drifted away from the flu theory. Jack relayed what he was hearing to Gina in the bathroom.

"It doesn't make any sense," he said in a raised voice. "Prescription opioids are synthetic. How could Orbis Novus have poisoned the supply?"

"It's possible if they have enough power and influence," she shouted above the noise of running water.

Gina left the hotel at 6 a.m. and walked over to the PHE building. The city streets, normally bustling at that hour, were ominously subdued. She passed only a handful of pedestrians, many of whom were wearing surgical masks. The situation room was anything but subdued. The number of occupants had doubled over the past twenty-four hours. The cast now included several busybodies dressed in blue and gray business suits who looked more like politicians than scientists. The city was clearly on high-alert. She couldn't locate Nigel within the throng, but David Hughes of the NCA waved her over.

"We're treating this as a criminal activity now," he told her. "The PHE is still trying to find the flu virus but we have to investigate other possibilities. Too many people are dying."

"You could buy some time just by doing what they're asking you to do."

"Who?"

"Orbis Novus. Tell people to stop using opioids."

"You think it's that simple?" asked Hughes. "People depend on those medications."

Gina started to smirk then curbed it. Hughes was completely unaware of his double entendre with the word "depend." She volunteered her services to help in any way she could then resumed her search for Nigel. A large whiteboard at the back of the room grabbed her attention. A young man was busily wiping away numbers and writing new ones under a scribbled title that read "Possible Deaths."

Britain: 67, USA: 24, China: 52, Brazil: 51, Columbia: 17, Canada: 9, France: 32, Germany: 9, Russia: 11, Thailand: 63, South Africa: 12.

Next to it was a larger list showing the fatalities per major city. Betty Wilshire approached and stood beside her, staring at the numbers.

"It just keeps growing," she said solemnly.

"Why does it say '*possible* deaths'?" asked Gina.

"All we know for certain is that they had similar symptoms of the virus."

"You've identified the virus?"

"Unfortunately, no," answered Betty. "But we have found the biomarkers."

"What does that mean?"

"Viruses leave evidence that they are present—specific proteins and RNAs. We've only tested a few of the victims so far, but the results are consistent."

"And opioids?"

"We have not confirmed opioid usage with all of them, but I'll tell you this—we haven't found one death that was not associated with opioid usage."

"Then there is a solid connection?"

"There's a problem there. The WHO has tested drug samples all over the world and hasn't found any known toxins. If they're poisoning the drugs, then they are using something we've never seen before."

They stood quietly together for a moment watching the man update the whiteboard numbers. "I hope to God it isn't a virus," muttered Betty. She appeared to be hypnotized by the statistics.

"Why?"

"We can deal with tainted opium, but a virus that goes from zero to sixty in about twelve hours—with a one hundred percent death rate? That would be a pandemic beyond biblical proportions."

Gina quietly walked away, leaving Betty in her gloomy trance. In light of the burgeoning focus on a criminal origin for the pandemic, she decided to go to the legat office at the embassy, though not before returning to her hotel for a quick shower and a change of clothes. She passed Nigel in the PHE lobby on her way out and told him of her plans.

"You'll have trouble finding a cab," he told her. "I'll take you."

At the Plaza on the River, shortly after Gina left, Jack filled a paper cup with hot tea from a dispenser in the hotel lobby and ventured out for a stroll on the chilly, deserted streets. He had come to realize that he had no business in London and needed to get back home. Nevertheless, he was divided by the notion of leaving Gina behind, though he knew that she was perfectly capable of taking care of herself. The way he saw it, she faced no danger as long as she avoided opioids.

He returned to the hotel restaurant and ordered the same breakfast he had fallen in love with since arriving: poached eggs, bacon, and the hotel's signature black pudding. The waiter's surgical mask did not faze him in the least, for the sight had become quite familiar over the past forty-eight hours. He wanted to tell every masked citizen he encountered that there was no need to panic, but it wasn't his place to do so. While awaiting his food, he searched for flight options on his smartphone, though he was still on the fence with respect to returning home.

There were plenty of available seats on outbound flights, and the airport website specified no government-imposed travel restrictions beyond screening for passengers displaying symptoms. Consumed by indecision, he closed the phone's app. He would need to confer with

Gina first. Perhaps it would help to call Grant at the *Chronicle*, he thought. They could discuss the latest message from Orbis Novus, and his boss would fill him in on the situation there. He would have to wait, as it was nearly midnight in Las Vegas.

A few minutes later, a text message lit up on his phone. It was his friend and coworker Jimmy.

"How r things in London?" read the message.

"Just thinking of u guys," wrote Jack. "Were ur ears burning?" There was no text response from Jimmy. The phone rang instead.

"Hey, man. What's up?" said Jack. He could hear the sounds of people bustling about in the background. "Are you at the office?"

"Yeah, it's pretty chaotic—a lot of people running around," said Jimmy. "All of the seniors are working this story. I'm supposed to fill in wherever I can."

"Really?"

"Yeah, haven't you heard? We had our first fatality here in Vegas tonight. Should I be worried?"

Jack was confused by Jimmy's question. "Geez, why are you asking *me*?"

"This is the work of your Orbis boys, right?"

"I think so, but there isn't any proof," said Jack. "They're eager to take credit but unwilling to give anyone a peak behind the curtain."

"People are starting to take them seriously. They need someone to blame, I guess."

Jack recounted his experiences since arriving in London, omitting the portions that included sharing a bed with an FBI agent. Jimmy provided details about the victim in Las Vegas. She was an addict living in a shared apartment in North Las Vegas. Two of her roommates were presently missing and also feared dead.

"Well, I better run," said Jimmy. "I just wanted to see if you were okay."

"Thanks."

"Oh wait, I almost forgot. A letter came for you a few days ago. It's sitting on your desk." Jimmy walked over to Jack's cubicle and picked up a legal-sized envelope. "There's no return address.... It's postmarked from Dallas."

The mention of Dallas rang a very recent bell with Jack. "Open it." He could hear the sounds of paper crumpling as Jimmy opened the envelope.

"It looks like a photocopy of an obituary," said Jimmy. "From the *Cincinnati Enquirer*… ten years ago… It's for a girl. She was eighteen… I'll scan it and send it to you."

"Great—thanks. Bye."

The email arrived on Jack's phone a few minutes later. He opened up the attachment and read the obituary.

"Huh," he muttered aloud as the story unfolded before him. *He really was from Ohio.* The startling development begat a need for further research. He could accomplish that much easier on his laptop, which was upstairs in his room. He couldn't wait to apprise Gina of his discovery and called her as soon as he stepped out of the elevator. After a few rings, her phone went to voicemail.

He spoke in a rushed, staccato cadence as he hurried down the corridor to his room. His mouth struggled to keep pace with his thoughts. "Hey, you're not gonna believe this—I know who he is—she sent me—I think it was Wu Lan—it's an obituary—he was a detective for the Cincinnati police—his daughter died of a heroin overdose."

Jack reached his room and swiped his keycard against the door lock. When the light flashed green, he opened the door and continued to speak into the phone as he flipped on the light.

"Anyway, call me. I know his name. It's…" The light suddenly revealed a well-dressed man sitting comfortably in a chair near the window. A hand reached from behind, grabbed his phone, and terminated the call. "… Frank."

"What brings you to London, Jack?"

The other man grabbed Jack by the arm and led him farther into the room. He wore a gray business suit that did little to hide his large, muscular frame. His shaved head contrasted with the image of his stately attire. Frank remained seated with one leg comfortably crossed over the other.

"How did you get into my room?" asked Jack.

"Does it really matter?" said Frank. "What you should be asking is *why* did I get into your room."

"What do you want from me? I did everything you asked."

"Did you really?"

Jack remained silent as Frank rose from the chair and approached him. "Are you just here on a holiday then?"

"I'm researching a story," Jack answered nervously. Something about Frank was different this time. Although calm, he seemed more resolute, irritated, and intimidating. The presence of the well-dressed goon fueled Jack's anxiety. A small part of him wished that they would throw a hood over his head.

Frank was growing impatient. "A story? I suppose you're collaborating with your girlfriend."

Jack felt his legs trembling. "I don't have a girlfriend."

"You don't?" asked Frank with an acerbic grin. He was within inches of Jack's face. "Gee, what were you two doing in each other's hotel rooms for the past two nights? Watching cartoons?"

"How did you even know I was here?"

"You can thank your FBI girlfriend for that, Jack. She was the one we were watching."

"I don't understand. Your plan is working. It's all over the world. What do you want from me—or her?"

"We need more time for the solution to… propagate, Jack. We can't afford for the FBI to intervene yet, and you're a little too chummy with them."

"Are you doing this because of your daughter, Frank?"

Frank's face broke character for an instant. He quickly collected himself, walked over to the window, and peered outside. "I don't know what you're talking about."

"I think you do."

Frank pivoted and exchanged a glance with his hulking cohort. "Alright, it's time to go." He pulled a surgical mask out of his pocket and placed it over his face. The bald man did the same.

"You don't want to catch something?" Jack asked facetiously.

"No, I don't want to be caught," replied Frank.

"What happens to me now?"

"That's not up to me. If it was, you'd already be dead," said Frank. He returned to within inches of Jack's nose. "Now listen to me carefully, Jack. You're gonna walk with us nice and easy downstairs, out the front door, and into a car—just like three buddies hanging out together. If you try to run, talk to anyone, or do anything other than look straight ahead, then your girlfriend, Agent Alvarez, won't live to see tomorrow. Am I clear?"

Jack nodded slightly.

"Am—I—clear?" repeated Frank sternly.

"Yes."

Nigel Peters waited in the lobby of the DoubleTree hotel as Gina cleaned up and changed her clothes. He spent the time glued to his cellphone, speaking with various Interpol contacts. Interpol was earnestly fulfilling its role of connecting law enforcements agencies across the world, as each country pursued its own criminal investigation of the epidemic. In parallel, the World Health Organization was attempting to coordinate activities and share data among the numerous national health ministries that were scrambling for a biological explanation. In spite of the integrated efforts, fatalities increased while answers remained elusive.

When Gina returned to the lobby at half past eight, Nigel told her that the death toll in England had surpassed one hundred. He dropped her off at the embassy then headed for his office at the NCA, to which he had been summoned. Before she hopped out of his car, Nigel asked Gina to keep him apprised of the FBI's findings. He was one of the few British authorities convinced that the League of Orbis Novus was somehow behind the crisis, and he knew they were supposedly located in the Western U.S.

Gina affirmed Nigel's request before heading upstairs to the legat office, where she found the legal attaché and all five of her deputies ardently working the case. Ties were loosened and sleeves were rolled up. An aura of urgency permeated the small office.

"Where have you been?" asked Courtney Roberts. This was the first time she showed any interest in Gina's whereabouts.

"Over at Public Health," replied Gina.

"What are they saying?"

"They're still trying to identify the flu strain."

"Well, we'll leave them to that," said Roberts dubiously. "We need you here now. Tell us everything you know about Orbis Novus." She led Gina into a small conference room where Nate Simmons and another deputy were listening to a conference call.

"We're on mute," said Simmons. He spoke quietly, as if he didn't quite trust the phone's muting capability. "Washington has all of the legat offices from affected countries on the line."

She took a seat at the table and listened to the concerted efforts and collective frustrations of her colleagues. She was surprised to hear Daryll Jameson's voice on the call, as it was the middle of the night in Las Vegas. He was bringing the other participants up to speed on the league.

Gina waited for an appropriate break in the dialogue and switched off the mute button. "Agent Jameson, this is Agent Alvarez in London."

"Alvarez, you're on the call—good," said Daryll. "You can pick it up from here."

Gina disclosed everything she knew about the league, which was not a whole lot. She discussed the timeline for the internet warnings, Jack Kurry's field trip to the lab, and the conversations with the informant. She also mentioned the alleged identity and recent death of the informant, to which Daryll added that the latter information had not been confirmed.

"Let's assume for now that this informant was who we think she was," said the voice of a senior director in Washington. "Her background might lead us to the facility. And the reporter, too—Kurry? We'll need to question him again."

"We've been trying to reach Kurry for a while now," said Daryll. "He's not answering his phone and we can't find him. He's not at his apartment."

"He's in London," said Gina.

"London? What's he doing there?" asked Daryll.

"He came here to write a story… I found out when I checked in with him the other day."

"Can you reach him? Do you know where he's staying?"

"I think so." She was wary of inadvertently divulging how cozy she and Jack had become. She sensed in Daryll's tone that he already suspected as much, and hoped that it was merely her own paranoia. "I'll get on it."

She left the room and pulled out her cellphone. She knew that Jack had left her a voice message while she was on the conference call. At the moment, she was more concerned about him accidently revealing their relationship to her FBI coworkers than anything else. As she walked over to her desk, she placed a call to Jack without listening to the message he had left for her. The call went directly to his voicemail greeting, indicating that his phone was either powered off or not within range of cellular service.

Neither explanation made sense to her, and she played the voicemail. Something seemed very odd about the way the message ended, or didn't end. The call was cut off for some reason. Gina knew that she needed to share it with her superiors, but something held her back. *Will this message reveal anything about our relationship?* She wanted to believe that Jack was merely overly excited about his discovery. She tried his phone again thirty minutes later, then again after an hour. After the third call went to voicemail, she grabbed her jacket and informed Roberts that she was going to look for Kurry.

"Take Agent Simmons with you," said the legal attaché. Gina preferred to handle the task alone, lest anyone discover her questionable relationship with Jack. However, her angst was increasing by the minute, and it made sense for multiple agents to be involved in the search. They could split up and follow separate leads if necessary. During the short drive in his car, Simmons debriefed Gina on everything she knew about the reporter.

"How did you know where he's staying?" he asked.

"I check in with him regularly. This was my case in Vegas, and he was my only witness." That was an easy bullet to dodge. Others might not be so avoidable, such as the voicemail message that was hidden on her phone and calling out to her like the tell-tale heart. She had already listened to the message twice more privately and determined that while it intimated a high-level of familiarity between them, it probably revealed nothing about their sexual relationship. Even if it did, she had no choice but to play it for Simmons now. Withholding it any longer could prove ruinous for her—and Jack. She feigned having forgotten about it.

"Wait—he left me a voicemail while we were on the con call. 8:47 this morning."

Simmons listened to the message attentively. "He identified somebody? Who's he talking about?" he asked.

"I'm not sure… probably the guy who threatened him."

As the day wore on, she became less concerned about the improprieties coming to light and more intent on finding Jack. The two agents were not surprised when nobody answered the door to Jack's room, or that there were no sounds emanating from within.

Gina started back toward the elevators. "Let's get the manager to open it up."

"Hold on, Alvarez," said Simmons. "We're in a foreign country. We don't have any jurisdiction here."

"So, what are we supposed to do?"

"I'll call the Met—the local police. But it might take a while to persuade them and the hotel to open up the room. The guy's only been gone for a few hours and there's no evidence of foul play."

"I've got a better idea," said Gina as she started to manipulate her phone. "This is a worldwide crisis, isn't it?" After a moment, she spoke into the phone. "Hi. I need your help. We've got a situation."

Twenty minutes later, Nigel Peters entered the hotel lobby with Inspector Hendricks and a uniformed female officer. They met the two FBI agents near the front desk. Hendricks spoke to the hotel manager while Gina provided Nigel and the constable with a description of Jack. It was not long before Hendricks returned with the manager and a member of the hotel security staff.

"We're ready," he said. The search party entered the room and found nothing blatantly suspicious. However, there were incongruities that suggested anomalous behavior. There was no luggage in the room, yet a t-shirt and pair of socks lay on the floor near the side of the bed. There was no laptop, yet a power supply for one was plugged into the wall. There was no cellphone, yet the charger was plugged into the lamp on the nightstand. A toothbrush and razor were found in the bathroom.

"It looks like he left in a hurry," said Hendricks. He turned to the manager. "We'll need to see what you have on camera, starting from this morning." Gina cringed inside, realizing that she might make cameo appearance in the video.

The group hurried down to the hotel's security office. There they huddled around a small monitor and studied the footage from multiple cameras beginning at 5 a.m., per Hendricks' request. When the timestamp reached 6:02, the figure of a woman in a professional pants suit could be seen traversing the otherwise empty lobby. Gina worried that Nigel might recognize her outfit from earlier in the morning, yet nobody seemed to notice, as they were not looking for a woman. Or so she thought—Simmons shot her an inquisitive look, complete with a furrowed brow. She shook her head ever so slightly in response, and he returned his gaze to the monitor.

At the 6:34 mark, a figure resembling Jack appeared. "That looks like him," said Gina, adding a hint of doubt to her tone, though she was quite certain that it was Jack. The man in the video filled a cup with coffee or tea before heading out the front door. An hour later, the same man returned and entered the hotel restaurant. This time, the footage revealed a much clearer view of his face.

"That's definitely him," asserted Gina. The videos showed nothing further of Jack until he emerged from the restaurant at 8:46.

"There he is," said Nigel.

"This is when he called me," added Gina.

The hotel manager pointed to the monitor. "He's heading to the elevators. We have a camera in the elevator lobby of every floor." As the security staff member pulled up the footage from the elevator lobby on the fourth floor, Gina replayed the audio from Jack's message for the group, then quickly added a few caveats.

"Jack is the person who tipped me off about Natalie Wu Lan," she said. "He must have found something else."

"A detective from Cincinnati?" asked Hendricks curiously.

"We'll look into it," replied Simmons.

The security staff member was ready with the surveillance footage from the fourth-floor lobby. Jack could be seen exiting the elevator and walking out of the shot. He was now speaking into his phone.

"Keep it there for a while," said Nigel. Several minutes later, the backs of Jack and two other men are seen entering the elevator. One of them, a large bald man, is towing a suitcase behind him. There were no cameras installed in the elevators, so they returned to the lobby footage with the hopes of obtaining a better view. The images were decent, but the men were wearing surgical masks and could not be identified.

"One of those men must be Frank," opined Gina.

"Kurry seems to be going along willingly," noted Hendricks. "Perhaps they've offered to show him something again—another field trip of sorts."

They reverted back to earlier footage and found no video surveillance of the two masked-men entering the building. There were no clear images of their faces.

Hendricks obtained copies of the relevant videos for the NCA and

FBI. Each would separately attempt to identify the men seen with Jack. The Met was tasked with tracking the men using surveillance footage from nearby neighborhood cameras and other means. Following a brief conference in the lobby, the three factions dispersed.

Gina and Simmons discussed Jack's reference to a mysterious detective from Cincinnati as they drove back to the embassy. Following a pause, Simmons abruptly changed the subject.

"That was you in the video, right?" Gina said nothing. "You know they're gonna pull his phone records at some point."

"We talked a lot," she said. "He was here to write a story about Orbis Novus."

Simmons nodded, yet his expression revealed some doubt. "Look, I'll keep this to myself for now, but if I see that your judgement is clouded, I'll have to step in. You need to focus on your job, Alvarez."

Gina nodded slightly, but her countenance made a full confession. "I know."

21

The morning of December 5th revealed an alarming increase in deaths and the number of locations reporting them. Statistics were no longer reported on a per city basis; tallies were aggregated into the number of victims per country. In England alone, the number had eclipsed eight hundred. There were more than four hundred reported deaths in the United States, where the illness appeared to spread in all directions from Kansas City, like the spokes on a bicycle wheel. Russia led the world with nearly a thousand cases. China was close on its heels.

Experts across the planet found little upon which to agree except for one consensus: the widespread illnesses likely shared the same underlying and unidentified cause. The U.N. and WHO convened a special conference in Manhattan, where bewilderment reigned over the world's foremost experts. There were as many working theories about the culprit as there were health ministries across the planet, though most opinions fell into one of two camps: a violent, flu-like respiratory virus and a toxic, as of yet undetectable, form of opioid that was somehow affecting both synthetic and natural products.

The spread of the contagion defied computer models and simulations. That the pathogen could spontaneously and simultaneously appear in disparate parts of the world contradicted the virus theory. However, the subsequent spread of the illness in those areas supported it. Strangely, the alleged superbug was apparently highly-contagious, yet there were no reports of caregivers contracting the illness.

In some parts of the world, the usage of opioids in hospitals and other medical facilities was temporarily banned. The prohibition proved nearly impossible to sustain. Critical surgeries could only be postponed for so long, and terminally-ill patients were suffering. General anesthetics typically used for surgery, such as Propofol, are not opioids. The problem was that patients were unwilling to accept that there was no risk with general anesthesia, or they were unwilling to endure the pain of recovery without opioids. Throughout the world there were reports of patients refusing opioids and demanding alternatives. An untold number of otherwise preventable deaths were indirectly linked to the epidemic, as people suffering serious injuries and ailments refused to seek medical treatment, in fear of contracting the mysterious illness. Many more of these cases would come to light in the days that followed.

A few smaller nations with no reported cases, including Jordan and Uruguay, shut down their borders in the hopes of preventing the pandemic from infecting their populations. Their lofty attempts would soon prove unsuccessful.

Governments that had once turned a blind-eye toward illegal poppy fields in their jurisdictions suddenly unleashed soldiers to burn them to the ground. In Afghanistan, the world's largest opium producer, the U.S. and Afghan armies stepped up efforts to destroy, or at least cripple, the Taliban-backed industry. Around the world, warlords fought back to protect their livelihood. Hundreds of soldiers, police officers, and thugs died in remote jungles, forests, and mountains within India, Thailand, Myanmar, Laos, Mexico, and Afghanistan. In the U.S., most of the small-time growers simply abandoned their poppy plants.

Much of the legal opium production was temporarily halted until the source of the epidemic could be identified. The Indian and Turkish governments shutdown all operations on December 4th and began to analyze the chemical composition of their products at all stages of production.

Whether caused by a pathogen or a toxin, governments agreed that there was a criminal element behind the crisis. That the pathogen could appear simultaneously in so many distant locations throughout the world defied the laws of mother nature. Biowarfare on a national level was ruled out early, as every world power had been affected, including countries that harbored terrorists. No known terrorist organizations had claimed credit for the outbreak; however, a heretofore unknown organization had predicted it months in advance: The League of Orbis Novus.

Epidemiologists in London worked quickly and tirelessly to trace the origin of the outbreak there. They mapped the locations of victims, interviewed friends and relatives, and fed the data into sophisticated computer algorithms. The computers estimated that ground-zero for the London epidemic was probably in the Soho area, and the conclusion made sense. The experts in London reasoned that the pathogen, probably an airborne virus, was likely released into the stifled air within multiple crowded areas, such as restaurants and bars. They also hypothesized that the pathogen was released several days before December 1st. Perhaps that was wishful thinking. They knew that if it had been introduced closer to December 1st and was able to spread so rapidly in just a few days, then they were facing a highly-contagious virus, the likes of which the world had never seen before.

In the United States, the data pointed to Kansas as the release point for the pathogen. The first identified cases were in Kansas City, and they spread quickly from there, forging paths along the busy interstate highways of 29, 35, 49, and 70. That the pathogen was released in only one location within the opioid-fueled nation suggested that the organization responsible had limited resources. Rather than introducing it within multiple large metropolises, they chose the geographic center of the country, from which it propagated rapidly.

Another theory supporting the single release point in the U.S. was that the culprits wanted to limit the damage. Experts opined that if the pathogen had been planted simultaneously in major cities such as New York, Los Angeles, and Houston, then the U.S. death toll could have skyrocketed to a half-million people very quickly. It was as if the parties responsible didn't need to press the accelerator all the way to the floor in order to make their point.

In all, there were twelve suspected release points throughout the world. In addition to London and Kansas City, the pathogen was ostensibly planted in Moscow, Shanghai, Paris, Berlin, Bogota, New Delhi, Tokyo, Johannesburg, Rio de Janeiro, and Bangkok. Australia and Antarctica were the only two continents to have been spared the initial release. Australians initially enjoyed a false sense of security, and there was talk of closing their borders during the first few days of the crises. The herculean task would have been nearly impossible to carry out, and the notion was squelched when cases appeared in Sydney on December 4th. Their patient zero was a tourist who had returned home from Thailand.

Most of the world now looked to the United States, and in particular the FBI, for answers regarding the surreptitious group. Over the past twenty-four hours, the Bureau had organized a nationwide search for the elusive faction. Agents coordinated federal, state, and local law enforcement agencies in casting a wide net over a circle centered in Las Vegas, and looked for clues to zero in somewhere. They had only a few leads, and one of their key witnesses was now missing. He was a reporter from the *Las Vegas Chronicle* who was last seen in London.

By December 6th, the worldwide death toll had reached thirty thousand, and would double by the end of the day. There were cases of victims who had used heroin between December 1st and 5th without incident, only to die from the illness after using heroin in the days that followed. Drug samples were tested and retested. Fentanyl and other substances were found in some heroin samples, but not on a large scale, and the superbug symptoms did not match those of traditional fentanyl overdoses.

Scientists were convinced of a viral presence. Symptoms and conventional wisdom pointed to a new strain of the influenza virus, though nothing had been found. The sharpest minds were employing the latest detection methods, including virus cultures, electron microscopy, and polymerase chain reaction. But those processes required days to complete, and worked better when a specific virus was being targeted. In this situation they were taking shots in the dark. There was a lot of circumstantial evidence and no smoking gun. Identifying the virus would only be the first step in solving the problem, yet little could be done until scientists knew what they were dealing with.

By this time, the correlation between the epidemic and opioid usage was undeniable, albeit still unconfirmed. The alleged relationship between a class of neurological drugs and an elusive respiratory virus baffled the experts. Furthermore, the number of victim deaths associated with illegal drug use, whether from opiates or prescription opioids, far outpaced those resulting from legally-administered medications. In Europe and the United States, where governments had not instituted nationwide bans, medical professionals took it upon themselves to curb opioid distribution. Some pharmacies refused to fill prescriptions, in fear of incurring lawsuits later.

Addicts flocked to rehab centers and many had to be turned away. Local governments scrambled to create temporary shelters for those wishing to detox, but the medications and personnel required to ensure a safe detoxification were in short supply. Some addicts attempted to quit cold-turkey, and a few succeeded—at least in the short term. Most opioid addicts lacked the resolve and support to even attempt quitting. They continued to use in spite of the rapidly-spreading pandemic, as well as the panic associated with it.

The widespread and ever-changing rumors didn't help. A new crop of urban legends proliferated throughout areas of high drug usage. One claimed that ingesting over-the-counter flu medication, such as NyQuil, prior to using heroin, rendered the superbug inactive. Another was undoubtedly concocted by enterprising drug dealers. It alleged that mixing heroin and cocaine—known on the streets as a "speedball"—made the user immune to the disease. As a result of hoaxes such as these, overdoses spiked during the first week of December, resulting in many more deaths. Health ministries scrambled to discredit rumors and clarify what they knew—or didn't know. All they could really do was implore their citizens to avoid opioids.

Overall, and in spite of the deceptive rumors, illegal opioid users seemed to be taking heed of the official warnings. Local governments in western nations soon discovered another challenge. Many users of legally-prescribed opioids failed to connect the threats seen on television to their own medicine cabinets. The crisis was viewed by some as a heroin problem that could never touch their lives. The number of fatalities from this category of users rose at a much higher pace than those resulting from illegal usage during the second week of December. Multitudes of volunteers took to the suburban streets in a zealous effort to warn citizens door to door. Some were authorized to collect prescriptions of Vicodin, Oxycodone, Percocet, and other commonly-prescribed opioids.

By the end of the first week, few people in the world were not touched by the worldwide superbug. If not directly affected by the death of a loved one, a person surely knew of a distant relative, friend of a friend, neighbor, or coworker who was. The catastrophe dominated conversations in every living room, classroom, and breakroom. It seemed odd to hear somebody talking about anything else.

22

In keeping with his word, Sydney Carter attended the group therapy session on his first day as an outpatient on the morning of December 5th. Rather than opening his mind to the shared threads underlying the addictions of his groupmates, he focused on the issues to which he could not relate, thus strengthening his preconceived notion that he was different. When asked to convey his story, he told the therapist and group members what they expected to hear. He recounted numerous stories about alcohol negatively impacting his life. Everyone listened intently except himself.

Of course, everybody was talking about the superbug before, during, and after the session. Many of the group members were recovering opioid addicts who were relieved at having gotten clean, and frightened by the dangerous prospect of slipping back into addiction. Sydney had not heard much about the crisis. The story had broken while he was detoxing and he had not watched the news or otherwise interacted with anyone during his first evening at home.

Upon returning to his basement apartment after the meeting, he turned on the television and watched the talking heads on cable news deliberate the sources of the pandemic. A few ideas crossed his mind, and he assumed that many of his colleagues at Emerson–Lee were already considering them. He was then overcome by a feeling of resentment. *Why haven't they called me back into the office to help?* He still thought of himself as Emerson–Lee's foremost expert on pathogenesis. In reality, most of his contemporaries sadly viewed him as a troubled soul and a has-been who could have accomplished great things if not for his personal demons. Sydney was oblivious to how others saw him, and his resentment soon graduated into anger. He switched off the television.

"Let them figure it out for themselves," he grumbled.

He knew that it was important for his sobriety to stay occupied. Feeling better than he had in years, he decided to improve his physical conditioning and took his bike out for a brisk ride around the neighborhood. The first thing he noticed was the number of people wearing surgical masks, and he reckoned that they were overreacting. From what he had seen and heard on television, the so-called superbug was not behaving like an airborne virus. This was obvious to him because of the pattern, or lack thereof, regarding the spread of the illness. Too many people who should have been contracting it were not. Even if a virus was released simultaneously in multiple parts of the world by a criminal faction, which he seriously doubted, the resulting proliferation did not adhere to expected patterns.

He had developed a working theory. Perhaps there was a genetic predisposition within certain people that made them either susceptible or immune to the new strain of the influenza virus—if there even was one. He also had not reconciled the correlation with opioids, or even considered it much. He had more personal issues to deal with, and figured that the rest of the world could handle its own problems. As such, he took a seat on a park bench and phoned his wife.

"Can I see the girls tonight?"

"You're not giving me much notice," replied Pam.

"Is there anything you need to do? I can watch them while you go out."

Sydney's days of babysitting his daughters had been over for a while. He had no expectation of Pam agreeing to his proposal. It was merely his starting point for negotiation, in hopes that his wife might offer a counterproposal. His strategy worked.

"You can stop by around five," she said. "But just for an hour. You're not staying for dinner."

He readily accepted the offer then biked around the park for another hour before returning home to clean up. At 4 p.m. he walked to the station and caught a train north to Dunwoody. It was just a short Uber ride to the house from there. The girls were excited to see their father.

Pam consciously hid her bitter feelings and frustrations regarding Sydney from her children. She didn't want to sour their relationship in the hopes that he might one day be a capable father to them once again. She had no aspirations for rekindling their marriage and had already commenced with divorce proceedings. She had not yet mentioned this development to her husband, though in her mind, even *he* couldn't be so self-absorbed to not see it coming. Actually, he was, but Pam chose not to bring the subject up just yet.

"I'm surprised you're not in Kansas City or some other place dealing with the pandemic."

"Yeah, they've got me working the case from Emerson–Lee," lied Sydney. "In fact, I'm going straight back to the office from here. I'll be working on it all night." Prior to this evening, he had neither the opportunity nor the desire to tell his estranged wife about his mandatory leave of absence. *Why tell her when everything is already under control?*

On the train ride home, he reflected on his day, and particularly the evening. He felt that the visit went well, notably because he and Pam did not argue. He interpreted it as a sign of her recognizing his self-control. In her mind, she was simply tired of fighting and there was nothing left for them to discuss.

Sydney felt emboldened by his recent victories and pondered ways to parlay them into more successes. Alone and bored on his couch, his brilliant, scheming mind concocted a win–win plan to prove to himself and the world what he already knew. A firm believer in the scientific method, he decided to test his hypothesis regarding his penchant for alcohol, or as he viewed it, a lack thereof.

His logic made perfect sense to him and went something like this: Having transitioned himself to an outpatient program with the Breland Recovery Center, he was now the steward of his own recovery—although he never used that specific term in reference to his situation. As a biochemist, who was more qualified than he to understand the chemical interactions between alcohol and the human body? He was convinced that he had no issue with alcohol; now he needed to prove it scientifically. The test was simple. He would drink three beers—no more, no less—and go straight to bed. That was something any "ordinary" person could do.

The plan required a quick trip to the corner grocery for a six-pack.

He drank the first two with a frozen pizza and the third shortly thereafter. It was too early for bed, so he remained on the couch and watched a documentary about cheetahs in the African savanna. He wondered if a normal person would have a fourth beer in this situation. *No—that was not a condition of the test. But then again…*

The ringing of his cellphone interrupted the internal deliberation. He didn't recognize the number of the incoming call, not even the area code.

"Is this Sydney Carter—Doctor Sydney Carter?" asked the woman's voice.

"Yes."

"Hello, Doctor Carter. I'm sure you don't remember me. I attended a lecture you gave at UCSD two years ago. I teach there. My name is Muriel Smithson. We spoke briefly afterward."

Sydney wasn't sure if he had heard her correctly. "UC San Diego?"

"Yes. I hope I'm not interrupting anything."

"No, um… that's okay. How did you get this number?"

"You included it on the brochure two years ago."

Sydney remembered the trip to San Diego—not the lecture so much as the festive evening he spent afterward in the famous Gaslamp District. He could not recall handing out his cellphone number, though he obviously had done so. Nevertheless, he was grateful for the company—and the distraction.

"What can I do for you?"

"I'm calling about Orbis Novus."

The name sounded familiar to him yet he couldn't place it. "Orbis what?"

"The pandemic."

"Oh, right. They're the people claiming responsibility for it."

"I think they *are* responsible," said Muriel. She went into detail about her meetings with a reporter from the *Las Vegas Chronicle* and an agent from the FBI. Like everyone else, she had doubted the validity of the internet warnings. She recounted her hypothetical discussions about vigilantes targeting the criminals that created and distributed the supply of illicit opiates. The developments over the past week had convinced her that Orbis Novus was real, and she regretted not taking the threats more seriously. Furthermore, something the reporter had mentioned at their last meeting prompted her to approach the problem from another angle.

"He was told to look at the people, not the plants," she said.

"They *are* looking at people," responded Sydney. "They have a lot of dead bodies at their disposal."

"True, but what if they're looking for the wrong thing, and in the wrong place?"

"Okay, I'm listening."

"They're looking for a virus resembling influenza because that's what the symptoms point to," continued Muriel. "I get it. Then this morning, something occurred to me, and I thought about you—your lecture, that is."

Sydney still had no recollection of the conference. "What did I talk about?"

"Most of your presentation was about the genetic mutation of viruses, but toward the end you mentioned a theory of yours." She proceeded to read from her notes. "You called it spontaneous viral transmutation."

"Oh, that was just something I cooked up way back—" The epiphany suddenly rushed over him like a wave crashing down on the beach. It could explain some things, though it was only a theory, and one that nobody had ever seriously pursued—including himself. He sat up straight on his couch and leaned forward.

"If that's happening," he said, "then there would be two different viruses."

"Could that explain such a rapid death after contracting it?"

"No—not by itself. You would need a trigger."

"Opioids?"

Now it was even more obvious, as the remaining pieces came together in Sydney's clouded brain. He stood up and began to pace around his small living room. "It's definitely feasible."

The two biochemists discussed the possible scenarios for about an hour, mostly with Muriel serving as an intelligent sounding board for Sydney's stream-of-conscious hypothesizing. He grew more resolute and assured by the minute.

"I guess I should let you go," said Muriel. "I'm sure you'll want to get working on this right away." A silent pause followed. "Are you still there?"

"I'm here," replied Sydney in a soft tone. He slumped back down onto his couch. "The thing is, I'm on a sort of sabbatical at the moment." His excitement of the discovery had completely obscured the fact that he was suspended from Emerson–Lee.

The notion that one of the CDC's leading experts in pathogenesis was not already working on the pandemic bewildered Muriel. Her imagination of a sabbatical conjured an image of Sydney studying abroad somewhere. Surely, he would have been called back home to assist by now. "Where are you?" she asked.

"I'm in Atlanta," said Sydney. He struggled to fabricate a plausible explanation. He was not about to admit the embarrassing truth to a near-stranger. He couldn't even admit to himself that he had a problem. He decided that he would figure it out on his own, and the less she knew, the better. "You know what? It isn't a problem. I'll get on this right away."

"Great."

"You've been a big help—thanks. I'll keep you posted." He couldn't get her off the phone fast enough.

"Sure. If you need me to—"

"Is this the best number for you?" interrupted Sydney.

"Yes."

"Great. Talk to you soon."

Sydney had been to Phil Rogers' house twice before for holiday parties in years past, and he was able to figure out the address using an internet map. Thirty minutes later, an Uber car dropped him off at the foot of his manager's driveway. It was just after 10 p.m. when a teenaged boy answered the door. He looked at Sydney inquisitively and said nothing.

"Is your dad home? Tell him it's Syd from work."

The boy did not have to tell his father anything. Phil had already entered the atrium to see who might be calling at such a late hour. A combination of dread and disappointment washed over his face when he saw who it was. He dismissed his son, walked outside, and pulled the door closed behind him.

"Jesus, Syd. What are you doing here?"

Sydney was exuberant. He had connected a few more dots on the way over. Phil thought his employee looked crazed.

"I think I've figured it out, Phil. They need to look at the blood more closely," exclaimed Sydney.

"What are you talking about? You're supposed to be in rehab. Have you been drinking?"

"No—I mean, yes, I had a few beers, but that's irrelevant. The superbug—I know how to find it. I know how it works."

Phil took a moment to size up the man who stood before him. He did not appear intoxicated, just excited. In fact, he had not seen Sydney this enthusiastic about anything in months. It was worth hearing him out. "Okay. Tell me what you're talking about."

Sydney took a deep breath. "It probably looks like an ordinary rhinovirus. That's why they haven't found it."

"A common cold? I don't understand."

"Do you remember that study I was doing on fish viruses a few years back? The research suggested that a particular virus was mutating when it moved into the bloodstream. I called it spontaneous viral transmutation."

"Vaguely," said Phil. Sydney had researched a lot of cutting-edge theories over the years, many of which led nowhere. That was common in the field of viral pathogenesis, and medical science in general. "There's no evidence of that ever happening in humans."

"But what if it could? Let's assume there's a new strain of rhinovirus—maybe it was a natural evolution, or maybe not. Let's say that the virus is harmless—it lies dormant in the respiratory system."

"Okay, you're suggesting that the immune system ignores it?"

"Yes—it stays under the radar—maybe gets a little attention—a few T-cells but nothing unusual. Assume it could live there indefinitely or for a very long time. Now, suppose it migrates into the bloodstream."

"And mutates there?"

"Into a completely different virus—probably something resembling a lentivirus, and it's also dormant."

Phil was skeptical, yet he found it difficult to refute the intellectually superior man's thinking, even in his current state. "So, we have *two* dormant viruses," he summarized. "One in the respiratory tract and one in the bloodstream. It's a stretch, Syd."

"Yeah, and lot of the crap I'm hearing on T.V. about this superbug is a stretch too. We're in uncharted waters here, Phil."

"It's viral then? It has nothing to do with the opioids?"

"If I'm right, it has everything to do with the opioids. They trigger the viruses—at least the bloodborne virus, I think. I haven't worked that part out yet."

"People don't die from cold viruses."

"They do when the body overreacts to them. What if the blood virus somehow kicked the immune system into overdrive—freakin' hyperdrive. It might attack the rhinovirus too, but with the wrong antigens, and boom—it can't shut itself down. It's like using a nuclear bomb to remove a hangnail."

"You're suggesting that these people are dying of viral sepsis?"

"I think so. These viruses are new strains, right? There's no acquired immunity to dial up." Sydney took a moment to catch his breath. "I still have to figure some things out. The opioid must trigger some kind of chemical reaction in the blood. I don't know how, but it has to. There's no other explanation."

"I suppose it explains why the victims die so quickly—and violently," added Phil. "And you think this is all man-made?"

"It's too precise not to be. It's ingenious—evil yes, but ingenious. Geez Phil, I could have dreamed this up, so why couldn't somebody else—or a whole team of people?"

Phil walked down the sidewalk for a few paces as the information infiltrated his brain. He turned and pointed to Sydney. "The airborne virus would have to be highly-contagious for this to work."

"What better choice than a rhinovirus? It probably took them years to develop the perfect strain—weak, highly-contagious, and mostly-dormant."

"A common cold with no symptoms."

"You and I might already have the virus inside us," suggested Sydney. "They say that caregivers aren't contracting it, but they are. It's just sleeping inside them."

The men started to fire off of each other.

"It's the last thing they would look for," said Phil. "I don't know whether it was intentional, but the flu symptoms acted like a red herring of sorts, throwing us off the scent of the real culprit."

"Which is hiding in the blood," added Sydney.

Phil was now fully onboard. "We have to get this in front of the CDC."

"I can start working on it right away," said Sydney. "I just need to get into the lab."

Phil rubbed his forehead and looked down at the sidewalk before responding. "Syd, I can't let you in there. It's going take some time to get your… situation sorted out."

"How much time do we really have, Phil?"

"Did you even go to rehab?"

"I did. I got cleaned up and now it's under control. I only had a few beers tonight before—"

"Listen to yourself, Syd. You're saying exactly what an alcoholic would say."

"Just let me into the lab. I'll grab my notes and my laptop and work from home."

"Come on, Syd. You know I can't do that." He continued after a heavy sigh. "Look, I'll make some calls. Maybe I can—"

"Molly," interrupted Sydney in a quiet voice, as if he was thinking out loud. He clasped his hands on top of his head.

Phil shook his head and shrugged. "What?"

"It doesn't have to be me," continued Sydney excitedly. "There was a woman who worked with me on H3N2 a few years ago. Her name was Molly something… Thompson, Thomas…"

"Molly Tompkins?"

"Yes! Molly Tompkins. She can identify the viruses—and the opioid connection too. Just tell her everything I told you. Get her working on it!"

Phil placed his hand on Sydney's shoulder to calm him down. "I will, Syd. We'll get Molly and a whole team looking into this. But I'm worried about you. You need help."

"Don't worry about me. Just find the answers."

The men went inside the house, where Phil picked up the phone and put a plan to test Sydney's theories into motion. He tracked down the phone number for Molly Tompkins and roused her out of bed. Like most of the pathogen experts at Emerson–Lee, Molly was already assigned to the pandemic. She spent an hour on the phone with Phil and Sydney, then decided to head over to the lab and start working, as she was too excited to wait until the morning.

It was nearly 3 a.m. when Phil dropped Sydney off on the street outside his basement flat. As Sydney was walking away, Phil lowered the passenger door window and called out to him.

"I'm going see about getting you back into the lab, Syd. You hang in there."

Sydney turned around and nodded. "Okay, thanks." Deep down, they both knew that Sydney would not be returning to the lab.

23

Several hours after Muriel Smithson phoned Sydney Carter at his basement flat on the night of December 5th, Gina Alvarez was sitting a few miles away in the Hartsfield-Jackson Atlanta International Airport, awaiting her connecting flight to Las Vegas. Daryll Jameson, the special agent in charge of the FBI office in Las Vegas, had ordered Gina to return home and help with the search for the elusive League of Orbis Novus. The move made sense; there was no reason for her to remain in London—no professional reason, at least. Britain's National Crime Agency was leading the search for Jack Kurry, and the legat office in the London embassy served as a liaison to the FBI personnel in Washington and Las Vegas.

Gina's plane from London had been barely half full. Most of the chairs in the boarding area in Atlanta were empty, and nearly everyone seated there wore a surgical mask. It was easy to hear the sound from the television monitor above her. The host of a cable news program was discussing the impact of the superbug on the worldwide economy. People were afraid to travel, go to movies, restaurants, and shopping malls during what should have been a busy holiday shopping season. Teams in the National Football League were making final pushes for the playoffs in front of half-empty stadiums. Many parents pulled their children from schools and most extracurricular activities were cancelled. It was if a giant blizzard had blanketed the entire world. Most people remained indoors, glued to their televisions and scouring the internet for the latest news.

The program on the airport monitor aired clips from a press conference with the U.S. Surgeon General, in which the nation's top medical advisor did her best to assure citizens of their safety. She referenced the correlation with opioids, suggesting that abstinence from the drugs would protect them. Yet there was an uncertain tone in her voice, for none of the experts working for the U.S. government could confirm a connection to opioids.

There was no mention of Jack Kurry in the news broadcast. British and American authorities thought it best to keep the identity and status of their crucial witness under wraps. Gina kept her hopes up. The group had taken Jack once before and released him unharmed. Then again, she strongly suspected that they were responsible for the death of Natalie Wu Lan in Dallas. The FBI had opened an investigation into the supposed suicide of the research scientist and had since confirmed that she was indeed the voice of the informant. This information was also withheld from the public.

Gina finally arrived at McCarran Airport in Las Vegas on the evening of December 6th and found it even more desolate than Hartsfield. Most conventions, the lifeblood of the city's economy, had been postponed. Those that hadn't were sparsely attended, and few vacationers were willing to risk contracting the deadly superbug in exchange for a few fun-filled nights in Sin City. The line of taxis waiting outside the airport terminal was much shorter than usual, and the line of passengers waiting for one was nonexistent. The city, so dependent on visitors, was quickly spiraling into an economic meltdown that would rival the Great Recession.

It was after 8 p.m. when her plane touched down, and she was exhausted. But instead of going home to her warm bed, she instructed the driver to head north toward downtown. During the long flight home, and in the wake of Jack's abduction, something else had begun to weigh on her conscience. She surmised that the odds were favorable, yet she was compelled to know for certain. The taxi pulled into the parking lot of a seedy, motel-style apartment building where she instructed the driver to wait. She approached the door to the apartment hesitantly, second-guessing her impulsive decision. After a moment, she knocked.

"Who's there?" came a mistrustful voice from behind the door.

"It's Agent Alvarez."

"Who?"

"Gina Alvarez, from the FBI."

"What do you want?"

Gina couldn't determine if it was the same voice she remembered from her previous visit, when she investigated the overdose of the woman attached to the human trafficking case known as Poison Ivy. "Can I speak with you for a minute? You're not in any trouble." She heard the sound of the chain lock sliding across its track. The door cracked opened to reveal Sarah's weary, wrinkled face.

"I remember you," said Sarah. "You were here when Jenny died." She opened the door wider but did not invite Gina inside.

"I just wanted to see if you were al—alright," said Gina, skirting the word "alive" at the last second.

"What, do you mean that virus thing?" replied Sarah, as if the worldwide catastrophe couldn't be farther from her doorstep. "I'm fine."

"Are you using?"

Sarah looked at Gina dubiously. She was not in the habit of discussing her illicit drug activities with law enforcement personnel.

"You can't use heroin," implored Gina. "It will kill you."

"I told you I'm not sick," responded Sarah.

"Listen to me," continued Gina. She was astonished that Sarah was oblivious to the link between the superbug and opioids. "You need to stop using heroin, or you will die," she said emphatically. "If not tonight, then tomorrow, or the next day—but it *will* happen."

Sarah's eyes suddenly peered over to something inside her room then quickly returned to Gina. That's when Gina realized that she couldn't leave the woman alone. "Can I take you somewhere—just for tonight?"

"I know what I'm doing," replied Sarah. "I'm not gonna overdose."

Gina sighed in frustration. She pleaded with Sarah for another minute or two before finally threatening to arrest her for possession. Sarah fell for the bluff, and subsequently packed a small bag as Gina flushed the packet of heroin she found on the coffee table down the toilet.

Gina had no idea where to take Sarah, but the cab driver did. He knew of a special treatment center that had been hastily set up by the state health department in response to the crisis. He drove the women to a warehouse in an industrial section of North Las Vegas. Gina was shocked to find a long line of people queued outside.

"You're the third person I drove here today," noted the cabbie.

She paid the driver and escorted Sarah to the back of the line. A man with a clipboard soon walked over to them and began the intake process. He told Gina that Sarah would be admitted that night.

"We'll make room for everyone," he assured her.

Worried that Sarah might take off, Gina remained for an hour until she was safely inside. "They'll take care of you," she told the young woman before leaving.

"Okay," replied Sarah. It wasn't exactly a thank you, yet Gina could see the relief in Sarah's eyes. The sight of the overwhelming crowd at the warehouse had apparently affected Sarah as well, and she knew that she was where she needed to be. Of course, the makeshift facility was only a temporary solution, a first aid reaction to the crisis. For most of the addicts inside, the nightmare would continue for some time. Many would get clean and others would continue to struggle with the trials of addiction. The league had merely removed a means to an end. There were still plenty of non-opioid alternatives available to enslave them until the root causes of their addictions could be properly addressed.

Gina was soon inside another taxi and headed for her home in Southern Highlands. On the way she left a message for Daryll Jameson, informing him that she was back in the city and would be present for the morning briefing. Her house was exactly as she had left it a week earlier—clean, quiet, and empty. Under the circumstances, she preferred it that way. She didn't feel like answering a lot of questions from nosey roommates, friends, and family members. As their only connection to law enforcement, she was always the one they called when something big happened. She typically knew little more than they did about major cases. In this particular case she happened to know a lot, though there was nothing she could disclose to them.

They had all called while she was in London—plus her ex-husband—but she had been too busy or too unmotivated to call them back. Now she lay on the couch, exhausted yet unable to sleep. The guilt of not returning the messages finally reached its breaking point and she sent a few text messages before retiring to the bedroom, where she eventually managed a few hours of light sleep. As usual, she downplayed her role in the investigation and did not mention that she had ever left town. Before nodding off, she lay in bed wondering about Jack's family. Jack had spoken highly of his father and the positive changes in their relationship since the death of his mother. His family likely had no idea that he was missing.

She arrived at the office the next morning an hour before the eight o'clock standup meeting and caught up with some busywork at her desk. One silver lining of the Orbis Novus case was a reprieve from the Poison Ivy phone records, if only temporary. Daryll popped his head into her office a few minutes before eight.

"How was the flight back?" he asked, then continued without waiting for an answer. "Are you ready?"

Gina could see that Daryll was in his legendary "big case mode" as it was referred to reverently (yet behind his back) by the agents who reported to him. The no-nonsense special agent had worked his way into a senior position by leading prominent cases into successful resolutions, and there were none in his illustrious background more prominent than this one. She followed her boss into the conference room, where a standing-room-only crowd of agents awaited, along with several more who had dialed in from Washington and other parts of the world.

She soon learned that the first item on the agenda was an update from her about the last known whereabouts of Jack Kurry. She ended her brief summary with a question.

"Has anybody been in touch with his family?"

An agent informed her that he was in contact with the father and sister, and that neither had known that Kurry was in London. Gina felt a slight relief in hearing that Jack's family was at least aware of his situation. In a strange way, it helped to know that there were others out there who cared about him and missed him. She glanced around the room to see if anyone was eyeing her curiously or otherwise, possibly indicating an awareness or suspicion of her improper relationship. The coast appeared to be clear. Nate Simmons had not betrayed her secret.

"Thanks for the update, Agent Alvarez," said Daryll. "NCA in London has the lead on finding Kurry. You'll remain our liaison to them."

"Understood," replied Gina. "I'll check in with Nigel Peters as soon as we're finished here." She maintained her businesslike visage when she learned that there were no new leads on Jack's whereabouts.

Internally, she felt a stress-induced rush of adrenalin flow through her gut.

The next order of business was to discuss the information recently obtained from a co-worker of Kurry's at the *Chronicle*, a man named Richard Forsby. Gina soon figured out that he was the same guy whom Jack referred to as Jimmy. Forsby had provided the agents with a copy of an email he sent to Kurry just before his disappearance. The agent projected its contents onto the conference room screen. It contained an obituary dated ten years earlier concerning the death of an eighteen-year-old girl from Cincinnati.

"The letter was sent to Kurry anonymously from a post office in Dallas," said the agent. He was one of the "blue suits" who had met with Jack the last time he was there. "We suspect that it came from Natalie Wu Lan, but the partial prints found on the envelope and letter were inconclusive."

The agent proceeded to display photos of a surly-looking man. Having just read the contents of the obituary for the first time, Gina knew immediately that she must be looking at Jack's captor, the mysterious character known as Frank. The suspect's full name was James Francis Cole, Jr. He had been called Frank since the day he was born in order to avoid confusion with his father, James Cole, Sr. Cole Jr. retired as a detective from the Cincinnati police department at the age of forty-five, two years after his only child, Amber, was found dead of an accidental heroin overdose. The incident occurred during a high-school graduation party at a neighbor's house. It was Amber's first time using heroin. She had snorted the drug, and friends testified that she might have thought it was cocaine.

Cole and his wife divorced around the same time that he retired from the police force, and the two soon lost touch. He bounced around jobs with various private security firms in Cincinnati for a few years before disappearing for good five years after his daughter's death. Former neighbors, friends, and coworkers told the FBI that Frank was never the same after his daughter died. He had mentioned starting a new life in Alaska on several occasions, and they assumed that he had finally followed through with it. None of them expected to hear from him again.

Gina studied the photos of Frank. The most recent was a police ID headshot that was taken shortly before he retired. Even without the influence of his backstory, she surmised that she would still have recognized the anger and sadness in his eyes. She also noted that he was in remarkable physical condition—at least when the photos were taken.

"We compared these photos with the surveillance footage from the Plaza on the River Hotel in London," continued the agent as he displayed a still photograph from the hotel video. He used a laser pointer to highlight portions of the photo. "The size and build of this man here are consistent with the photos and descriptions of Cole. It is our working theory that he's the man who brought Kurry to the Orbis Novus lab last month, and he's also the man who abducted him in London, along with this other gentleman."

Gina added that this was likely the reason Kurry had called her just before his disappearance. She chose her words carefully, emphasizing her professional relationship with the witness. "He was in London to write a story on Orbis Novus," she said. "He checked in with me on a regular basis." This was not new information; she simply felt compelled to mention the reason for her numerous phone calls with Kurry.

"Have you been able to find any record of Cole's travel in recent months?" Daryll asked the blue-suited agent.

"Negative. He's likely using an alias."

"Any record of him living in Alaska or anywhere else?"

"No. He's off the grid."

"Let's focus on Wu Lan's whereabouts over the past few years," said Daryll. "If she was a member of the organization then she must have left a trail somewhere." Although it sounded like a suggestion, it was clearly an order. He then turned to a female agent seated next to him. "Agent Goldsmith, have you located the aircraft yet?"

"We're running down every flight plan filed on November 5th at every airport within an hour's drive of Las Vegas, excluding the big commercial jets." replied Goldsmith. "We've ruled everything out so far. I highly doubt that we'll find a flight plan."

"Wouldn't the jet have been tracked by the FAA—picked up on radar somewhere?" asked another agent.

"Not necessarily," said Goldsmith. "Even if the jet had a transponder, they could have turned it off. And if the plane stayed below five thousand feet it wouldn't show up on air traffic radar."

"Keep on it," said Daryll.

Following the meeting, Gina returned to her office where her officemate Shawn grilled her on the latest developments with Orbis Novus. He was one of the few agents in the Las Vegas field office that was not officially working the case, though he spent most of his time tracking related events on the internet. During her subsequent phone call with Nigel Peters, Gina noticed that Shawn was paying close attention. She didn't mind. She understood his interest in the monumental crisis and even felt a little sorry for him not being involved in the hunt for Orbis Novus. Cases like this were the reason they joined the Bureau.

"It's funny," she said to Shawn later. "A week ago, I was the only agent in the Bureau assigned to this, and even I didn't think much of it."

Nigel did not have much to tell Gina regarding the search for Jack. The FBI had provided their British counterparts with Frank's identity several hours earlier and the lead had generated nothing yet. There was one piece of evidence found near the Plaza on the River: Jack and his two escorts were captured on video entering a car outside of the hotel, and the license tag on the car was clearly visible.

"The car was stolen from a nearby parking garage," explained Nigel over the phone. "We found it parked a few blocks from the hotel. The owner didn't even know it had been stolen."

There was a bit of good news too. The death toll in Great Britain was still rising but the rate of increase was leveling off. Britain's National Health Service had stopped administering opioids except for use in hospices. In London and other major English cities, police were sweeping the streets to intercede with opioid addicts and deliver them to one of the makeshift detox facilities that were recently established. There were even reports of a few conscientious drug dealers refusing to sell heroin. Evidence of the disruption of the opiate supply in faraway countries was starting to appear in London and other western drug markets. It was not just the supply-side being affected; demand was rapidly diminishing as well.

Twelve hours after the morning standup meeting in the FBI's Las Vegas field office, the evening status meeting commenced. Most of the discussion centered upon the comings and goings of Natalie Wu Lan. The blue-suited agents presented some interesting findings.

"Wu Lan made six trips to Las Vegas over the past two years," stated one. "There is no record of her staying in a hotel anywhere near the city. On four of those trips she rented a car from McCarran Airport."

The second blue suit jumped in. "A little while ago, the rental car company provided the following data." He projected some numbers onto the screen. "You can see here that she put less than a hundred miles on the car each trip."

The group discussed the implications of the new findings. It was inconsistent with the information Kurry had provided about his trip to the Orbis Novus facility, and raised several questions. If Wu Lan was driving herself to the facility, then why was her trip less than fifty-miles one way when Kurry claimed to have flown in a jet for two to three hours? Several theories arose: She was meeting up with others and continuing to the facility in a separate vehicle; she was flying from Las Vegas to the facility in a separate aircraft; maybe she wasn't even going to the same facility.

Agent Milford, the veteran behavioral analyst who had participated on the second phone call with Wu Lan, proposed an alternate theory. "Wu Lan didn't expect anyone to ever investigate her travels," she told the group. "She had no reason to be deceptive. Maybe we should re-examine Kurry's plane ride. The men escorting him had the motivation to deceive." Milford rose from her chair and walked over to a large whiteboard. "They went to great lengths to prevent Kurry from seeing anything along the way, even placing a hood over his head for most of the trip." She drew an "X" on the board. "Why not take extra precautions to throw him off the scent?" She started drawing a giant curve extending from the X.

"Are you suggesting that the plane flew around in circles to make it seem like the facility was farther away than it actually was?" asked Daryll.

"It's possible," replied Milford. "Maybe the facility is only an hour or so away. But I think it's even more deceitful than that. I believe they flew in one giant circle and landed in the exact same spot they took off from." She finished drawing her circle, ending it back at the X.

"Think about it Daryll," said another senior agent. "Look how much time we've wasted searching over a thousand-mile radius. We could be playing right into their hands."

"There's more," continued Milford. "We know that Jack didn't land at a municipal airport. There was no car ride between the plane and the facility. They flew directly to the site, which means it could be out in the desert somewhere."

"Hold on a second," said Gina, as she began to scramble through some loose pages that lay on the table in front of her. "Wu Lan said something on her last phone call. Here it is. She said she was close to us. 'Maybe closer than you think'."

"You think she was at the facility when she called?" asked Daryll.

"I do," replied Gina. "There was something in her voice. She was trying not to be overheard. There were some strange background noises before we were cut off."

"Play the recording again," Daryll said to an agent sitting behind a laptop. The agent played the brief conversation over the conference room speakers. "Is it possible that we're hearing Wu Lan being found-out at the end of that call?" pondered Daryll.

"That was the last time we heard from her," said Gina. "Her body was found two days later."

"But in Dallas," added one of the blue suits.

"Well, they wouldn't want her to just disappear," suggested Milford. "That would prompt an investigation."

"So, they take her back to Dallas and staged a suicide," said Daryll. "It buys them a little extra time, even if the suicide story doesn't hold up."

The alleged suicide of Wu Lan wasn't holding up. Another agent subsequently briefed on a report from Dallas of a large bald man seen entering Wu Lan's apartment building on the day of her death. One witness described him as having a "very intimidating" demeanor. Comparisons to the bald man seen in the London hotel video were inconclusive.

"I think we have enough here," summarized Daryll. He issued new directives to nobody in particular. "Let's zero in on Vegas and work our way outward into the desert. Assume the plane flew in a giant circle, and that Orbis Novus is right under our noses."

At 10 p.m., Gina was in her office scouring internet maps when Daryll stepped into the doorway.

"Gina, I'm going home to get some rest. I suggest you do the same."

She knew that Daryll's advice constituted an order. She wasn't contributing much anyway. There were other agents already working the problem who were more experienced with these types of searches. Her primary responsibility was to assist London in finding Jack, and not to search for the Orbis Novus facility. She wondered if the two tasks were not one and the same.

Presuming that she would be unable to sleep, Gina avoided the freeway in favor of a slower route home. Curious to see how the heartbeat of the city was faring, she drove south on Las Vegas Boulevard right through the four-mile Las Vegas Strip. Traffic was extremely light, and she breezed past one resort after another in a fraction of the time it would normally have taken. All of the lights, fountains, and music were on in full-force, entertaining a smattering of tourists traversing the wide sidewalks and pedestrian overpasses. The city's economy depended almost entirely on tourism, and the impact of the superbug was visibly devastating.

She switched her car stereo over to a local news station and learned that 102 deaths in Nevada were now linked to the pandemic. All were in Clark County in the southern part of the state. The superbug had not yet reached vast regions of the United States, including Idaho, Montana, Maine, Vermont, and Northern Alaska, yet Gina knew that it was only a matter of time. Even Hawaii had reported several deaths on Oahu. A week after the first victim was discovered, flustered scientists seemed to know little about the virus or how it was spreading.

Not long after 11 p.m. she sat on her couch and flipped through the television channels in search of something interesting and unrelated to the superbug crisis. She was continuously distracted by the small piece of paper lying on the coffee table in front of her. It contained a phone number that she had copied from some documents at the office. The lure of the paper finally won out, and she turned off the television. She told herself that it was three hours earlier there, as a way of pushing herself off the fence. She knew that the call would border on unprofessionalism, but she had already crossed that line. She needed some kind of connection and figured that he did too.

"Hello?" came the voice on the end of the line.

"Yes, hello. Is this Mr. Kurry?"

"Speaking."

"Mr. Kurry, my name is Gina Alvarez. I'm a special agent with the FBI."

The voice became more animated. "Have you found my son?"

Gina felt compelled to sugarcoat the news. "No sir, we haven't, but we're making progress—good progress."

"Do you need something from me? I want to help, but I don't know what else I can tell you that I haven't already told the other agents. I didn't even know that Jack was in London."

"No, Mr. Kurry. That's not why I'm calling." A brief silence ensued as Gina contemplated how to proceed. She purposely had not rehearsed the conversation beforehand, opting to dive in head-first instead of chickening out. "I was with Jack in London."

"Do you know Jack?"

"I do. I was in charge of the case before… before December 1st."

The name suddenly rang a bell with Don. Jack had mentioned her before. "So, what can I do for you, Ms. Alvarez?"

Gina hesitated again. "I just wanted you to know what Jack was doing in London. I spent quite a bit of time with him there."

"I spoke to his editor earlier today," said Don. "He told me that Jack had taken a leave of absence."

"Yes. He went to London because he thought that nobody was paying attention to Orbis Novus. I think it went beyond just writing a story. He wanted to help in some way."

"Well, everybody's paying attention to them now," remarked Don.

Gina sensed his embittered tone but did not take it personally. They spoke for a few minutes more. Gina was careful not to reveal her relationship with Jack, and Don did not let on that he had mostly figured it out. It was not difficult for him to fathom that Gina was a factor in Jack's decision to go to London. He also recognized that the purpose of her call was to convey that information to him, even if she did not consciously intend to. There was no other apparent reason for their conversation. He tried to relieve her of the burden she might be harboring.

"I'm glad you called, Ms. Alvarez," he said at the end of the call. "It's good to know that Jack went to London with the best intentions. He's a grown man and I trust his decisions."

"We're gonna find him, Mr. Kurry."

24

Jack Kurry couldn't remember much of what happened immediately after he left the hotel on December 4th with Frank and the large bald man. He recalled entering the back seat of a sedan parked just outside the hotel entrance and sitting in between his two captors. They drove for only a few blocks before the car pulled into an alley where Jack was ordered to exit and climb into the middle row of an SUV parked in front of the sedan. Frank followed him in while the bald man entered from the other side, thus sandwiching him between the two imposing figures once again. The driver of the sedan remained in the car.

Jack could not see the face of the man driving the SUV, but the woman in the front passenger seat turned around and greeted him. She had dark brown skin and short black hair that was covered by a colorful headscarf. He guessed that she could not be older than forty.

"Hello, Jack," she said with a thick accent that sounded to Jack to be African. Then she looked at Frank. "Hold him."

Jack expected Frank to slip a hood over his head. Instead, Frank and the bald man held his arms firmly as the African woman pulled a hypodermic syringe from a small leather case.

"Time to sleep now," she said, then forcibly stuck the needle into Jack's thigh. As she pushed the liquid into his body, she smiled and added, "Don't worry. It isn't an opioid." The last thing Jack could remember thinking was how perfectly straight and bright white the woman's teeth were.

He recalled waking to a semiconscious state and having no idea how much time had elapsed since being injected. Although groggy, he knew instantly that he was on a small, fast-moving powerboat. The vertical bobbing caused by the bow thrusting into the waves and the loud drone of the engine left no doubt. He could see the shape of the bow in the small cabin in which he lay. The firm bed with a foam mattress matched the shape of the boat and encompassed the entire forward section of the cabin. He turned his head to find the African woman sitting a few feet away in a chair near the door. He tried to from a few words but his mouth would not obey his brain. The woman displayed her perfect smile and injected him again.

His next memories seemed more like a collection of still photographs than a continuous recollection of live events. The first was being lifted off the bed by Frank and the other man. The next was being carried over the larger man's shoulder like a soldier might carry a wounded comrade off the battlefield. As his head dangled downward, he could see the man's black leather boots walking on a wooden pier. Next was the vision of a small white jet with a blue stripe on the vertical tail. The final memory was that of being strapped into a cushy leather seat, before everything went dark once again.

When he reached a full state of awareness some unknown number of minutes or hours later, the woman's face was once again the first thing he saw. She was seated in a chair across from him, entranced with a book she was reading. It took him a few moments to sort through and organize the few memories he had collected over the past several hours. When the mental puzzle pieces were finally in place, he deduced that he was flying on the jet with the blue stripe. There were a few other seats in his field of vision. All were empty except for the one facing him.

The woman had not yet noticed that he was awake. She was dressed in white slacks, a red blouse, and trendy shoes. Gold earrings protruded from behind her headscarf. Her appearance was disarming to Jack, if not quite attractive. He was unfamiliar with the book she was reading. The title on the cover read, *A Piece of Cake*. While turning a page, her eyes lifted and realized that she was being watched.

"Ah, there you are," she said. Her accent was heavy yet not difficult to understand. "I'll fetch you some water."

Jack soon discovered that his wrists were strapped to the armrests. While the woman was gone, he twisted and craned his neck to obtain a better view of the small cabin. There seemed to be someone sleeping in a chair behind him—maybe two people. The woman returned to find him squirming around.

"Jack, I am not going to have to sedate you again, am I?" she said with a hearty laugh. He stopped fidgeting and remained quiet. She lifted a paper cup to his lips and gave him a few sips of water before returning to her seat across from him. "Now, let's have a conversation."

"Who are you?" asked Jack. He felt scared yet surprisingly tranquil under the circumstances. Perhaps it was merely a residual effect of the sedative, though he also recalled Frank's words back in the hotel room. Somebody must have wanted him alive, at least for the time being.

"You can call me Adimu," replied the woman after a brief pause. The way she said it made him think that it wasn't her real name.

"Where are we going?"

"Perhaps I should make myself clearer," said Adimu. "It is I who will ask the questions." She crossed one leg over the other and leaned forward. "What did she tell you?"

"Who?"

Adimu smiled again. "Jack, I am trying to make this easy for you, but you cannot play games with me. The woman who called you—what did she tell you?"

"You mean Natalie Wu Lan."

For a fleeting moment, Adimu's face revealed surprise in hearing the name. Jack instantly regretted saying it, having allowed obstinance to cloud his judgement. Orbis Novus was apparently unaware that he knew the identity of the informant.

Adimu quickly disguised her reaction. "I do not know who that is," she said. "I am referring to the woman who called you on the Sunday before last."

Jack inferred that Adimu only knew of the second call from Wu Lan. He also reckoned that he had little to gain from lying. His captors seemed to hold all the cards. "She said something about London, then the call terminated."

"And that is why you were in London?"

"I was working on a story about… your organization—for my newspaper."

"And I suppose your girlfriend, Agent Alvarez—she was working on your story too?"

Jack looked at Adimu solemnly and said nothing. He recalled the threat Frank had made regarding Gina.

"We asked you nicely not to speak with the authorities," continued Adimu. "We *warned* you."

Jack was growing more nervous and anxious. Adimu's persistent charm and composure was beginning to make her seem terrifying. He couldn't think of a reply.

"Why did the FBI go to London, Jack?"

He began to stammer. "They approached me in Las Vegas… I had to tell them something."

"And that is when you decided to sleep with Agent Alvarez?"

"That has nothing to do with… I don't understand. Everything you wanted to happen is happening. I didn't mess anything up."

Adimu laughed. It was no different than her earlier laugh, yet it now seemed less charming and more sinister. "How could you possibly know what we wish to happen? What else did the woman say to you?"

"She said something about killing. I didn't understand what she meant. I guess I do now. Everybody does now."

"What else?"

"That's all. London—and killing. I swear that's all."

Adimu uncrossed her legs and leaned in closer. She clasped her hands gently around Jack's left hand. "I like you Jack, but I cannot help you unless you are completely honest with me. There are people here that want to kill you, and I want to protect you from them."

Jack tried to calm himself and repress his tears. "I don't understand. The superbug is already out there. You've accomplished your goal. Aren't you finished?"

Adimu chose her words carefully. "Our solution requires more time in order to achieve the results we desire. We cannot be discovered before then." She wiped a tear from Jack's cheek with her thumb and returned her hand to his. "Perhaps when we are finished," she continued, "I would be willing to die. Now tell me, Jack, does the FBI know where our facility is?"

"I don't know. I don't think so. They wouldn't tell me if they did."

"Your girlfriend did not tell you?"

"She wouldn't say, but she implied that they didn't know where it is." He hoped that the woman could see that he wasn't lying.

Adimu looked into his eyes for a moment, as if deciding whether to believe him. She released his hand and leaned back into her chair. "You said something to Frank about his daughter. What were you talking about?"

"Nothing. I was just guessing."

"You see, Jack? This is what I am talking about. If you are not honest with me, then I cannot protect you." She gave him a few more sips of water. "Who told you about Frank's daughter?"

"Natalie."

"And you told the FBI? You told your girlfriend, yes?"

"No," lied Jack. "I was about to. They took me before I could call her." He could see the skepticism in her face and he wondered how much Frank and the other man had heard before they grabbed his phone in the hotel room. Adimu sighed, cocked her head back against the seat and studied Jack.

"What happens to me now?" asked Jack.

"We have to keep you with us for a while. You know too much, Jack—too many people. You cannot be trusted."

"Then what?"

"When we are satisfied that our solution cannot be reversed, we will release you."

At that moment, the large bald man emerged from behind and stood near them in the aisle. He looked to Adimu, as if awaiting instructions.

"I believe you have met Cedric," Adimu said to Jack. She nodded to Cedric. He produced a black hood from inside his jacket and placed it over Jack's head.

"I am sorry Jack," said Adimu, "but I am sure you would prefer this over the sedative. We will be landing shortly."

It sounded to Jack that both she and Cedric walked away, leaving him alone. He sat quietly and tried to eavesdrop on any conversations that might be underway nearby. He heard nothing except the monotonic hum of the engines. After a while he could feel the plane starting to descend. The engines began to vary in speed and he heard the sounds of flaps and landing gear extending.

The plane landed, taxied for a minute or two, then came to a halt. The engines spun down. He could hear Adimu, Frank, and a man with a French accent speaking softly to each other. Soon a couple of other voices joined in, and he heard the hatch door opening. Various voices and footsteps traversed the cabin for a half hour, then the door was closed. The engines powered up, then the plane taxied and took off. He felt a hand on top of his head.

"That was only a refueling stop," said Adimu. "Do you need to use the lavatory?"

Hours passed before the plane began to descend once more. Adimu and the man with the French accent were speaking nearby. Jack couldn't make out the words, but he sensed that they were debating something. Suddenly, the hood was whisked off of his head, revealing Adimu and Cedric standing before him. Cedric held the hood and Adimu held a syringe.

"We are almost home," said Adimu in a motherly tone. "I am afraid the hood will not be enough this time."

Jack looked at Cedric with a forlorn expression of fear. Cedric returned an emotionless stare.

Adimu glanced at them both and said, "Cedric is a man of action and very few words, Jack. He does what he is told." She held up the syringe. "This was *my* decision." She pressed the needle into his upper arm and emptied its contents inside him.

For the third time in an undetermined period of hours or days, Jack awoke in a muddled haze. He lay on a cot in a small room, less than ten feet by ten feet square. There were no windows on any of the cinderblock walls, which looked to have been painted with several coats over many years. Stringy remains of old cobwebs dangled from a vent on the ceiling and danced in reaction to the incoming flow of air. Next to the vent was a single incandescent lightbulb emitting no more than forty watts of illumination. A short chain hung down from the light socket, and a longer string was tied to the end of the chain.

Jack sat up and rested his head in his hands. The memories slowly returned to him, with the most recent being the sight of Adimu holding the syringe. He waited for a few minutes to regain full cognizance before taking stock of his surroundings. It didn't take long. An old sink was attached to the wall opposite the cot. The inside of the basin was covered with the colors of permanent grime and various paints. The cement floor appeared to have been swept, though streaks of dirt remained. He guessed that he was in a recently-cleared janitorial closet.

A small metal trash can stood under the sink. Next to it was a larger copper pot. Both were empty. The door was hollow but metal. He tried to turn the nickel-plated doorknob. As he presumed, it was locked from the outside. He banged on the door for a few seconds to let his captors know that he was awake.

"Hey! Who's there?" There was no sound of any response outside the door, so he turned and looked back at the cot. A small mattress sat on top of springs that stretched across the portable bed frame. It was covered in fresh sheets and an army blanket. *It looks like I'm gonna be here for a while*, Jack thought. He began to feel a little queasy, so he returned to the bed and lay down on his back. As he stared into the dim light, the same two questions looped repeatedly in his mind. *Why did they need to capture me* and *why am I still alive?*

An hour—maybe two—passed before he heard the sound of a key entering the outside doorknob.

"Lay down on the cot," said Frank's voice. Jack was already there. The door cracked open for a moment before swinging to the wall. Frank stepped inside carrying a tray of food which he placed on top of the sink.

"Are you gonna tell me anything?" asked Jack.

"Yeah. Here's a cup for water. You can piss in the sink or the pot. Makes no difference to me. Use the pot for everything else. If I find a mess on the floor, I won't be happy."

"You know what I mean," said Jack boldly. He was beginning to feel as if he had nothing to lose.

"Adimu already told you everything you need to know. Have you told us everything *we* need to know?"

"Yes."

"Then just sit tight and keep quiet," advised Frank as he headed for the door.

"I know why you're doing this," blurted Jack. Frank turned toward him and said nothing. "I'm sorry about your daughter," continued Jack. He had seen enough movies to know that it was important to establish a personal connection with his captor. "My mother died last year, and—"

"Shut up," said Frank. He pointed his index finger at Jack. "Don't you ever mention my daughter again." He promptly walked out and shut the door.

Jack had no way of accurately measuring the passage of time. Frank was the only person with whom he had any contact. Each time he visited, he brought a tray of food. On every other visit, he also donned rubber gloves and replaced the copper pot with an empty one just like it. Jack guessed that the pot was being emptied once per day. On the third day, he ventured to engage Frank in a dialogue.

"Do you guys have any books or anything I could read to pass the time?"

Frank looked at him curiously for a moment. "I'll look around."

"So, I'm gonna be here for a while then?"

"Do you want a book or not?"

"Yes."

"Then shut up."

"Are you still a cop?" Frank said nothing as he retrieved the pot. Jack pushed him further. "Do you think what they're doing is right?" He purposely used the word "they" to distinguish Frank from his fellow members of Orbis Novus.

Frank set the pot down. "Did your mother die of a heroin overdose?"

"No, she died of cancer."

"Then you wouldn't understand."

"I understand that a lot of innocent people are dying."

Again, Frank said nothing.

"How many are you willing to sacrifice?" pressed Jack.

"I'd have no problem sacrificing *you*," said Frank, "so you should keep your mouth shut." Jack adhered to Frank's advice, having already pushed his luck further than he had thought possible.

A short while later, Frank opened the door and tossed a paperback book onto the cot. "Here. You can thank Cedric."

"Thanks," mumbled Jack.

Frank eyed Jack through the opening of the door for a moment then entered the room, closing it behind him. He leaned back against the door and folded his arms.

"I told you I was from Cleveland," he said. "That's true, but I didn't grow up there. I spent most of my childhood in San Bernardino, California. My father was with the Del Rosa Hotshots. Do you know what hotshots do?"

Jack nodded slightly. "They fight wildfires."

"Yeah, it's a dangerous job," continued Frank. "Sometimes my father would be gone for weeks at a time. We'd never be sure if he was gonna make it home, but we were lucky—he always did."

"That's good," Jack said awkwardly. He really didn't know what to say.

Frank ignored the response and continued. "One of their principal tactics is to establish a control line to keep the fire from spreading. It's a barrier that the fire can't cross over. Sometimes they get lucky, and they can use a natural barrier, like a river, or a rocky terrain. Most of the time they have to create their own control line. They have to burnout the trees and brush to consume the fuel in the barrier before the wildfire can get to it."

"Fight fire with fire?"

"Yeah. That could mean burning several acres of healthy trees in order to save tens of thousands more—not to mention cities and towns." The analogy was obvious, and Frank left the room before Jack could respond.

Jack picked up the thick, worn paperback. The front cover was missing. The title page read, "Les Misérables par Victor Hugo." It was in French. Jack grunted an expletive and flung the book into the opposite wall. He stared at it lying on the floor for a few minutes then decided that it was better than nothing. He was familiar with the plot, having once played in a high school production of the musical based on the novel, and had twice seen a Broadway revival of the show while living in New York. He proceeded to decipher the French as best he could and soon found that the mental exercise passed the time rather adequately, especially when compared to the alternative of staring at the ceiling.

The next day, he was ardently deciphering the story and temporarily distracted from his precarious status when he heard the key unlocking the door. Frank had delivered a tray of food just a short while ago—this was something else. Frank entered and immediately placed the familiar hood over Jack's head.

"Let's go."

A thousand thoughts traversed through Jack's vivid imagination, ranging from being released unharmed to being executed. Frank led him out the door and along the floor of what he envisioned to be a corridor. He soon felt carpeting beneath his feet as they turned into a room. The sound of hushed voices cropped up from all directions, and he sensed that there were several people in there with him. Frank guided him into a chair. It felt like a conference room chair in that it swiveled and rested upon wheels. He could feel the thick edge of a well-polished table in front of him. He waited for the hood to be lifted but it remained in place.

"Mr. Kurry, I did not think our paths would cross again." The voice was familiar. It was the same elderly, German-sounding woman who greeted him on his first visit. Her tone was cool and deliberate. "It is important that you tell us everything you know."

Jack was tempted to tell them that he had already done so, then reconsidered and remained silent.

"She told you something specific about the virus," continued the older woman.

"Who?" asked Jack.

"You are skating on very thin ice, Mr. Kurry," said the woman. "We have no time for your games."

Adimu's voice chimed in just a few inches from his year. "These people will hurt you, Jack," she said softly. "Please tell her what Doctor Wu Lan told you about the virus."

Jack was overcome by an ominous revelation. His captors were now acknowledging the identity of the informant in his presence. He sensed that his chances of being released alive were fading quickly.

"I don't know anything about a virus," he said nervously. "She didn't say anything like that."

"Jack, I cannot protect you if you lie to them," said Adimu. She was practically whispering in his hear.

"Did she instruct you to look for a virus in the bloodstream?" asked a Latino man. Jack recognized his voice from his first meeting with the league.

"I'm telling you," implored Jack. "She didn't mention anything about a virus."

A few more people peppered him with scientific-sounding questions while ignoring his denials in between. Some of the voices were familiar and others were new. One voice was notably absent—that of the younger Asian woman. Eventually, the older matriarch quelled the discussion.

"They could not have discovered it this soon unless they were told where to look," she said. "I do not believe you, Mr. Kurry, and we have given you every opportunity to cooperate. Now listen carefully."

Jack had no idea who "they" were and what it was they had discovered.

"Did Doctor Wu Lan talk to the FBI?" asked the Latino man.

"No—only me." Jack sensed the tension level in their voices rising.

The man pressed further in a condescending tone. "She didn't talk to Gina Alvarez?"

"No. Wu Lan called me and I told the FBI everything she told me. But she said nothing about a virus."

"Please, Jack," whispered Adimu. She put her arm around his shoulders. "They will hurt you."

"Did the FBI introduce you to any scientists or doctors?" asked the voice of an American woman.

"No, why would they—"

"I have heard enough," interrupted the older matriarch. "Frank, take him."

Two hands grabbed each of Jack's arms just below his armpits and yanked him forcefully from his chair. The men walked him hastily into another room, where they stood silently until Jack heard a few more people enter, followed by the sound of the door closing. Frank then removed the hood.

Jack stood in what resembled a medical examination room, illuminated by tubular fluorescent lights that projected a cold white hue onto everything within. In the middle of the room was a black padded table, just like the ones he had sat on many times before when visiting a doctor, only without the roll of disposable white paper covering it. In the room with him were Frank, Cedric, Adimu, and two other middle-aged men. One appeared to be Latino and the other Caucasian.

"Put him on the table," said the Latino man. Jack recognized his voice as one of the conference room interrogators.

Cedric led Jack to the table. "Lie down," he demanded in his French accent.

"What's going on?" asked Jack as Cedric pressed him into a prone position, then affixed straps to his arms and legs.

Adimu hurried over to stand behind Jack's head and placed her hands upon his cheeks. "Just tell them what they need to know." She appeared to be on the verge of tears. Cedric removed Jack's shoes and socks.

"Hey… Hey! Just slow down guys," pleaded Jack. "I've already told you everything I know. What are you doing?"

"I'll ask you only once," said the Latino man. "What did Doctor Wu Lan tell you specifically about the virus?"

Jack could see that Cedric now held a large pair of pliers. "Okay, okay," said Jack, trying to speak as calmly as he could. "Just hold on a second." He tried to fabricate something that he could tell them but drew a blank. "I swear to you that she didn't say anything about a virus."

The Latino man nodded to Cedric.

"Oh, Jack," said Adimu softly. She held his head firmly in her hands. Cedric gripped the toenail on Jack's left baby toe and yanked it off in a single tug.

Jack shrieked in pain as his body convulsed and wriggled in a reflex response. The straps held firm. The fourth man in the room walked over to the foot of the table and began to wipe away the blood with a white towel.

"That's just the baby toe," he said in a gruff American accent. "The big toe's the worst, but we've got a few more to go before we get there."

Adimu bent her head down so that her nose gently brushed against Jack's. "Just tell them what you know, and I can stop them." Then she wiped his tears of pain with a soft cloth.

"But I don't *know* anything else," whispered Jack desperately.

The Latino man nodded again, and Cedric extracted the next toenail. Jack screamed in agony. When Cedric removed the third toenail, Jack passed out. When he came to, the American was injecting a clear liquid into his forearm.

"A little epinephrine should keep you from going to sleep on us," said the man. "We still have seven more toes to go."

"Okay, look, let me think for a second," said Jack in desperation.

"You have had enough time to think," replied the Latino man. Cedric grasped the fourth toenail.

"Wait," said Adimu. "Let him speak." She stroked Jack's head. "Go on, Jack."

Jack told them every last detail he could recall. He admitted that Gina and two other FBI agents had listened in on Wu Lan's second call.

He described the final conversation with Wu Lan, and how he had conferenced-in Gina. He talked about his second meeting at the FBI office, and he insisted that Wu Lan said nothing about a virus.

When Jack was finished with the disclosures, the Latino man walked over to him and said, "We don't like being lied to, Jack." Cedric began to pull on the fourth toenail, but the Latino man held up his hand and stopped him. "Not that one." He pointed to the big toe. "That one."

Cedric struggled to separate the toenail from the toe. By the time he succeeded, the levels of pain and bloodshed resulting from the extraction of the big toe had far surpassed that of the previous three combined. Blood now covered the table and surrounding floor. Dissatisfied with the results, the men extracted three more nails, including the one covering his other big toe. Jack eventually reached the point where his screams were silent and his tear ducts were empty. Cedric positioned himself to extract another.

"Stop it!" Adimu said to her cohorts in a stern voice. "Leave us."

The four men filed out of the room. Adimu walked over to Jack's feet and applied fresh towels against them. They quickly turned red with blood. The initial shock had worn off, leaving Jack with a pulsating pain. He drew heavy breaths in response.

"Look at me," said Adimu. "Calm down." Jack did his best to focus on the attractive African woman. "Are you telling me the truth?" she asked.

"I swear on the life of my family," said Jack.

"Do not say that unless you mean it. Life and death mean nothing to these people. They will kill your family in a heartbeat."

"I mean it."

Adimu studied him for a moment then walked out of the room. A few minutes later, Frank entered with a younger woman wearing a white lab coat. She had shoulder-length blonde hair and wore trendy eyeglasses with blue plastic frames. The woman went over to a cabinet and withdrew a bottle of hydrogen peroxide.

"I'm sorry, but this will sting," she said in a Russian accent. After applying the hydrogen peroxide to each exposed toe, she spent several minutes carefully bandaging them as Frank looked on. Not another word was spoken, though Frank and the woman exchanged glances from time to time. When the woman was finished, Frank pushed a wheelchair over to the table and removed the straps from Jack's arms and legs. He helped Jack into the chair and placed the hood over his head.

They returned to the storage room, where Frank assisted Jack out of the wheelchair and onto the cot. As Frank was leaving Jack asked, "What happens now?"

"To you?" asked Frank.

"Yeah."

"Good question. I really don't know." He opened the door to let himself out then turned back toward his prisoner. "Nobody here is your friend, Jack."

25

Muriel Smithson gathered with several of her students and faculty peers in the cafeteria of her building at UCSD to watch the latest press conference on a wall-mounted television. Every day for the previous week, the airwaves had been saturated with breaking news and special reports, yet this one was different. For seven days there had been nothing but questions. Now, on December 8th at 5 p.m. Pacific Time, there was an answer—a breakthrough of sorts. It was more of an explanation than a solution. Still, it felt as if the world had turned a corner.

The assemblage of scientists, doctors, and bureaucrats in Atlanta (plus a few opportunistic politicians in search of a photo-op) spoke in layman's terms. Muriel recognized that their simplistic explanation precisely matched the deliberation in which she and Sydney Carter engaged a few nights earlier. Clearly Sydney had identified the missing puzzle pieces and placed them into their proper positions.

But where was he? The Sydney she met briefly a few years back appeared to embrace the role of public speaker. His reputation on the lecture circuit was that of an engaged and enthusiastic evangelist who loved to share his discoveries and theories with others—and he was quite good at it, too. Surely, he would be the CDC's first choice for a spokesperson on television. Instead, a Dr. Tompkins delivered the news and fielded most of the questions from the press. She appeared capable and confident, yet there was no way she could have known what she knew without Sydney's input.

Muriel soon discovered why Tompkins was chosen to speak in the wake of Sydney's presumed unavailability. The forty-something woman exuded confidence and intelligence, despite a smaller-than-average physical stature. Her caramel-dyed hair was cropped into tight curls, and modern eyeglasses covered her eyes. She even wore a white lab coat for effect, as if she had rushed directly from the lab to the press conference. Muriel guessed that she probably had.

Dr. Tompkins spoke of a new kind of virus—one newly discovered, that is. A similarly-behaving virus was known to exist in a few primitive species. She said that before today, it was never considered a possibility that such an organism could exist in mammals, let alone humans. An assistant placed a large poster board on an easel behind Tompkins. On it were two odd-looking drawings resembling alien creatures. Tompkins identified one as a virus from the family that causes common colds. She pointed out that it was very different from other viruses in the family in that it immediately replicates into the bloodstream and mutates into the virus depicted in the second drawing. She referred to the pair of pathogens as "twin viruses." You could not have one without the other. Only the first virus could exist outside of the human body and it quickly spread around the world like a relentless common cold. The second virus formed inside the human body, the result of a mutation of the first virus upon migrating into the bloodstream.

Tompkins told the press and television audience that the viruses were essentially harmless and would likely remain dormant in the human body for decades. Then she dropped the hammer. Everybody knew it was coming, yet they still wanted to hear it. They needed somebody with a PhD to drive the point home. Tompkins announced that the introduction of opioids into the bloodstream triggered the bloodborne virus into a mode of accelerated reproduction. That, in turn, prompted the body's immune system to kick into high gear. The lethal complication associated with this reaction had to do with the immune system being "confused" by the RNA signatures of the twin viruses, as Tompkins described it. The immune system somehow ends up attacking the first virus, in the lungs and other organs, with the wrong antigens. She had difficulty translating this portion of her narrative into words that the average person could comprehend. In short, she said that the immune system was overreacting, resulting in certain death within a matter of hours. The official cause of death was sepsis resulting from widespread and severe inflammation.

When the floor was opened to questions, every hand shot into the air, and reporters shouted over each other until a single voice won out. When one reporter's question was answered, the process repeated. The press conference went something like this:

"How soon will we have a cure?" There was no known cure, or even a path to a cure at this time. They had never seen anything like this.

"What about a vaccine?" This is a new kind of virus. Even if a vaccine were possible, it could take years to develop.

"How can opioids cause this to happen?" It's a very complicated answer, having to do with the chemical structure of opioids. The easy way to think of it is that the opioids are a fuel or "superfood" for the bloodborne virus.

"Is it just opioids, or could other substances trigger the virus?" It's possible, but they have no evidence. Much more research is required.

"Is it all opioids, or just heroin?" It's all opioids—synthetic or natural.

"Can the spread of the virus be halted or contained?" Unlikely. The rhinovirus was very robust and highly-contagious. It was then that Tompkins dropped another bombshell, speculating that most of the people in the room were probably already carrying the twin viruses.

"Is there a test for the viruses?" No, but they hoped to develop one soon.

The press conference continued for more than an hour. As they are prone to do, the reporters repeated questions that had already been asked—especially the ones that couldn't be answered. Finally, someone inquired about the origins of the twin viruses.

"Do you think that this was a natural occurrence, or is an organization such as the League of Orbis Novus responsible?"

Tompkins glanced at a well-dressed man standing over her shoulder, then hesitated, as if carefully contemplating her response. "It is our opinion that this could not have occurred naturally. There must have been some form of unnatural stimulus, and/or other methods of human intervention."

At this point, the well-dressed man stepped up to the podium and introduced himself as the Deputy Attorney General. His discourse was much less revealing than Tompkins', producing far more questions than answers. He acknowledged the existence of Orbis Novus and their status as the primary suspect, or suspects, responsible for the pandemic. He was reticent to provide further details, pending the ongoing investigation. He evaded most of the reporters' questions and repeatedly emphasized the need for everyone to avoid using opioids of any kind. Of course, this prompted a new line of questioning for Tompkins and the other scientists on the stage.

"Can we survive without opioids?" asked a reporter.

"We did for nearly a million years, give or take," replied Tompkins in a slightly acerbic tone. Questions about alternative painkillers were vaguely addressed. Some alternatives already existed; others would need to be developed. "Hopefully, less addictive ones," said Tompkins.

"Do you have any idea why they did this?" asked a young reporter.

The Deputy Attorney General stepped in again. "We don't want to speculate about motives at this time."

A man watching the broadcast in the UCSD cafeteria with Muriel broke the silence there. "Isn't it obvious?"

"Yeah, they did the world a favor," exclaimed a student.

"You think it's good that so many people have died?" shouted another.

"No, it isn't," said yet another student. "But since it's already happened, why would we want a vaccine now?"

"Opioids play an important role in healthcare," responded a professor.

"You mean 'played'," someone wisecracked.

And thus, the world shifted from panic to polemic, and the vehement debate commenced. It had been idling for a few days, lying in wait for a scientific confirmation of the opioid link. Across the planet in schools, pubs, homes, busses, stores, and anywhere else two or more people gathered, the question was raised, pondered, mulled over, and argued. Some waivered while others stood steadfast in their opinions.

Whether or not the world was a better place without the highly-addictive opioids was not the lightning rod—most people conceded that it was. The issue that sharply divided the world was the ageless question of whether the ends justified the means.

The future of the League or Orbis Novus, if its members could ever be found, was hotly debated as well. Strangely, world opinions of their fate were divided along different lines than those opinions regarding their actions. There were people who liked what the league did, who also felt that they should be put to death for doing it. Many conversations started with a phrase akin to "It's good that we no longer have the opioid problem *but* I do not condone how it was carried out." This disclaimer somehow relieved the speaker of feeling any guilt for approving of the result, implying that such an act of genocide was far beneath him.

"There was surely a better way to handle the problem," suggested others, without offering any details of their alleged superior solution. Nobody could point to any successful approaches to fixing the world's addiction to opioids that were in effect prior to December 1st.

"They saved more lives than they took," verbalized a few bold individuals, though millions more were thinking it. The notion was credible, yet difficult to prove empirically and even harder to stomach. It usually prompted a response along the lines of "Try telling that to the people who lost loved ones."

Within a week, a politically-correct position dominated all others. It stated that the opioid epidemic should have been dealt with in a better way and that Orbis Novus was nothing but a band of savage murderers. Suddenly, hundreds of these "better ways" to handle the problem appeared out of the ether. Blowhards took to the airwaves and blogs claiming that their approach would have solved the opioid crises without sacrificing lives. Of course, there was no way to prove them wrong. One could only wonder why they had not proposed their solutions earlier.

As with many polarizing issues, the average citizen landed on an unstable middle ground. They could appreciate the benefits of the league's harsh response to the crisis and also sympathize with the victims and their families. An editorial that ran in the December 12th edition of *The Washington Post* began with the following controversial line:

"In medieval times, nobody wanted to be the executioner, but everyone was glad that they had one."

Although the world had some answers, the pandemic was far from over. The death toll continued to climb, albeit at a slower rate. The virus quickly propagated into the far reaches of the planet, sparing nobody who injected or ingested opioids. By the end of December 10th, more than a hundred thousand deaths were directly attributed to what was now called the Gemini Viruses. In retrospect, one might note this day as the start of the healing process, though it was not very evident at the time.

The test for the Gemini Viruses (specifically, the rhinovirus) would be perfected several days after the Atlanta press conference. Soon after, the WHO guesstimated that more than forty percent of the world's population was already infected. This announcement had the curious effect of reducing panic rather than fueling it. People came to grips with the new world order and surgical masks in public gradually disappeared. Workers returned to the workplace, students returned to schools, and family vacations were rescheduled. Most people opted out of having their mucus tested for the virus. What was the point?

Medical professionals stepped up efforts to fill the void left by the disbandment of opioids. For acute pain, many returned to options that existed long before opioids displaced them as the go-to drug, beginning with acetaminophen and ibuprofen, or a combination of the two. Research into viable alternatives for chronic pain was underway long before Orbis Novus changed the world forever. Variants of medical marijuana were already emerging as effective alternatives when combined with other treatments. Pharmaceutical companies saw an opportunity to patent new medications. The extent to which they considered side effects and addictiveness was moot.

The illicit drug market was forced to adapt in a fashion that was oddly-similar to its legal counterpart. Unwilling to literally kill the demand for their business, cartels quickly abandoned their remaining supplies of heroin and prescription opioids in favor of pushing alternatives to fill the void. Crack cocaine and crystal meth were chief among the proxies, and the syndicates scrambled to saturate black markets in America and Europe with supplies of them. Prices on the black markets were heavily discounted in response to a dwindling demand and also to dissuade users from seeking treatment.

Unfortunately, the latter strategy proved to be remarkably effective as countless addicts could not overcome their disease and switched to another drug of choice. Nevertheless, the overcrowded rehab centers and emergency rooms indicated that many addicts had opted for an escape from the destructive illness. Some viewed it as a sign from God, and fundamentalist sects within all of the world's religions readily agreed. Several hardcore evangelists predicted the onset of the Apocalypse as documented in the Book of Revelation—and a of few them actually believed what they were preaching.

Muriel left the spontaneous and spirited debate in the cafeteria and returned to the quietude of her office, shutting the door behind her. She called Sydney's cellphone and it went directly to his voicemail. She decided against leaving a message, having concluded that Sydney was too busy in the lab to respond. Instead, she picked up her desk phone and dialed an extension that was scribbled on a yellow Post-it note stuck to her desk. As the phone rang, she briefly considered hanging up before changing her mind. After all, it was Mindy who had volunteered the information to her two days earlier.

"Hi Mindy, it's Muriel Smithson. I assume you've seen the news?"

"Yes. It's crazy, but not altogether surprising."

They spoke briefly about the developments before Muriel raised the true subject of her call. She said nothing about her role in identifying the pathogen.

"I couldn't help but notice that there was no mention of your brother at the news conference. Have you heard anything?"

"They're not telling us much," replied Mindy. "I guess they think it's better to keep things under wraps."

"I haven't said anything to anyone. I'm just very worried about him, and I wanted to know if there was anything I could do for you."

"No, thanks. I appreciate your concern, though."

"Maybe now that the truth is out, they'll have no reason to keep him."

"We hope so," said Mindy.

Muriel returned home that evening to find her husband and cat waiting there. The former had already prepared dinner for her, while the latter was impatiently demanding his own. True to her word, Muriel had not mentioned anything to her husband about Jack's disappearance. Conversely, he knew everything about his wife's conversation with

Sydney and the likelihood that it led to the recent discoveries. He also knew when something was bothering his bride of thirty-six years.

"Do you want to talk about it?" he asked as they sat quietly at the kitchen table.

"It's probably nothing... It's just that something seems a little peculiar with Sydney Carter. I think he started to tell me what it was, then stopped."

"Call him."

"I tried this afternoon but he didn't answer."

"Call him again."

"I will. Tomorrow."

26

On the same day as the Atlanta press conference, the FBI team in Las Vegas experienced a breakthrough of their own. Gina Alvarez arrived at the office at 7 a.m. to find it buzzing with liveliness and excitation. She encountered Daryll Jameson in the hallway en route to her desk. Contrary to the others, he maintained his no-nonsense expression.

"We think we've found their facility," he told her, before she could even ask about the commotion. "Be in the conference room in ten minutes."

Gina froze in her tracks, staring blankly as her boss walked past her. She had thought it might take a few more days for the team of investigators to locate the organization's hideout. After weeks of little progress, everything was now happening so quickly. Over the past few days, she had developed a strong inclination that Jack would be found at the Orbis Novus facility suspected to be in the western U.S. Now she was on the verge of finding out if her hunch was true. A flood of emotion and excitement poured over her, forcing her to gather her composure before continuing to her office. Once there, she encountered her equally-thrilled officemate, Shawn.

"They got it," he said exuberantly.

"We'll see," replied Gina calmly.

She joined a large group of agents convening in the conference room a few minutes later. It comprised the tactical operations team that would assail the suspected facility, plus other support and leadership personnel. Some were based in Las Vegas; others had helicoptered in from Los Angeles during the very early morning hours. Because she had been assigned to the case from day one, Daryll wanted Gina on site with the assault team in support of the effort.

Daryll opened the meeting, summarizing how his team of special agents had zeroed in on the facility using a process of elimination. There were only a few civilian and private airstrips within the search radius, including one adjacent to the alleged site. The suspected facility was nestled in a pocket north of Las Vegas surrounded by Nellis Air Force Base, Creech Air Force Base, and the infamous, highly-secure Area 51.

The building was an abandoned research facility built in the 1940s in support of nuclear weapons testing. The concrete airstrip had deteriorated over the decades, though satellite imagery indicated that it could still accommodate small aircraft.

The property had been under private ownership since 1967 and had changed hands several times over the years. The current owner had been tracked down in New Mexico, and was currently being held for questioning. He claimed not to have visited the property in more than four years.

"It's really an ideal location for them," concluded Daryll. "Just far enough from Area 51 and the other bases to avoid their attention, and just close enough to deflect any scrutiny from civilian authorities. Essentially, our own air force was unwittingly providing cover for them."

A rugged FBI agent from SWAT took over the briefing following Daryll's remarks. The SWAT members present in the room resembled Army Rangers more than special agents. They wore desert-colored fatigues, vests, and ammunition belts. Matching helmets were stacked neatly in a corner of the room. Gina did not see their assault rifles but suspected they were close by.

The SWAT leader stepped forward and projected several high-resolution satellite images onto the screen. They depicted a building next to a small airstrip, completely surrounded by the desert landscape. He next displayed photos taken less than an hour earlier by a reconnaissance team hidden on a nearby hill. Their photos showed three vehicles parked outside.

"You can see that we won't have the element of surprise," said the leader, pointing to a long access road that was fully-exposed in the desert sun. "But we don't expect heavy resistance—probably only small arms." He pointed to the vehicles. "These two cars haven't moved since we located the site, but we observed this van arriving two hours ago. We saw a single occupant carrying a box into the facility. The vehicle is there as we speak." He displayed a very recent photograph depicting a man carrying a small box. It was taken with a zoom lens from several hundred yards away.

The leader spoke for another thirty minutes, delving into the tactical details of the assault plan. It sounded fairly straightforward to Gina—the team had no option but to bull-rush the building. Daryll concluded the meeting by giving the assault team a twenty-minute warning for departure. Gina returned to her office where she donned a bullet-proof vest, followed by her trademark navy-blue windbreaker with "FBI" printed on the back in large block letters. She had mixed feelings of anxiety, excitement, and confidence in the prospects of finding Jack alive and well in the desert facility.

Her hope in finding him more than five thousand miles away from where he was abducted stemmed from a conversation she had with Nigel Peters twenty-four hours earlier. The NCA officer in London had disclosed news concerning where Jack was, or more accurately, where he *wasn't.* At the opening of their phone conversation, Gina had mentioned that the FBI was closing in on the Orbis Novus facility in Nevada, and that it was only a matter of time before they found it.

The dialogue continued:

"Do you think there's a chance we'll find Jack Kurry there?" she asked.

"Perhaps a better one than you think," replied Nigel. "We've managed to track him down to Portsmouth here in the UK."

"How did you do that?"

"We picked up James Cole on a surveillance video at a public dockyard."

"Frank."

"Yes. He was with the other man from the hotel, and a woman. The man was pushing someone in a wheelchair, who appeared to be unconscious."

"Kurry."

"Quite likely, indeed."

"What were they doing?"

"They moved out of the camera shot, but it stands to reason that they boarded a boat somewhere. There are only small craft docked there, so they couldn't have gone far—maybe France, or Guernsey. I doubt they went to France."

Gina quickly pulled up Google Maps on her desktop and typed in "Guernsey." A small island in the English Channel popped up on her screen. "Why Guernsey?"

"They could have easily taken a small aircraft from there. We're checking into it."

"So, you think he's left the country?"

"By all indications, yes. Unless this is just another one of their red herrings."

Now it was a day later, and agents were en route to the suspected home base of the League of Orbis Novus. Gina rode to the site with Daryll in a sedan trailing a caravan of black SUVs occupied by the FBI SWAT members. Just past Indian Springs, about fifty miles north of the city on state highway 95, the convoy veered onto a dirt road and headed north. She had difficulty seeing the road ahead, amid the dust cloud kicked up by the vehicles in front of them.

Suddenly, the convoy came to an abrupt halt, and SWAT agents scrambled out of their vehicles with weapons at the ready. Daryll and Gina exchanged curious glances, as they were not yet near the selected rendezvous point. Radio chatter quickly revealed the situation. The surveillance team on the hill had notified the SWAT leader that the mysterious van seen parked at the facility was now heading straight for them. As the SWAT members moved into positions to intercept the van, Daryll and Gina took cover behind the rearmost SUV. The SWAT leader came back to brief Daryll.

"As soon as we secure the vehicle, we'll need to move quickly to the facility," he advised. "We'll have to assume that the occupant or occupants of the van will tip off the suspects in the building before we can subdue them. This could make the operation a little messier than we had anticipated."

"Understood," replied Daryll.

"Do you want us to proceed?"

"Yes. What choice do we have?"

Visions of the infamous raid on the Branch Davidian compound in

Waco, Texas filled Gina's imagination. A bloody shootout would endanger the lives of her fellow agents and the hostage held inside. Orbis Novus had already demonstrated that they were willing to sacrifice thousands of lives for their cause. Perhaps they were also willing to sacrifice their own.

The van approached the blockade and slowed to a complete stop. The driver readily complied with the orders dictated by the SWAT leader to first extend his hands out the window, then slowly exit the van. The befuddled driver wore an expression of sheer terror as he knelt in the desert sand with his hands on his head. Once the SWAT team determined that he was unarmed and the van was otherwise empty, they signaled Daryll and Gina to approach. The driver seemed clueless, and Daryll wanted to question him before advancing, against the advice of the SWAT leader.

"Who's inside there?" Daryll demanded.

"I don't know," replied the nervous driver. "I just delivered a package."

Daryll questioned the driver for another minute before the apprehensive SWAT leader stepped in. "We should move immediately," he urged. "*Now!*"

"Okay, let's go," relented Daryll.

All but one of the agents hurried back into their vehicles and sped toward the facility. The remaining SWAT member remained with the handcuffed driver and watched his comrades disappear in a cloud of dust.

Approximately two minutes later, the vehicles reached the front of the facility where they fanned out and screeched to a halt. The SWAT agents took cover behind the vehicles then immediately executed a meticulous yet hurried assault on the building. Groups of two or three agents alternated between approaching the facility and covering their comrades in a leapfrog maneuver. Once they were in position, a large agent slammed a battering ram into the front door, after which several of his teammates poured inside.

As a result of their brief encounter with the van driver, Gina and the other FBI agents now suspected that the facility would be unoccupied. Their suspicions were soon confirmed. A few minutes after entering the building, a SWAT member emerged outside and gave the all-clear.

Gina and Daryll entered to find a stack of eight boxes placed neatly just inside the door. They would remain there undisturbed until the ordinance disposal team inspected and cleared them. All of the agents evacuated the building while waiting for the team to arrive; nobody thought the League of Orbis Novus to be above leaving a boobytrap for them.

In the interim, the van driver was brought up to the site for further interrogation. It only took a few minutes for the agents to determine that he was merely a pawn in the larger game. He earnestly volunteered every detail surrounding the mysterious job for which he had been hired a few weeks earlier. The self-employed driver was paid to make a series of deliveries to the facility. The gist of his assignment was to deliver one of ten boxes every other day. The man was also instructed to remain parked outside the facility for three hours after each delivery. He thought this additional task was a bit odd, though the extra thousand dollars he was paid to do it made it quite tolerable. The agents immediately recognized the purpose of the seemingly bizarre instruction. The league apparently wanted the deserted facility to appear occupied and attract the FBI to it. Their scheme worked. The building had been abandoned a few weeks earlier, if not longer. This theory was soon bolstered by the investigation into the two cars parked outside the facility. They had been stolen in St. George, Utah four weeks earlier.

The van driver disclosed that the man who hired him had also provided the ten sealed boxes. He quickly identified Frank as his client upon seeing a photo that Gina displayed on a tablet. The driver then handed over a key that Frank had given him. There was little else that he knew. A subsequent background investigation of the frightened man revealed that he had been truthful and cooperative. Once the bomb technicians determined that the boxes were innocuous, Daryll opened one after another to find that each contained nothing but an armload of desert rocks.

Although the building had most recently served as a diversion, there was enough evidence remaining inside to indicate that it was once a functioning lab for Orbis Novus, and the probable location of Jack's notorious field trip. The most telling sign was a message scribbled onto a large whiteboard in a conference room that read, "Resistance is futile." Gina was too young to understand the reference.

"Star Trek," said Daryll. "The Next Generation."

They found a room that had likely functioned as a laboratory. The smell of bleach still permeated throughout the sterilized room and it was devoid of equipment and containers that might reveal its purpose. Nevertheless, the layout of the long tables, the locations of power supplies, the presence of specialized lighting, and other clues suggested that it had recently facilitated the league's sinister experiments. Members of the FBI Hazardous Materials Response Unit swept the room for traces of any chemicals left behind and found nothing.

Orbis Novus had taken similar care with respect to sanitizing the rest of the building. Nothing was found that might identify its former occupants, as might be expected if they had left in a hurry. The agents did find plenty of evidence indicating that people had resided in the facility, if only for temporary stints. There was a kitchen, complete with a coffee machine, as well as bathrooms and showers. No DNA evidence was recovered.

Gina sat in Daryll's car as the senior special agent updated his superiors in Washington via a conference call.

"It's pretty obvious that they fully expected and even intended for the facility to be found," said Daryll. He filled them in on the faux deliveries of boxes full of rocks. "The time we've wasted searching for the Nevada facility was time taken away from locating their present base, if there is one."

The consensus opinion on the call was that there probably was no alternate facility. Having achieved their goal, the group had likely disbanded. That begged the question of where Jack Kurry was being held, or even worse. A voice from Washington sent a chill down Gina's spine.

"We have to consider the likelihood that Kurry is no longer alive," suggested the senior official. "The organization has killed before—even one of their own."

Gina's expressionless countenance disguised the anguish she felt inside. They were back to square one with respect to finding Jack and it was only a matter of time before the Bureau would call off their search. After all, his last known location was outside of the U.S., and they had just ruled out the most promising lead within its borders. Finding him now became secondary to identifying the members of Orbis Novus, as instructed by the officials in Washington. The most promising leads were the at-large James Francis Cole and the deceased Natalie Wu Lan. Agents continued to search for any possible connections to the two people.

During the drive back to Las Vegas, Gina's phone chimed with a text from Nigel Peters. "Call me when you get a chance." She called him immediately and turned on the speakerphone so that Daryll could participate.

"We've tracked down a possible jet in Guernsey," said Nigel. He proceeded to describe how an employee on the airport tarmac noticed two men and a woman board a small jet with a man in a wheelchair. The worker was too far away to identify Frank in photographs shown to him, but his descriptions of Frank and "a large bald man" were consistent with the surveillance videos from the London hotel and Portsmouth dockyard. The man described the woman in the party as being of African descent. He didn't get a good view of the person in the wheelchair.

"There's good news and bad news," continued Nigel. "We know who owns the jet and we know that it was headed for Ponta Delgada in the Azores."

"What's the bad news?" asked Gina.

"Nobody deplaned at Ponta Delgada. They just refueled and took off again. We don't know where the plane went from there."

"And the owner of the aircraft?" asked Daryll.

"It's a Brazilian company that leases out business jets. Interpol is working with the Federal Police in Brazil. We're cautiously optimistic that the client left a trail, but I'm afraid it might take some time to find it."

"Geez, Brazil?" These guys really get around," Gina said with a sigh.

"Probably by design," replied Nigel, then added with a hint of cynicism, "The only thing we can probably conclude with any certainty is that they are not presently in Brazil."

A few hours later, Gina sat at her desk studying Google Maps in her web browser. A small jet with a better-than-average flight range could leave the Ponta Delgada airport in the Azores and make landfall heading in almost any direction. North America, South America, Europe, and Africa were all within range. It could even fly under the detection of radar and return to Great Britain unnoticed, which would be consistent with the evasive and deceptive tactics previously executed by the league.

Her greatest fear was being unable to find Jack; second to that was being unallowed to search for him. The latter concern materialized later that evening when Daryll popped his head into her office.

"I need you back on Poison Ivy starting tomorrow," he instructed. "Washington is taking over the lead on Orbis Novus. Go home and recharge."

On her drive home from the office that evening, Gina wrestled with the idea of calling Don Kurry once again. The news about the facility had been released to the public an hour earlier. There was no mention of Jack, as the authorities were still withholding information about his disappearance. She knew that Jack's father would have questions and wanted to be the one to tell him, even if it meant violating protocol. She couldn't help but feel that she was abandoning Jack and his family, though it was far beyond her control. She decided to call him.

"You've probably heard about the raid on a suspected facility in Nevada today," she told Don. "I know that you didn't hear anything about Jack. I just wanted to tell you that he wasn't found there, nor was there any evidence that he had been held there."

"Then where do you think he is?" asked Don.

"Honestly, Mr. Kurry, I don't know. I wish I did." She couldn't reveal that Jack was last seen boarding a plane headed for the Azores, nor did she want to.

Don did not return the wall-mounted kitchen phone into its cradle following his conversation with special agent Gina Alvarez. Instead, he pressed the disconnect button then selected the speed dial number for his daughter. Following some brief pleasantries, he told Mindy why he was calling.

"I just spoke to an agent named Alvarez. She said that they didn't find any signs of Jack at the facility outside of Las Vegas."

"Was the agent a woman?" asked Mindy.

"Yes—why?"

"I think she's the same one who visited my friend at UCSD with Jack."

"She was with him in London too," added Don.

"That's interesting…" said Mindy, allowing her voice to trail off.

"It's strange. I got the feeling that her call was sort of… unofficial. I don't think she wants me to mention our conversation with the other agents I've been speaking with."

"Do you think there's something going on between her and Jack?" asked Mindy.

"I don't know and I don't care. I just want to find Jack."

27

On December 12th, the day that the world death toll eclipsed 200,000 souls, the University of California conducted townhall-style meetings for students and faculty on all of its campuses. The chancellor of UC–San Diego asked Muriel Smithson to participate on a panel of university professors for the session on his campus scheduled for later that morning. Originally slated for the 800-seat Mandeville Auditorium, the meeting was relocated to the 5000-seat RIMAC Arena in response to overwhelming interest, concern, and anxiety surrounding the superbug pandemic. Before entering the arena, Muriel felt unequal to the task of assuaging the fearful students and employees.

"What are we supposed to tell them?" she asked a colleague on the panel.

"We just need to be honest. If we don't know something, then we should admit it," suggested the colleague.

"Do we really know very much?"

"We know more than they do at this point. At least we can explain what's happening from a scientific perspective."

The chancellor kicked off the meeting with a brief statement. He ambiguously pledged the university's commitment to the safety of its student body, faculty, and staff. There wasn't much more he could offer, and he eagerly turned the floor over to the panel. The question-and-answer session commenced after the panel members declined an invitation to make opening remarks.

Nobody questioned the link between opioids and the twin Gemini Viruses. The first few questions fixated on the development of a vaccine, as might be expected by a generation raised in a world of immunization.

"Even if we developed a vaccine," said a doctor from the medical center, "it would generally only help people who haven't yet been exposed to the viruses. Given that hundreds of people in the San Diego area have died, it's reasonable to assume that most of you—most of *us*—are already carrying the viruses."

Muriel did not enjoy pouring more rain onto the parade, yet she felt compelled to share her somewhat unique viewpoint. "I have spoken with one of the top scientists working at the CDC," she told the audience in reference to Sydney. "He indicated that this particular family of rhinovirus does not respond effectively to vaccines. Maybe future generations will find a way to utilize opioids again, but we should get used to a world without them."

"Good riddance!" shouted a voice in the crowd.

"We need them!" retorted another.

The raucous assertions and rebuttals quickly escalated into a verbal frenzy which the chancellor eventually quelled. Similar commotions erupted several times throughout the session.

In response to a student asking how he might avoid catching the viruses, a professor responded, "Live in a plastic bubble. I see no other way."

One panel member was simultaneously booed and cheered when she boldly suggested that the world was a better place going forward, though she vehemently denounced the methods of Orbis Novus.

"They're murderers!" yelled someone.

"They cleaned up our mess!" claimed another.

When the crowd quieted once again, a young female student asked if anyone on the panel knew how many people died of opioid overdoses in the U.S. during the previous year. None of the panelists had the answer.

"72,327 during last year alone," said the young woman, reading from her smartphone. An eerie silence followed as people mentally compared the death counts of overdoses and the superbug. Everybody was doing the math; nobody was brave enough to say anything about it.

Eventually, the chancellor picked up his microphone and proclaimed that they were not there to discuss the League of Orbis Novus, then he wisely steered the questioning into the realm of opioid alternatives.

"Free weed!" shouted a clown from the upper rows of the arena, prompting a spirited cheer from the audience.

"Marijuana is a viable alternative for many forms of chronic pain," said a panelist. "I suspect that we'll develop many others in the years to come."

The chancellor wrapped up the meeting two hours after it started by thanking the panel members. As any good educator would do, he shared his own takeaways from the session in the form of parting remarks.

"I learned tonight that we have no choice but to move forward and adapt to the changes. We cannot undo them. History will judge the merits and demerits of what has happened. For now, we need to come together as a people and help each other cope with the aftermath." After a smattering of applause, the audience emptied out to the campus where raucous debates continued long into the night.

The panel members remained on the arena floor for a few minutes talking among themselves and addressing individual questions from lingering audience members. Muriel caught sight of Jack's sister approaching and excused herself from a conversation to greet her friend with a hug.

"Have you heard anything about Jack?" asked Muriel.

"No," replied Mindy with a sigh. "I'm beginning to lose all hope of ever seeing him again."

"You shouldn't think that way," reassured Muriel, though she too wondered if there was any chance that Jack would be found alive. The women conversed for a few minutes before Mindy asked Muriel about her most recent meeting with her brother.

"What was the name of the FBI agent who was with him?"

"Um, Alvarez—a younger woman," replied Muriel.

"What was she like?"

Muriel was puzzled by the peculiar question. "She was nice… professional… Why do you ask?"

"I don't know. Never mind," said Mindy. Her eyes were beginning to swell with tears. "I should get home." They embraced again and parted ways.

Muriel had not forgotten to call Sydney Carter, but she had

successfully procrastinated placing the call in favor of less awkward tasks. The sad exchange with Mindy now inspired her to check in with him, and she dialed his cellphone as soon as she returned to her office. She was surprised when he answered the phone.

"Hello?" said a groggy voice. It sounded as if he had been sleeping, though it was only 4:30 in the afternoon on the East Coast.

"Doctor Carter? It's Muriel Smithson."

After a brief pause, Sydney replied, "Yes. Hello." Muriel sensed that he needed a moment to recall their conversation from a few days earlier.

"It looks like everything turned out the way you thought it would with respect to the viruses," said Muriel.

"Yeah."

Muriel waited for Sydney to say something else, then filled the awkward void. "Anyway, I just wanted to check in with you. You seemed… well, you sounded like maybe you weren't feeling very well the last time we spoke."

For Sydney Carter, the 12th of December began somewhere around ten o'clock that morning when he awoke to the sound of someone pounding on the door to his basement apartment. He cursed as he flipped over onto his back and rubbed his eyes, having no intention of answering the door. The knocking continued intermittently for five minutes before Sydney grudgingly rose to see who was disturbing his sleep. He briefly searched for his robe amid the clutter covering his bedroom carpet, then proceeded to the door clad in nothing but his boxer shorts. He soon discovered the culprit to be his manager at Emerson–Lee University.

"You haven't been answering my calls," said Phil Rogers. "Can I come in?" Sydney stepped aside and gestured his boss inward with a sweep of his arm. "Did you even listen to my voicemail messages?" asked Phil.

"I was getting to it," replied Sydney. "I might have heard the first one."

The men walked into the pigsty that served as Sydney's living room, dining room, and occasional bedroom. Empty food containers, beer cans, and various other forms of litter covered the coffee table. Sydney caught Phil eyeing the cans.

"I'm only drinking beer now," he announced diffidently. "And those there are about a whole week's worth. I have a system for controlling it."

Phil ignored the hollow proclamation. "Have you been watching the news? Your theory proved to be true." He cleared a spot for himself on the couch and sat down, though not before stealthily brushing away some crumbs.

Sydney followed Phil's lead and sat down in a folding chair that was next to the couch. "Yeah, I saw that. Good for Molly and everybody else."

"'Everybody else' includes you, Syd. You should be proud of what you discovered."

"Why? I didn't save anybody's life. I just told them how the people were dying." He rose from his chair and stepped into the adjacent kitchen area. "Do you want a beer? I allow myself one or two before lunch."

"No, thanks," replied Phil. "Syd, what you did was important. We have to know what we're dealing with in order to stop it."

"Stop it?" said Sydney derisively. "There's no way in hell you're gonna stop it." He sat back down, flipped open his can of beer, and took a swig. "I thought I was pretty clear about that."

"We proved the connection to opioids. That will help convince people to stop using them," said Phil.

"Yeah, good luck with that."

Phil realized that his flattery was ineffective and moved directly to the purpose of his visit. "Syd, I met with the board of regents yesterday and explained your role in discovering the viruses. They've agreed to take you back on the condition that you return to treatment today."

"They'll take me back?"

"Yes, but you have to show them something first—you have to commit yourself to it."

Sydney leaned forward and stared blankly at the drink in his hands. The defensive façade slowly faded from his face and he wiped a tear from his eye.

"Are you okay?" asked Phil.

After a brief period of silence, Sydney set the can on the table and buried his face in his hands. "I don't think I can do it," he mumbled through his fingers.

"Sure you can, Syd. Let's go right now."

"Now?"

"Right now. Get dressed and I'll drive you there."

"But what if I can't?"

"There are people who can help you stay sober," said Phil.

"It's not just that. What if… what if I can't do it anymore?"

"Do what?"

"My job. Sometimes my head... my head feels so foggy."

"Look at what you just did. You were the only one who thought of it."

"No, I wasn't. I never would have thought about it if that woman hadn't called me."

"Who? What woman?"

Sydney started sobbing. "My wife isn't gonna take me back."

"You don't know that," said Phil. "And even if she doesn't, you should still get sober. Think about your daughters."

"What if I can't do it?" mumbled Sydney. "Ugh! I can't think straight!"

"That's because you're sick. They'll help you clear your mind."

Sydney suddenly sat up straight and looked at Phil with a look of emboldened courage. "I'll do it. But I can't go right now."

"Come on, Syd. You're making excuses again."

Sydney sprang up and walked over to refrigerator. "I promise I'll go. You have my word. I just need to see my daughters first, because I'm doing this for them."

"You'll see them when you're better. We should go right now."

Sydney grabbed a half-empty twelve pack of beer and a second, unopened one from the refrigerator. "I'm telling you the truth. Look, take these with you. That's all the beer I've got." He laid the cardboard containers on the floor in front of Phil. "Come back at six o'clock."

"This isn't a good idea, Syd."

"Take them. Come back at six. I promise I'll be here and ready to go."

Phil pressed his objections for a few minutes longer before conceding to Sydney's stubbornness. "Okay," he said with a heavy sigh.

"But I'm gonna call you every hour between now and then. If you don't answer, I'm coming back here straight away."

"Deal."

As Phil walked toward the front door, Sydney picked up the packages of beer and shoved them into Phil's unsuspecting arms.

"Take these," implored Sydney.

Phil reluctantly accepted the beer, then said, "I'm agreeing to this against my better judgement. Don't let me down."

"I won't."

A strange mix of surrender and determination circulated throughout Sydney's body as he washed up. For the first time, he admitted to himself that he was not smart enough, strong enough, or steadfast enough to resolve his problem on his own. In fact, he was soon overwhelmed once again with feelings of deficiency and frailty. While in the shower, he wondered if he should have left with Phil, and worried that he might not make it through the day.

"You can do this," he said to himself repeatedly as he stared at his reflection while shaving. "It's time." The emotional rollercoaster ride continued throughout the day, alternating between confident highs and disheartening lows.

He knew that his wife, Pam, would not allow him to see his daughters on such short notice, so he didn't bother to ask. Instead, he rode a MARTA train north and walked to the school where his older daughter, Lexi, was attending kindergarten. The assistant principal was sympathetic to Sydney's situation, but she could not accommodate his request to see his daughter without first contacting her legal guardian—Pam.

Sydney didn't want to go down that rathole. "Don't worry about it," he told the woman, and exited the school. He stood just beyond the school property and watched classes of children come and go from the recess area. At one point he thought he recognized Lexi, though the girl was too far away for him to be certain.

"I'll see you in a month," he said to himself, then lumbered slowly back to the train station. Lexi had been his best chance for seeing one of his daughters. There was no hope of visiting Amanda at her daycare facility, where the security rivaled Fort Knox. Sydney's crestfallen ego tried everything in its power to convince him that he had earned the right to have a beer or two, yet he managed to make it home sober.

Phil's hourly phone calls helped.

Back in his basement flat, Sydney contemplated calling Phil and asking him to come over earlier than six o'clock. He decided to tidy-up his apartment instead, so that he would come home to a clean environment following rehab. The place was nearly spotless when Phil called for the four o'clock check-in. Sydney once again considered asking him to come over right away, then figured that it was already close enough to 6 p.m. He packed a bag and fell asleep on his bed soon after—the first sober sleep he had experienced in days.

The sound of his ringtone roused him from a deep slumber about thirty minutes later. He was still semiconscious when he answered his phone in a groggy voice.

"Hello?"

"Doctor Carter? It's Muriel Smithson."

"Yes. Hello."

"It looks like everything turned out the way you thought it would with respect to the viruses," said Muriel.

"Yeah."

It was a minute or so into the conversation before he was fully-alert and cognizant of Muriel Smithson's inquiry about his general health.

"Oh, I'm fine," he told her. "I was just sleeping." He then realized how odd that might sound, and included, "I'm off work today."

"I'm so sorry to bother you. You've certainly earned a vacation day," said Muriel.

"Yeah, we seem to have figured it all out—and thanks very much for your help," Sydney said politely, then added a small fib to his larger pack of lies. "I told everyone at the CDC about our conversation."

"Well, thank you, but that isn't why I called," she said shyly.

"They just need to find those Orbis Novus guys now," opined Sydney. "But I guess most of the damage is already done."

"Yes, I suppose…" Muriel hesitated for a moment. "I probably shouldn't tell you this, but they're holding a hostage somewhere. He's the brother of a coworker of mine. A reporter."

"Really? I hadn't heard anything."

"No, the FBI is keeping it under wraps. They don't want to give Orbis Novus any kind of advantage."

"Oh. I won't say anything."

"Between you and me, Doctor Carter—"

"Call me Syd."

"My coworker is convinced that her brother is being held at a secret facility somewhere, but between you and me, Syd, I'm afraid the young man might be dead. I suppose he knew too much about the organization. He was in London doing research on them when he was captured. He even interviewed me a couple of times, through my connection with his sister."

"I'm sorry to hear that."

"It's strange," Muriel speculated. "I wonder how these Orbis Novus people could have known about spontaneous viral transmutation, let alone perfect it. They'd have to be scientists—and very good ones at that."

"They would. Definitely." The gears in Sydney's sober brain slowly began to spin up to speed.

"I just wonder," continued Muriel half-seriously, "if maybe some of them attended one of you lectures, like I did."

"It's funny you say that," replied Sydney, "I ran into a guy recently who—" The lightning bolt struck at that very instant. "Oh my God."

"What is it?"

"I can't believe it didn't occur to me. Jesus—it makes perfect sense."

"What does?"

"Guatemala. It must have been a test run." The phone call became less of a conversation and more of a monologue as Sydney thought out loud. At one point, his phone indicated that there was an incoming call from Phil, but he was completely oblivious to it. He explained to Muriel that the virus outbreak he studied briefly in Guatemala was likely a precursor to the one that Orbis Novus eventually released across the world. Other pieces began to fall into place.

"I thought that Rudy was doing me a favor because I was hungover," he said to Muriel. "He was just trying to get rid of me."

Muriel was having trouble keeping up with the story. "Rudy?"

"Rudy Jimenez. He worked as a grad student under me at Emerson–Lee. He was there."

"Where?"

"Guatemala. Emerson–Lee sent me to help with the outbreak."

"And you were hungover?"

"Yeah, I—" Sydney froze in reaction to a second lightning bolt of realization. Was it possible that his drinking problem had inhibited his ability to recognize what was happening in Guatemala? Maybe that was why Jimenez had requested him by name when Emerson–Lee offered to help. Perhaps his tarnished reputation had proceeded him.

His voice softened. "Muriel," he said nervously, "I haven't been completely honest with you."

He disclosed everything to her, including his drinking, suspension, and untimely exit from rehab. As his words flowed in a rapid stream of consciousness, he pondered the notion that he was responsible, at least partially, for the thousands upon thousands of deaths. A healthier man might have dismissed the suggestion, but Sydney's imagination was fueled by the depression and paranoia spawned by his disease. In his mind, the pandemic was his fault. The league took his own scientific theory and dangled it right in front of him. And he was too drunk to see it.

"I can still save one," he grumbled aloud.

"What are you talking about?" asked Muriel.

"What's the reporter's name?"

"Jack. Jack Kurry. Why?"

"I've got to go. Thank you, Muriel, thank you." He hung up.

Seconds later, he was on the phone with an operator manning the FBI's tip line. His mind was racing at a pace that his mouth couldn't match, and he struggled to convey his thoughts, blurting out each before the previous one was fully-articulated. His side of the conversation sounded something like, "It's Guatemala!... Sydney Carter—I'm a scientist… No, you don't understand. I was there… Guatemala! Spontaneous viral transmutation… at my lecture! I don't know where… Rudy! No, I'm Sydney Carter… You need to talk to Phil… Phil Rogers!" In his frenzy, he neglected to mention the name Jack Kurry.

After a few minutes, the frustration reached its boiling point and he abruptly ended the call. Sydney's incoherent rambling was the one-thousand-and-seventeenth tip about Orbis Novus that the FBI received on that day alone. There was no follow-up.

Phil Rogers arrived at Sydney's apartment just before 5:45 p.m. He banged on the door for ten minutes, then walked around to the front of the house and rang the doorbell. There he convinced Sydney's landlady, an elderly woman in a bathrobe and curlers, to open the door to the basement flat.

"I don't see much of Doctor Carter," she said as they walked around to the back of the old Victorian house. "He mostly keeps to himself." She stopped abruptly and faced Phil. "Maybe we should call the police first."

"You can call them if you want," said Phil. "But you need to let me in there first. It's an emergency, and I'll take full responsibility."

"Well, okay. Just this once," she replied reticently. After knocking on the door and waiting for what seemed to Phil like an eternity, she unlocked it.

Phil was astonished to find the apartment in near-immaculate condition. The landlady seemed unimpressed, as if she had expected nothing less. Phil quickly searched the premises, fearing that he would find Sydney passed out on his bed or in the bathroom. All he found was a hastily-scribbled note on the kitchen counter.

"Phil—sorry, but I had to leave. Don't worry about me. Everything is good, Syd. P.S.—I didn't go to rehab but I promise that I will go when I get back."

28

Sydney sat alone in the molded plastic chair, wearing nothing but an old t-shirt and faded jeans. It was 3 a.m. in Mexico City and he was the only person waiting near the gate from which his flight to Guatemala City was scheduled to depart in four hours. The entire terminal was deserted save for the cleaning crew and a few other travelers who were forced to spend overnight layovers sleeping on the unforgiving chairs or the cold floor. Sydney was physically drained but his mind was too active for sleep. He was also famished. The airport restaurants were closed, and the vending machine had rejected his credit card. The expensive last-minute airline ticket had maxed it out. In his pocket was the $500 in cash he had emptied from his checking account via an ATM in the Atlanta airport. He attempted to exchange some of his dollars for pesos with the janitor, but the language barrier was impregnable.

Much more than food, he craved a drink—just one, to calm his nerves. Unfortunately, there would be no opportunity for that until he reached Guatemala City. The minutes ticked by as slowly as would be expected in such a wearisome and agitated situation. Over the ensuing hours, the waiting area slowly filled with travelers. The sound of the gate agent boarding the plane eventually roused Sydney just as he was nodding off for the first time since departing Atlanta. He lumbered down the aisle of the aging airplane and found his seat. Two hours after the jet airliner's wheels went up, they touched down in Guatemala.

Minutes later, Sydney sat on a bench outside the airport in

Guatemala City and stared into the bright, sizzling day. This juncture marked the extent of his pre-planning. He had intended to figure out the rest of his plan when he reached Guatemala, and now he was there. He silently weighed his options for a few minutes, then picked up his small bag and walked to the back of the taxi line.

The cab dropped him off in front of the same hotel at which he stayed during his previous trip. Instead of going inside, he walked down to a cantina he had spied on the drive over. The small watering hole was practically empty, and a gray-haired bartender fixed his eyes on the gringo from the moment he walked in the door. Sydney took a seat on a barstool.

"Cerveza, por favor." This was the extent of his Spanish. The bartender opened a bottle and placed it in front of Sydney. "Do you speak English?"

"A little," replied the bartender.

"I need some help," said Sydney. "Some… protection. I have money." He flashed a few twenty-dollar bills. The puzzled bartender stared at him blankly then disappeared into a back room. He returned a few minutes later with a young man donned in a San Antonio Spurs tank top. The younger man looked Sydney over carefully before speaking.

"You want coke? Meth?" he asked in a soft, heavily-accented voice.

"No, I need a gun—a pistol," said Sydney, shaping his thumb and forefinger accordingly. Then he added, "It's just for self-defense," as if that might make a difference to the Guatemalan drug dealer.

The young dealer looked at the bartender, then back at Sydney. He contemplated the gringo's request for a moment, then grinned and said, "Wait."

By the time Sydney finished his second beer, the dealer had returned with another man. This latest participant was a chubby, middle-aged man with long hair. He wore a plain white, tank top undershirt that was two sizes too small and appeared as if he had come straight from his bed. He sat on a stool next to Sydney as the dealer stood nearby.

The chubby man spoke to Sydney's reflection in the mirror behind the bar. "Two hundred dollars." His English was remarkably intelligible.

"Do you have a gun?" asked the naïve scientist.

"Show me the money," replied the chubby man.

Sydney cautiously removed ten twenty-dollar bills from his wallet while trying to conceal the complete wad of cash he had within it. The man subsequently produced a tattered nine-millimeter handgun from the crotch of his pants and placed it onto the bar. Then he pulled out an ammunition clip.

"Thanks," said Sydney. He slid the gun toward himself and looked it over. The chubby man pocketed the cash, then stood up and took a few steps toward the door before turning back.

"Do you know how to use that thing?" he asked.

"Not really."

The man provided a two-minute tutorial which ended with him pointing the loaded gun at Sydney's reflection in the mirror, before handing it over to his student.

"Good luck, my friend. You got fifteen rounds in there. I can sell you another clip if you want."

"No, thanks. I'm good."

The man looked at Sydney curiously. "Are you in some kind of trouble, man?"

"No. I mean, I hope not. This is just in case."

Sydney stuffed the handgun into his pants as the chubby man walked out the front door and the young drug dealer returned to the back room. The old bartender watched with a befuddled expression as Sydney took the final swig from his bottle. The bartender nodded and pointed to the empty bottle, as if asking Sydney if he wanted a third.

"No, thanks," said Sydney. He placed a ten-dollar bill on the bar and left.

Sydney felt emboldened by the relative ease of the gun transaction. He was ready to execute his next step, and he knew that it would be even riskier. This phase would involve a huge leap of faith, yet one that he couldn't do without. He pulled out the frayed business card from his wallet—the one that Manuel had given him on his visit last summer in support of the outbreak in the village.

He ran the logic through his head one last time: Manuel had been hired by Emerson–Lee, and not by Rudy Jimenez or anybody else on the Guatemalan staff. Manuel had seemed just as perplexed as he was on that morning when the team left him behind in the trailer. And most importantly, he would not be able to find the site without Manuel. He dialed the number on his cellphone.

Manuel seemed genuinely delighted to hear from Sydney, if not a little surprised. He had a previous obligation but insisted on canceling it, and he told Sydney that he could pick him up in front of the hotel in an hour. He arrived right on schedule and jumped out of his car to greet Sydney, grasping his hand in a firm handshake.

"Hello Doctor Sydney. You will be happy to know that I have fixed the air-conditioning."

"Excellent."

Sydney sat down in the front passenger seat and removed all of the money from his wallet. Handing it to Manuel, he said, "This is every penny that I have. It's nearly three hundred dollars. I hope it's enough for today."

Manuel smiled and replied, "Just keep it for now, Doctor Sydney. You can pay me later."

There were few words exchanged between the two men during the long ride north. Sydney did not want to reveal anything about the purpose of his trip—he wasn't exactly sure what it was anyway. He pretended to sleep for most of the drive, though his heartrate increased with each mile. He periodically felt for the gun lodged between his pants and his hip while mentally reviewing the instructions for using it, provided by the hefty man in the bar. The sun was low in the sky when Manuel's car pulled into the compound that hosted Sydney on his previous visit. The field was empty this time.

"Are you sure this is the right place?" asked Manuel.

"Yes. I'll walk from here."

"Where are you going?"

"I'm just… I'm meeting someone in a building over there."

Manuel eyed Sydney curiously and struggled to form a response. There was no building in sight, but it wasn't his place to question his client, even one whom he considered a friend. "Would you like me to come with you, Doctor Sydney?"

"No, that's okay. It's just over the hill." In truth, Sydney only had a vague notion of where he was headed.

"Should I wait here?"

"No, I might be gone for several days. I'll call you when I'm ready." He handed Manuel all of the money he had left. "Here you go. Thanks Manuel."

Manuel looked out into the field and the desolate jungle beyond, lit only by dusk, then returned his eyes to Sydney. "Are you sure this the right place?" he repeated.

"I'm positive."

Manuel leaned over and opened his glove compartment. He pulled out a small hunting knife and held it by the blade, offering the handle to Sydney. "You might need this." When Sydney hesitated to accept it, Manuel added, "There are coyotes and other animals out there."

Sydney took the knife, exited the car, and began to walk resolutely toward the horizon. When Manuel had driven out of sight, he stopped and took in his surroundings, hoping to guess the direction of the suspected facility. For the first time since leaving Atlanta, he wondered if there even was one.

Gina Alvarez began her work day with a call to Nigel Peters in London. The British NCA officer had spent the preceding two days chasing leads into stone walls. Each sounded promising to Gina until Nigel dropped the second shoe. NCA identified the man who leased the Brazilian business jet, but it turned out to be a false identity. The jet filed a flight plan before departing Ponta Delgada in the Azores, but it turned out to be false as well. Nigel seemed impressed by the league's ability to cover its tracks, yet he remained guardedly optimistic about locating them.

"I believe that we'll find them," he told Gina. "They can't hide forever."

Gina was less hopeful, and Jack didn't have forever. "Isn't it likely that the league has already disbanded?"

"It's possible," replied Nigel, "but that doesn't mean that we won't find them. We've already identified two—Natalie Wu Lan and James Francis Cole. We're looking into all of their associations."

The FBI was taking a similar approach, though the urgency of the case was slowly waning. At the daily standup meeting, Daryll Jameson announced that it would be the last such gathering. The Bureau would continue to support the NCA in the search for Jack Kurry, whose whereabouts were presumed to be outside of the United States. James "Frank" Cole was added to the FBI's Ten Most Wanted list, and the suspicious death of Wu Lan remained under investigation. There was no longer a time sensitivity with respect to addressing the pandemic from a criminal perspective, for the origins and impact of the league's so-called solution were now understood in the medical and scientific communities.

The WHO, CDC, and national health ministries across the globe shouldered the burden of dealing with the aftermath and forging a path forward into a world without opioids. The world seemed much more interested in what happened versus finding those who did it. Nevertheless, national police agencies, loosely connected by Interpol, would continue to search for those responsible, though it was not the top priority for any particular agency.

The Bureau's strategy made sense to Gina from a professional standpoint, yet it did nothing to assuage her worries that stemmed from her personal feelings for Jack. Compounding her anxiety was the necessity to keep those feelings to herself. There was nobody with whom she could commiserate, though she had found a little solace in her ambiguous conversations with Jack's father.

The assignment of a new case did not provide much of a distraction. In addition to the interminable phone records of the Poison Ivy case and her duties as liaison to the NCA regarding Orbis Novus, she now supported a drug-trafficking investigation with ties to a Las Vegas gentleman's club. Despite the heavy case load, she still found time to spend fruitless hours studying online maps in the hopes of identifying possible destinations for a business jet departing the Azores. The problem was that the aircraft could have made several more undocumented refueling stops, and could plausibly be anywhere in the world. She knew that the task was practically hopeless and not exactly on her to-do list, yet it was also cathartic. It was during one of these searches that her desk phone rang.

"Agent Alvarez? This is Muriel Smithson from UCSD. We met several weeks ago."

"Yes, of course, Doctor Smithson. What can I do for you?"

"Well, maybe there's something I can do for you," suggested Muriel. "I might have some useful information."

"Is this regarding Orbis Novus?"

"Yes, it's…" Muriel hesitated, then proceeded to ramble nervously. "I'm afraid it's a little… odd. I'll need to give you some background first, then you can decide whether it makes any sense. It's probably a longshot, but I won't be able to sleep unless I tell someone, and you left me your business card, so…"

"No, no," interjected Gina. She was happy to entertain longshots at this point. "I'm glad you called."

Muriel provided some background on her intermittent, albeit consequential history with Sydney Carter. She told Gina about his theories regarding pathogens and viruses, doing her best to summarize his ideas in layman's terms. She described in detail her phone conversation with Sydney that ultimately led to the recent identification of the Gemini Viruses and their biochemical relationship with opioids.

As an agent assigned to the case, it was Gina's job to be up-to-speed on the scientific discoveries regarding the superbug and the key players responsible for them. "How come I've never heard of this guy?" she wondered aloud.

"That's where the story skews a little," said Muriel. "There's something going on with Doctor Carter. He has some personal issues, but I have no doubt that he's responsible for discovering the twin viruses."

"As well as yourself," added Gina. She couldn't see Muriel frown in response to the kudos. Muriel's intentions were truly selfless and she had no desire to take any personal credit.

"Doctor Carter is considered to be a genius," said Muriel. "I simply repeated his own theory back to him."

"And like many geniuses, I suppose he possesses some kind of tragic flaw," opined Gina.

Muriel hesitated again. She presumed that Sydney had told her about his personal struggles in confidence. She was nonetheless compelled to disclose the full context of the information she was providing to the FBI. It was certainly possible that Sydney was delusional. She took a deep breath while forming her response. "Doctor Carter confided to me that he was suffering from alcoholism and is currently on a leave of absence from work." She couldn't see Gina grimace and roll her eyes in response. "But I have to tell you, Agent Alvarez," continued Muriel, "that he knows what he's talking about."

"What is the new information?" asked Gina.

"Do you remember an outbreak in Guatemala this past summer?"

"No. An outbreak of what?"

"That's just it. The pathogen disappeared before they could figure out what it was. The CDC sent Doctor Carter to help. He told me that they sent him back home after one day and never sent him the blood samples he had requested."

"Who's 'they'?"

"The response team in Guatemala. Doctor Carter mentioned a man named Jimenez. I don't recall his first name."

"Why does he think this has something to do with Orbis Novus?"

"Again, this is where it gets a little shaky. You'll want to ask him yourself, but he seemed convinced that they were hiding a facility there. He thinks the outbreak in the village was some kind of test case."

"And this guy Jimenez is a member of the league?"

"I have no idea, but I got the impression that Doctor Carter thinks so."

As Muriel relayed everything Sydney told her, Gina's skepticism slowly transformed into genuine zeal. Suddenly, she couldn't wait to speak with Dr. Carter herself, so she thanked Muriel for the information and politely ended the conversation. Subsequent calls to the phone number Muriel provided went directly to voicemail. Her officemate, Shawn, listened to her leave two detailed messages, just as he had eavesdropped on the conversation with Muriel.

"What have you got?" he asked Gina.

"A lead on the facility—maybe nothing."

Shawn had already pulled up information about the Guatemalan outbreak in his web browser. "This article says that the Guatemalan authorities believe the cause might have been something called the Marburg virus."

"Does it mention someone named Jimenez?"

"No."

The two agents spent the next hour researching Dr. Sydney Carter, the deadly Guatemalan outbreak, and someone associated with either of them named Jimenez. It was Shawn who found Sydney's name in an international travel database.

"Look at this," he told Gina. "Carter left for Guatemala yesterday, by way of Mexico City. Maybe that's why he isn't answering his phone."

"Why would the CDC send him back there—especially if he's on a medical leave of absence?" asked Gina.

"Only one way to find out," replied Shawn.

Within minutes, Gina had tracked down a representative from the human resources department at Emerson–Lee University. The woman was polite but unauthorized to disclose much about Sydney—even to the FBI.

"I understand," said Gina. "But could you at least confirm whether he was sent to Guatemala yesterday on university or CDC business?"

"Let me get back to you," said the HR representative. She called Gina back fifteen minutes later, and conferenced in a man named Phil Rogers. She introduced him as Dr. Carter's manager.

"I can tell you that Doctor Carter is currently on a leave of absence," said the HR rep, as if reading an official statement. "He was not sent to Guatemala or anywhere else on official business yesterday."

"What is this about?" asked Phil. "Is Syd okay?"

"We believe that Doctor Carter might have information relevant to an ongoing investigation," said Gina, as if reading from a statement of her own.

"Yeah, I know this has something to do with the Gemini Viruses," said Phil. "Syd helped us figure out what was going on. What does that have to do with Guatemala?"

Gina dodged the question. "Mr. Rogers, did Doctor Carter investigate the outbreak of an illness in Guatemala over the summer?"

"He did."

"What did he find out?"

"Not much, as I recall. It was more of a courtesy visit. The problem was already under control."

"Did he do any follow-on investigation after his return?" inquired Gina.

"I don't think so—I doubt it. That's when he started to… um…"

The HR rep came to Phil's rescue. "Doctor Carter was assigned to other tasks before taking his leave of absence," she noted, and Gina understood what she meant. The conversation ended shortly thereafter. There wasn't much more that the representatives from Emerson–Lee could tell her, and she wasn't interested in answering Phil's questions. She looked at Shawn curiously after hanging up the phone.

"They don't know why he went to Guatemala?" asked Shawn.

"Nope."

The agents agreed that it was time for Gina to brief Daryll Jameson on the new lead. She found the senior agent in his office where she disclosed everything she had learned about Sydney Carter and the

Guatemalan outbreak. Daryll acknowledged that there might be some validity to the lead, then reminded his subordinate that the Las Vegas field office was no longer leading the Orbis Novus case.

"Let's get on the phone with Washington," he said. "They'll get in touch with the Guatemalan authorities."

"If there actually is a facility there, then you're going to want some boots on the ground," suggested Gina. "We already know that we've got at least one U.S. citizen in hot water down there."

"No, Agent Alvarez, we *don't* know that. We don't know why Doctor Carter went to Guatemala. All we know is that it wasn't for official business. Maybe he's taking a vacation."

"You know that isn't true, Daryll," said Gina forcefully. She rarely referred to her boss by his first name, and her chutzpah caught him by surprise. "We don't have a legat office there," she continued. "We need somebody there to spur the action. Time could be running out."

"Let me guess—that person should be you?"

"My Spanish is very good," lied Gina. "Shawn can go with me. He's fluent." At least the part about Shawn was true.

Daryll rubbed his eyes with one hand then slowly dragged it down to his chin. "This isn't even our case, Gina." He stared at her in the way that a father might look at his persuasive daughter, then caved. "I'll call Washington and see what I can do. Give me an hour."

It was nearly an hour to the minute when Daryll entered the office of Gina and Shawn.

"I guess it's your lucky day, agents Alvarez and Zuroski," he said. "Washington tells me they're spread too thin, and they want us to investigate the Guatemala lead."

Gina inferred that Daryll was spinning his explanation and that he had requested that his office handle the assignment. "Thanks," she told him.

"Don't thank me. I don't think you'll find anything down there, other than maybe a drunken scientist." He pulled out a small piece of paper from his pocket. "This is your point of contact for the PNC—the Guatemalan national police. And this is the name of our embassy contact. He'll be with you every step of the way. Touch base with both of them immediately, then get on a plane. Call me in the morning."

"Got it."

"And remember," added Daryll. "Your official purpose is to advise the police on the Orbis Novus case. If you play your cards right, they might let you tag along and observe the operation. Safe travels."

Gina and Shawn waited until Daryll was out of sight before they allowed smiles to crack through their sober expressions. They quickly launched into the preparatory phone calls, with Gina holding a conversation with the state department official from the embassy in Guatemala City, and Shawn conducting a discussion with a senior officer in the PNC—entirely in Spanish. Afterward, Shawn formed an itinerary with the FBI travel office, and Gina updated Nigel Peters in London via email. It was too late at night to call him.

"The Guatemalans told me that they'll try to track down Sydney Carter overnight," said Shawn. "They'll have an update when we arrive."

"It's gonna be a long night," replied Gina.

29

The sun rose in the eastern hemisphere on December 14th and shed the first rays of light onto the downward slope of the superbug pandemic. Reports of new deaths would significantly decrease that day, as the explanation of the opioid connection began to spread faster than the virus itself. Parochial authorities in villages took it upon themselves to destroy what remained of the opium poppy fields, and they met no resistance from the gangs that once cultivated and defended them. In the cities, police forces, bureaucrats, and community outreach organizations loosely banded together to ferret out the remaining supplies of heroin and other illicit opiates, while granting unconditional amnesty to anyone who cooperated.

The WHO had taken on the grim task of aggregating death counts from around the world. On December 14th, their confirmed death toll for the Gemini Viruses exceeded three hundred thousand. Tens of thousands more were suspected. The number of deaths reported on that day was lower than the previous day, marking the first time that the worldwide death rate decreased from day to day. A rapid decline would continue for weeks until no new deaths were reported.

Hospitals, clinics, and pharmacies surrendered their remaining prescription opioids to authorities. Some nations held their supplies in storage, in the event that a vaccine or some other solution might render them useful once again. Most countries destroyed their supplies immediately under the advice of their health ministries. Not a single scientific expert foresaw a future that included opioids—at least not for several decades.

Universities and government agencies sponsored hastily-scheduled conferences around the world to discuss new techniques and approaches for managing chronic pain. Researchers scoured through medical journals written over the past twenty-years in search of alternatives that had been tossed to the wayside in favor of the cheap and effective opioids. They discovered that there were indeed healthier and less-destructive options.

Pharmaceutical companies also surrendered their stockpiles of opioids and scrambled to step up production of alternative pain-relief medications. They funneled millions of dollars into the research and development of new products to replace the billions in revenue streams that had evaporated along with the opioid demand. Stock prices for the major producers of prescription opioids plummeted.

The world's stock market indices also fell considerably during the first week of the pandemic. Following the discovery of the Gemini Viruses and confirmation of the opioid connection, the markets bottomed-out and slowly began to rise. Speculators recognized the long-term positive implications of a world without illicit opiates. By Christmas Eve, the S&P 500 index was on the upswing and down only four percent from its level on November 30th.

Some legislatures in western countries considered adopting regulations banning the production of opioids, though only a few followed through. There was little need to legislate against the production of a lethal chemical that served no practical purpose and generated no demand. In a matter of two weeks, the black market for illicit opiate products had completely dissolved.

Each day that the world waited for a blood test to confirm the presence of the Gemini Viruses, fewer people clamored for it. When a French company finally developed a test, even fewer people bothered to take it. Most had accepted the estimates released by the WHO. Even as early as December 14th, scientists speculated that half of the world's population was already infected. The estimate was more than eighty-five percent for people living in the cities and suburbs of western countries.

As one talking head put it, "Even if I tested negative for the virus, I still wouldn't risk taking opioids—not that any are available." That was easy for a non-addict to say. For the addicts, there was simply no supply.

The persons responsible for developing and releasing the deadly virus were still at-large. Law enforcement agencies around the world pursued leads generated mostly from anonymous tips. The tips typically arose from alleged sightings of the two known Orbis Novus members. Photos of James "Frank" Cole appeared on televisions and in newspapers worldwide, as well as being plastered all over the internet. He was supposedly spotted in a nightclub in Jerusalem and in a laundromat in Melbourne—on the same day. Authorities also distributed photos of Natalie Wu Lan in the hopes that someone might have seen her somewhere outside of her hometown of Dallas in recent months. Instead, random people from around the globe called into hotlines with claims of having seen her alive and well—weeks after her death. As of December 14th, none of the leads had proved useful.

In the early morning hours of that day, only the FBI, NCA, and Guatemalan government were aware of a possible site for the League of Orbis Novus within the tiny Central American nation. They considered the intelligence to be weak and its source unreliable. He was a troubled, shunned research scientist who had investigated a small outbreak of an illness in a northern village several months earlier, and now suspected a connection. He disappeared before authorities had a chance to question him. Nevertheless, no stone would be left unturned.

30

Since Jack's painful meeting with the League of Orbis Novus, Frank had brought him eight meals and emptied the copper pot four more times—all without saying much of anything. On one occasion, Jack was taken to a small locker room and permitted to shower while his clothes were laundered, yet even then the two men exchanged few words. On the day before the shower, Frank left two quasi-recent copies of Sports Illustrated magazine in the room. Jack had since studied every word cover to cover, though most of his time was still consumed by the French version of *Les Misérables*, which he was nearly halfway through. That morning he deciphered enough to know that young Cosette and Marius were meeting secretly in her garden, and that she informed her new boyfriend that she might be moving to England. He couldn't help but picture himself and Gina in the roles, though he recalled that the two protagonists never make it to England.

Fear of the unknown had slowly yielded to boredom. The only person other than Frank with whom he had had any contact since the agonizing day of his toenail extractions was the blonde Russian woman. She came into his room two days after the ordeal and changed his bandages. When she asked Jack how he was feeling, he responded with a question.

"How much longer will I be here?"

"I don't know," she replied. "Not long, perhaps."

"Why are you all still here?"

"No more questions."

Now it was two copper pots later, and his toes were feeling a little better. He was able to put his dirty socks and shoes over the bandages and move around the room without too much pain. He decided to implement an exercise routine consisting of pushups, sit-ups, and knee-bends. There was just enough room in the storage closet between the cot and the sink to accomplish the maneuvers without banging his head on one or the other.

He had also implemented a routine for turning the light on and off, in the hopes of keeping his circadian rhythm intact and improving his sleep. He would turn the light off following the second meal, and turn it on again upon waking. He had no idea if his cycle was in sync with the outside world, but he felt as though he was sleeping a little more deeply during his artificial nighttime hours.

It was during his seventh night that he woke to the sound of the key unlocking the door. He quickly sprang up and sat on the edge of his cot. This was an unexpected visit, and he was somewhat relieved to see that it was Frank's silhouette in the dimly-lit hallway. He didn't know why Frank's presence invoked a feeling of security—he certainly had no reason to trust him. Frank entered the room and quietly closed the door behind him before turning on the light.

"Put your shoes on," he said quietly.

Jack did not ask why. He didn't think Frank would give him an honest answer, and a part of him didn't want to know anyway. He tied his shoelaces and stood up. He noticed that Frank was wearing the same stylish jacket he had worn in London. It was very warm in the building, thought Jack—there was no need for a coat.

"Sit down," said Frank. He leaned back against the door and folded his arms while Jack sat down on the bed and stared at the floor. "And stay quiet."

Jack could no longer contain his curiosity. "What's going on?" he whispered.

"We're getting out of here," replied Frank.

"You're releasing me?"

"No. You and I are leaving."

"I don't understand."

Frank turned and put his ear to the door, then carefully locked it from the inside using his key. He took a step toward the bed, causing Jack to recoil instinctively. "I'm supposed to kill you in a few hours.

And after you're dead, Cedric will kill me."

"Why would he kill you?"

"Those are his orders. I'm a liability now—just like you. You and I know too much, and too many people know who we are."

Jack took a moment to process what Frank was saying. "The obituary that Wu Lan sent to the *Chronicle*?"

"Yeah. My face is plastered on every television in the world."

Jack's heart began to race. The notion of escaping energized him, though he inferred from Frank's demeanor that it would not be easy. Frank had always appeared indomitable and unflappable; now he looked nervous, if not frightened. Nevertheless, Jack was grateful to have an ally, even if the alliance stood on the shaky foundation of a common enemy.

"What's the plan?" asked Jack.

"The plan is that you shut up and we wait. I'll tell you what to do when the time comes."

They waited in silence for a few minutes. It seemed like hours to Jack. His nerves got the better of his judgement and he broke the silence with a misguided attempt to solidify a bond with his captor.

"I understand why you did this," he whispered. "but did you know that so many people would die? Do you regret it?" He definitely regretted asking the question as soon as the words left his mouth. He winced in response to his recklessness, as if bracing for Frank to strike him. To his relief, Frank merely stared at him inquisitively for a moment. Jack knew he had dodged a bullet and returned his gaze to the floor.

A soft knocking on the door came a few minutes later, in the form of three evenly-spaced taps. Frank reached into his inside jacket pocket and pulled out a matte black nine-millimeter handgun. Then he carefully unlocked the door and cracked it open. After peering into the hallway, he opened the door halfway and a large figure scurried inside, after which he closed the door and locked it.

Jack recoiled in fear and confusion upon seeing Cedric's hulking body engulf the room. Here was the very man that Frank said would kill him, yet Frank did nothing except return his gun to his pocket. Frank must have noticed Jack's apprehension.

"Relax," said Frank. "He's with us."

The two henchmen whispered back and forth for a couple of

minutes. Jack could only make out a few of the murmured words, but it was obvious from their facial expressions that their scheme was very intricate, very risky, or both. When their conversation concluded, they drew their weapons and loaded rounds into the chambers.

Frank turned to Jack. "Stay behind me, do exactly as I tell you, and don't make a sound."

Cedric turned off the light in the storage room, then opened the door slowly and slipped out into the hallway. Frank immediately followed and motioned for Jack to do the same. Jack could see very little while his eyes adjusted to the darkness. There were no windows in the corridor and the overhead lights were off. The only source of light came from around the corner in the opposite direction whence they headed. Jack's toes began to throb with each step and he tried to favor the back of his feet. The three men walked softly and deliberately to the end of the hallway, where Cedric stopped in front of a closed door. He tapped on it softly three times. When there was no response, he looked at Frank, as if asking for guidance. Frank nodded.

Cedric slowly turned the doorknob and gently pushed the door open as Frank motioned Jack to move away. They waited against the wall as Cedric slipped into the dark room and closed the door behind him. Jack could see the light come on from the space between the bottom of the door and the floor. Then it quickly went off again. Cedric cracked open the door, extended his arm through the opening and gestured to Frank. Frank and Jack went inside. When the door was closed once again, Cedric turned on the light.

The room appeared to be a small office. There were two desks, two chairs, and whiteboards on two walls. The whiteboards were clean, and the desktops were bare, save for a coffee mug full of pens and pencils on one. There was a single window on the far wall. The venetian blinds covering it were closed, though Jack could still see that it was dark outside. Standing next to the window was the Russian woman who had bandaged Jack's toes. She was wearing black jeans and a gray sweatshirt. She appeared to be far more jittery than Frank or Cedric.

"Why didn't you open the door?" asked Frank quietly.

"I'm sorry. I thought that you would just come inside," replied the woman.

"Put on your coat," said Frank. The woman picked up a white lab coat that was draped over one of the desk chairs and put it on.

Cedric checked his wristwatch. "We must go now."

"Sit there," Frank said to Jack, pointing to one of the chairs. Then he looked at the woman. "We'll be right back."

The woman sat down in the opposite chair while the two henchmen turned off the light and slipped back into the hallway, closing the door behind them. There was just enough moonlight seeping in between the horizontal blinds to illuminate the woman's face. Jack wheeled his chair close to hers.

"What's your name?" he asked in a whisper.

She hesitated. "Katarina."

"Katarina, I might be less of a liability if I knew exactly what was happening."

"We have to leave here."

"I got that part already. Why can't we just walk out of here?"

She froze once again. "It isn't safe. The group is divided."

"Divided how?"

She ignored his question and sighed. "It was not supposed to be this way."

"How so?"

Now she looked at him squarely and continued as if she was relieving her conscience of a heavy burden. "We started out working on a virus that would simply make opioids ineffective—harmless. Then everything changed… and now, this. This is not what I agreed to do."

"What are you talking about?"

Before Jack could pursue his line of questioning further, the door opened once again. He presumed that the division to which the Russian woman referred was the question of whether he and Frank would live or die, and that Cedric and Katarina were apparently on the side of the good guys. He had no idea how many others there were inside the building, and how many of them wished him dead. The question he most wanted to ask his new confederates is why the league still existed at all, given that their mission was accomplished days ago. Perhaps it was finally disbanding, which explained their desire to tie up loose ends, and included killing Frank and him.

The answer would have to wait. Frank shined a flashlight on Jack and signaled for him and Katarina to follow. Cedric led the way back down the corridor in the direction of Jack's janitorial closet. Frank walked directly behind Cedric while holding his handgun at the ready.

Jack noted that he resembled the highly-trained law enforcement officer that he once was. Katarina and Jack followed a few steps behind. The four insurgents passed Jack's room and headed toward the corner from which the light emanated. Cedric stopped just short of the illuminated intersection and carefully peeked around the corner. He turned back to Frank and whispered, "He's there."

Frank stowed his pistol into his jacket pocket and grabbed Jack's arm just underneath the shoulder. "You're my prisoner," he said. "Look the part." After exchanging glances with Katarina and Cedric, the group proceeded around the corner.

The corridor was empty except for a large man standing guard near a door. The sentry wore black boots, pants, and a sweater that matched his thick hair and dark beard. Jack instantly recognized him as the man from the park bench in Dayton—the guy who held his father's dog while he met with Frank in the SUV. The man greeted the others in an accent that suggested Middle Eastern origins. Cedric returned the greeting as he passed then suddenly pivoted and struck the man squarely in the jaw, knocking him to the floor. Before the stunned victim could regain his senses, Cedric dove on top of him and locked his head in a chokehold. Jack could not determine if it was the result of asphyxiation or a snapped neck, but the man soon lay lifeless on the cold floor. Katarina walked over to the man with a hypodermic syringe at the ready. Cedric shook his head, and she returned the needle to a pocket in her lab coat. It wasn't needed.

Jack had never seen a person die in his presence. He was not at the hospital when his mother passed away, and her death was all but expected by that time. Under ordinary circumstances, he might have been overwhelmed with consternation; however, the flow of adrenalin spurred by his own precarious situation helped him to discard the violence in front of him, or at least delay its impact. Still, he wondered why Cedric could not have simply rendered the man unconscious.

"Did he have to kill him?" he whispered to Frank.

"Yes."

The door which the sentry had guarded led to the grounds outside the facility, as seen through a small glass window on it. Despite the chain and padlock on the door, Jack assumed that they would depart through it, and was surprised when the group continued down the corridor.

"We're not leaving through there?" he asked.

"It's not that simple," replied Frank as he grabbed Jack's arm again. "Now shut up."

In spite of his increasing curiosity and anxiety in the wake of Frank's vague response, Jack thought it wise to hold his tongue. The group turned a corner and opened a door into another hallway. This one was short, with just two doors on either side before dead-ending into a cinderblock wall. Another burly man, albeit a little smaller than the previous victim, stood with his back against the wall.

The redheaded guard seemed surprised to see Jack. "What's he doing here?" he asked in a British accent.

Cedric quickly approached the man. "Doctor Scott wants to see him." As soon as the words left his mouth, Cedric thrust his fist into the man's throat. The man sunk to the floor, slowed by the friction of his back rubbing against the wall. Katarina hurried over and injected him with the syringe. He died within seconds.

Suddenly, and as if they had rehearsed the tactic hundreds of times, Frank and Cedric each kicked open one of the two doors on either side of the hall, then simultaneously bounded into the rooms. They appeared confounded to find them both empty. Frank quickly corralled his three cohorts into one of the rooms. It was a small bedroom with no outside windows. In addition to a single bed, there was a small dresser and desk. A few sundry items lay on the dresser.

Frank spoke in his normal volume. "Do you think they know?"

"They must be waiting for us," said Katarina. She was clearly more distraught than her male companions.

"It is possible they have left the facility," suggested Cedric.

"We can leave too," said Katarina. "Let's go right now, Frank." She was almost pleading with him.

"We can't leave without it," said Frank. "No matter what the cost. We knew that going into this."

Jack was not about to interject himself into the deliberation, nor did he need to inquire about what the "cost" was. He had no choice but to trust his captors-turned-protectors.

"Let's go get it," said Frank. He reached into another pocket and pulled out a small handgun, which he gave to Katarina. She reluctantly accepted the offering, then checked the sidearm with the comportment of an experienced handler. Frank and Cedric re-checked their own weapons as well, before venturing back into the hallway.

The foursome backtracked toward the first corpse, which still lay on the floor undisturbed. From there Frank led them in the opposite direction and stopped outside a large metal door. He retrieved a key from his pants pocket and looked to the others for confirmation before putting it into the lock. He threw the door open then quickly stepped to the side, as if anticipating a violent response to his action. There was none.

The room was completely dark. Cedric took a few steps inside, followed by Frank and Katarina. Jack had no desire to remain alone in the hallway, so he stuck close to Katarina's heels. Rather than switching on the overhead light, Cedric turned on his flashlight. The narrow beam of light revealed a shocking scene in its path. Facing Cedric and about ten paces away, was a man holding a gun pointed directly at him.

The man fired as soon as the light hit him. The muzzle flash briefly revealed a room full of people brandishing weapons. Cedric fell immediately upon absorbing the bullet. His flashlight crashed to the floor and went dark. Within a second of the first shot, others rang out, each alighting the surroundings for a microsecond, like a vivid lightning storm or a strobe light. The two factions traded gunfire, with each shot aimed in the direction of an opposing muzzle flash. Each burst of light briefly illuminated the contents of the room, revealing it to be a scientific laboratory.

Jack dove to the floor and took cover next to a cabinet that he felt in front of him. He considered crawling to the door, then decided it would be too dangerous. He instinctively covered his head with his hands, as if they might somehow deflect an incoming bullet.

After about thirty seconds and more than forty rounds of blind fire, the room lights came on. Jack peeked upward to see Frank near the door, still standing. It was he who had flipped the light switch. Frank quickly darted and ducked while firing at targets Jack could not see. Next, he ran out of Jack's sight line and fired several more shots. Then everything went quiet, except for the gurgles and groans of people clutching to life.

"Jack," said a familiar voice from across the room. "Get up." Jack slowly rose to see Frank as the lone person standing. The room was strewn with bloodied bodies. One near Frank was attempting to crawl toward the door. Frank pointed his nine-millimeter at the man's head and pulled the trigger. Then he walked over to another wounded person and repeated the task. It was the older woman—the presumed leader of Orbis Novus. Jack recognized some of the other bodies as well. Both of the men who had presided over his torture were among them—the Latino and the American.

Cedric's lifeless body lay in the exact spot where it fell upon turning on his flashlight. A pool of blood surrounded the gunshot wound in his head. Jack took a step toward Frank but was distracted by the sound of heavy breathing to his left. There, Katarina sat on the floor with her back propped up against the wall. Her hand covered a wound on her lower chest, desperately trying to stem the flow of blood. Jack stooped down to offer whatever aid he could, but Frank rushed over and pushed him aside.

"Where is it?" he asked her urgently.

Katarina looked down toward her wound.

"There's no time for that. You need to tell me where it is, right now," Frank demanded.

Katarina slowly gestured toward a locked cabinet nearby with a nod of her head. "There," she murmured. Frank rushed over to the cabinet and shattered the glass with the butt of his pistol. He grabbed a plastic container and quickly returned to Katarina.

"Is this all of it?"

Katarina struggled to respond.

"Is this all of it?!" repeated Frank.

"Yes," gurgled Katarina as her mouth filled with blood.

Frank shoved the plastic box in front of her face. "Look! Are you sure?" Katarina's eyes rolled up into her head as she drew her last breath. Frank stood up and relaxed for the first time since he entered Jack's janitorial closet less than twenty-minutes earlier. After a heavy sigh, he laid his gun on a nearby table, then broke the seal on the plastic box and opened it.

"What is that?" asked Jack.

"Something bad."

Despite Frank's ambiguous reply, Jack surmised that the contents of the box were the likely cause of the league's dissension and the reason it had not disbanded following the release of the opioid superbug. Frank lifted a vial from the container then looked around the lab, as if searching for something.

"We have to destroy these," he said. He put the vial back into the box, which he carried over to a nearby sink. "But I'm not sure how to do that."

Jack walked over to him. "Can't you just dump it down the sink?"

"Some of this stuff isn't in a liquid form."

"What is it?"

The men were too distracted to notice that someone else had entered the room.

"It's the answer to humankind's greatest blunder," said the woman's voice. Jack looked up to see Adimu standing just inside the door. She pointed an Uzi submachine gun directly at them, hanging from her shoulder by a narrow strap. "Put it down and step away from the sink," she added calmly. Frank complied with her order and backed away slowly.

The sight of Adimu befuddled Jack. She had earned his trust with her profound sympathy in the wake of his torture. Although she was now pointing a weapon at him, a part of him felt that she wouldn't hurt him. She merely wanted what was in the plastic box. Conversely, Frank had risked his own life to protect and free him. He also seemed willing to give his life in order to destroy the contents of the box. Jack's two supposed allies were now at odds.

Adimu carefully entered the room and surveyed the carnage. "Did you forget to count the bodies, Frank? You missed one."

"I can't let you leave here with that," said Frank, gesturing to the plastic container on the table.

"And yet I am the one holding the weapon," Adimu said coolly. There was no sign of the tearful empathy she displayed earlier. Jack now suspected that it had all been an act. He had fallen hard for her good-cop routine.

"You know that this is the right thing to do," continued Adimu. "You signed up for this."

"Not for this," said Frank. "It was only supposed to be the opioids. This thing will kill millions of people."

Adimu laughed. "Of course, it will. And your President Truman knew that he would kill thousands with his atom bomb to save a million more. This is no different. We will save hundreds of millions."

Frank glanced at Jack. Jack sensed that he was looking for some kind of assistance—perhaps a distraction.

"What is this stuff?" asked Jack.

"A new virus," said Adimu. "It will rid the world of its deadliest pestilence."

"What's that?"

"Alcohol."

"Alcohol?"

"Ethyl alcohol—beer, wine, and spirits," said Adimu. "This was our ultimate goal all along."

"How can you do that?" implored Jack. "You've already killed thousands of people."

"No, Jack. We've killed *hundreds* of thousands of people, but how many more have we saved?" said Adimu. Jack could see that she would be more than willing to sacrifice one or two more for the cause.

"Imagine a world without alcohol," she continued. "Look at all of the evil things that happen under its influence: murder, rape, child abuse, spousal abuse, traffic fatalities, unwanted pregnancies, fetal alcohol syndrome—just to name a few. Millions of lives will be saved every year. This is the world's panacea."

"How many people will die?" asked Jack.

"Including the two of you? Millions. But you are sacrificing yourself to save countless others. You should be very proud. You are the—"

Before she could finish, Frank lunged for his pistol lying on the table nearby. Adimu reacted swiftly and riddled him with bullets. Frank fell to the ground, already near death. When Adimu walked over to his body, Jack bolted for the door. He made it to the corridor as bullets struck the wall behind him. Remembering that the door he passed earlier was locked, he headed in the opposite direction from which they had come, in the hopes of finding the front entrance. He could hear Adimu slamming a new magazine into her gun as he rounded a second corner. A large glass door stood fifty feet in front him.

In that very moment the nerves in his toes reminded him that they no longer had toenails protecting them. Adrenaline had effectively blocked the pain for the initial moments of his flight, yet now it took every ounce of will he could muster to stay on his feet. He began to bounce, as if running over hot coals.

And suddenly there was something peculiar about the door—so strange a sight that he thought it was a trick of the light. As the door grew closer, he could see that the vision was real. There was a man peering in from the outside. The man tried to open the door but it was locked from the inside by a deadbolt. Jack reached the door and unlocked the bolt. As he opened the door, the stranger started to enter. Jack recoiled upon seeing that the man was brandishing a small gun. For all he knew, this was just another thug hired by Orbis Novus.

The man slipped inside. "Are you Jack?"

"Yes," replied Jack as he winced in pain. His toes began to throb as soon as he stopped moving. "We have to get out."

The man remained in the doorway. "I'm here to help you," he said.

Adimu's voice squelched their introduction. "Stop." She stood at the far end of the corridor and aimed her Uzi at the men. "Come inside." Her sober expression turned to astonishment upon seeing the new arrival, whom she appeared to recognize. The look of amazement quickly morphed into a wry smile. "Doctor Sydney Carter. I never expected to see you here. Did you come to revel in your creation?"

Sydney appeared equally perplexed as he entered the hallway. He surrendered, raising his hands high in the air. One still held his pistol. "Adimu? You're behind this?"

"We merely built upon your theories, doctor. You are the genius behind all of this. You taught us well."

"I didn't teach you to murder people."

"It is not murder. It is an unavoidable sacrifice, and a small price to pay for the good that we have done for the future of mankind."

"And the outbreak here last summer—that was you?"

"That was one of several variations we tested. It reacted with opioids effectively but was too weak to survive outside of a host. I trust Rudy took care of you during your visit? I was in Nevada at the time."

"He sent me home after one day."

"Yes, yes," Adimu said with a laugh. "We could not allow you to get too close. But why are you here now? Frankly, I am surprised you are not sleeping in a gutter somewhere."

"I came to get him," replied Sydney, pointing to Jack. "You've done what you wanted to do, so let him leave with me."

"But we are just getting started, Doctor Carter. Oh—are you unaware? We have a new virus to unleash."

"It reacts with alcohol," added Jack.

"Yes, it does," said Adimu. "I think you would be most interested in it, Doctor Carter."

"Alcohol? That's impossible," said Sydney.

"But you know that it *is* possible," said Adimu. "Imagine how your life would have turned out without the demons of alcohol. You would still have your job and your family. You of all people should understand why we are doing this."

Sydney looked around the empty corridor. "Who is 'we'?" he asked. "Where is Rudy Jimenez?"

"I'm afraid our family had a little squabble. It's a shame, really. We had some of the brightest minds from all over the world. Who knows what else we might have accomplished together?" She took a deep breath. "I'm sorry, Doctor Carter, but I have no more time for this reunion."

"Let Jack go. I'll be your hostage."

"Hostage? Why on Earth would I need a hostage?"

Sydney looked over his shoulder at the dark, early morning sky. "I've alerted the police. They're on their way."

Adimu paused in thought. Sydney's bluff appeared to be working. "Do as I say," she told Sydney, "and I'll release Jack."

"Okay."

"Put down your pistol and slide it toward me."

Sydney complied. Adimu kicked the handgun farther behind her.

"Now," said Adimu, "walk toward me—slowly."

Sydney stepped toward Adimu as Jack looked on near the front door. Sydney stopped less than two feet away from the muzzle of Adimu's machine gun. Adimu reached into her pocket and pulled out a device resembling a large pen. She immediately sprayed mist all over Sydney's face and her own. Sydney jumped backward, but it was too late.

Adimu drew in a deep breath and stepped closer to Sydney. "Ah, now we are the Adam and Eve of a new civilization."

Sydney began to tremble. "Now let him go," he murmured.

"I am afraid I cannot do that," said Adimu as she pointed her weapon toward Jack. Sydney reached his hand behind his back and underneath his shirt, then stepped toward Adimu and spoke softly into her ear.

"You shouldn't trust a man who has nothing left to lose."

He then thrust the hunting knife into her abdomen. She released her Uzi and it dangled from the strap on her shoulder. Sydney pulled out the knife and stabbed her again—this time in the chest. She fell to the floor in agony.

"Thanks Manuel," Sydney mumbled to himself.

Jack started toward Sydney.

"Stay where you are," said Sydney. He extended his hand toward Jack while his eyes remained fixated on the dying woman.

"You know her?" asked Jack.

Sydney knelt down beside Adimu as she drew her final breath. "She worked for me a long time ago."

"I'm sorry."

"Don't be," said Sydney as he picked up the Uzi. "Who else is here?"

"I think everybody else is dead."

"Then you need to get out of here," Sydney said sternly. "Go get the police or whatever it is they have around here."

"Aren't they on their way?"

"No. I was bluffing."

"Are you coming?"

"I'm infected."

"What are you gonna do?" asked Jack.

Sydney turned and looked at Jack. "I don't know."

31

Gina Alvarez managed to wedge a few hours of sleep into her compacted travel schedule. It was well after midnight local time when she and Special Agent Shawn Zuroski arrived at the hotel in Guatemala City. Less than five hours later she and her partner sipped from paper cups of coffee in the hotel lobby, awaiting their ride.

"The coffee is really good here," said Shawn. "The Guatemalan highlands produce some of the world's finest coffee."

"How do you know that?" asked Gina.

Shawn showed her his smartphone display. "Wikipedia."

Gina took an analytical sip from her cup. "I can't tell any difference."

"I've acquired a taste for fine coffee," proffered Shawn. "You wouldn't understand."

"That explains why you spend six dollars for a cup in Vegas."

Shawn ignored her jab and pulled up another page in his browser. "Maybe we can visit the Coffee District while we're here."

"Sure. We can check out the emperor's new clothes too."

Shawn noticed a Toyota Camry pull up to the hotel's main entrance, which was otherwise deserted. An Anglo-looking man dressed in a gray suit hopped out. "I'm guessing that's our contact," he said. Sure enough, the young attaché entered the lobby and made a beeline for the agents.

"Agents Alvarez and Zuroski?" he asked. After the agents confirmed, he introduced himself as Gerald Patterson with the State

Department. "Call me Pat," he said.

Pat drove them a short distance through the moderate, pre-dawn traffic to a police station that also served as the barracks for Guatemala's PNC SWAT. Waiting for them there was the Director General of the PNC and the leader of the SWAT group, a major by the name of Gutierrez. The latter updated the agents on the situation, as Shawn translated for Gina. The PNC had been unable to locate Sydney Carter, but they had narrowed down the list of possible Orbis Novus facilities near the village of Tanchi to two buildings. It must not have been too difficult, thought Gina, as there were only two buildings visible on the satellite map image. The major had his sights set on a particular building because it was deep in the jungle and not far from where the medical response team had set up its camp for the outbreak during the previous summer. It had been built in the eighties as a training facility for the army and had long since been sold to a private owner.

Shawn asked if the PNC had contacted any of the members of the outbreak response team, particularly a man named Jimenez.

"We did not," replied the Director General in English. "We did not wish to tip him off, in case he is involved. We confirmed that he has been seen in Tanchi lately."

Gina wondered how they could confirm his location without tipping him off, but kept her skepticism to herself. "Is there any reason for him to be up there?" she asked.

"Not according to the health ministry," said the director. "But Doctor Jimenez works for a private international firm. He could be there for any number of reasons."

Shawn and Gina looked at each other, sharing the same thought. The fact that Jimenez worked for an international firm was a significant red flag. It would have been nice to investigate his employer, but there was no more time.

The major took command of the conversation once again, and briefed the Americans on his plan for taking control of the suspected facility. The SWAT members and observers would helicopter to the city of Coban, where vehicles would be waiting to take them to the site. Timing was critical for the daylight assault, and the major hoped to secure the building before 8 a.m. They were soon making their way to nearby choppers.

Gina was impressed by the polish and professionalism of the SWAT members. They were equally impressed by the attractive FBI agent and insisted on addressing her in Spanish. She directed them to her fair-skinned partner of Irish and Polish descent to translate. Major Gutierrez was the latest to engage her.

"He says that his team trained in New York," Shawn translated to Gina as they boarded one of the three Blackhawk helicopters. "He loves the Yankees."

Everything went more or less in accordance with the major's elemental, brute-force plan. In Coban they transferred into a squad of jeeps and traversed a narrow road into the jungle highlands. Forty-five minutes later they passed by a small pasture, and the major said something to Shawn.

"This is where the medical team set up their trailers last summer," he relayed to Gina. "It's only a little farther."

Sure enough, the convoy came to a halt less than a mile down the dirt road and the SWAT members sprang into action. The sight of their tactics invoked a feeling of déjà vu within Gina. Although the terrain was vastly different, the scene seemed eerily similar to the raid on the desert facility in Nevada. That operation had yielded nothing, and she knew that this one was a greater longshot. Even if it was a facility for Orbis Novus—itself a remote possibility—she surmised that they would find nothing but another box of rocks. The league always seemed to be two steps ahead of them.

She jogged along the rear of the assault formation with Shawn and Pat. The Guatemalans didn't seem to mind that the Americans were practically shoulder-to-shoulder with them. Although she carried no weapon, Gina felt very safe amid the well-armed unit. The team entered a cleared area, where an old brick building came into view. Rather than surround the facility in accordance with the plan, the SWAT members suddenly stopped and dropped into defensive positions with their automatic rifles at the ready. There was a man sitting in the grass about twenty meters before them. He sat next to a walkway leading to a large glass door at the front of the building. The man seemed unfazed by the arrival of the police and did nothing other than slowly raise his hands in the air. There were no signs of any other activity in the area.

"Oh my god," proclaimed Gina. "That's Jack Kurry."

Shawn looked at her in disbelief. "Are you kidding me?"

"Maybe it's a trap," suggested Pat.

The Americans walked over to the major, who was barking out commands to Jack in broken English.

Jack's eyes lit up when he saw Gina. He stood up on his painful toes. "Gina?"

The major asked Shawn if the man was Sydney Carter. Shawn informed him that it was Jack Kurry, then he turned to Jack and shouted, "Mr. Kurry, is anybody there with you?"

"They're all dead," replied Jack. "I mean, all but one."

"Is it safe for us to approach you?"

"I guess so," said Jack indifferently. The agents started toward him, then a sudden realization poured over his face. "Wait!" he implored. "Don't come near me. I might be infected."

"We're all infected, Jack—uh, Mr. Kurry," said Gina. "It's okay." She now stood a few meters away from him. The other two Americans were just behind her, while the SWAT members held their positions several meters back. They appeared content to allow the Americans to interrogate Jack, especially after hearing the now-universal word "infected." Gina maintained a professional demeanor in front of her peers, though inside she was brimming with relief and joy in finding Jack alive and well.

"No, this is something different. Stay there," demanded Jack. He appeared hesitant to elaborate. "I need to speak with you in private."

"How can we do that if I can't come any closer?" asked Gina.

"Who are these guys with you?"

"This is Special Agent Zuroski, and this is Pat... um…"

"Gerald Patterson, from the embassy," added Pat.

Gina glanced at Pat apologetically for forgetting his name, then returned to Jack. "Just talk to us quietly. The soldiers will stay back there."

"First of all," began Jack in a loud whisper. "Where am I?"

"You're near the village of Tanchi," said Pat.

"That really doesn't help me. *Where* am I?"

"Guatemala," answered Gina.

Jack proceeded to convey everything he had witnessed since his abduction in London. The eyes of his small audience widened when he told them about the rift in the league. Their jaws dropped as he described the bloody firefight that had transpired just a few hours earlier. Shawn and Pat took a reflexive step backward when Jack informed them of the new virus. After a few minutes, the major had grown impatient.

"We can't tell him about this new virus," Gina whispered to Shawn and Pat when she saw the SWAT commander approaching. "Speak to him in generalities while I try to get in touch with Daryll." She looked at her phone and sighed. "I have no signal here."

Pat pulled a device out of his pocket. "Here. Use my sat phone."

Gina walked away and spoke to Daryll while Shawn brought the major up to speed. Jack sat down again, remaining isolated in his self-imposed quarantine. Shawn told the major that there was a deadly contagion inside the building, and that it was probably anthrax. He said that Sydney Carter was last seen in the building, and added that he was likely infected with the anthrax bacteria. In response to the major's inquiry about the man sitting in the grass, Shawn told him that Jack probably was not infected, but they needed to make certain.

The major had heard enough. He ordered his men to surround the building at a safe distance, then radioed back to PNC headquarters for guidance. Within two hours, several helicopters landed nearby and the area was soon swarming with police, scientists, and government officials. An armed hazmat team prepared to secure the building while two other men in futuristic-looking protective suits fetched Jack and escorted him into a large white tent they had hastily pitched.

Gina, Shawn, and Pat stood by as spectators. "You told him it was anthrax?" said Gina.

"I had to think on my feet," replied Shawn. "I didn't want them entering the building."

"Yeah, but *anthrax*?" she repeated.

"Hey—it worked. The higher-ups can handle it from here."

Pat pointed to the tent into which Jack was sequestered. "What happens to him?"

"I don't know," replied Gina.

"Do you think he has it?" asked Shawn. At that moment the gravity of their secret set it. In the grand scheme, it really didn't matter if Jack was infected. The real issue was containing the new virus. They exchanged mortified glances with each other.

"If it ever got out…" Pat wondered aloud.

"Yeah, I know," said Gina. She managed to peel herself away from

Shawn and Pat after a while and made her way over to Jack's containment tent. The door was zipped shut, so she walked around to the rear.

"Jack?" she called out softly.

"Hey," came his voice from the other side of the plastic.

"Are you alone?"

"Yeah."

"It's really good to see you," she said. "Although, it might be a while before I can see you again."

"I know. This really sucks. How did you find me?"

"The man you said is inside the building—Sydney Carter. He told us."

"Who is that guy? I'm pretty sure he saved my life."

"He's a scientist. We have no idea what he's doing here, but we hope to have a chance to speak with him real soon."

"Yeah—don't get too close to him," said Jack.

"Do you think you might be infected too?"

"No. I just didn't want to take any chances."

They spoke for a few minutes before Gina heard Pat calling her name. The U.S. ambassador had arrived with an entourage of state department lackeys.

"I have to go," she told Jack. "I'll be in touch as soon as I can."

"Thanks," said Jack, then he quickly followed up. "Hey, is this a date?"

"Why, are you keeping count?"

"I just want to know how well our relationship is progressing."

"Hmm. I'd say that finding you alive is a big step forward. See you later."

"I feel obligated to tell you that I have no toenails. Hey - would you do me a favor and call my father?"

"Of course."

Gina kept her word and contacted Don Kurry as soon as she returned to the hotel. She tried to sound as professional as she could, though Don's elation was contagious. The conversation was brief, for she was unable to tell him much about the schedule for Jack's return home. Some of that was due to secrecy, though it was mostly because she didn't know.

Later that evening, Gina and Shawn sat in Gina's hotel room and spoke with Daryll Jameson on the phone. Despite being the two FBI agents on site in Guatemala, their boss now seemed to know much more than they did. He told them that the facility had been completely sanitized, meaning that it was burned to the ground. This was done in defiance of protestations from the U.S. State Department, which had requested the site to remain intact pending the arrival of their investigative team. Instead, the Guatemalans chose to rid themselves of the suspected anthrax threat. Nevertheless, the hazmat team took hundreds of photographs before torching the building. The local authorities also decided to incinerate the twelve bodies found inside. They were cremated on site, though not before DNA samples were carefully collected.

The purported existence of the new "alcohol virus" was now held at the highest levels of secrecy within the U.S. government. As expected, Daryll reminded his junior agents of their obligations and said little more about the subject. Gina figured that the matter was already in the President's hands. She asked about the fate of Jack Kurry. Daryll told her that arrangements were being made to transport him to the States, where he would remain in quarantine until it could be confirmed that he had not contracted the new virus. Gina wondered how they could possibly know, other than the obvious test, which could prove deadly.

"And what about Sydney Carter?" asked Shawn.

"There's still no trace of him," said Daryll. "He's gone."

32

Two weeks later, Gina found herself back in Las Vegas and nearing the onset of a well-earned vacation. She planned to head to the airport directly from the office, leaving promptly after lunch. She was supposed to be wrapping up her analysis of phone records for the Poison Ivy case, yet she found it difficult to focus. Her officemate was equally distracted, though he had no vacation pending.

"They finally identified the last one," announced Shawn while pointing to his web browser. "Doctor Martyna Lehmann. A sixty-three-year-old chemist from Berlin. They think she was the ring leader."

Gina walked over and perused the article over Shawn's shoulder. "I wonder what her motive was?"

"Doesn't say."

"That can't be all of them. There must be others out there who participated one way or another but weren't in Guatemala that night."

"Probably," agreed Shawn. "From what I hear, all of the leads have dried up. They'll keep searching, though, at least until the world forgets."

"Is there any mention of… you-know-who in that article?"

"Nope."

Gina lowered her voice. "At this point… I mean, you would have to assume that he's dead, right?"

"Let's hope so," whispered Shawn. "Something would have happened by now."

"*Something?* That's an understatement."

"I'm pretty sure we're in the clear," said Shawn with no hint of conviction.

Gina nodded, if only to reassure her coworker. She had no knowledge of Sydney Carter's status and hoped that she never would. If he ever surfaced alive, it would likely prove cataclysmic for the world—a catastrophe hundreds of times worse than the Gemini Viruses. She returned to her desk and continued to fidget. Shawn could see how anxious she was, and he had long since suspected why. It had nothing to do with Sydney Carter.

"Why don't you just go to the airport now and eat lunch there?" he suggested.

"Good idea." It was the final ounce of persuasion she needed. She immediately packed her things and shutdown her computer. "See you next week."

Shawn offered one final morsel of advice. "You might want to stop and see Daryll before you go—if you know what I mean."

Gina shrugged, then nodded. She had been avoiding the inevitable conversation, yet Shawn was correct—it would make her trip a lot more relaxing if everything was out in the open. A minute later she sat in a chair in front of the senior agent's desk. She told him the truth, though not without a little spin.

"I've been corresponding with Jack Kurry on a personal level," she blurted.

Daryll kept his eyes fixed on his computer and drew a sip from his coffee mug. "Is that a fact?" he said in a rhetorical monotone. He already suspected as much, and he wanted her to know it. "And how long has this personal correspondence been going on?"

"Well, we spent several hours together in my car before December, but that was strictly professional. That is to say, we *might* have talked about some personal subjects to pass the time… Um, we also spoke in London… and I *think* we even got together for dinner before he—"

"You know what, Agent Alvarez?" interrupted Daryll. "I don't want to know. In fact, I'm gonna pretend that this conversation never happened." He turned his attention back to his computer. "Enjoy your trip to Georgia—I assume that's where you're going."

"Okay, but should I—"

"Whoa. What part of 'I don't want to know' did you not understand?" His eyes once again conveyed the frustration of a father trying to talk sense into his beloved daughter. "Look, I hope that you and whoever you're meeting there hit it off. Maybe you'll have a nice relationship going forward." He leaned in. "Did you hear me? I said '*going forward*'."

Gina stood up to leave. "Roger that—and thanks."

Daryll held up his hand and returned his gaze to his computer display. "Uh, uh, uh—no, no, no. Don't thank me. I didn't *do* anything because I didn't *know* anything."

"Understood." She looked as if she wanted to say something else.

Daryll finally looked at her. "Alvarez! Why are you still here?"

She hurried out with an irrepressible grin on her face.

It was nearly 11 p.m. when Gina's plane landed in Atlanta on December 22nd. The scene at the airport sharply contrasted with her experience the last time she passed through it, barely a few weeks earlier. It was once again brimming with scurrying travelers who appeared oblivious to the fateful events that had so recently scarred the world forever. She stood for a moment and took in a panoramic view of the activity surrounding her, simultaneously admiring and lamenting the human capacity to adapt and forget.

She spent the night in an airport hotel then rented a car and drove down to Fort Benning in the morning. The young guard posted at the gate checked Gina's identification against a list of registered visitors in his database before granting her access to the army base. He also graciously provided her with directions to the post hospital.

There was a little confusion at the hospital's reception desk. Gina mistakenly asked to see a patient named Jack Kurry. When the nurse was unable to find anyone registered under that name, Gina remembered that she had been instructed to ask for a specific woman, a Colonel Jacobsen.

"Oh," said the nurse as her face lit up. "You're on *Colonel Jacobsen's* list." She reached into a drawer and retrieved a single piece of paper containing a short roster of names. "Yes, here you are. I'll call them right away. Would you like some coffee?"

Gina was a little embarrassed by the sudden VIP treatment. "No, thank you."

Several minutes later, a corporal arrived to escort her. He led her down a back stairwell and into the basement, where they traversed a labyrinth of corridors until they reached a door guarded by a military policeman. The corporal entered an access code and the door lock clicked open. Inside was a small waiting room.

"Please have a seat, ma'am," said the corporal. Then he disappeared through the only other door in the room—directly opposite from whence they entered. A few minutes later, Gina heard the sound of voices coming from behind the same door. It soon opened and four adults and a child entered the room. One of them was obviously Colonel Jacobsen, as indicated by the nametag on her uniform. The others were civilians—one older man and a younger couple with a small girl. The colonel engaged Gina immediately.

"You must be Gina Alvarez," she said as she extended her hand. "I'm Nancy Jacobsen."

Gina rose to greet her. "Yes. It's nice to meet you."

"I assume you've met Jack's father, and his sister and brother-in-law?" asked the colonel.

Gina was visibly awash with embarrassment. She had not expected to encounter Jack's family and it threw her off kilter. "No," she said nervously, "We've spoken on the phone, though. That is, Mr. Kurry and I have."

"Hello, Gina," said Don with a smile. "I'm glad to finally meet you. This is my daughter Mindy and her husband Ron." Then he picked up the toddler. "And this is my granddaughter, Bella."

"I've heard about all of you," stammered Gina. "A little bit." She felt compelled to explain her presence, though nobody in the room seemed the least bit concerned. "You're probably wondering why I'm here."

"Not really," replied Mindy. "Jack told us you were coming."

"Yes, this is a big day for Jack," added the colonel.

"Oh, I doubt that he's *that* excited to see me," said Gina sheepishly.

"What I meant was that he's being released this afternoon," clarified the colonel.

"Yes, of course," said Gina as she stared at the floor in embarrassment. "That's definitely great news."

"We're heading out to grab an early lunch," said Don. "I hope we can catch up later."

"Jack said that you'll be having dinner with us," said Ron.

"Oh, that would be nice," replied Gina.

The colonel escorted Gina through the door and around a corner where she found herself looking at Jack through a thick glass wall. The colonel then excused herself, leaving them to speak through an audio system. Jack sounded as if he was on an old AM radio.

"Hey," he said excitedly. "How are you?"

"You could have warned me that your whole family was going to be here."

"Oh, yeah. I forgot. I did tell them that you were coming, though."

"That doesn't make it any better." She soon forgot about her awkward confrontation in the waiting room, and the subject turned to Jack's release.

"They ran a lot of tests," said Jack. "They must have taken a gallon of blood out of me over the past two weeks."

"Army doctors?"

"No. It's mostly been people from the CDC. They seem to be in charge. This was the closest secure facility they could find."

"And everything is positive—I mean, negative, right?"

"That's what they tell me."

"How do they know?" asked Gina.

"They seem pretty confident that they could recognize the new virus based on the signatures of the Gemini Viruses. They apparently performed a lot of tests with my blood samples and ethanol, but they wouldn't tell me much else. The only real way to find out will be when I have a shot of Jack Daniels later today."

Gina laughed for a moment, then became quite serious. "Wait, do you think there's a chance that…"

"No," laughed Jack. "It's fine. But just in case, I've decided that it will be the last drink I ever have. You might want to do the same."

"Ha—sure."

Jack inched closer to the glass and looked at Gina solemnly. "Have they found out anything about… *him*?" he asked softly.

Gina was reticent. She was now very far removed from the need-to-know with respect to Sydney and the alleged virus he might carry. She had no business discussing it—even with Jack. She shook her head slightly, and mouthed, "I don't know."

"Yeah, that's what I figured," said Jack quietly. "Two guys in suits came by here the other day and swore me to secrecy. I had to sign a bunch of papers. I guess I won't be writing any articles about it."

The name Sydney Carter had been mentioned in several news reports regarding the League of Orbis Novus, but only in reference to his role in discovering the Gemini Viruses. A few stories even noted his mysterious disappearance, though it was attributed to the sad denouement of a man's struggle with the disease of alcoholism. The U.S. Government had managed to extinguish all traces of Sydney's trip to Guatemala and had even leaked false stories of him being sighted in a Key West bar in late December. There was no mention—anywhere—of a new virus.

Oblivious to Sydney Carter's role in the saga, the world seemed satisfied to have the final pieces of the Orbis Novus puzzle in place. None of the villains (or heroes, depending on which side of the fence one's opinion fell) could do anything further to harm (or help) civilization. The biggest fear among the talking heads on the twenty-four-hour news stations was that a copycat organization might attempt to engineer a similar pathogen.

"But then again," said one blowhard, "they've already tackled our biggest crisis: opioids. What more could they hope to accomplish?"

About the Author

C.C. Prestel lived most of his childhood and adult life in the heart of Maryland's Baltimore-Washington corridor. He relocated to Las Vegas upon retiring from a career as a software engineer and small business owner. There he decided to finally write down some of the story ideas that had been bouncing around his head for decades.

In addition to writing novels, he enjoys hiking, playing guitar, and Texas Hold'em.

Acknowledgements

Thanks to Beth Dorward for another great editing job.

Dad, Jan, and Greg: thanks for taking the time to read the early versions of the manuscript and providing useful feedback.

Thanks Kit, for your support. I hope you like this one.

Also from C.C. Prestel

Shaker chronicles the odyssey of Michael Taylor, an unassuming English teacher who wakes up to find himself a prisoner on a mysterious ship with more than forty strangers. Neither he nor his companions have any recollection of how they got there. Those who survive the voyage soon learn that their lives will be forever changed. Taylor struggles to survive against lethal enemies and his own internal conflicts in a distant, hostile world that has been ravaged by decades of warfare. This story details his saga and transformation from an ordinary man into the legendary warrior known as Shaker.

Made in the USA
Coppell, TX
27 April 2020